DUNCAN FALCONER
THE OPERATIVE

sphere

www.duncanfalconer.com

SPHERE

First published in Great Britain in 2006 by Time Warner Books
This paperback edition published in 2006 by Sphere

Copyright © Duncan Falconer 2006

The moral right of the author has been asserted.

A CIP catalogue record for this book
is available from the British Library.

ISBN-13 978-07515-3633-1
ISBN-10 0-7515-3633-4

Typeset in Bembo
by Palimpsest Book Production Limited,
Grangemouth, Stirlingshire
Printed and bound in Great Britain by
Clays Ltd, St Ives plc

Sphere
An imprint of
Little, Brown Book Group
Brettenham House
Lancaster Place
London WC2E 7EN

A member of the Hachette Livre Group of Companies

www.littlebrown.co.uk

To Tristan and Barty

Duncan Falconer is a former member of Britain's elite Special Boat Service and 14 Int., Northern Ireland's top-secret SAS undercover detachment. After more than a decade of operational service he left the SBS and went into the private security 'circuit'. *The Operative* is his third novel. He has also written a non-fiction bestseller, *First Into Action*, which documents the real-life exploits of the SBS.

Author's note

In a work of fiction it will be no surprise to anyone that none of the characters in this book are other than the product of my imagination. If there are any resemblances to any living persons, they are entirely accidental and unintended. Equally readers will appreciate that for obvious reasons I have deliberately disguised a number of technical details of the composition of the explosives.

Chapter 1

Stratton climbed from a local taxi outside a row of detached homes just off the Wareham road in Poole, Dorset, paid the driver, and headed along a gravel track towards the front door of the largest house. His battered old leather jacket was draped over an arm in the crook of which he held a bottle of inexpensive wine. A large present splendidly finished off with a red-ribbon bow rested in the other. Stratton owned a car, an eight-year-old Jeep that he'd had for several years, but he had been away on an assignment for the past three months and when he'd tried to start it that morning for the first time since his return the engine wouldn't turn over. He wasted little time with it, refusing to squander his first day home tinkering with his ride, so he called a mate in the camp's motor transport department who said he would take a look at it the following day. Then Stratton spent the morning shopping for a new pair of trousers, a shirt and a pair of shoes, getting a trim for his tussled dark hair, and generally being self-indulgent.

Spending a day shopping in Bournemouth, or anywhere for that matter, was not normal for Stratton, and devoting that amount of time to his personal attire and appearance was downright unusual. This man could never be accused of hedonism by anyone who knew him: in fact, in higher circles, specifically among his bosses in the SBS and Military Intelligence, he was considered unkempt. That was not a complaint, of course, not from those he worked for directly. It was an unkempt world he operated in and Stratton could often be found in its darkest and most dingy parts.

Stratton could not say for sure why he had woken up that morning feeling entitled to a day of decadence. But he assumed it had a lot to do with having spent the last phase of a boring operation holed up in a camouflaged observation position in a pile of large, unstable boulders on the side of a mountain overlooking the summit of a ski lift a few miles outside the town of Almaty, Kazakhstan. He'd been waiting for a caravan bringing a supply of heroin over the mountain range from Afghanistan.

Drug smuggling was not Stratton's usual area of operation but it was true to say that anyone who worked in anti-terrorism ops was by default connected with the drug-smuggling business. Finally, after three weeks of eating American MREs (meals ready to eat), getting a hot drink only during daylight hours for tactical reasons and breathing air with a markedly reduced oxygen content due to the altitude, the caravan had finally arrived and Stratton had carried out his task – which was to do nothing more than film it. He was glad that the task had not gone on any longer and that he had made it back home, and on this day in particular. It was Josh Penton's birthday, a six-year-old boy whom Stratton had known since the day the kid had been born, son to one of his oldest friends in the SBS – and Stratton's godson.

There were a number of cars jammed along the usually quiet gravel drive and as Stratton approached the front door he could see several people in the large kitchen. As he raised the hand with the wine in it to push the front doorbell the door opened. Jack was standing in the hallway looking somewhat sombre and holding a bottle of beer, which he immediately thrust at Stratton.

'You're adrift,' Jack said accusingly.

'Car wouldn't start,' replied Stratton with equal gravity.

'We don't accept excuses in this business. Take the bottle and drink the contents.'

'You're a beer behind, laddy,' a voice barked behind Jack. It was Smiv, a tall, red-headed Scotsman with a bull neck and a build to match.

Jack pushed the beer closer to Stratton, frowning. 'Refusing will not help your case,' he said.

'It's not even one o'clock,' Stratton pleaded.

Jock and Smiv were joined by Bracken, a dark-haired *hombre*-moustachioed brute whom many called Turk because of his highly suspect ancestry, a heritage which he flatly denied. 'How's it going, Stratton?' he asked.

'He's a beer behind,' Smiv told Bracken.

'That right?' Bracken said as he put a bottle to his lips and took a swig. 'Who does he think he is?'

Stratton rolled his eyes, took the bottle and put it to his lips.

'You don't get in this door until that's emptied,' Jack added.

5

Stratton sighed, tipped back his head, and slowly emptied the glass container, not as adept as most at divesting a bottle of its contents in one go. He handed it back to Jack who beamed as if all negative issues had been suddenly resolved.

'Come inside,' Jack said, stepping back to allow Stratton entry. As he closed the door he gave Stratton a bear-hug, then stepped back to look him over. 'Everything in order? No bits missing?'

'No. The most boring job I think I've ever done. I had piles from sitting on cold, damp rocks for a couple of weeks, but otherwise no complaints.'

'Always take a packet of Anusols with you on ops,' Smiv advised like an old sage.

'Might as well shove 'em up your arse, all the good they do,' Bracken chimed in as he took another swig from his bottle.

'Sad thing is he's serious,' Smiv confided to the others.

'Go say hello to Sally,' Jack said, nodding towards the kitchen and taking Stratton's wine. 'And then go see Josh. He's been going on at me all week about when you're coming home and if you'll be in time for his party.'

''E 'asn't gotta beer again,' Bracken noted and one was immediately held out to Stratton.

'I haven't had a drink in a month. I'll be trashed on another of those.'

The other men remained unmoved by his plea, as did the bottle. Stratton took it, rolled his eyes again and went into the kitchen where several wives were helping to prepare food.

'Stratton!' Sally yelled on seeing him. She quickly put down the tray of sausages that she had just removed from the oven, tossed her gloves onto the kitchen counter and hurried over with outstretched arms. 'Come 'ere, you handsome bastard,' she said, a northern twang discernible even after more than a decade living in the south of the country. 'We've missed yer.'

She gave him a bear-hug. Stratton wrapped his laden arms around her, and gave her a fat kiss on the lips.

'Doesn't greet me like that when I come home,' Jack said, feigning hurt.

''Im or 'er?' Bracken asked.

'Oh, shot op, Jack. 'E gets the same,' she said to Stratton. 'Except in lace underwear.'

'Ooooh,' the men cooed in chorus.

'I'll 'ave to try that,' Bracken said.

'She wears the lace underwear,' Smiv explained.

'Oh.' Bracken nodded, understanding.

'Let me take a look at you,' Sally said, standing back. 'All in one piece?'

'We've been through that,' Jack said, stepping forward and taking over. 'Now get yourself down and see Josh before she starts checking for herself.'

Sally gave Jack a little smack on the arm. 'Go on,' she said to Stratton. 'Get down to the garden. I'll talk to you later. And take that rabble with yer.'

Stratton headed through the kitchen to a set of double doors that led out on to a balcony overlooking a large back garden surrounded by leylandii. A barbecue was smoking away in a corner where some two dozen adults stood chatting, drinks in their hands, and a dozen children. Stratton picked out Josh. The boy was wearing a set of oversized military-camouflage clothes and leading several of the children in an attack against an enemy position with his plastic M16 assault rifle.

Stratton made his way down a flight of steps to the bottom where a man turning chicken legs on the barbecue saw him. 'Stratton,' he called out.

'Seaton,' Stratton replied. 'Long time no see.'

'Fallujah,' Seaton reminded him, his accent southeast-coast American. 'What happened to you? You left right after.'

'Our job was only to lift Maqari for you guys. Interrogations bore me,' Stratton said. 'What are you doing here?'

'Well,' Seaton said, lowering his voice and looking to make sure that no one was within earshot. 'The job you just came back off – you were working for us. Great footage, by the way. Sorry it wasn't more exciting for you.'

'That's how it goes sometimes.'

'I'll make it up to you soon,' Seaton said.

'How soon?'

'Pretty soon, I think.' Seaton winked.

Stratton didn't know Seaton very well. He was aware that the man was in CIA operations in the Middle East but was not a field operative like Stratton.

'I have a present to deliver,' Stratton said, holding up the gift.

'We'll catch up later.'

Stratton headed across the garden, wondering what kind of operation it would be that Seaton had hinted would be 'pretty soon'. But his thoughts were quickly interrupted. Most of the men greeted him as he passed and when Josh saw him he stopped in mid-battle and sprinted over at full speed.

'Stratton!' he shouted as he dived into his god-father's arms. 'When'd you get back?'

'This morning.'

'Where'd you go? Are you allowed to tell?'

'Only you, Josh.'

Josh looked around at his mates who had come over to join them. 'Sorry, guys. Stratton can only tell me.'

The others looked downhearted as Josh pulled Stratton away from them. Stratton crouched so that his and Josh's heads were close together.

The other kids looked on jealously as Josh nodded while Stratton talked. Then the boy's eyes lit up and he looked at Stratton in disbelief. 'True?' he asked. 'Bloody 'ellfire,' he exclaimed, a bit of his mother's northern accent sneaking into his despite the fact that he spent only a few weeks of each year with his grand-parents in Manchester.

'Promise not to tell anyone,' Stratton asked.

'On pain of death,' Josh said with immense sincerity. Stratton gave him the present and stood up as Jack joined them.

'Thanks, Stratton,' Josh said as he crouched to open the gift, quickly surrounded by his mates.

'What crap did you spin him this time?' Jack said into Stratton's ear.

'I took over a battle from a dying Afghan warlord and led a thousand of his men on a cavalry charge against a band of rogue Taliban insurgents coming over the border from Pakistan.'

'Christ. He probably thinks his dad's a complete loser while his godfather goes around winning every war single-handed.'

'Yup,' Stratton agreed.

Josh stood up holding the contents of his package. In one hand he held a *pakol*, a traditional Afghani mujahedin hat, brown and shaped like a large pie, and in the other a Russian Army belt with a black buckle from the Second Armoured Division, a relic of Russia's Afghan war.

'What are they?' Josh asked.

'The hat's from a certain Afghan warlord,' he said, winking. 'And the belt's from a Russian soldier he killed in hand-to-hand combat.'

'Wow!' Josh exclaimed while his father rolled his eyes and shook his head.

'Right. We've got a new game,' Josh said, facing his troops with great seriousness. 'I'm an Afghan warlord and you're all my men. And we're going to do a cavalry charge.' Josh put the hat on, winked at Stratton and then ran away, followed by his obedient soldiers.

Jack sighed as he watched Josh race off. 'If I told him you were his real dad he'd just shrug and say, "Okay, see ya, let's go home, Stratton."'

'Stratton?' a voice called out from behind.

Stratton turned to see Bracken, Smiv and Smudge walking towards him. Smudge was a lanky SBS operative with an unusually large nose not unlike the keel of a yacht, and in his hand was a small green plastic briefcase.

'I think I've got you this time,' Smudge said.

'Got me?'

'Party trick,' Smudge said, holding up the green briefcase. 'I brought the fat.'

'Here?' Stratton exclaimed. 'You must be joking.'

'Joke I do not . . . Over here,' Smudge said, heading across the garden.

'No,' Stratton said.

'Just take a look,' Smudge urged. 'Come on – I've got some money to win back.'

'Go on, Stratton,' Bracken said. 'At least take a look. It's a good one.'

Stratton looked at Jack who simply shrugged, evidently in on whatever was going on.

Stratton reluctantly followed the group to the far corner of the garden where a small table stood all on its own. In the centre was a small tower of glass made of an empty champagne bottle and a slender champagne flute balanced upright on top of it.

They all stared at it in silence, the others glancing between Stratton and the table as if he knew what this was all about.

'I don't get it,' Stratton finally said.

'You've got to get the glass inside the bottle,' Smudge revealed.

'What?' Stratton asked, unsure whether he had heard correctly.

'The champagne glass inside the bottle . . . May I remind you that you were the one who said that the use of explosives was not brutality but a delicate science and that with the right formula and chemistry anything could be achieved.'

'I never said that.'

'Something like that,' Smudge insisted.

'The universe was started with a big bang,' Bracken commented. The others ignored him.

'All you have to do is get the glass into the bottle,' Smudge repeated. 'And there has to be a recognisable amount of the bottle left.'

'The glass inside the bottle,' Stratton said, unable to stop himself from calculating a solution.

'One hit only,' Smudge added, sensing that Stratton might already have a plan.

Stratton looked around at the garden, estimating the dangers. But Smudge was ahead of him.

'Everyone goes into the house,' Smudge said. 'Won't be more than like a large banger going off.'

Stratton looked at Jack who shrugged his indifference. Then he peered closely at the bottle and flute again. 'The glass inside the bottle,' he said.

''E 'as a plan, methinks,' Bracken said, grinning, the comment denting Smudge's confidence.

'You can't touch any of the glass other than with fat,' Smudge said. 'One explosion, and the flute has to end up inside the bottle . . . You owe me a chance to get my money back.'

'For what?' Stratton asked.

'That Sunni cleric in Mosul – what was 'is name?'

'Mohamed Sah,' Jack offered.

'That's 'im. You had to blow his car off the street and onto the roof of his house.'

'He did that,' Jack said.

'Yeah, but I should've won on a technicality,' Smudge argued. 'The guy was supposed to have been in it at the time.'

'You're a sore loser, Smudge,' Smiv chimed in.

12

'I accepted it, didn't I? I'm moving on. Stratton was the one who said he could do anything with explosives and I'm offering him another chance to prove it. What do you say? Double the Mosul bet? Two hundred quid says you can't do it.'

Stratton was more interested in the challenge than the money.

'I'll match Smudge's two 'undred,' Bracken said.

'I'll 'ave some of that,' added Smiv. 'I can't see how he can do that.'

'You in, Jack?' Smudge asked.

'If Stratton says it can be done,' Jack said.

They all looked at Stratton who was still studying the problem.

'What do you think?' Smudge asked him.

'The question is not if, but how,' Stratton answered.

'No,' Smudge said, challenging him. 'The question is, my friend, *can* you do it?'

They watched Stratton study the table, the glass, the air above, and even the surrounding area. Finally he stood back, put his hands on his hips, exhaled deeply and nodded to himself.

'Is that a yes?' Smudge asked.

'Yes,' Stratton finally said.

Smudge immediately looked concerned. He knew that Stratton was a master when it came to explosives but he was also canny and Smudge did not trust him. 'One bang only,' he reiterated.

Stratton nodded.

'No touching any of the glass afterwards,' Smudge added.

Stratton nodded again.

'No picking the glass up with anything and putting it inside the bottle,' Smudge added, trying to cover every possible catch he could think of.

'No picking the glass up afterwards,' Stratton said, his eyes never leaving the table as he finalised his solution. 'Any more rules?'

Smudge looked around at the others in case they had any to add, hoping that someone had thought of something. But there was only silence. 'Okay,' he said.

'I'll match the two hundred, then,' Jack said. 'But my money's on Stratton.'

'Easy money.' Smudge smirked.

'Gotta go with the track record,' Jack said.

'Can I get in on this?' Seaton asked, making his way into the group.

'Absolutely,' Smudge said. ''Ow much?'

'What's the going bet?' the American asked.

'Jack has two hundred,' Smudge said.

'Two hundred it is, then,' Seaton said, getting out his money.

'Right. Two hundred against,' Smudge said as he reached for the notes.

'No. I'd never bet against Stratton,' Seaton said, handing the money over.

Smudge's confidence was rocked a little once again, but he recovered. 'Your money ... Right, then,' Smudge said as he picked a flower from the tree and put it into the flute. 'That has to stay in the glass that ends up in the bottle.'

'You can't add on things after the bet,' Jack said.

'The flower doesn't matter,' Stratton said. 'Nice touch, Smudge.'

Smudge frowned as he held out the briefcase, insisting to himself that Stratton was bluffing.

Stratton took the case, placed it on the table and opened it up. Inside was a series of neatly organised compartments, a pristine surgical pack filled with an assortment of micro-explosives that included: a metre reel of detonator cord or cortex no thicker than a piece of spaghetti, a two-metre reel of very fine slow-burning fuse, a cartridge of four micro-detonators, a pack of PE5 (Super-X) plastic explosive packed in thin cellophane sheets like sliced processed cheese, three timers, one electronic, one mechanical and one chemical, two radio-receiver detonators, a ceramic surgical knife (non-metallic), a heavy-duty multi-tool 'workman' that included pliers, scissors and various other utensils, a roll of electrician's tape, a spool of nylon fishing line, an assortment of screws and tacks, several paper-thin magnetic strips, and a remote-detonation transmitter and continuity tester.

Stratton removed the detonating cord, unravelled a short length which he cut off using the ceramic blade, then began pulling it carefully through his fingers.

'Why's he doing that?' Bracken asked.

'He's stretching it to thin it out,' Jack informed him.

'I see.' Bracken nodded. 'Why?'

'He's making it a weaker charge, I suppose.'

Stratton eased the cortex through his fingers, being careful not to break it. When it was half its original thickness he wrapped it once around the neck of the bottle, just above its widest point, and cut it precisely where the ends met. The men were joined by several others and they watched with interest as Stratton removed a small piece of electrician's tape which he stuck to the face of his wristwatch. Then he cut two lengths of slow-burning fuse, one twelve inches long, the other double that. He attached the shorter fuse to a micro-detonator and carefully placed its tip where the two ends of the cortex met, securing it in place with the tape where it sat like a bracelet.

Stratton reached for the glass.

'Uh-uh,' Smudge quickly interrupted. 'You can't move anything. You gotta leave it in place as is.'

Stratton didn't appear bothered about the rule revision and went back to the briefcase. He removed the reel of fishing line, unwound a couple of metres and looked up into the tree that loomed over the table. The men followed his gaze and watched the end of the line float skywards over a branch and back into his hand. He flicked the line along the branch until it was above the glass. Then he cut it, tied a slip knot and pulled it to the top of the line where it tightened in place. He released the line to check that it dangled directly above the glass, which it did nicely, then turned the line several times around the thickest part of the glass and tied it off with a knot.

'What's he doing?' Smudge asked.

'Shut up, Smudge,' Smiv said. 'He's not doing anything you said he couldn't.'

'Whose side are you on, anyway?' Smudge asked him.

'I still don't think he can do it but I'd like to see him try.'

Smudge frowned.

Josh's head rose up between the men beside Stratton. 'What you doing, Stratton?'

'I'm going to blow some fat.'

'Wow,' Josh replied, eyes wide.

'Would you like to light the fuse?'

Josh's eyes lit up even more. No other reply was necessary.

The final touch was the long piece of fuse, which Stratton wrapped one end of around the nylon line just above the champagne glass. He placed the other end beside the end of the smaller fuse-line attached to the detonator.

Several discussions immediately broke out among the men – descriptions of what was meant to happen and estimates of varying degrees of success. The general consensus seemed to be that it was an interesting idea but a doomed one.

'You want to get everyone inside?' Stratton asked Jack.

A moment later the children and wives were being herded into the house. A man with a well-developed gut and a decidedly un-special-forces-like bearing who had been talking to several of the wives and not paying attention to the goings-on in the corner of the garden joined the men heading into the house. 'What's happening?' he asked.

'A party trick,' Jack said.

'Oh, great. What is it?'

'The explosive kind,' Bracken explained.

'Explosive. Inside the house?' The man chuckled, not believing them.

'No. Outside. That's why we're going inside,' Bracken said.

The man stopped in the doorway, looking as if he'd misheard. 'Not real explosives, surely?'

'Yeah. As in boom boom,' Smiv said.

'Real explosives?' the man asked again.

'Which is why we're going inside,' Bracken repeated patiently.

The man looked across the garden to the table where Stratton was crouched with Josh, talking about something. 'Are you *mad*?' he exclaimed. 'You can't blow things up. This is a private neighbourhood.'

'If anyone complains we'll say it was just a big banger,' Bracken said.

'Big *banger*?' the man echoed, looking astounded.

'So who's gonna know?' Bracken asked.

'*I'll* know,' the man said, his voice rising to its highest pitch. 'May I remind you that I'm a police officer.' He was from the Dorset Police Firearms Unit which the SBS occasionally instructed.

'Relax, Bob. It's all under control,' Jack assured him.

'Relax? If anything goes wrong it'll be me who gets it in the neck.'

'Bob,' Smiv said, putting a large hand on the man's shoulder and squeezing it a little. 'If you don't shut up I'm going to shoot you in the leg tomorrow when we're on the range. Now get in the poxy house and do as you're told.'

Bob looked at the hardened faces staring at him, all belonging to men a head taller than him. 'I'm going to deny all knowledge,' he said as he went into the house.

'Is everyone inside?' Jack asked. 'Shut the balcony door, please,' he shouted and someone complied. 'Stratton? All yours.'

18

'Don't you break any of my windows, Stratton,' Sally called out from the patio doors.

Jack closed the doors on her, cleared various items off a garden table and tipped it on its side.

Stratton took a small battery-ignited gas lighter from the briefcase and pushed the button on the side a couple of times, initiating it for Josh to see how it worked. 'You have a go,' he said to Josh who took the lighter and pushed the button. The small portal instantly glowed red and blue without a visible flickering tongue of fire: it looked more like the rear of a miniature jet engine.

'That's perfect. Now, you remember the last time we lit a fuse?'

'Yes.' Josh nodded.

'This is just the same. When you light the ends of the fuses and they start to crackle we'll walk slowly back to the table where your dad is. Okay?'

Josh nodded again. 'What do we count up to?' he asked.

'Twelve inches is sixty seconds. You remember how we count?'

'Thousand and one, thousand and two, thousand and three,' Josh said, nodding his head at each number.

'Perfect . . . You ready?'

Josh held up the lighter.

'Okay. Light it.'

Josh ignited the lighter and carefully aimed the jet at the ends of both the short and the long fuses lying beside each other. They immediately crackled to life and began to give off a thin wisp of smoke.

Josh began to count. 'Thousand and one, thousand and two, thousand and three, thousand and four . . .'

Stratton took the lighter from him, pocketed it, closed the briefcase, stood up and took Josh's hand. Josh looked up at him, still counting, and Stratton winked, emphasising how calm and cool they should be. As Josh got to a thousand and ten, they strode off together to where Jack was waiting for them behind the table.

'Thousand and twenty-one,' Josh counted as he got down beside his dad. He glanced over at the patio doors where his friends were pressed against the glass, watching him.

'Is my money safe?' Jack asked Stratton while his son continued counting.

'I'm relying more on luck than judgement but I'd say we're in good shape.'

As Josh got to one thousand and fifty-seven, there was a sharp crack, hardly louder than a normal firework banger, and a moment later the three of them stood up to see what had happened.

The patio doors opened and Smudge led the others out as a small cloud of smoke dissipated. They walked over and stood around the table. The champagne bottle was in precisely the same position but its top was missing. Swinging like a pendulum above it on the nylon line was the champagne flute containing the flower. The longer fuse wire was still burning up towards it.

Everyone gathered around, watching the glass swing less and less as the thin wisp of smoke from the fuse drew closer to it. Smudge was at the other side of the table, facing Stratton, the swinging glass between them. He looked unsure. But the odds on the fuse burning through the nylon at the precise moment were surely in his favour.

The seconds ticked away and as the fuse got shorter no one said a word. Even Bob the police officer stared in anticipation.

The fuse reached the nylon and burnt through it. The glass fell, the bottom of the stem hitting the edge of the bottle and breaking off. But the rest of it dropped inside the bottle.

Jack leaned over the bottle, reached inside it, and lifted the glass out. Apart from its stem it was intact, with the flower inside. 'I'd say that was a winner.'

There was instant applause from everyone and Josh hugged Stratton's legs.

'Wait a minute,' Smudge said. 'The bottom of the glass is broken.'

'Shut up, Smudge,' Bracken said. 'He did exactly what you asked him to. Cough up.'

'But technically—' Smudge whined on.

'Just give 'em the money and stop your whingeing,' Smiv said as he took out his wallet and duly counted out a hundred pounds into Jack's hand. Smudge reluctantly took out his wallet and handed his payment to Jack who beamed as he took his cut before handing some to Seaton and the rest to Stratton. 'Never a doubt,' Jack said. 'Beer?' he asked both Seaton and Stratton.

'Beer,' they agreed. They broke into laughter as they headed for the house, Jack and Seaton putting an arm around Stratton.

The sound of a beeper going off filtered through the laughter and conversation as people discussed the feat. Every man heard it but Sally was the first to react, looking up from Josh, her smile fading as her gaze met Jack's.

Smiv pulled his pager from his pocket. 'It's me,' he said as he read the slender information bar on the top of the device.

Sally sighed, looking relieved. 'If there's one sound I hate it's that one,' she said to one of the wives beside her.

Another beeper then sounded off, followed by another. Within a few seconds there was a chorus of them and practically every operative was reading his pager.

Sally went instantly sullen. 'They'll be gone in about five seconds,' she said.

Jack looked across at his wife, his expression saying it all. 'Sorry, Sal. We have to go.'

She nodded.

'Anyone need a lift to the camp?' Jack called out. No one answered and Jack took Sally in his arms. 'I'll call you as soon as I know what's happening.'

She nodded, trying to hide the disappointment on her face.

Jack kissed her and headed for the house. 'You not been called or you left your pager at home?' he asked Stratton as he passed him.

'I just got back.'

'When has that ever stopped 'em?' Jack said.

'Someone's being considerate for once,' Stratton replied.

'Enjoy the party,' Jack said as he disappeared into the house.

'I will,' Stratton said as Seaton strode past him.

'Don't bet on it,' the American said as he followed the men inside.

Stratton watched him go and took his beeper out to see if it was operating. Within seconds the men had all gone, except for him and Bob. The wives and children stood around, looking as if they had just been mugged.

'Where's dad going, mummy?' Josh asked.

'I don't know, Josh. He'll be back soon.'

'It could be an exercise,' Stratton offered, aware of how limp it sounded as soon as he'd said it.

'When's the last time the lads had an exercise? You've been doing the real thing for so many years now you don't need one.'

She was right to a certain extent. Stratton was only trying to make it easier for her to bear, although he didn't know quite why he needed to. It wasn't as if the lads died like flies every time they went away. Yes, it was a dangerous job but the number of fatalities over the years was low, considering the nature of the work. The wives had been complaining lately about the amount of time their men had been spending away from home. Most were bored with being left alone so much while others suspected that the men had too much of a good time when they were away. Stratton wouldn't have put Sally in either category and knew that for the past year or so she'd been experiencing genuine fear about Jack going away. She had mentioned it to Stratton more than once and although she knew that it was silly to take any notice of what was, at the end of the day, just her imagination she couldn't help how she felt.

Sally smiled at Stratton, trying hard not to be a wet rag. 'I'll go get you that beer,' she said. 'You're not leaving this house until you and I are drunk, John Stratton. Understood?'

As she stepped towards the house a beeper cut through the air. Sally stopped in the doorway and turned to look at Stratton as he pulled his pager from his pocket to check the readout.

'I'd better hurry and catch a ride,' he said as he approached her. He opened his arms and she wrapped hers around his body, resting her cheek on his chest.

'I know it's what you all do,' she said with a sigh. 'I'll just never get used to it, that's all.'

Stratton released her as Josh came up to them. 'You going too, Stratton?' the little boy asked, adjusting the oversized *pakol* on his head.

'Yes. I have to go with your dad. You have a happy birthday, and look after your mum.'

Stratton bounded up the steps to the kitchen balcony and as he went inside the house Sally called out his name. He popped back out and looked down on them.

Sally had picked Josh up and was holding him in her arms. 'Take care of him,' she said, suddenly looking quite worried.

Stratton nodded and she smiled bravely. But all Sally could hear were the voices in her head warning her that she would never see Jack alive again. Even though she had heard them before, this time they seemed more compelling. She wanted to tell Stratton her fears but knew it would only make her feel stupid and put him in an uncomfortable position.

She watched him disappear and was suddenly filled with the urge to run through the house, out onto the street, and see Jack one last time before he went away. But she took control of herself.

'Don't worry, mum,' Josh said.

'I'm not,' she lied and held him tightly in her arms.

Chapter 2

Stratton and Jack stepped in through a doorway cut into a large grey metal sliding door that was closed across the entrance to what, from the outside, looked like a small aircraft hangar. It was one of the Special Boat Service's operational squadron hangars inside their sprawling headquarters on the edge of Poole Harbour. Gathered in the hangar were the men from Jack's party plus half a dozen others. Most had some kind of facial hair: a moustache, a goatee, or simply a few days' growth of stubble.

The door to the operational offices that were constructed on a suspended platform above the floor of the hangar opened and an officer and the squadron sergeant-major stepped out. They were wearing desert-camouflage uniforms. The sergeant-major led the way down a metal staircase where he stopped halfway to address the men.

'Listen up,' he barked. 'Teams Alpha, Bravo and Charlie should all be here. Team leaders speak only if there are members who are not present, otherwise your silence will be taken as affirmative.' His stare scanned the group and paused on Stratton and Seaton, the only two men who were not assigned to teams.

He nodded to them and looked back at the officer. 'All present, sir.'

'Thank you, sergeant-major,' the young officer said, looking up from a clipboard that he was reading from and scribbling notes on.

'I'm sorry about the call-out,' the officer said in his well-bred accent. 'I know that most of you are on local leave but we're the standby squadron for fastballs such as this. There'll be a detailed brief on the plane but the location is Iraq. One of the deck of cards has been located. Mohammad Al-Forouf. He's a Sunni cleric from Ramadi and quite an important force behind the resistance movement within the Sunni Triangle. He's also the man behind the UN and Red Cross headquarters bombings in Baghdad as well as numerous others. He's recently been using the dilapidated but still functional rail system to move ordnance around the country. This has been working for him quite well, mainly because trains are so rare and somewhat autonomous about their movements that coalition forces have been lax with stop-and-searches. Sources have revealed that Forouf will be travelling from Mosul in the north and heading south towards Tikrit and Baghdad in the next twenty-four hours. He's very elusive, obviously, since he hasn't been caught yet. Coalition forces have made three attempts against him since the war, all without luck. He's rumoured to be heavily guarded and goes nowhere without serious protection. This is the first time we've had int that he's actually on one of his trains. If it proves to be true, then that gives us a tactical advantage insofar as he and his men will be in a confined location, on a predictable route, and out in the open. The source is apparently very reliable and quite valuable to military intelligence who want him left in mint condition and – this is from them – the deal is we can't just vaporise the train, which suggests that the source is going to be with Forouf. That means it's going to require some surgery . . . Stratton?'

'Sir,' Stratton said, raising a hand.

'This is an explosive op. You'll be running that side of it.'

Stratton nodded.

'As I said, we'll have a detailed brief on the flight and any up-to-date int when we get to our forward-base location at Camp Victory. Get your kit sorted. We leave from the lower field in thirty minutes.'

'Listen up,' the sergeant-major boomed as the officer headed back up the stairs. 'For those of you who can't remember where Iraq is, think desert – sand and heat, and a lot of both. Pack accordingly. Don't forget mozzy nets and insect repellent – Yanks have so far reported six hundred and fifty cases of leishmaniasis which is a flying tick-borne disease. Smith? Don't bring your hammock this time. There ain't any trees where we're going.'

Smudge rolled his eyes as some of the men looked round at him. 'I packed it by mistake,' he mumbled.

'You heard the boss,' the sergeant-major continued. 'Thirty minutes. That means I want everyone down on the lower field to load the choppers in twenty and ready to go in twenty-five. Let's go.'

Everyone immediately headed for their personal equipment cages.

'You want to work with me on this one?' Stratton asked Jack.

'I'd be offended if you didn't ask,' Jack said. 'I'll go grab the boom-boom soon as I have my kit together, which'll take three minutes. What do you think you'll need?'

'A lot of linear, methinks. Stacks of L–Ones and Twos. I'll pick up the console and the RT devices.'

'Right.'

'P for plenty,' Stratton said as Jack walked away.

'Always.'

Stratton walked to his equipment cage, unlocked the combination, took hold of his large backpack that was already good to go other than for a few changes for desert conditions and paused to deal with a major distraction. He hadn't done a train before, not a moving option like this, and it posed some interesting problems. He was eager to solve them but pushed all thoughts of it out of his mind for the time being. Stratton no longer feared failing to find a solution to problems such as these as much as he used to. There had been a time when he would have been worried about fulfilling such a hugely pivotal role in an operation, but after so many years he knew that there was always a solution: it just had to be found. It was not complacency or smugness on his part, but a confidence in himself, his team, and the tried and tested system that was Brit special forces. He was looking forward to the journey to Baghdad, every minute of which would be spent going over details, calculating how he was going to blow the train without killing those on board, and then looking for all the things that could possibly go wrong.

Less than eleven hours later at 5:55 a.m. local time the fiery tendrils of dawn stretched skyward from the Iranian border little more than a hundred miles to the east as Stratton lay beneath one of several railway carriages. They were attached to a narrow, none too magnificent yet surprisingly clean and well-maintained diesel locomotive. Its engines hummed loudly, ticking over enough to convey electrical power to the carriages as Stratton shuffled slowly on his back over grimy, oil-stained sleepers separated by jagged gravel, moving between the heavy cast-iron wheels from one carriage connection to the next. He was wearing a pair of dirty old trousers with a matching jacket and worn boots with nylon packing-string for laces. His head was wrapped completely in a grubby red and white *shamagh* or scarf, with only his eyes visible.

Stratton was working quickly, placing slender, shaped linear explosive charges – pre-cast hollow triangular lenghts of lead filled with RDX – moulding the strips to the metal links where they would cut them like sugar cubes when the devices were detonated. To complete the charges he attached a remote-control detonator to the tail end of each strip and secured them neatly to the bottom of the links so that they would not be noticed. The dull lead was ideal, not only as a dense tamping device to direct the force of the blast against the surface to be blown: it also blended well with the dirty metal. As a final touch he scraped old grease from the bearings and smeared it over the charges to complete their camouflage, careful not to cover the short, slender antennas of the devices' receivers.

As Stratton completed the last charge-placement for that coupling, a pair of dirty brown feet inside worn sandals shuffled along the length of the train towards him. He froze, following the feet through the massive spoked wheels with his stare, quickly considering his options if he were seen. Getting caught at this stage would undoubtedly lead to the discovery of the explosives, thus ending the mission. The target would bolt and remain even more difficult to catch and – top of Stratton's list – getting found out would have serious implications as far as his immediate chances of survival were concerned, particularly if the man had an AK47. But something about the lethargic manner in which the man walked reduced Stratton's alarm.

His instincts were vindicated as the feet ambled past, away from the train, across the tracks and out of sight.

Stratton took hold of an old canvas bag beside him that contained more linear charges and detonators. He checked to see that the area opposite where the man had passed was clear and rolled out from under the carriage, over the rail between the wheels, onto the grimy, caked sand and to his feet.

The train stood in a dilapidated station, battered by both wars with Britain and America and peppered with bomb craters and scattered wreckage of all kinds, from cranes to rolling stock as well as military hardware. Several of the station's buildings spaced out at either side of the tracks had been completely destroyed while others remained nominally functional, though none had their windows or doors intact. Like so many government-owned buildings in the country, the station had been extensively looted after the fall of the

Baathist regime. There was no raised platform, the buildings being at ground level and set well back from the tracks. Vehicles were dotted about: lorries and fuel trucks, some functional, some wrecked by the war, others gutted for spares.

A dozen or so men hung about the largest of the station buildings: drivers and labourers, all taking part in the morning ritual of smoking, talking, eating bread and drinking *che*, a sweet tea, provided by a boy who had set up a tea shop in one of the destroyed buildings, the flickering fire reflecting off the roofless walls. Several of the men carried AK47 assault rifles. Some of them were station guards, others simply those who preferred to be armed, but none of them were taking any notice of Stratton who would have been difficult to see in the low light conditions or hear because of the locomotive engine.

There was a chill in the air that was noticeably cooler when the wind picked up. But within a few hours, if the fine sand did not rise with the day to filter the sun's rays – not uncommon at this time of year – the temperature would quickly climb.

The carriage that Stratton had been beneath was one of three French-made third-class passenger cars built and shipped to Iraq in the early 1970s. They were connected to the locomotive and behind them were a dozen or so dilapidated open trucks. As Stratton reached the coupling between the first and second carriage from the engine he ducked beneath the heavy linkage and lay on his back as before. He opened his canvas bag, removed a length of shaped charge, and repeated the procedure of bending it snugly around the coupling and securing it in place. After attaching the detonator and initiator and smearing the device with grease he closed his bag, ensured he had not left anything lying around and checked that the ground was clear at both sides of the carriage. The charge-placing phase was complete and as the sun began to rise above the buildings it was time to go.

Stratton rolled out and got to his feet. As he brushed himself down the sound of vehicle engines broke through the hum of the locomotive, announcing the arrival of a small convoy. There were half a dozen or so, a mixture of 4x4s and pick-up trucks packed with men. Bringing up the rear, amidst the thick dust being kicked up, he could make out a large lorry.

Stratton turned his back to them and headed towards the locomotive as the lead vehicles came to a halt on the edge of the station. The lorry overtook the other vehicles under the direction of men from the pick-ups, drove across the tracks and down the side of the train.

It stopped alongside the third carriage from the locomotive. The back was promptly opened, accompanied by a lot of shouting by those in charge as dozens of large wooden boxes were hauled out of it.

Just before Stratton reached the locomotive cab where two engineers were occupied with their preparations he turned away across a stretch of open ground. He headed for a shattered, imploded building that looked as if it had received a direct hit on its flat roof from a mortar or artillery shell.

He stepped inside and over the rubble of plaster-coated breeze-blocks and concrete that covered the floor, concealing himself beside a jagged hole in a wall that a window frame had once filled. Another vehicle arrived and Stratton peered around the corner to take a look. It was a dust-covered black Mercedes saloon and it immediately became the focus of attention.

The car stopped at the head of the convoy and three men climbed from the back and front passenger seats, all well-dressed compared to the coarse patchwork of Bedouin attire worn by those from the pick-ups and 4x4s: two in traditional robes and *shamaghs* and one in an expensive western-style suit. They were immediately surrounded by men with AK47 assault rifles and, with a modicum of order, though still looking like little more than an organised rabble, the group made its way towards the carriages.

Stratton raised a small pair of binoculars that had been hanging from his neck inside his jacket to his eyes and focused on the new arrivals.

'Mister Al-Forouf,' he muttered as he picked out the man with the sharp suit, slick black hair and well-groomed goatee.

Stratton watched the three VIPs move ahead of the others, climb the narrow steps of the centre passenger carriage and pass inside, followed by a handful of the armed followers. The rest divided up and clambered aboard the other two carriages at either end of Forouf's.

Stratton trained the binoculars on the crates being loaded onto the carriages. The last dozen or so caught his attention. He carefully focused on the side of one of the boxes waiting to be loaded and recognised the English writing on the side. The words *Flower Engineering* were stencilled in plain black capitals on a green background, an image fresh in Stratton's mind: he had seen the same markings only a week ago on several of the boxes that he had photographed when they'd been strapped to the sides of donkeys being led over the mountain pass in Almaty, Kazakhstan.

Stratton checked his watch. It was time to leave. He stepped from the back of the building and walked away into the desert, keeping parallel to the railway line and out of sight of the train as much as possible. A hundred yards or so away he made a sharp right-angle turn back across the rail tracks, glancing at the locomotive that now had thick black smoke issuing from the exhaust at its nose. He kept up a brisk pace across an expanse of open ground speckled with sad, dilapidated vegetation, aiming for a collection of mud huts.

He passed a sleeping dog and a small herd of roaming goats that were futilely searching the dust for a morsel, and stepped over some partially flattened coils of brittle razor wire. He continued on past a crippled, rusting artillery piece, its barrel frozen in a skyward tilt as if in defiance, its breech and undercarriage shattered, and around the corner of the first mud hut where he stopped dead in his tracks.

In front of the next hut was Stratton's transport, an old Russian Army M72 motorbike and sidecar. But sitting on it, inspecting it like baboons examining an unfamiliar fruit, were two Iraqis, both armed with AKs.

A young barefooted boy in grubby shorts and a T-shirt stood watching them. When he saw Stratton he walked over to him and immediately began claiming dramatically in Arabic that he'd told the men that the bike belonged to someone. He begged Stratton to understand that if he was bigger and stronger he would have stopped them.

'*Maalek*,' Stratton said, telling the boy that it was okay. He kept his stare fixed on the two Ali Babas, the affectionate local name for crooks, who had an unmistakable aura of thuggery about them. One was sitting in the sidecar, searching the inside, his AK47 resting across its top in front of him while the other, his assault rifle slung across his back, was trying to start the engine. He was pushing down the crank pedal with great effort but no result and periodically fiddling with a switch on the handlebar as he mumbled obscenities.

The boy started to explain again how sorry he was but Stratton held his hand out to stop him.

'*Maco muchkila*,' Stratton said quietly, reassuring the boy who was clearly upset at having failed in his intention to look after the bike while Stratton was gone.

Stratton looped his canvas bag over his shoulder and under an arm to free his hands. As he walked forward, he took hold of the end of a stout iron bar leaning against the building, moving it out of sight behind his back.

The man in the sidecar looked up with dark, narrow eyes as Stratton closed in while his friend continued his efforts to start the bike.

'*Hazih al darrajah lee*,' Stratton said slowly, putting on a gravel voice in an effort to disguise his poor Arabic as he relayed to them that the bike was his.

The one trying to start the engine paused to wipe his brow before giving Stratton a scowling look. '*Egleb wajhek,*' he cursed. Then he ignored Stratton and went back to his efforts.

Stratton understood the comment to mean roughly 'Take your eyes away.' Or perhaps, under the circumstances and more basically, 'Fuck off.'

He sized up the two criminals – Iraq had been plagued by these types since Saddam had emptied out the prisons, releasing thousands of them just before the war – and decided to deal with the one in the sidecar first since he was watching Stratton more closely. The man relayed a warning by resting his hands on the AK47 lying horizontally across the car in front of him but Stratton could clearly see that the safety catch was on and the stock folded. This was significant insofar as the AK47 had a safety catch that was notoriously difficult to push down when the stock was in the collapsed position. The bad news was that unlike nearly every other assault rifle in the world the first position after 'safe' was 'fully automatic'.

A screaming hoot from the locomotive indicated that its departure was imminent. Stratton relaxed his shoulders, firming his grip on the bar behind his back. As the man in the sidecar glanced in the direction of the train Stratton chose that moment to act.

He sprang forward, swinging the iron bar up in both hands. As the man jerked to life, surprised by the sudden attack and pulling up the gun, the thumb of his right hand trying to force down the safety catch behind the stock, Stratton brought the bar down onto his skull with such force that it caved in the bone around one of his eyes, bursting the eyeball. The man gave out a stifled squeal and went instantly limp, his

37

weapon clattering to the ground, his head dropping forward inside the car, his arms dangling over the sides.

The other man was no stranger to an ambush and, with the agility of a monkey, dropped off the seat to hit the ground on his right shoulder, rolling onto his back and over onto his knees while pulling his weapon strap over his head. But Stratton had not slowed the speed of his advance and maintained his momentum, planting a foot firmly behind the bike's rear wheel to make a tight turn around it, raising the iron bar on the upswing. The Arab remained on his knees and moved the business end of the AK47's barrel to point at Stratton as his fingers pushed down on the safety catch. Stratton heard the click and, knowing that he would never cover the short distance in time to strike the weapon aside, launched the bar with all his strength. It turned one revolution as it shot through the air and the end struck a glancing blow to the man's face, tearing open the side of his cheek and momentarily stunning him.

Stratton closed the gap and as the man levelled the weapon at him again Stratton stretched out a leg, the toe of his boot connecting with the barrel and kicking it aside. His momentum brought him on and the instant before they collided he raised a knee that connected with the man's jaw, sending him flying back. The man hit the ground but did not release his weapon and as he began to raise it once more Stratton dropped a foot onto the barrel, pinning it to the ground. At the same time he picked up the iron bar. A second later it came crashing down on the man's forehead. The Iraqi faltered under the heavy blow but there was fight left in him and Stratton, giving no quarter, raised the bar again and brought it down with all his strength. The top of the man's skull caved in like an eggshell and he died instantly.

Stratton breathed heavily as adrenalin coursed through his body, his gaze darting to the man in the sidecar before scanning the immediate area. The only human in sight was the boy who had taken to his heels the moment Stratton had begun the fight and was now watching from behind the corner of a mud hut.

Stratton dropped the bar, went to his bike, reached down under the tank, turned the small fuel-cock lever, straddled the seat, placed his foot on the crank pedal and pushed it down firmly. The engine didn't start and Stratton rose up and dropped all his weight onto the crank once again. By the third attempt fuel had passed through the system into the carburettor and the engine burst into life with a throaty rumble. Stratton reached down the other side, removed a heavy metal pin, took a firm hold of the handlebars and placed a foot on the sidecar, yanking the handlebars fiercely to one side while at the same time pushing hard with his foot. The sidecar, now disconnected from the bike, rolled over, the limp Iraqi inside it hitting the dirt, pinned beneath its weight.

Stratton moved his satchel comfortably in front of him, revved the engine, and was about to put it into gear when the boy ran up to him, holding out his hands.

'*Aatini flus,*' he said, more hopeful, demanding money. '*Aatini flus.*'

Stratton looked at the raggedy youngster who, although he had failed to fulfil his task, had at least remained with the motorbike. Stratton reached inside his pocket, pulled out several US currency notes and handed a five-dollar bill to him, enough to feed the boy and his family for a week if they were careful.

'*Shakran*,' the boy said. Then, as an afterthought, he reached into his pocket and removed an object which he held out in front of Stratton. It was a small, crude wooden carving of a camel that was wearing a probably unintentional wry smile. '*Ishteri*,' the boy said, asking him to buy it.

Stratton took the carving and inspected it. Then he looked at the boy who could not have been much older than Josh. He had large brown eyes and, judging by his matted hair, had not had a wash in a long time.

'*Khemsa dollar*,' the boy said, looking hopeful, aware that he was asking a hundred times its value though a good a price to begin negotiations.

'*Ante sewete?*' Stratton asked, suspecting that the boy had indeed made it himself since he had a small rustic knife sticking from his pocket and had been whittling a piece of wood with it when they'd first met.

'*Nam*.' The boy nodded. '*Ha thihe. Lel haz*,' he said, describing it as a good-luck charm.

Stratton inspected the camel once again, decided that it did have a kind of charm about it and handed the kid another five-dollar bill. He placed the camel in his pocket, put the bike in gear and revved the engine.

'Thank you,' the boy said in heavily accented English, a broad smile on his face.

Stratton looked back at him, unable to stop his own smile forming. 'Some master of disguise I am,' he said as he revved the engine once again. Then he released the clutch and roared away as the boy watched him go.

Chapter 3

Stratton manoeuvred the heavy bike along a dusty track for a short distance to the main road that headed south from Mosul towards Tikrit. Over his left shoulder he caught a glimpse of the train between the eucalyptus trees and dilapidated buildings that lined the road as it chugged out of the station. Stratton opened the throttle fully, made his way up through the gears and roared down the two-lane highway, which was moderately busy.

After several miles, he reached into an inside pocket, pulled out a GPS and switched it on. Seconds later a detailed coloured map of Iraq appeared on the screen showing his position on the road as heading for Baiji, the next major town before Tikrit. It also showed the railway line paralleling east of the road. The Tigris river crossed his path halfway to Tikrit to parallel the road's west side.

Stratton weaved around a battered orange and white taxi that was hogging the outside lane and overtook a line of oil tankers. Then, seeing the road clear ahead for half a mile, he toggled the GPS control panel until he found a specific waypoint – a pre-programmed location – which was a deserted spot west of Baiji, far out in the desert, the rail track clearly indicated less than a kilometre from it. He hit the 'go to' button and the information panel instantly indicated that it was a hundred and twenty kilometres away as the crow flew – more like a hundred and forty by road. The GPS also calculated that at his present speed he would arrive at the waypoint in an hour and thirty-nine minutes and he added another fifteen to allow for the road curvature which was ample time to get into position before the train arrived. That did not, of course, allow for any hold-ups.

Eighty kilometres further on, near where the railway line crossed the road, the traffic had slowed considerably and become denser. As Stratton made his way down the outside of the traffic he saw that the lead vehicles half a mile ahead had halted. That meant either a checkpoint, an IED (Improvised Explosive Device), exploded or not, or a traffic accident of which there were many in this country due to the terrible condition of the majority of vehicles combined with the atrocious standard of Iraqi driving. They had scant regard for highway codes, driving regulations and sensible speeds.

As Stratton closed on the tail end of the halted traffic he could see that it was an American military checkpoint. He slowed to cut in between the vehicles to get to the outside where he could head for the front of the line. To avoid the countless potholes and piles of trash on the verges he sometimes had to leave the road completely.

Two M111 armoured vehicles provided the main protection for the checkpoint, their 25mm heavy machine guns covering north and south of the road. There were half a dozen armoured Humvees, some a fair distance into the desert, their roof-turret M60 and .50 machine guns pointed at the line of traffic, and a couple of dozen soldiers on foot manning the vehicle funnel and supporting positions in various nearby locations.

As Stratton slowly made his way to the front of the line two soldiers reacted to his queue-jumping arrival by raising their M4 assault rifles and aiming directly at him.

'Hey, asshole,' one of them shouted as he moved forward. 'Stop where you are.'

Stratton stopped immediately, took the bike's engine out of gear and raised his hands. American soldiers were not famous for their politeness, tolerance or diplomacy. As far as persons or vehicles approaching their space were concerned, even the remotest suggestion of the presence of a weapon or a suicide bomber meant that an immediate response of the bullet kind could be expected.

'Where you goin' in such a hurry, ass-wipe?' the soldier shouted as he closed in, keeping his rifle aimed at Stratton's head. Stratton noted his shoulder flashes designating him a member of the 4th Infantry Division, based in Tikrit, that controlled this area.

The Arab occupants of the vehicles close by watched the proceedings with some interest, not that it was anything new to them. But it was of some concern to Stratton as he had a few miles to go after the checkpoint and did not want to take the chance of any local suspecting that he was a westerner. If they were to pass through the checkpoint soon after him they might be a threat and he was vulnerable on a motorbike. He decided to keep his mouth shut until the soldier got closer – although that too had its dangers.

'I'm talkin' to you, asshole,' the soldier yelled as he approached, his buddy staying back to cover him. It was not unheard of for Coalition forces to be attacked by a lone fanatic carrying a concealed weapon or explosive charge and, having lost a great number of fellow countrymen during the past couple of years, the soldier's aggressive reaction was understandable. However, things were not made any easier when soldiers assumed that every Arab could understand English.

'*Salam alycom*,' Stratton said as the soldier stopped a couple of metres in front of him, the rifle still aimed at his face.

'Yeah, fuck you too,' the soldier said. 'Shut the engine and get off the bike.' He gestured with the barrel of his gun, his finger curled warily around the trigger. 'Off!'

Stratton slowly lowered one hand to kill the engine, then the other to grip the handlebars so that he could climb off the bike. He dropped the stand with his foot and as soon as the bike was balanced upright he raised his hands again.

'What you got in the bag?' the soldier asked.

Stratton wasn't concerned so much about the explosives he was carrying. They were most uncommon and would only be recognisable to a special-forces operative. Even an Army explosives engineer would have to study them carefully before becoming suspicious. Stratton remained quiet.

'Search the motherfucker,' the soldier shouted to his buddy who walked briskly over, slung his weapon over his shoulder and reached out to pat Stratton down.

'I'm a British soldier,' Stratton said, quietly but firmly.

'What?' the soldier said, continuing with his task, his hands patting Stratton's shoulders and down the front of his chest.

'I'm a Brit,' Stratton repeated quietly. 'A British soldier.'

The soldier's hand touched something solid under Stratton's left arm and stopped dead.

'What he say?' asked the soldier doing the covering.

'Says he's a Brit,' the searcher said, his hand still on the metal object that he was certain was a pistol.

'That is a gun you can feel,' Stratton said, looking the searcher in the eye in case the man was unsure.

The soldier was going through his own possible scenarios that included Stratton being a fanatic who could speak English and waiting for his chance to strike. He had just a couple more weeks left out of a year-long tour of duty and wasn't about to end up in a body-bag after all that time. If that meant blowing away even a remote suspect, so be it. All he had to do was roll away while yelling 'Bad guy!' and his partner would empty his magazine into Stratton.

'I have ID in my jacket,' Stratton said.

The soldier looked into Stratton's pale eyes and knew they were not those of an Arab. 'Let's see it,' he said. 'Nice and easy.'

Stratton slowly reached inside his jacket, into the breast pocket of his shirt, and pulled out the plastic ID card that bore a hologram image of the Union Jack across its front, a gold information chip in a corner, and his picture. The soldier inspected the card, then looked at Stratton, only able to see his eyes. As if Stratton had read his mind, he slowly took hold of the *shamagh* where it covered his nose and pulled it down to reveal most of his face.

'You SF?' the soldier asked.

'Yes.'

The soldier took a moment to compare the ID thoroughly with Stratton's face, then his tension visibly lowered. 'Wait here,' he said before stepping back and walking away to leave his buddy to watch Stratton.

He was conscious of the minutes ticking away but there was no point in pushing these guys. They would let him get on his way in their own time once they were satisfied that he was kosher and nothing he could say would change that. Pushing them would only make it worse.

Stratton turned his head slowly and looked into the distance to where he expected the train to come from eventually. There was no sign of it.

The traffic slowly moved through the checkpoint, each car searched for weapons and other devices. A military interpreter, an Iraqi dressed the same as the soldiers and wearing body armour but not carrying a weapon, questioned the occupants. Some vehicles were allowed to proceed while others were directed off the road to an area where they were searched more thoroughly by soldiers using dogs.

Stratton watched the soldier with his ID show it to his commanding officer who inspected it, glanced over at Stratton, said something to the soldier, then handed it back.

The soldier returned and gave the ID back to Stratton. 'You're outta here,' he said dryly, unimpressed.

'Thanks,' Stratton said as he pocketed the card and climbed onto his bike.

'So, what are you, Lawrence a' fucken' 'Rabia?' the soldier asked.

Stratton started up the bike. 'You take care of yourselves,' he said, meaning it.

'You too, Lawrence,' the soldier said in his dry country accent, a smirk on his face.

Stratton cruised through the checkpoint. When he was clear of it he opened up the throttle and sped away.

Half an hour later he slowed to consult his GPS. He checked the lie of the land ahead, pulled off the road and steered along a track that led past a dilapidated village – a collection of mud huts, several battered vehicles, starved-looking dogs, ducks and goats, with raggedly dressed children playing amongst it all.

The uneven rock-solid ground that would be impassable mud for a bike in a couple of months' time when the rains arrived prevented a speedy passage. He had little choice but to bump slowly along, avoiding the deeper ruts as best he could.

A mile further on, as the track became smoother, Stratton stopped to check his GPS once again, comparing its information to the desert ahead that was flat as a billiard table. Across his front as far as the eye could see in either direction were electricity pylons, all bent over as if some great storm had tried to blow them down. The clue that the damage was man-made was provided by the missing cables and terminals, which had been stripped clean by criminals to be sold as scrap metal. Behind him he could just about make out the clump of trees that surrounded the village he had passed through while ahead the orange-yellow earth with its sporadic bumps and clusters of brittle vegetation ran on for ever.

Following the GPS he left the track and drove out over the hard-packed ground. After a mile he stopped again but this time he turned off the engine. The sudden silence was like a loud shout.

Stratton climbed off the bike, laid it down on its side with some care, removed his bag from around his neck and walked on into the desert towards several sandy mounds. It was not until he was a few metres from one that he spotted the tell-tale signs of a military hide: a whip antenna and a patch of camouflage net covering one side of the mound.

Stratton climbed under the back of the net and joined Jack who was looking out at the desert through a pair of high-powered binoculars.

'Watch out for the memorabilia,' Jack said, indicating an anti-personnel mine a few feet away.

Stratton glanced at the small Russian-made Pog that resembled a cast-iron corn on the cob half buried on the edge of the hide.

'The place is festering with mines,' Jack added. 'That one's probably from the Iraq–Iran war. Everything go okay?'

'Pretty much,' Stratton said as he put down his bag,

grabbed a bottle of water from a six-litre pack and drained most of it in one go. 'One locomotive,' he said, taking a breath, 'three passenger carriages, and a dozen or so trucks . . . Forouf is in the centre carriage.'

'Complicated?'

'Interesting,' Stratton decided as he finished off the bottle. Then he opened what appeared to be a small laptop inside a protective plastic jacket. He checked the power leads, plugged in the whip antenna that protruded through the cam net and turned the computer on.

'The junction is 500 metres ahead,' Jack informed him. 'I've rigged the charge and programmed it in as device zero one zero.'

Stratton flicked through several data screens on the laptop, stopped at a page labelled 'device queue' and studied it.

Jack picked up a radio handset. 'Alpha one, this is Mike four zero, the deck is loaded.'

A moment later the radio speaker crackled. 'Alpha one, roger that. We have a visual that gives you an ETA in approximately three minutes.'

'Roger that,' Jack replied.

'How did you rig the track change in the end?' Stratton asked.

'Well, I played with the two choices we discussed. I first went for the lever-throw option but then it started to look too complicated and so I ended up going for the push charge to shove the exchange rod directly across.'

'Good choice.'

'You sure?'

'I would've gone for that.'

Jack nodded, privately pleased. 'How about the carriages? How'd you rig 'em?'

'Some interesting combinations,' Stratton mused as he typed commands into the data queue. 'Gave myself a few options.'

Jack glanced at him, then back to the open desert. 'I'm looking forward to this.'

Stratton remembered something. He reached into his pocket, took out the small carving and placed it on a stone beside Jack. 'Here,' he said.

Jack looked at Stratton, then at the carving. 'What's that?'

'What does it look like?'

Jack stared at it. 'A camel with a harelip.'

'It's a present for Josh . . . he still collects animals, doesn't he?'

'He doesn't play with them as much since you started giving him all that military crap,' Jack said as he picked up the camel and inspected it. 'I hope you didn't pay for this.'

'It's a present from you.'

'Oh, I see. Dad comes home with the penny camel and what do you have for him? No, let me guess. A glistening scimitar you wrested from Saddam himself just before you single-handedly destroyed all his body-guards and brought him in.'

'No more military crap, I promise . . . Since we're not going to have a chance to go ashore and do some shopping other than at the PX on the airbase, which only sells military crap, I didn't want you going home empty-handed.'

'That's nice of you,' Jack said with unguarded sincerity.

'He'll love it.'

'Yeah. He probably will,' Jack agreed, placing it in his pocket and going back to his binoculars. 'Thanks.'

Stratton highlighted a list of eight device codes on his data queue with marginally different signal frequencies beside each.

'Here she comes,' Jack said, picking up the handset. 'Alpha one, Mike four zero has the obvious visual,' he said into the radio.

Stratton looked through his own binoculars and found the train beneath a black trail of smoke issuing from its nose. 'That's it,' he said as he went back to his laptop. 'Give me a nod at a thousand metres?'

'Roger that,' Jack said as he raised the handset to his mouth again. 'Mike four zero, we're standby, standby.'

'Roger, you're standby,' the voice repeated.

'Give me a countdown,' Stratton said as his fingers played the laptop with surprising agility as he went through a systems check.

'Will do,' Jack said, studying the train.

Stratton moved the cursor down the device queue, carrying out a receiver continuity test. When he reached the last code a red marker flashed a warning. He hit the test key again with the same result. 'Zero one zero . . . Jack? I'm showing no continuity on your charge.'

'What?' Jack exclaimed, horrified, and moved to where he could see the screen.

Stratton ran another test. 'That's a negative,' he said

as he grabbed his bag and started to head out through the back of the hide.

'No,' Jack said, taking Stratton's arm. 'I laid it, I'll fix it. You need to stay and play the board in case I can't get back in time.'

Stratton knew that it was the wisest choice and didn't argue.

'What a wanker,' Jack mumbled as he picked up his own demolitions bag and ducked under the cam net.

'Don't rush it,' Stratton called out. 'You have time.'

'I'm still a wanker, though,' Jack called back as he broke into a trot to the bike, raised it onto its wheels, straddled the seat and after the second crank, gunned the engine to life. He quickly snapped it into gear and shot away across the hard ground, kicking up a thin trail of dust behind him.

Stratton looked through his binoculars to gauge the progress of the train, then moved them to check Jack's progress. It was a risky move. Jack had to get to the charge, fix it, and get out of there before the train arrived. The engine driver would probably see the bike cross his front and his reaction would depend on how suspicious he was. Jack was wearing desert camouflage fatigues but the dust would make it difficult for anyone on the train to be sure of that until they were practically upon him. Stratton was confident that Jack would succeed but as he watched his friend and the train slowly converge he felt a twinge of fear for him.

Stratton and Jack had first met while on the same SBS selection course as young Marines many years ago. They exchanged hardly a word during the first three months of the course that began with a hundred and thirty-seven men. They only began to get to know each other during the last few weeks when the numbers were down to just twelve.

Their friendship was cemented during the final week-long exercise in Scotland when they partnered a two-man Klepper canoe along with one other pair to carry out a demolition raid against a power plant at the head of a loch. The underside skin of their canoe had been damaged during the final leg of their three-night portage across country to the foot of the loch from where they would paddle to the target. After patching it up as best they could by using a couple of oyster clamps they elected to press on, hoping that they could complete the twenty-kilometre paddle before the craft, an extremely durable wood and canvas construction, became unseaworthy. In truth, they feared the clamps would not hold for long and they put their fates in the hands of the gods simply because it would have been unthinkable not to make an attempt. The selection course was less about achieving the objective and more about tenacity and initiative in the face of extreme odds and exhaustion.

The gods, however, did indeed smile down on Jack and Stratton, for a while at least. They succeeded in planting their explosives on the target but as they made their way across the loch to the landing point where they were supposed to meet up with the other canoe one of the oyster clamps dramatically failed and water gushed in. With more than a thousand metres to the rendezvous they quickly changed direction and paddled as fast as they could to the nearest shore, which was still two hundred metres away. But within seconds the canoe was completely submerged and although it had built-in flotation tubes, their equipment, which included rifles as well as rations for several more days, was too heavy and they abandoned it as it sank. The water was near-freezing but they were forced to ditch their jackets, boots and trousers in order to stay afloat and not follow their canoe to the bottom which was a good hundred metres below them at that point.

As they briskly swam side by side through the calm black water that had a frozen mist hovering just above it Jack and Stratton were keenly aware of the seriousness of the problem. They were in a severe survival situation that would not necessarily be solved when they reached the shore — if they *could* reach it, that was. They tried to distract each other from the biting cold with inane chatter as they breast-stroked towards the black line below the silhouette of trees that indicated the shore. They discussed the possibility of drowning and how probably no one would know their fates for several days since the procedure, if they failed to meet up with the other members of the team, was to make the next rendezvous some twenty miles east across country.

The exercise was run as realistically as possible and if they could not make that location they were expected to head for the final emergency escape rendezvous another twenty miles beyond that. Only then, if they did not show up, would the alarm be raised and a search party sent out to trace their route from their last known position. It could be several days on top of that before it was assumed that they had gone down in the loch and God only knew how long before a dive search was organised. In short, if they didn't make the shore and find an immediate way of getting warm again they were screwed. To add to their problems the area was deserted for miles in every direction apart from the power station. But to seek aid there would mean, as far as the exercise was concerned, giving themselves up.

Ten minutes after bidding farewell to the canoe the pine trees that lined the distant shore seemed as far away as ever. Jack and Stratton were aware that their core temperatures were dropping dangerously low. Their limbs had long since gone numb and though it was getting more difficult to operate their muscles they increased their efforts, as much to generate body heat as to speed up their swim.

Stratton's hand suddenly hit something which turned out to be a rock and they were instantly rejuvenated: unlike most of the loch's shoreline that dropped almost vertically where the land met the water they had been heading for a point with a shallow gradient.

A few minutes later they were helping each other stagger up the rocky beach, unable to feel the stones beneath their bare, numb feet. As soon as they hit the shoreline they broke into a hobble, moving as fast as they could up the slope and into the wood where they stopped to take off their T-shirts, their only clothing other than their underpants, squeeze out the water and put them back on, a task that was exceedingly difficult in their condition.

'What do you think?' Jack asked, shivering fiercely.

'We don't have much choice,' Stratton said with

difficulty, his face and neck numb, the muscles almost rigid.

Stratton was referring to the power station and Jack had to agree. It was out of sight from where they were but finding it would not be difficult since all they had to do was follow the edge of the loch. The problems were the distance and if they would have enough time to get there before they collapsed.

'There's a road that follows the loch this side,' Stratton said. 'Let's head west until we strike it.'

They headed uphill and after pushing through the dense pine wood, which was overall easier on their bare feet, they emerged onto a track that, although muddy, was fairly level and, as such, a godsend. They broke into a brisk pace along it. The track met the tarmac road ten minutes later and they pressed on without stopping, keeping to the soft verges to save their tender soles that were already lacerated. The lights of the power station became visible in the distance through the trees.

Half an hour later Jack and Stratton paused at a sharp bend in the road as it veered away to follow a river that fed the loch. The power station was less than half a mile away as the crow flew but the road showed signs of diverting along the inlet for possibly a couple of miles before crossing it and turning back towards the station. They chose to save time by going cross-country against the distance of the road and made their way down the rocky incline and into the freezing water. They swam across as quickly as they could and scrambled up the steep, rocky bank the other side and back onto the tarmac road.

By now they were literally turning blue and were well aware that hypothermia was fast setting in as their bodies closed down all extremity blood-flow to preserve what energy and heat they had left for their brains and organs. They forced conversation as best they could, talking about anything: upbringings, school, girlfriends, whatever came to mind. Once they lost control and succumbed, delirium would be followed by collapse, coma and then death.

As they rounded the final bend to the power station and stepped from gloom into the glow from the security lights that surrounded the complex they continued to question the wisdom of giving themselves up, despite their serious situation. It was the equivalent of surrendering to the enemy and, although the training team would understand it to be a life-or-death situation, in their own hearts, and in the minds of the others, they would have failed. The charges they had laid were part of a coordinated attack and were intended to detonate at the same time as others in the area. A check of their watches showed that there was a good hour before the devices were supposed to blow. Their surrender would alert the 'enemy', giving them time to search and perhaps find the charges, raise the alarm that special forces were about and compromise the other teams. That would be an unforgivable failure and one that neither man would want to live with. But it was also clear that they would not survive much longer in their present condition.

As Jack and Stratton approached the power station they saw a military four-ton truck parked part-way down the slope towards the main entrance and recognised it as one used by the SBS Directing Staff. The DS would no doubt be inside in the control office with the duty civilian engineers, taking advantage of the warmth and the tea and coffee facilities while watching the loch for signs of the attackers who were expected to get in and out without being seen.

Stratton and Jack made their way to the lorry and Stratton checked the cab to ensure that it was empty. The back was secured by a tailgate with a length of canvas rolled down from the roof to meet it. The canvas was not strapped to the tailgate and they reached up to pull themselves inside. But they were shocked to discover that they could not use their hands – their limbs were so cold and numb that their nerves had ceased sending information to the muscles. As they looked at each other in the stark illumination of the security lights, long past the shivering stage and stunned by the level to which their bodies had deteriorated, they began to laugh, even though they were horrified as well as amused at their ridiculous predicament. They had come this far, almost frozen to death, dripping wet, inches from possible sanctuary and couldn't help themselves.

'I hope I'm not as blue as you,' Jack said.

Stratton raised one of his feet to inspect the bottom of it. 'I think we've lost the soles of our feet,' he said, and they laughed even more.

'How long do you think we have before we die?' Jack asked, grinning.

'I don't know, but not long,' Stratton replied.

The laughter dried up and they looked soberly at each other.

'Better get in the back of the lorry and see what's inside, then,' Jack suggested.

'Let's get the tailgate down,' Stratton said and each took a side to take out the pins that held it in position. Stratton's was loose and popped out immediately so he went to help Jack who was having trouble with his. They pushed on it together but it was jammed solid. Stratton managed to pick up a stone and after a couple of taps the pin came loose and they pushed it out to let it dangle on its chain. Noise was not a concern since the buildings were some fifty yards away and the wind was blowing strongly.

Together they pulled at the tailgate and, unable to hold it as it lowered, they let it swing down with a clang. After helping each other inside, they attacked the bags and boxes. The Directing Staff always carried emergency gear that included clothing, sleeping bags, rations, fuel cookers – everything that Stratton and Jack needed to survive.

They had to help each other out of their wet, near-frozen T-shirts and pulled on the dry clothing as quickly as they could, not bothering with buttons since that was impossible at that moment. The DS kept their own field kit in the lorry and Stratton and Jack raided their bags for footwear which fortunately fitted. A few minutes later they were climbing out of the back of the lorry with a backpack each, filled with necessary stores. They hobbled across the road like two old men. But it was still not over for them. They were still cold to the core and had to find a secure place where they could get into the sleeping bags and make a brew of hot, sweet tea before they could even begin to start getting back to normal.

They headed straight up a pine-covered hillside that loomed over the power station. After walking only a hundred yards into the dense wood they dropped their packs, unwrapped their sleeping bags and wriggled into them. Jack placed a petrol cooker between them and got it going while Stratton rigged a poncho across their feet to cover the glow from the cooker in case any of the DS should venture out to the truck. Within a few minutes both men were lying back, enjoying a hot brew while a meal was heating up on the cooker.

It took a while before the throbbing from the cuts on their feet began to increase – which was not all bad since it indicated that their circulations were returning. After the meal both men fell into a deep sleep despite the pain. When they woke up at dawn, having missed the first rendezvous, they decided to get going for the next later that morning despite it being daylight. They could take it nice and easy, get there by dark the following day and continue the rest of the operation. Walking would be painful but, considering the suffering they had already endured on the selection course, the fact that this was the final exercise and the last hurdle would make it that much easier, knowing they could rest all they wanted at the end of it.

Jack and Stratton remained close friends from that day on and five years later Stratton was best man at Jack's wedding. As he watched Jack tear across the desert on the old Russian motorbike towards the track junction with a force of militia bearing down on him he knew that Jack would not give up until he had succeeded in his task – and that was what worried him most.

Stratton forced himself to look away to concentrate on his own task as the train closed on the thousand-metre point of the track. He pulled the laptop in front of him, moved the cursor down the column of devices, highlighted one of the codes, and positioned two fingers over the two detonation keys that had to be pressed simultaneously. He looked up to check the train's location and as it reached the point he hit the keys.

Stratton watched the coupling between the second and third carriage flash brightly as it blew apart. A second later a thunderous boom engulfed the hide and echoed across the desert.

Forouf was in the middle of a conversation with his associates when the blast shook the carriage to its wheels as it hammered the rear door from its hinges, throwing it into the long, narrow space where it slammed into a row of seats. He was first to recover and hurried to the gaping hole in time to see the carriage behind separating from his. Several of his fighters appeared, bunched in the opposite doorway, staring helplessly at the widening gap as their master gradually moved away from them.

Alif Hammad, one of Forouf's associates, had dropped to the floor to cover his head with his hands and remained waiting for a devastating assault that he expected to follow any second. When it did not come he got to his knees and looked out of a window to find nothing but the open desert. He had been waiting for an attack since leaving Mosul and prayed that it was not a cock-up. He did not care if they killed Forouf in the process although the man was of some importance. But Hammad was particularly concerned about his own well-being.

Stratton highlighted another device code on his laptop and hit the keys.

Forouf watched in horror as another explosion beneath the trailing carriage blew the wheels off. Its front, now unsupported, dropped. Several of his militia fell from the doorway onto the track to be instantly grated, then the carriage spun sideways and flipped over. The occupants were brutally tossed as if in the spin cycle of a washing machine before the carriage disintegrated and they were thrown away or crushed beneath the tumbling undercarriage. The trucks following behind completed the destruction as they ploughed through what was left of the carriage.

Forouf pushed angrily back into his carriage and went from side to side, searching through the windows for the enemy who had done this. But because of the angle he could not see the motorbike cutting across the front of the train.

The locomotive driver and his engineer had heard the explosions behind them that shook the train and were straining to look back out of the windows at either side of the cab. They saw the final destruction of the carriage and turned in to look at each other, shocked and completely clueless as to what they should do. The engineer then saw the motorbike ahead as it arrived at the rail junction. He shouted for the driver to look. It only served to add to their dilemma, leaving them with just two options: stop, or keep going. But since they had no communications with the boss two carriages away and were scared to make a decision that could get them shot they agreed to do nothing and keep going. One thing they were sure of: this was not a good day.

Jack leaped off the bike as it slid to the ground and hurried to the charge on the outside of the rail up against the end of the ramrod that levered the track change. It was exactly how he had left it and he studied it quickly without touching anything, unable to identify the fault. A distant crack and another explosion turned his attention to the train as a ball of smoke rose from behind the engine. Then he looked back down at the charge.

The door at the front of Forouf's carriage blew in as the coupling between his carriage and the leading one disintegrated, separating it from the rest of the train. The wind immediately ripped through uninterrupted with no doors now at either end and as Forouf hurried forward to see what this new destruction was he saw several of his men lying dead in the doorway of the leading carriage as it moved away.

Confusion, frustration, anger and fear brought him to the boil as the locomotive gradually pulled away and one thing became obvious to him. He had been deliberately isolated from his men and the engine.

Forouf hurried to the front of his carriage as some of his men appeared at the rear of the one moving away from him. '*Awkef al qetar!*' he yelled to one of them who responded by running back through the carriage to the other end where he opened the door to reveal the rear of the locomotive. The man jumped across the coupling and grabbed at the handle of the door that led into the engine compartment but it was locked. He banged on the window and shouted in futile competition with the wind, the clattering wheels and the throb of the engines. He was joined by a colleague who nudged him and indicated the ladder that led up onto the roof of the locomotive.

Jack gave up on the charge and with no time to replace it he cursed loudly at his bad luck or ineptitude. Whichever, it was his fault. There was nothing more for it than to throw the junction switch manually. The only good news was that at least the job would get done since he'd had niggling doubts about the charge actually achieving the desired effect in the first place.

He dropped to the ground as the train closed on him and glanced up at the cab as it went past to see the engineer in the window looking down at him. As the back of the locomotive shot by he saw men climbing onto its roof. A second later the back of the carriage passed and he jumped to his feet, grabbed the heavy track-change lever and heaved on it. But the rusty joint was tight and barely moved.

Forouf's carriage was seconds away.

Jack slammed a foot against a sleeper and with a

supreme effort, his shoulder behind it, the lever started to move.

Suddenly, bullets peppered the ground around him, zinging off the rails and slamming into the wooden sleepers. Jack glanced up in mid-effort to see the fire coming from the rear of the carriage attached to the locomotive. His instincts were screaming at him to take cover but Forouf's carriage was almost upon him and, ignoring the shots that were fortunately poorly aimed, he invoked every ounce of his strength. An explosion suddenly destroyed the back of the loco-motive, killing the men who were firing at him and Jack knew that Stratton had seen the shooting. He yelled out loud and as his strength peaked the lever gave in and the ramrod shunted the internal rack across, an instant before the front wheels of the carriage touched it.

Jack hit the ground and rolled away as the carriage flew past but he was not out of danger yet. Forouf had seen him from the window and had grabbed a weapon from one of his men, hurried to the rear of the carriage and opened fire while his men shot from the windows.

Jack was exposed where he lay and, since the carriage was slowing down, he decided that a moving target was better than one lying still and leaped to his feet, pulled the bike up, started it and sped away. Gunfire raked the ground in front of and behind him and he opened the throttle while keeping his head low.

Stratton watched his friend through his binoculars, clenching his teeth, willing him on. Then he grabbed the handset. 'Mike four zero, go, go, go!' he shouted.

Two Chinook helicopters carrying the reaction teams had been hovering on standby just above the ground a mile away and immediately raised their tails as the pilots applied full power, their twin rotors grabbing the air and pulling the heavy beasts forward. Within seconds they were screaming at full speed feet above the ground towards the lone carriage trundling across their front.

Stratton stepped from the hide and stood on the mound, his attention focused on Jack as he watched him speed across the desert leaving a broad trail of dust in his wake. 'Come on, old buddy, keep it going,' he muttered.

The choppers covered the ground in half a minute and a short distance from the carriage both of them rose up sharply and banked in opposite directions to split their attack formation. The lead chopper manoeuvred sharply in front of the carriage while the door gunner, seated behind a .50 calibre heavy belt-fed machine gun, let rip, sending a hail of fire across its front and down the sides, the intention being to frighten the occupants into ceasing fire. The second chopper came in low behind the carriage, fired a burst across the rear to scare the men with weapons in the wrecked doorway, then turned up the side, crossed beneath the other Chinook, moved ahead several hundred metres and reared up as it made ready to hover, kicking up dust that practically hid it from view. Before the rear wheels touched down, men toting M4 assault rifles and wearing desert combats, loaded webbing, and goggles against the dust, streamed down the rear ramp and split into groups. One of the teams, carrying a long roll of heavy wire mesh, ran to the track, placed it across the rails to cover the width, ran it out for twenty metres and then hurried away to take up firing positions as the carriage drew closer.

Fifty yards from the mesh another team fired grenades in through the carriage's windows as it rolled past and seconds later it was filled with a dense white smoke. The front wheels rolled over the mesh, which wrapped around and locked them.

The second Chinook landed a team at the first crash site to secure it in case anyone had survived. Then it went in pursuit of the locomotive that was already slowing down, the engineer frantically waving a stained white rag out of the window.

As Forouf's carriage came to a halt the men inside practically fell out of its front and rear, coughing and spluttering, eyes streaming and mucus pouring from their noses. Forouf was among them as they were immediately leaped upon, dragged to the ground, hooded and cuffed. Hammad was treated with the same courtesy to avoid him incurring any suspicion and though he was relieved that it was over and that he had lived through it he vowed never to make such a deal again, certain that his survival had been purely by chance.

Stratton jumped off the mound and exhaled with relief as Jack headed towards him.

Jack was elated, not only with the success of the operation but with the rush of having survived the gunfire. He raised a hand and waved, then, deciding to celebrate with a bit of showmanship, climbed up onto the bike's seat and stuck a leg in the air, balancing the machine carefully over the rugged terrain. Feeling even more confident, he took a hand off the handlebar and raised that too.

The front wheel started to wobble and Stratton shook his head, fully expecting his friend to take a tumble any second.

Jack didn't see the small anti-personnel mine the size of a cigarette packet half buried in the sand. It had been there for a decade and a half, and had that been all he might well have survived the blast of just a few ounces of explosive hitting the bike's wheel. But it was a not uncommon trick played by many armies to place an anti-personnel mine directly on top of a vehicle or anti-tank mine, which was the case on this occasion.

The explosion threw Jack high into the air, the bike spinning in pieces beside him. Stratton broke into a run before Jack hit the ground, ripping the *shamagh* from his head and screaming Jack's name as he sprinted as fast as he could, uncaring that he could meet a similar fate.

He slid to a halt on his knees beside Jack's horrendously mutilated body, aware that if by some miracle Jack was still alive he would not live long, not out here, miles from a hospital. There was a medic pack back at the hide but it would be of pitiful use against these injuries. He put a hand to Jack's throat, searching for a pulse, but there was none.

Stratton remained motionless beside his friend, barely aware of the dune buggy tearing across the desert towards him, until something in his subconscious let out a warning cry.

He jumped to his feet, took out his pistol and fired it towards the buggy, the bullets striking the ground either side of it.

The buggy came to a halt and Seaton climbed out, leaving Smiv at the wheel.

'Mines,' Stratton shouted.

Seaton instantly realised what had happened. He glanced around the immediate area, then back at Stratton.

Stratton knelt again beside his friend and it was only then that he noticed the little wooden camel on the ground next to Jack. He picked it up and held it as memories of their times together swept through his head. Then, suddenly, he could see Sally's face as she heard the news. And then he thought of poor Josh.

Stratton heard his name being called and looked around at Smiv who was standing in the vehicle and shouting as loud as he could.

'Do you want a chopper?' Smiv repeated.

Stratton understood what he meant. The chopper could hover feet off the ground while Stratton lifted Jack inside. But there was no need for that now. He would carry his friend back to the hide, retracing his footsteps, and even though there were still dangers in doing that he did not give a damn. He wasn't about to leave Jack out in this shit-hole for the hours that it would take to clear a route wide enough for a vehicle to get to them.

He signalled a negative response that relayed the worst. Seaton watched as Stratton crouched down, picked up Jack's body, and walked away.

Chapter 4

Sally sat alone in her kitchen at the dining table, wearing a black dress and staring through unfocused eyes at a pile of sympathy cards and letters, most of them from members of Special Forces units around the world.

She was numb, and unhappier than at any time in her life. Her world had been thrown on its ear and it was only in the last couple of hours, since Jack's ashes had been poured onto the gently lapping waters of Poole Harbour from a jetty on the Hard, the landing point used by the SBS down the road from their head-quarters, that she had begun to think beyond this day. She was surprised by how clearly she could suddenly see the way ahead once she turned her attention to it and how obvious it was what she needed to do. She wondered if the clarity was some kind of illusion but her plan, which was arguably extreme, was in char-acter and she would stick with it unless a better one presented itself.

The doorbell rang but Sally didn't move other than to blink her red-rimmed eyes. She didn't want to speak to anyone else that day. The funeral had been bad enough. It was the small talk that was so frustrating.

She'd hated the colonel's eulogy, going on about how great Jack was. She knew that better than anyone but all it did for her was to prolong the pain. There was nothing more to say as far as she was concerned. Jack was dead, gone from her life for ever and her son was fatherless. Those were the cold facts and although she would miss him terribly nothing would bring him back.

Josh had been quiet during the ceremony but otherwise normal until he saw Smudge with tears rolling down his face. Then he started to cry and so did she. It was horrible and she couldn't wait to get home and be alone.

The doorbell went again. Sally got up and walked to the window but the visitor was out of sight in the small alcove. She wondered how long they would keep pushing the bell before they got the hint and went away. Then, as if he had heard her thoughts, Stratton stepped backwards into view and looked at her. She would never have been so rude as to wave anyone away once they had made eye contact but Stratton was probably the only person she would genuinely welcome inside. He was different and practically family, away all the time, it seemed, but when he was home he always came to visit and always had a gift for Josh who loved him.

She went into the hall and opened the door. Stratton stood looking at her, wearing a dark suit and looking unusually tidy.

'Why aren't you at the mess with everyone else?' she asked, forcing a smile.

'I was on my way . . . Can I come in? I won't stay long.'

Sally stood back to let him in.

Despite their close relationship he felt awkward as she closed the door behind him. It was a different world inside the house now and Sally was a different person now that Jack was gone. As she stared at him it was as if his presence had finally broken the dam she had built in her heart. Her expression changed suddenly as the tears began to well up in her eyes. She fell into his arms and sobbed like a child.

'I'm sorry,' she said. 'I've been trying to brave it out all week but I can't any more.'

'It's okay,' Stratton said, feeling uncomfortable with the closeness. It was this kind of emotional contact that he had difficulty with. Whenever he indulged it felt insincere though it was not. It was the physical display that he had trouble with. That had always been the main problem behind his unsuccessful relationships with women. Sharing this moment with Sally should have been different, it should have been natural despite the circumstances. But it was not.

She pulled away as if sensing his discomfort. 'Right. No more tears,' she said, wiping her eyes and heading back into the kitchen. 'I'll put the kettle on.'

Stratton followed, wanting to say something to comfort her, but he couldn't think of anything intelligent. Not that it would have made much difference. Sally was a tough and stubborn woman and would do things her own way, even more so now that she was without Jack's soothing common sense.

Stratton sat on one of the stools at the island breakfast bar and watched her make the tea. His gaze wandered around the room, to the cards on the table and the toy basket in a corner. 'Where's Josh?' he asked.

'Downstairs, watching TV, but he's not really watching it. Poor lad. I don't think it's truly sunk home yet that his dad's never coming back.'

'Maybe he's tougher than you think.'

Sally hoped that Stratton was wrong, though she feared otherwise. The truth was she didn't want Josh to be that strong, like his father, or worse, void of emotion like his godfather. She didn't want him to become a soldier like them. It suddenly dawned on her that her plan was based on that very fear. She didn't want Josh to grow up around soldiers any more or be influenced by them.

'We're leaving Poole,' she said matter-of-factly, pouring the milk into the cups.

Stratton detected something in her tone that suggested there was more to the statement. 'Going up north?' he asked.

'No. Well, for as long as it takes to sort out things with my mum and dad. Then we're leaving the country.'

Stratton masked his surprise.

'We're going to the States,' she went on. 'I've got a cousin in California. They're always asking us over.'

It sounded to Stratton she was talking about more than just a short break.

Sally took a moment to put her thoughts in order while filling the mugs with tea, placing one in front of Stratton. 'I want to get away. I mean, really away.'

'Sounds like a good idea,' he said, saying it for the sake of talking but not sure.

'I'm going to sell the house,' she said. 'My dad'll take care of everything.'

Stratton sipped his tea. Sally was not one for making idle statements and he did not doubt her sincerity.

'I'm sorry,' she said.

'For what?'

'Josh won't be able to see you.'

'I'll always visit.'

She looked at him and smiled. A part of her wanted Stratton to remain in their lives but she could never begin to tell him her fears about that. It was counter to what Jack would have wanted and although that made her feel guilty she believed she was doing the right thing. Anyway. Much as Stratton might want to visit as often as he could she doubted he would make it to somewhere as far away as California very often. They saw him little enough as it was, even living in Poole.

'When are you leaving?' Stratton asked.

'Soon as I can pack everything into boxes, pile them in the hallway for my dad and pack a couple of suitcases . . . Will you keep that to yourself? I couldn't take fifty service wives beating on my door . . . I'll call our close friends when I get to my dad's.'

'Sure . . . I'll give you a hand.'

'I'd rather do it alone. There're a lot of things in this house that are going to be tough to say goodbye to.'

Stratton understood and got to his feet. 'Can I go to see Josh?'

'Sure. I need to make him something to eat,' Sally said, standing up and going to the fridge. 'Can I get you anything?'

'No, thanks.'

Stratton left the kitchen and walked along the corridor and down the stairs lined with framed family photographs, one of which included him. He stepped quietly into the living room.

Josh was seated on a couch, watching a cartoon show, and did not look at Stratton as he sat down beside him.

'Hi, Josh'

Josh moved closer to Stratton without looking away from the television and leaned against him. Stratton put an arm around him and they sat for a while, watching the TV.

Stratton eventually moved forward to face the little boy. 'I have something for you, Josh. It's a present from your dad,' he said as he opened his hand to reveal the little camel.

Josh took it and examined it, instantly appreciating the strange smirk. 'Thanks,' he said. 'Is there a story with it?' he asked.

The irony of the question struck Stratton. So many of the gifts he had brought back for Josh over the years were accompanied by fictitious tales of derring-do but he could not tell the boy the truth behind this one.

Stratton made a move to get up but Josh took hold of him. Stratton held him close and kissed his head. 'I'm going to go and see your mum,' he said, pulling away and getting to his feet. 'I'll see you later. Okay?'

Josh slouched forward as if to study the camel but he was actually hiding his disappointment.

'You look after that, Josh. It's a very special little camel.'

Stratton left the room.

As he walked back into the kitchen Sally was busy cutting up vegetables into a saucepan. He picked up his tea and took a sip, unsure what to say to her, then saw her mobile phone on the counter and picked it up.

'You can use it in the States.'

'I know. I'll take it with me in case of emergencies until I can sort something out over there,' she said.

Stratton punched in his name starting with three 'A's and followed by his number. 'My number's at the top of your phone list. You call me if you need anything. Any time of the day or night. Okay?'

'I will.'

He stared at her, unable to hide his sadness. 'I'm gonna go, then . . . I'll call round tomorrow.'

'I want to leave first thing in the morning,' Sally said, wiping her hands and coming over to him. 'Dawn if I can get Josh to wake up that early.'

Stratton looked into her tired, reddened eyes, the pain clearly etched in them. He placed his arms around her and they held on to each other in silence for a moment before he released her and stepped back.

'Let me know when you get there,' he said.

'I will.'

'Promise?'

'Why wouldn't I?' she replied, unable to hold his gaze as firmly as she would have liked.

Stratton walked out of the room and a few seconds later the front door closed.

Sally watched him through the kitchen window as he headed down the gravel path and wondered when or even if she would ever see him again. 'If' seemed like a strange notion but she could not help thinking it.

Stratton drove directly to the sergeants' mess in Poole Camp, which was crowded with practically every current member of the service who was not on operational duty and even more retired hands who, although many of the old and bold did not personally know Jack, had turned up to pay their respects. He spent an hour chatting to various people and before slipping out cornered his Squadron Commander to ask for two weeks' leave, effective immediately. Under normal circumstances the operations officer would have had to be consulted in case there was anything that had come up on the boards. But considering that the request came from Stratton – bearing in mind, too, the circumstances, and the fact that he was owed several weeks' leave from his previous two operations – the OC granted it.

Stratton returned to his cottage in Lytchett Matravers on the outskirts of Poole and the following morning packed a bag and drove his Jeep to the ferry terminal in Poole Harbour where he caught a boat to Cherbourg. He had planned nothing more than a drive across Europe. Where, he cared not. East sounded appealing, across France, Germany, perhaps the Czech Republic, then down into Austria, and perhaps further still.

But he would reach as far as Salzburg in Austria

when a cry for help would send him tearing six thousand miles west to face a conflict he could never have imagined.

when I've told you, you don't have the right, from
Saul, unless there's a ... ' Maybe this could never have
happened.

Chapter 5

Sally stepped out of the Bradley Terminal at LAX, Los
Angeles International Airport, pushing a trolley loaded
with baggage, Josh holding on to the side, and headed
for the shuttle stop where transport would take them
to the car-hire depot. Half an hour later she was sitting
behind the wheel of a Cherokee 4x4, acquainting
herself with the controls.

It was late in the afternoon. Because of the distance
from LAX to her cousin's house near Sacramento –
according to the lady at the car-hire place, a good six
to eight hours' drive north, depending on whether she
took the scenic coastal route or the freeway – she
decided to spend the night in LA. An early start the
following morning would also avoid the heavy late-
afternoon freeway crush of traffic heading out of the
city. Sally had been recommended to find a hotel in
Marina Del Rey which was only a few miles from
the airport and a safe area, or Santa Monica a few
miles further up the coast where there was a large
British population and an English pub. Sally found no
attraction in an English connection but she decided
to head in that direction anyway since the map indicated that the freeway north to Sacramento started

near Santa Monica: she could hop right on it and avoid getting entangled in the traffic hassles of the city.

Unfortunately, a combination of heavy traffic and her unfamiliarity with left-hand driving caused Sally to miss several turns. Fifteen minutes later she was lost. However, she was confident that Santa Monica was not far away. A street sign indicated that she was on Sepulveda Boulevard which was marked on the map as a major road. But although it passed close to Santa Monica after it became Lincoln Boulevard it appeared to run north and south for miles and she was unclear about precisely where she was on it. She could calculate west by using the sun, having had Jack explain it often enough when they'd been on camping trips, so she decided to head that way until she hit the ocean. It seemed straightforward enough.

She waited for a gap in the traffic, pulled across the road and headed down a side street.

The houses immediately became shoddy, the streets dirty and the population predominantly Latino and black. As Sally passed a group of youths one of them shouted something and ran into the street, waving for her to stop. She accelerated past and watched him in her rear-view mirror as he made what appeared to be an obscene gesture. An uncomfortable feeling washed through her but there was nothing for it but to press on to the beach, which she hoped was not far away. A quick glance over her shoulder revealed Josh playing with some toys on the back seat.

'You tired, Josh?'

'Yes,' he nodded while assisting one of his Action Men to wrestle with a small tiger.

'We'll be at a hotel soon,' she said, although as she drove on there was no sign of the neighbourhood improving. She assured herself that the beach would be a completely different kettle of fish once she found it. No doubt it would be developed and bustling, just as in the television programmes on LA she had seen.

Sally crossed an intersection and passed a block of predominantly wooden bungalows with cracked paint-work and old shingle roofs. The buildings were even more dilapidated than those on the previous street. The number of tramps or homeless-looking people also seemed to increase and as she came to the end of the street she passed a long row of what could only be described as makeshift kennels on the sidewalk. Built of debris, driftwood and plastic sheets, they were inhabited by humans, not animals. It was as if she had travelled back in time to the Depression.

A boy suddenly ran out onto the road up ahead, followed by others, forcing Sally to brake suddenly. But she didn't stop completely and steered around them as they banged on her window and shouted in guttural Spanish. Josh looked up, suddenly uneasy.

She came to a T-junction and stopped to look both ways. Neither direction showed much promise so she turned north, looking for the next road heading west. Every block was penetrated by dirty, rubbish-filled alleyways. As she arrived at a small intersection she took the left turn, hoping that the sea would soon come into view. But the ground rose sharply as the road headed uphill. The quality of the houses improved slightly but they all had security gates, as well as bars on the lower windows. Some had barbed wire along

82

the tops of their outer walls. It seemed as though every person she passed, none of them white, looked at her suspiciously. This made Sally conscious of the fact that she was a lone white woman in a nice car and obviously in the wrong place.

Cars were parked on both sides of the street, most of them in a run-down condition. This was not the LA that she had seen on TV – it was closer to a shanty town in a Johannesburg suburb.

As Sally came to the crest of the hill she could see that several cars were double-parked, making the street barely wide enough for one vehicle to pass along. She slowed to navigate between the cars when suddenly a sedan shot backwards out of an alleyway and reversed along the street towards her. She braked hard.

The sedan screeched to a stop yards in front of her and a large man in a leather jacket jumped out of the passenger side, ran over to a shorter man walking along the pavement and started to beat the living daylights out of him.

Sally could not believe what she was seeing.

'Where's the fuckin' money, asshole?' the big man yelled as he kicked the other who had dropped to the ground to protect himself from the vicious blows of the thug's fists.

Sally looked around at the road behind. She considered reversing back down the hill but did not trust her driving skills with a left-hand-drive vehicle. Her anguish increased and, feeling helpless and scared, she pushed the centre of her steering wheel and gave a blast of her horn.

The man doing the beating paused while holding

on to the collar of his near-unconscious victim whose face was by now bleeding badly. He looked at Sally with a murderous glint in his eyes. 'Leka! Take care a' that bitch,' he shouted.

The sedan's reversing lights were still on. To Sally's shock it suddenly accelerated backwards and hit her car hard enough to make her fly forward and bang her chin on the steering wheel, stalling her vehicle.

Josh started to cry and call out for her, increasing her anxiety. Then the driver's door opened and Leka climbed out. He was a large man, dark-skinned though not Latino. His features were more Slavic or Eastern European.

As Leka reached her car, Sally quickly hit the central locking system, securing the doors. She watched the man as he moved with relaxed ease, wearing a malicious expression that she found immediately frightening. As he reached her door he slammed the side of her vehicle with his hand and then ripped off a wing mirror.

'Move the fucking car, bitch!' he shouted.

Sally's panic rocketed and she tried to start the car as Josh cried behind her. 'It's okay, Josh,' she said. She turned the key in the ignition and the starter motor turned over. But the engine failed to come to life.

Leka banged on her window as if he was trying to break in. 'I said move it, bitch!' he shouted.

Sally's efforts to start the car became desperate as she turned the key repeatedly without luck.

The man yanked hard on the door handle and then violently kicked the car, incensed at being denied entry.

'Move the fucken' car, bitch!' he yelled again as though her efforts were not enough.

The man beating his victim unconscious on the sidewalk stepped back, and straightened his shirt and jacket, as if he had finished for the time being. 'Next time I cut your legs and arms off, you understand? You got twenty-four hours, then we don't talk no more,' he said. The brute was as tall as his friend Leka but broader. He appeared to come from the same part of the world.

Sally looked around, hoping for help. Although there were a handful of people looking on with interest, none of them appeared to want to come any closer.

Sally pushed on the horn once again and this time held it down.

'Turn that off!' Leka yelled venomously. 'Turn it off!' he repeated, kicking out at the car again. Then something in the man snapped. He walked between the parked cars to a pile of rubbish on the sidewalk, picked up a large chunk of concrete and came back with it.

Sally released the horn to try and start the car once again but the engine was dead. Leka raised the concrete slab above his head and brought it crashing down onto the windscreen, cracking it so that it crazed in all directions. Sally screamed and leaned on the horn once more.

Leka raised the slab and brought it down again, this time shattering the windscreen completely and showering Sally with glass. Desperate and beside herself with fear she grabbed her handbag and fumbled inside.

She found her phone and struggled to hold it steady while she hit the keys.

Leka reached inside the car and grabbed hungrily for her like a wild beast. 'Come 'ere, you fucken' bitch!' he yelled as he clutched a piece of Sally's clothing which tore as she pulled back.

Stratton was asleep in his hotel room when he heard his mobile phone chirping in the pocket of his jacket, which hung across the back of a chair by the bed. He looked at the window and saw that it was dark outside. Then he reached for his jacket and pulled it onto the bed. He took the phone out of the pocket and when he saw the name on the phone's screen he hit the receive button swiftly. What he heard sent a chill through his entire body. A woman was screaming hysterically and in the background he could hear a man's voice shouting.

'Sally! Sally!' he shouted as he leaped out of bed. But it was evident that Sally no longer had the phone and was probably fighting for her life.

Sally had dropped the phone and was scrambling over the back of the driver's seat to protect her son. But Leka was already halfway in through the destroyed windscreen and reaching for her with his long, powerful arms. He caught hold of her ankle and yanked her back with brutish force, ripping her grip from the back of the seat as he pulled her towards him. He grabbed her by the hair with his other hand and with the same awful violence kept dragging her back, twisting her painfully so that she was now on her back halfway out through the windscreen and feeling as if her spine was about to break. She could no longer scream, the position of her body making it difficult even to breathe.

'You still wanna fuck with me?' Leka shouted, sliding down off the hood and dragging her to the side of the shattered windscreen, his face close to hers. The other thug walked over calmly and joined his partner to look down on Sally's contorted face. 'What you wanna do with her, Ardian?' Leka asked. Obviously his friend was the dominant one of the two. 'Shall we fuck her, or fuck her?' He laughed at his sophisticated use of the language that was not his mother tongue.

'Bitches don't get outta line,' Ardian said coldly. He brought his fist up into the back of Sally's neck with such force that something snapped. She went limp in Leka's arms and he released her.

Sally remained still, dangling awkwardly halfway out of the windscreen, facing the sky and gurgling gently.

'Guess we fucked her,' Leka said, smirking.

'Guess we did,' Ardian agreed. The two men looked along the street. The handful of youths who had remained at a distance to watch turned to head away, some of them moving at a run. The two men were neither fazed nor panicked by what they had done. They walked calmly back to their car, climbed in, and drove slowly away.

Josh was covering himself and crying in the back seat. He looked up once it had gone quiet to see that they were alone. He stood up, climbed over the seat, and looked at his mother. 'Mummy,' he sobbed. But she did not move. He took hold of her leg and shook it. 'Mummy!' She remained still. Josh wrapped his arms around her and continued to sob heavily and inconsolably.

Chapter 6

Stratton impatiently paced the small waiting area at the end of the corridor that led back to the entrance to the Santa Monica Police Department. A few yards away a line of people waited outside a glass window built into a wall behind which a police officer stood dealing with enquiries. Stratton checked his watch and tried to calm his growing frustration that threatened to turn into uncontrollable anger. It had been twenty minutes since the desk officer had told him that a detective would be down to see him in a few minutes since the officer himself knew nothing about Sally or Josh.

Stratton had no doubt that the call had been from Sally but he had not been able to get a reply from her phone since. Sally's parents had given him her cousin's number though Stratton had not said why he needed it so urgently. The cousin in Sacramento had not seen or heard from Sally and did not expect to until the following day. Stratton had been unable to contain himself and had caught the first available flight that morning. From the second he'd put down the phone in the hotel room in Salzburg everything had been done with maximum haste. The flight had been unbearably long and he had called Sally's number a dozen times, using the on-board payphone. Stratton was usually a patient man but now that he was finally in LA and, he hoped, within reach of finding out what had happened to her the waiting was starting to get to him.

A door halfway along the corridor opened and a portly man in civilian clothes stepped through, holding a file. He walked to the waiting area, stopped short of Stratton and looked around. 'Is there a John Stratton here?' he asked.

'I'm Stratton.'

The man, in his forties, was without doubt a cop: he looked as though he had been in the job for most of his life. He glanced at Stratton over the rims of his glasses, weighing him up. 'How can I help you, sir?'

Stratton held his frustration at bay. He had pain-stakingly explained every detail of his concerns to the desk officer and now this guy was acting as if he knew nothing. 'I'm looking for a woman named Sally Penton and her son, Josh. I believe she was in some kind of trouble and she may be hurt.'

'And where are you from, sir?'

'England.'

'And how long have you been here in the United States?'

'I flew in today.'

'You can prove that?'

Stratton dug into his pocket and pulled out his UK passport. The stub of his boarding pass was inside it and he handed both items to the officer, who inspected each page. 'They also took my fingerprints and photo-graph at Immigration.'

The officer ignored him until he got to the end of the passport and compared Stratton's photograph with the man himself. 'Are you a relative of this woman, sir?'

'No. She's a close friend.'

'Why do you think she's been in some kind of trouble?'

'She called me on my phone. She was screaming. It sounded like a scuffle, a fight, then all I could hear was crying which I think was Josh, her son.'

'She called you at your home?'

'My mobile phone.'

'What's the number of your phone?'

Stratton dug it out of his pocket, hit a key, and showed the face to the officer who took it and wrote the number in the file. 'Do you know anything about her?' Stratton asked.

'And you flew in from England, you said?'

'No. Austria.'

'You got here pretty quick.'

'There's a nine-hour time difference between Central Europe and the USA's West Coast. Look, do you know anything?'

The officer removed his glasses and squeezed the bridge of his nose with his fingers as if he was tired. 'I'm afraid your friend . . .' He paused to check the name on the file. 'Your friend Sally Penton is dead.'

The statement hit Stratton like a bolt of lightning although outwardly he remained unmoved. More than a decade and a half of wars and violent conflicts had hardened his reaction to any kind of bad news but this revelation stretched his control to its limits. 'How?'

'Was Sally into drugs?'

'What?'

'Drugs. She was driving through a pretty rough neighbourhood.'

'She was not into drugs. What happened?'

'We don't know much. Looks like gang-bangers.'

'Was she raped?'

'Doesn't look like it. This ain't official, but the initial report on the scene was that her neck was broke. Looked like someone bust in the windshield and dragged her outta the vehicle onto the hood.'

Stratton was shocked. This was very different from a friend dying in combat. 'What about Josh?'

'The boy's okay. Shaken up but he wasn't hurt.'

'Where is he?'

'Child-protection agency.'

'Where's that?'

'You gonna be in town long?'

The thought had not occurred to Stratton but the way things looked the answer was obvious. 'As long as it takes to get Josh home,' was all he could think to say.

'Where you staying?'

'I don't know.'

The officer took a card from his pocket, scribbled something on the back and handed it to Stratton. 'That's the protection centre. It ain't far from here. I'm Sergeant Draper. Those are my numbers. Let me know where you're staying.'

The officer's mobile phone rang in his pocket. He took it out and put it to his ear. 'Draper here.'

Stratton walked over to a chair where his backpack was, picked it up, and walked away.

'Hey, check back in a day or so and we may have something,' Draper called after him, but Stratton was already halfway along the corridor and heading for the exit.

Half an hour later, Stratton climbed out of the back of a yellow taxi, carrying his backpack. He faced a gate in a high fence that ran along the front of an open grassy area beyond which stood a large 1960s-style single-storey building. The taxi pulled away as he approached the gate and pushed it open.

Lights were on inside the building that had bars on all of the blind-covered windows. But there was no sign of life.

Stratton checked his watch. It was after six p.m.

As he approached the wooden entrance doors they opened and a young, conservatively dressed woman walked out, carrying a laptop case over her shoulder and an armful of files. She glanced at Stratton as she closed the door behind her. Then she made a point of checking it was firmly locked, as if she had decided that he was a suspicious character.

'Excuse me,' Stratton said.

'Can I help you?' she asked in a serious tone, looking him up and down.

'I'm here to see a boy who was brought in today or last night, I don't know which.'

'The facility is closed to visitors right now. You'll have to come back tomorrow.'

'Do you work here?'

'Yes,' the woman said, sounding tired and eager to get going.

She was attractive despite her frumpy clothes. Her fatigued eyes made her look older than she probably was.

'Could you just tell me if you know anything about a young English boy who was brought in today or last night?' Stratton asked, restraining his temper.

'We get a lot of children brought in every day. Like I said, you'll have to come back tomorrow,' she replied, impervious to his persistence. She was not a tough woman by nature but years of practice dealing with hostile parents and guardians had inured her to confrontations.

Stratton could see that he was up against a wall because of the way he was handling this so he took his attitude down a couple of notches. 'I know it's late but I've come a long way – is it too much for you to tell me if he's okay? That's all I want to know and I'll go. He's six years old, English, his name's Josh—'

The door to the centre opened and a stout black lady wearing thick bifocals leaned out. 'Oh, Vicky, you're still here. Do you know where the DCS 4334 forms are? I've looked everywhere.'

Vicky looked around at her.

'They're the court medical-consent emergency worksheet forms,' the black lady said.

'I know what they are, Dorothy,' Vicky sighed, frustrated at her unsuccessful efforts to get away from the building. 'Have you tried the bottom drawer of the second filing cabinet to the right of my desk?'

'Uh-huh. They ain't in there.'

'I'll come and look,' Vicky said, heading back to the door.

'That's okay,' Dorothy said. 'It can wait till tomorrow. You run along and have yourself some fun. You spend too long in this building as it is.'

'I'll look for them,' Vicky said as she reached the door.

'No,' Dorothy said, trying to act firm though she was obviously a subordinate. A grin crept onto her face. 'I didn't know you had company.'

'Dorothy,' Vicky said, feigning anger through clenched teeth.

'Okay, okay,' Dorothy said, stepping aside to let her through. 'Sorry. She won't be a minute,' she said to Stratton, the grin remaining on her face as she checked him out.

Dorothy followed Vicky inside and Stratton considered joining them. But he decided against it and looked out onto the street.

It was a clean, quiet neighbourhood, the centre surrounded on three sides by well-tended bungalows, the garden dotted with tall, slender palm trees and with a kids' climbing frame in one corner. It might have been quaint had it not been for the back of a row of unattractive three-storey non-residential buildings across the street. There was no brickwork anywhere to be seen: all the buildings were less than fifty years old and were made from stucco-coated, earthquake-spec frameworks, wood for the houses, steel for the non-residential places. This was still Santa Monica, some thirty blocks from the ocean and in a nicer part of the sub-city.

It would be dark soon and Stratton directed a thought to where he would stay. But he couldn't get Josh out of his mind for long enough to think straight. It was safe to assume that getting the boy back to the UK was going to involve a lengthy bureaucratic battle and at some stage Stratton was going to have to call his boss and let him know what he was doing. He told himself he was going to have to be very patient and work with the system, whatever that entailed.

He heard the door close behind him and turned to see Vicky walking back down the steps and onto the path.

'You were going to tell me about the boy.'

'No, I wasn't. Look, I've had a long day—'

'Nothing compared to his,' Stratton snapped, practically barring her way.

Vicky felt the sting of his sudden attack and looked into his steely eyes. Although she did not feel threatened by him his stare had an intensity she could not ignore.

'Are you a relative?' she asked.

'No.'

'I can't give information about any child in this centre to anyone other than a close relative or a court-approved guardian. I'm sorry but those are the rules,' she said, moving past him to open the gate.

'All I want to know is if he's okay,' Stratton said. 'Why is that breaking any rules?'

It was clear that this guy was not going to give up easily: he was obviously concerned and was not actually asking for very much. 'There was a young English boy brought in this morning,' Vicky said, relenting slightly. 'I don't know anything about him yet. We've had a busy day moving a dozen kids out to new homes and admitting over a dozen more. If he had been physically hurt then I would have known about it. Any child brought to us is here for a reason and it's never good, but I promise you that he's being well taken care of . . . Come back tomorrow and I'll be able to tell you more.'

'What time?' Stratton asked, his hand remaining on the gate latch.

'Not before nine a.m. Does he have any relatives in this country?'

'No.'

'Will any be coming over to get him?'

'He has grandparents, but they're old – I'm all he's got right now.'

Vicky nodded, understanding the situation far better than Stratton did. 'It's not going to be easy, mister . . . '

'For him or for me?'

Stratton saw the irritation return to her face, signalling that he had gone as far as he was going to get. 'I'll be back tomorrow,' he said as he pushed open the gate for her. 'Name's John Stratton.'

Vicky walked through the gate and down the sidewalk, feeling his gaze on her. She concentrated on putting Stratton and the boy out of her thoughts. It had the hallmarks of another difficult case but there were so many. This was just another in an endless line that she had to deal with every day. After ten years as a social worker in the child-protection agency she had almost managed to do what she knew she had to in order to preserve her sanity: disconnect herself from the job as soon as she left work – *almost* managed, that was. Had she known that it was going to be such a depressing, distressing vocation she might have chosen a far less 'noble' line of work after leaving college. Quitting was always an obvious option but even though she had often thought about it, desertion – for that was what it would really have been as far as she was concerned – was not something that she was prepared to contemplate. Only one other way of life was likely ever to get her away from the centre and that was having a child of her own. But that was so far off her life's radar that it was almost as depressing to think about.

Stratton watched Vicky walk around the corner at the end of the block as he let the gate close behind him, shouldered his pack and headed in the opposite direction. There was clearly scant chance of a taxi coming by in this area so he crossed the road and headed for the corner where another street led to Wilshire Boulevard, a main traffic artery that ran east from the coast and into the heart of Los Angeles.

A few minutes later Stratton was in a taxi, heading for the beach area.

'Any suggestions for a hotel?' he asked the taxi driver, an old, mellow man wearing a battered straw hat.

'How much you wanna pay?' the man asked in a relaxed Midwestern drawl.

'What are my options?'

'You new in town?'

'Yes.'

'Well, you got motels. They're around fifty bucks a night. Then there's places along the front. There're some fancy hotels. Don't know exactly what they cost but it's a few hundred dollars, easy. There's others not so fancy that you can get for something like seventy or so. How long you stayin' in town for?'

'Don't know.'

'If you're stayin' more 'n a week, there's an apartment building that sometimes does short lets. It's an old building they did up a few years back. You don't get room service but they have a launderette and Santa Monica ain't short o' good eatin' places, that's for sure.'

Stratton was attracted to the idea. The one thing he didn't like about hotels was the fact that someone came into the room every day. 'Where are these apartments?' he asked.

'Ocean Avenue, on the cliff front. Beach is a minute's walk.'

'Can we take a look?'

'Sure thing.'

The taxi took a left at the lights on Second Street a block before the end of the boulevard, then second right towards Ocean Avenue, the main boulevard running along the top of the tree-lined cliffs. It pulled over in the middle of the block and stopped at the kerb outside a large pink building with a neon sign advertising Pacific Towers Apartments. Stratton paid the man, climbed out with his backpack, and looked up at the sixteen-storey structure.

Stratton walked in through the glass doors of the entrance. A Chinese restaurant took up the ground floor on the left side and he went on through a short lobby and out into an open-air courtyard. The building took up three sides of a square and was open on the beach side. An old, dribbling fountain stood in the centre of the courtyard and a modern health club behind full-length glass windows was located on the right-hand side. Stratton crossed to a corner and went to push through another set of glass doors into what was obviously the reception area but they were locked. He could see a reception desk tucked away in the corner of a small lobby but there was no sign of life.

There was an electronic registry fixed on a wall to one side of the doors with a call button beside a small LED screen. He pushed the button. The screen requested him to enter an apartment number. One of the options he scrolled through was 'manager' so he selected it and hit the call button again. A moment later a dial tone purred from the small speaker followed by the electronic beeps of a number being dialled and then a ringing tone.

Seconds later a click was followed by a man's voice. 'Manager,' it announced.

'Hi. I'm looking for an apartment.'

'We got no full-time apartments available.'

'Short-term would be fine.'

'It's six-fifty a week plus utilities. How long you want it for?'

'I don't know. Couple of weeks, maybe.'

'You pay weekly plus a two-week deposit up front.'

'What floor's it on?'

'Fourth. In the back.'

Fourth was fine, Stratton thought.

'You want it or not?' the voice croaked.

Stratton had an image of a crusty middle-aged man who chain-smoked. 'I'll take it,' he said.

'I'll be out in a minute.'

The phone went dead and a buzzer in the door sounded. Stratton pushed it open and walked into the lobby that was clean and devoid of furniture apart from the reception desk. A pair of elevators occupied the centre of the lobby with a fire escape opposite and two corridors leading off in opposite directions, disappearing around corners and into the wings. A door slammed along one of the corridors and an overweight man in his forties with a cigarette hanging out of a large stubble-surrounded mouth walked around the corner where a sign indicated the entrance to the health club. He stepped behind the reception desk and produced a sheet of paper from a drawer.

'Fill this in,' he said, placing a registration form on the counter, a pen beside it. 'That'll be nineteen hundred fifty. You get the deposit back minus any damage and breakages when you leave.'

'You take a credit card?'

'Machine's broke, cash only.' The man reeled off the phrase as if he'd said it a thousand times.

Stratton had bought a couple of thousand dollars with his debit card at the airport but the taxis had eaten into it a bit. 'Can I give you nineteen and the rest tomorrow?'

'Tomorrow's fine. Room 411,' the manager said, placing a ring with two keys on it on the counter as Stratton counted out the money. 'The small key fits the lobby entrance. You gotta car?'

'No,' Stratton said, pushing the money towards him.

'If you get one, parking's fifty more a week. The

health club's free for you, ten dollars for guests,' he said as he deftly counted the hundred-dollar bills. 'We gotta launderette next floor down or if you want your washing done there's an old lady lives down the corridor. 103. Barbara. She's cheap. Been here twenty years and 'cause o' rent control she pays only two-fifty a week. Can you believe that? Can't get rid o' the old crate. We'll have to wait till she dies,' the manager said, producing a grin that revealed two rows of brown, distorted teeth.

Stratton completed the registration form without revealing his true home address and picked up the keys.

'You have any problems, I'm in 116 around the corner.'

'Thanks,' Stratton said, picking up his pack and heading for the elevator. While he waited for one to arrive the manager left the desk and went back the way he'd come. Stratton looked at the red fire-exit door and pushed it open. A grubby, dark, grey concrete stairwell led up, all the way to the roof no doubt, and down, most likely to the underground parking.

The elevator announced its arrival with a ding and the doors slid open. Stratton stepped inside and hit the button for the fourth floor. The doors closed and the elevator ascended.

Stratton stepped out into the fourth-floor corridor that resembled those in the lobby, both ends disappearing left and right around corners into the building's wings. It was clean and fresh-looking, the carpet either new or very well maintained. The number on the door in front of him was 408 so he took a guess and turned right. Large windows on the elevator side of the corridor revealed the dark ocean in the distance beyond the street-lamp-illuminated palm trees that lined the top of the cliff.

Stratton stopped outside apartment 411, the one nearest the corner. A glance along the brightly lit corridor into the wing revealed that it extended to a fire exit at the far end with a further half-dozen apartments staggered either side. He would check the fire exit later. He unlocked the door, pushed it open and walked inside.

The apartment wasn't as small as he had expected. It looked clean and the furnishings, though inexpensive, were functional. There was a separate bedroom and bathroom and a tiny kitchen – behind a partition in the living room – had a sink, fridge, cooker and a few cupboards squeezed into it.

Stratton placed his pack on the floor and went to the living-room windows that flanked the room's corner. The city was brightly lit and there was a view of the beach and the Santa Monica pier that had a large Ferris wheel on it set among funfair buildings decked in coloured lights. The cliffs melted away a short distance past the pier and the brightly lit Ocean Avenue continued south, separated from the beach by what appeared to be a row of expensive hotels. The view east, which could not be described as spectacular, was of the city itself, stretching as far as the eye could see.

Stratton went into the bedroom which was basic but adequate, as was the bathroom. It would do fine but he was already looking forward to leaving and going home.

He suddenly felt tired and checked his watch. It was almost four in the morning back home but experience had taught him to stay awake until at least past ten p.m. local time to help adjust to the time difference. The plan for the rest of the day was to find a cash machine, get some more dollars, then grab a bite to eat. He would follow that with a walk around the neighbourhood to familiarise himself with it. The following day all his efforts would be focused on Josh and what he would have to do to get the boy back to England.

Stratton's thoughts drifted back to poor Sally and his heart was suddenly filled with sadness. The only family in the entire world that he had been close to – and it had been shredded in the space of a couple of weeks. Getting Sally's body back to the UK was another issue that he would have to deal with. He suddenly felt overwhelmed. Although he'd planned a variety of special forces operations around the world during the past decade or more he'd never had to do anything like this. Its smooth running would depend on the cooperation of the authorities, though he had no doubts that the bureaucratic obstacles would be a pain. Kidnapping Josh and getting out of the country undercover would have been easier and more in line with his expertise. But that would mean leaving Sally's body here and it was out of the question for a number of other reasons too.

Stratton went to the apartment's entrance and stepped out into the corridor. He closed the door behind him and walked to the fire escape. The stairs led down to a door that opened from the inside only and led out onto Ocean Avenue, which was busy with pedestrian and vehicle traffic. He walked north to the corner and turned along Santa Monica Boulevard. It was lined with shops and restaurants and was bustling with the sort of night-time activity that one would expect in a popular tourist town.

Chapter 7

At nine a.m. the following day Stratton walked through the gate of the child-protection centre and along the path to the front doors. A black armed security guard wearing a crisply ironed shirt, slacks, a large badge on his chest and a baseball cap sat beside the entrance on a white plastic deckchair.

'Mornin', sir,' he said as Stratton passed him.

'Hi,' Stratton replied as he pushed in through the doors.

Two little Hispanic children sprinted past Stratton, causing him to pull up sharply as the door closed behind him.

'Come on, you two,' a woman in a nurse's uniform said as she hurried into the lobby and shooed the kids into a corner where she took hold of their hands. 'No playing in the corridors,' she said good-naturedly. 'Back we go to the playroom.' And with that she led them away.

Stratton crossed the narrow lobby to a reception desk and watched the nurse take the children along a corridor and in through a doorway.

'Can I help you, sir?' asked the lady at reception. It was Dorothy from the night before and she grinned on recognising Stratton. 'Oh, it's you. Did you have a nice time last night?'

'Yes, thanks,' Stratton said, aware that Dorothy was still under the impression that he had some kind of relationship with the social worker. 'Is Vicky in?'

'Yes. I think she's busy – but then, hell, she's always busy. I'll give her a call,' Dorothy said, reaching for the phone.

'I'm actually here to see a young boy who came in last night. Josh Penton.'

'You have a kid in here?' Dorothy asked, looking surprised.

'I'm a friend of the family. I stopped by to see him.'

'And Vicky knows all about this, right?'

'She knows I'm coming to see him this morning.'

'Em . . . Okay, I guess,' Dorothy said looking a little confused. 'Maybe I should give her a ring.'

'I'm only here to say hello. Is he in the playroom?' Stratton asked, indicating down the corridor.

'Nice try, Mister . . . Stratton, is it?' Vicky was standing in the doorway of an office near the entrance.

Dorothy looked even more confused. 'I thought—'

'It's okay, Dorothy. Would you come into my office, please?' Vicky asked Stratton coolly.

He walked past her into the office. Vicky went to her desk, leaving the door open. Stratton waited for the ticking-off that he was expecting but there was no sign of anger in her expression. Quite the opposite, in fact.

'I'm sorry about what happened to Josh's mother. I didn't find out until I got in this morning . . . I understand your concern for Josh and I'm here to help in every possible way, but can I ask you to please respect the way we do things around here. There's a reason why they call this place a child-protection centre and why we have an armed guard at the entrance. Many of the children in here have been forcibly removed from their families, some of them for quite horrific reasons. It's not unheard of for some of those families to ignore the court's decisions and try and kidnap the children. Two weeks ago a woman came in here with a gun to get her daughter back, a little girl who for the past year she'd kept locked in a cupboard without any hygiene facilities and with barely enough food to live on. That,' Vicky said, pointing at the wall behind her where a neat hole was ringed by a marker, 'was where she fired her gun when I told her she couldn't have her daughter. Then, merci-fully, she was overpowered by the guard . . . This place is all about the children and not their families or guardians. Do you understand, Mister Stratton?' Her statement sounded as much an appeal as a lecture.

'I understand,' Stratton said, genuinely humbled.

'Where's Josh's father?'

'He died a week ago.'

'Oh,' Vicky said, lowering her head as if receiving bad news about a friend. She was used to dealing with cases where children had been exposed to dreadful experiences but even after so many years she was still unable to put the painful details to one side quickly enough.

Vicky took a form from a drawer and placed it on the desk in front of Stratton. 'Would you fill in this questionnaire, please? The first section is about Josh

108

and the second section is for you. Fill it in as accurately as possible. Any details found to be deliberately incorrect will negate any chances you have of gaining custody of the child.'

'Miss Whitaker – a word, please,' a man's voice interrupted rudely behind Stratton.

Stratton looked around to see a skinny, balding, bespectacled man in the doorway. He was clutching several files.

'I'll be one minute, Mister Myers.'

'I need to speak to you right away,' Myers insisted.

'I said I'd be a minute – *if* you don't mind, Mister Myers,' she said firmly.

Myers frowned, stepped back into the lobby and started neurotically flicking through a file.

'Excuse me,' Vicky said to Stratton as she headed for the door. 'Some people just don't know the meaning of manners.'

Stratton took a pen off the desk and started filling in the form. It took several minutes to complete the pages that requested detailed information – he had to get several of the numbers and addresses from the small Filofax he carried in his breast pocket. When he had finished the form he left it on the desk and stood in the doorway to see Vicky still in conversation with Myers who looked as though he was telling her off about something. He seemed like an irritating little man and when he walked away Vicky folded her arms and looked at the floor in agitated thought for a moment.

Stratton walked over to her, deciding that he would be nothing short of cooperative and friendly, especially since the young woman appeared to get flack from all directions. Her kindness and compassion for her wards were apparent and he reckoned that she could be a useful ally if he got on the right side of her. 'He your boss?' he asked.

She looked up at him. 'Head administrator – thinks he owns the centre. Technically he's my superior but I run the childcare. He holds the purse strings but in fairness to him I have to admit that job requires a certain level of coldness. As he's always pointing out, if I ran this place it'd be bankrupt in a month.'

'Miss Vicky, Miss Vicky,' a small boy called out as he headed towards her, holding a model helicopter.

'George. You're not supposed to be out here,' she said without a hint of scolding.

'I know,' George said. 'But my helicopter's not working and Mister Myers said he didn't have time to handle someone else's goddamned case load and—'

'Okay,' Vicky interrupted. 'Go back to the playroom and I'll come by later and see if we can fix it.'

George's expression fell with immediate unhappiness at all the rejection he seemed to be receiving. 'Okay,' he said, kicking the floor and turning to go.

'Can I take a look at it?' Stratton offered.

George stopped and looked up at him suspiciously.

'Do you know what kind of helicopter it is?' Stratton asked.

'It's a Hip M1-8,' George said. 'It says so there,' he said, showing Stratton the bottom of it. 'Soldiers can get in the back that opens,' he explained as he demonstrated the unusual rear-entry doors that were hinged like crab claws.

'Do you know where it's from?' Stratton asked, crouching so his head was at the same level as the boy's.

'It's American.'

'Nope. It's Russian.'

'Russian?' George asked, surprised. 'How'd you know that?'

'Because I can fly one.'

'You can fly one of those?' George exclaimed, immeasurably impressed. 'Wow.'

'Well, I'm not really a pilot and I wouldn't like to try taking it off and landing it by myself, but I can do all this kind of stuff,' Stratton said, holding George's hand around the helicopter and banking it left and right and then into a dive, adding sound effects where appropriate.

'Wow,' George repeated as his imagination took over.

'Let's see what's wrong with it,' Stratton said, holding out his hand.

George gave him the helicopter. 'The rotors are supposed to turn,' he said. 'I got new batteries for it but it still don't work.'

Stratton opened the battery housing and inspected the terminals. They were dirty. He reached around his back and produced a small folding tool-set from its pouch, selected a small blade, and scraped the terminals carefully. He replaced the batteries, closed the housing, and turned a switch on. A light immediately flickered on the tail and the main rotor started to turn. He handed the model back to George who took it gratefully.

'Thanks, mister,' he said. Then he turned on his heel and flew the helicopter, complete with sound effects, back along the corridor and in through a set of double doors.

Stratton stood up, smiling as he watched George go.

Vicky had watched him throughout and when he looked at her she realised that she was staring at him and looked away. 'You completed the form?' she asked.

'It's on your desk.'

She nodded. 'What happens now is I submit it to administration and then Mister Myers will decide if you can see Josh.'

Stratton put his hands in his pockets and looked at the floor in disappointment, biting his lip. 'Okay,' he said.

'However,' she said, lowering her voice. 'I'm going to break the rules and let you see him now.'

Stratton looked up at her.

'A reward for fixing George's helicopter. I'm a soft touch, Mister Stratton, but don't push it.'

'I won't.'

'Follow me,' she said, leading off down the corridor past Dorothy behind her desk. The receptionist gave him a wink.

Stratton followed Vicky to the double doors which she pushed open. They went inside.

At least two dozen young children were spread around the large room. Some were seated around a staff member who was reading a book to them while others were drawing or just playing with the numerous toys that covered the floor. Every wall was plastered with some kind of childish drawing or painting.

Stratton spotted Josh immediately. The boy was sitting by himself across the room, his head down. He looked dejected.

'He's been like that since he got here,' Vicky said. 'It's too early to try and get him involved in any activities. We don't leave him alone for too long at a time – he's had a very traumatic experience. He'll visit a child therapist this afternoon who'll decide how best to care for him.'

Stratton left her, walked across the room to the boy and crouched down beside him. 'Josh?'

Josh looked up, sprang to his feet and dived into Stratton's arms. In one of his hands was the little carved camel.

Vicky was touched by the reunion and watched as Josh kept an iron grip on Stratton, nuzzling into his godfather's neck.

A nurse stepped into the room behind Vicky and saw Stratton with Josh. 'That his father? Poor kid.'

'Let him stay as long as he wants,' Vicky said. 'If Myers asks about him send him to me.'

Vicky left the room.

An hour later Stratton appeared in her office doorway. 'Thanks,' he said.

She looked up at him and smiled.

'What now?' Stratton asked.

Vicky's smile faded. 'There are several scenarios,' she said, sounding as if some of them were not going to be welcome to Stratton. 'I should warn you that these things can take time. Because of the number of children we get rolling into these centres we like to get them placed outside as soon as possible.'

'You talking about a foster home?'

'That's the general routine here. It may take a while to get you cleared as a legal guardian. They're going to have to check your records back in England, make sure you are who you say you are, and that you have no criminal record. I don't know how long the bureaucratic snail takes in the UK but if it's anything like ours . . . I'm being straight with you because I don't want you to get your hopes up. I can only promise you that I will expedite my side of things but I don't have much to do with the administrative process. Josh has grandparents,' said Vicky, glancing at his form.

'I talked to them this morning. They're getting on a bit. The old girl would find the trip hard. I told them I'd take care of things. They trust me. When can I see Josh again?'

'I get the feeling I can trust you too. Can I?'

'Yes.'

'We'll work something out . . . Do you have a number I can call?'

Stratton took out his phone, hit a key and placed it in front of her. She scribbled the number down on a pad.

'That a UK number?'

'Yes.'

'Maybe you should check in with me. Our budget doesn't stretch to international calls.' She handed him a card. 'Call me tomorrow.'

Stratton nodded. 'Thanks.'

Vicky was suddenly filled with sympathy for him. He was in a strange town, knowing no one and uncertain how long he was going to have to go through all this. A little boy he clearly loved was in terrible emotional pain and Stratton was unable to help the child as soon as he'd like. But her heart was already pretty much filled with the woes of so many other children: she warned herself that there was little room there for a grown-up who could look after himself.

Stratton walked away. A second later Vicky heard the front door close. She looked through a gap in the window blinds and watched as he walked out through the gate and away down the street. Then she sat back for a moment, dismissed him from her thoughts, and got back to her pile of work.

Chapter 8

Twenty minutes after Stratton arrived at the Santa Monica Police Department, Sergeant Draper elected to grace him with his presence. The policeman was wearing the same suit as he had the day before.

'How's it going?' Draper asked, his tone uncaring.

'Fine,' Stratton replied, remaining polite despite his annoyance with the man. On the drive over he had considered calling his boss back in Poole to see what could be done at that end to move things along. But he doubted that such a move would be effective at this early stage. The British Consulate in LA would be worth a visit and he could probably engineer a useful introduction there by using his contacts in military intelligence. That would be his next move, he decided, as soon as he had gathered a little more information to provide a baseline of knowledge to work from.

'You shoulda called me, like I said, before you came down here. You'd've saved yourself a trip. I don't have any more to tell you than I did yesterday.'

'You don't have a single thread of information?' Stratton asked, unable to hide completely the contempt that he was beginning to feel for the man.

'Like I said, it was gang-bangers. They ain't exactly gonna hand themselves over. We have people who work the streets but it's gonna take time for word to get back to us. We may eventually get a name we can start on, a witness if we're lucky. People in that neighbourhood are always wanting to make deals with us for one thing or another.'

'That's it? That's how you work?'

'That's how *it* works, pal,' Draper said, not liking Stratton's tone.

Stratton couldn't guess at the number of unsolved crimes in LA but he imagined it must be high. 'Can you tell me where it happened, at least?'

'Venice. In back of Gold's Gym. That area is getting cleaned up, big money moving to the beach, but there's still a lot of lowlifes there. Hey, twenty years ago even *we* wouldn't go in there at night. Sorry, pal. Check in before you come down, okay? Save us both a hassle.'

Draper's mobile phone rang.

'What about Sally's body?' Stratton asked.

'See the desk officer and he'll give you the paperwork,' Draper said as he checked the screen of his phone. 'I gotta take this,' he said, raising it to his ear and walking away.

Half an hour later, having lined up to see the desk officer, Stratton stepped onto the street outside the police department, folding several sheets of a form into his pocket. He looked at a map of the city that he had bought the night before. Venice was less than a mile from the Police Department and he decided to walk.

He took Main Street south. It paralleled the beach

a couple of blocks east of it and was lined with restaurants, bars, and various clothes, art and antique shops. A window cleaner washing a shopfront gave Stratton directions to Gold's Gym. It was tucked into the backstreets a couple of blocks past the last of the shops and after finding it he headed around the back into a more decayed residential part of the city. The multicultural atmosphere of Main Street gave way to a predominantly black and Hispanic one: graffiti was everywhere and each house and apartment block, new and old, had some kind of visible security, usually heavy-duty bars over windows and entranceways.

Stratton saw a group of Latino kids sitting on the front steps of a house and crossed the road towards them. They stopped talking as they watched him approach and remained seated as he stopped in front of them.

'You lookin' for drugs, man?' one of them asked. He couldn't have been more than fourteen years old.

'No – I'm looking for something else,' Stratton said, deciding that the drug pusher was not the leader.

'What would that be, man?' another boy asked, getting to his feet and circling behind Stratton, an expression of contempt on his face that looked more forced than natural. The others got to their feet to look at Stratton in a similar fashion.

Stratton didn't sense that the move was entirely hostile. He reckoned that they were simply fluffing their feathers. He concentrated on the boy, probably the leader, who was circling him, and when the youngster eventually stopped in front of him Stratton looked him straight in the eyes. There was not a great deal of intelligence behind them, the lids drooping halfway across the eyeballs, but there was a maturity beyond the boy's years in his posture and also confidence.

Stratton went for the direct approach. 'A woman was killed here two days ago,' he said.

'You a cop?' the boy asked, dryly.

'No. I'm not American so I couldn't be a cop. She was my sister.'

'That was your sister?' one of the other boys asked. 'Man, she took a bitchen''.'

The other boys agreed, some of them grinning.

'You see it?' Stratton asked the boy who appeared to be the youngest. His age was probably in single digits.

'Never said I saw nothin',' the boy said, already developing his street wisdom.

One of the others uttered some Latino phrase and the whole group laughed.

Stratton studied them for a moment and had a rethink. Dealing with near-morons required a certain approach. 'I'll give you fifty dollars if you show me where it happened,' Stratton said.

'Fifty dollars?' the leader asked, appearing unimpressed. But Stratton knew that he was undoubtedly interested.

'Just to show me where,' Stratton said, reaching into his pocket and plucking out a note. It was a hundred-dollar bill.

'We ain't got no change, mister,' one of them laughed.

'Then I'll give you a hundred,' Stratton said. 'If you tell me more than just where it happened.'

The leader looked around the street, instinctively cautious. Then his slow eyes came back to focus on Stratton's face and he blinked. 'Maybe we'll just beat you and take your money,' he said.

'You can try,' Stratton said, rolling up the bill into a ball. 'But I'll eat it before you can get it. Or you can just give me what I want and you can have it without any trouble.'

The leader looked into Stratton's eyes and saw no trace of fear and, if anything, amusement. 'We can't tell you nothin'. That's the way it's gotta be, *pinchi,*' he said, unsure about this gringo.

'So, you can show me where it happened?' Stratton asked.

'Down there.' The boy indicated with his chin.

'Show me,' Stratton said.

The leader did another check around, then looked at the smallest kid in the group. 'Show him. And be cool.'

'Why do I gotta take him?'

''Cause I said. Walk down there in front of him, then pick up the money and come back here.'

The kid reluctantly obeyed his master, walked down the steps and stopped in front of Stratton, his head no higher than Stratton's waist. 'Come on,' he said and set off.

Stratton followed the kid for a block and a half until the boy broke into a short run, stopped, made a point of turning on the spot and walked back towards Stratton. Stratton opened the hand with the wadded-up note in it. The kid took it as he passed and jogged back up the street towards his pack. The leader checked the note and then they all walked away around a corner.

Stratton looked down at his feet. They were surrounded by bits of car-window glass and he imagined Sally lying on the car's bonnet, dead, with Josh watching her. The broken glass was spread over the street as if her vehicle had been in the centre of the road and not parked against the kerb. Whatever had happened had taken place while she was in transit. He doubted that she would have stopped in a place like this for anything less than a breakdown.

He scanned the sidewalks and houses on either side but the place was deserted, as if everyone knew his purpose and wanted nothing to do with him. Then his gaze fell on a corner shop further up the street where an oriental man was standing in the doorway, looking directly at him. As soon as their stares made contact the man went inside. Stratton wanted to talk to someone and since banging on doors didn't seem like a good idea round here he decided to start with the only living person in sight.

Stratton stepped onto the sidewalk and headed for the shop that was very much in keeping with its surroundings: grubby, grille-covered windows and in desperate need of a paint job.

He paused in the doorway to look inside. Every bit of space was packed with product apart from a narrow path from the entrance that led around an island of shelving in the centre. The counter was near the front door and two convex mirrors in the opposite corners covered the blind spots at the back of the store. The oriental man was stacking cigarette packets onto shelves behind the counter while a fat white woman at the far end sorted through some vegetable racks.

Stratton stopped in front of the counter and took a packet of gum from a box, all the while staring at the shopkeeper to catch his eye. But the man appeared determined not to look at him.

'How much is the gum?' Stratton asked.

'Fifty cents,' the shopkeeper replied in a thick Korean accent.

Stratton held out a dollar bill and as the man reached for it Stratton drew it back a little. The man's eyes flashed at Stratton and held his unblinking gaze for a moment, a hint of anger in them. Then he stretched for the bill and took it.

'A woman was killed two days ago in front of your shop,' Stratton said in a low voice so that the woman in the back could not hear.

The man did not reply, avoiding Stratton's stare again, and put the fifty cents change on the counter.

The overweight woman shuffled from the back of the shop, stopped beside Stratton and plonked a bag of vegetables down on the counter. 'This produce is crap,' she announced, a fearsome look on her face.

'That why they half-price,' the shopkeeper replied dryly, as if the complaint was a normal occurrence. 'Two dollar, please.'

'If they're half-price then they're twice the fucking price they are at the market.'

'This isn't the market.'

'Fucking Chinks,' she said to Stratton as she tossed two dollar bills on the counter, grabbed her bag, and walked out of the store, muttering to herself.

The shopkeeper walked around the counter and looked out of his door to watch the woman walk away and see if there was anyone about. When he turned back to face Stratton he was glaring angrily. 'Why you people come here again? I tell you everything last night.'

The man was obviously confusing Stratton with someone else and for the time being Stratton wasn't about to let him think otherwise. 'Are you sure you didn't miss anything?' he asked, grabbing at the first thing he could think of that might induce the man to talk.

'Go ask your friends,' the shopkeeper spat, glancing out the door again. 'I tell them all I know!'

He was not threatening Stratton but he was clearly nervous about something as he went back behind his counter to continue stacking the shelves.

'I need to double-check,' Stratton said, wondering who the man could be referring to.

'You promise you leave me alone when I tell you. I dead if they know I talk to you. I told you I not go to court or go downtown with you. I tell you the man who kill the woman and now you come for more. What more you need? I not talk to you any more. Fucking FBI. Get out of my shop!' He paused to glare at Stratton long enough to reinforce his demand. Then he turned his back on him.

The Korean man was determined to end the conversation, out of fear or anger. Whichever it was, Stratton was up against a wall: short of physical violence there was no other way through as far as he could see at that moment. He picked up the fifty cents, deposited the coins in a children's-charity box and walked out of the store.

Contemplating the shopkeeper's revelation, Stratton walked back to the spot where Sally had been killed. The FBI had apparently interviewed the man the night before whereupon he had revealed the name of a suspect. Yet this morning Sergeant Draper had said he knew nothing. The police had responded to the incident within a few hours and the FBI had interviewed the shopkeeper a day later. The question was why the FBI had become involved in what looked like a local police matter. It might explain why Draper knew nothing or wouldn't tell what he did know.

Stratton's first thought was that he should go to the FBI, not that he expected any more joy from them than he'd had from the police – unless, of course, there was someone he could get help from. He walked down the road, racking his brains for anyone he knew or had known in the past who might be useful. By the time he arrived back on the bustling Main Street a name had struck him. There was one person who might be able to help although Stratton did not know him well enough to assume that he would. However, he was, in a very tangential way, connected with this and perhaps a favour could be coerced from him. It was worth a try.

Stratton took out his address book, flicked through the pages, found the number and tapped it into his phone. As soon as it started to ring he turned it off, realising the lack of wisdom in using his own mobile to make this particular call.

He saw a payphone on the other side of the street and darted through a gap in the traffic. He dug into his pocket to pull out the small pile of coins he had amassed, picked up the receiver, put all the silver into the slot and dialled the number.

A moment later the phone at the other end was answered by a voice he recognised.

'Seaton?' Stratton asked.

'Who is this?'

'Stratton.'

Seaton was in the living room of his comfortable suburban home, an open file on his lap. He was seated on a leather recliner. The room, like the rest of the house, was carefully furnished with reproduction veneer items and was glowing with middle-class ostentation. Unmistakably the creation of a self-obsessed wife it was full of framed family photographs, mainly of two smiling boys, the older of whom was in his very early teens. There were also plaques from various military intelligence outfits and special forces, not all of them American. One was from the SBS and it hung beside another from Navy SEAL Team 6.

'Stratton? Hey, good to hear from you. How you doing?'

'Fine. Where are you right now?' Stratton asked – he'd called Seaton's mobile phone.

'I'm at home,' Seaton said, having redirected his mobile to his home number.

'Can you talk?'

'Sure. Hey, I'm glad you called,' Seaton said, sitting up and putting down his file. 'I'm sorry I never made Jack's funeral. I was ordered straight home after the op to do some follow-up. I tried to call Sally a couple days ago but I couldn't get hold of her.'

Stratton paused to consider the best way of breaking the bad news that would also prompt a favourable reaction to a request for help. 'I understand. Your card was much appreciated,' he lied.

'I still should've been there, but, well, I suppose I don't need to explain to you . . . So, what can I do for you?' Seaton asked.

'I need a favour.'

'Shoot,' Seaton said, getting to his feet. He went over to his desk where a read-out on a small digital screen displayed the number of the phone Stratton was calling from and beneath it the location: Venice Beach, California.

'I'm in California.'

'California?' Seaton said, feigning surprise. 'Getting some sun and a taste of those famous babes, I hope.'

Stratton decided to get to the point. 'Sally was killed a couple of days ago,' he said.

'What?' Seaton said, dumbfounded. 'Jack's Sally?'

'That's why I'm calling.'

'I can't believe what I'm hearing . . . How'd she die, for God's sake?'

'She was murdered.'

'*Murdered*? Where?'

'Here – in Los Angeles.'

Seaton pushed his hands through his short, mousy hair as he walked to his patio windows. The view beyond the wooden fence surrounding his groomed garden was of a dense collection of tall, deciduous trees belonging to Dranesville District Park, a small, pretty patch of green that hugged the south bank of the Potomac river in Maryland. 'I can't believe it,' Seaton said. 'What was she doing in LA?'

'Getting away. Josh was with her. He's okay. I'm working on how I can get him back to the UK.'

'What do you need me to do?' Seaton asked, sounding genuinely concerned.

Stratton was still reluctant to ask directly, mainly because he didn't know Seaton that well. It wasn't a small thing and Stratton had not made up his mind whether Seaton was a team player, one of the guys, or a career man – no one got far up the promotional ladder by being one of the guys. Career-minded people didn't stick their necks out without some self-interested reason.

'How'd it happen?' Seaton asked.

'I don't know exactly. She rented a car at the airport and somehow ended up in the backstreets of Venice. I'm guessing that she was looking for a hotel for the night. The police say she was attacked by a gang but they don't know who. Thing is, the FBI does.'

'I don't understand. Why's the FBI involved?'

'Beats me. When I got no joy from the cops I went down to the crime scene and found out that the Feds have got hold of a name.'

'I hear what you're saying,' Seaton said. 'You want me to see if I can help you get custody of Josh?'

'No,' Stratton said, slightly irritated that Seaton appeared to have missed the point. 'I want to know that whoever did this to Sally is going to pay.'

'Why wouldn't they?' Seaton asked, not getting Stratton's drift.

'I want to know why the Feds have taken over the

case and are withholding the name of the killer from the cops. It bothers me.'

Seaton considered the request for a moment. Stratton could almost hear him thinking on the end of the line. He kept quiet in the hope that Seaton was heading in the right direction.

'I might be able to find out something. I'm heading into the office in an hour. I'll see what I can do.'

A computer voice broke into the conversation: 'You have thirty seconds remaining for this call.'

'You still there, Stratton?'

'I don't have any more change,' Stratton said. 'I'll call you later.'

'Hey – why don't you come over?' Seaton suggested. 'Stay a couple days. You know some of the guys here. Where you staying?'

'Santa Monica.'

'Getting Josh outta there isn't gonna be an overnight job. You can hop on a plane. Only take a few hours. We can talk about it when you get here.'

Stratton's immediate thought was to stay close to Josh. But he knew that he had a better chance of getting help from Seaton if he spent some time with him. 'Sounds like a good idea,' he said.

'Great. It'll be good to see you. We'll work this out. Let me know your flight soon as you can and I'll pick you up.'

'Will do,' Stratton said as the phone automatically disconnected.

Seaton lowered the phone and pondered the situation. He had been a CIA agent for a couple of years longer than Stratton had been in special forces and his natural cunning and wit had been honed by those years in the business. He didn't know Stratton very well but he had spent enough time with the SBS to know that the man was one of their top go-to operatives and had also made the Secret Intelligence Services' full-time roster, which was unusual for anyone still in SF. Seaton reasoned that it was perfectly natural for someone to want to know who had killed a close friend of theirs. But when that someone was a man like Stratton the picture had the potential to get darker. Seaton was aware that he was probably being overly suspicious, a natural enough response in his line of work, but there was still always a need to be cautious. For instance, he did not ignore the fact that Stratton had called from a payphone.

Seaton decided that he would help Stratton but only in a way that would keep his own profile way out of any snooping spotlight.

Stratton carried on down Main Street towards his hotel, wondering if Seaton would change his mind once he had thought it through – not that Stratton reckoned he had asked for anything too unreasonable. Snooping around the FBI was only wrong because the FBI wouldn't like it, but there had to be some perks to the business of clandestine ops and that was what the old-boy network was for. Stratton dearly wanted to know who was responsible for Sally's death, but more importantly he wanted to ensure that they were going to pay for it, preferably with their lives. But if there was no other option he would accept indefinite incarceration for the killers.

The top floors of the pink towers came into sight. Stratton checked his watch as he picked up his speed, estimating that he could get his bag, catch a taxi, and be at the airport in about an hour – ample time, he hoped, to catch a domestic flight to Washington DC.

Chapter 9

Stratton made it to LAX in time to catch the 1:55 p.m. US Airways flight that arrived at Ronald Reagan National Airport at twenty minutes to midnight local time. As he stepped through the gate Seaton was waiting at the far side of the arrivals hall watching him, a welcoming smile appearing on his face as they made eye contact.

'Good flight?' Seaton asked as Stratton approached.

'Quiet,' Stratton replied. They shook hands.

As the plane touched down both men had begun to feel uncomfortable about meeting each other, and not just because of Sally's and Jack's recent deaths. Seaton and Stratton were very different animals. Although they were compatible in their work they were not well matched socially. Seaton was essentially a suit, although he had the option to join his men in the field on occasion, as he had during the Iraq operation. Whether or not he did depended on the risk rating, which needed to be fairly low. He was a planner and information collator by trade, having entered the organisation with an MBA in Middle East studies, and he had risen through the ranks, gaining enough experience over the years to become a consultant on East

European and Middle Eastern anti-terror affairs. He was a little bigger than Stratton, as fit as him and probably stronger physically, but front-line operators always left him with an unmistakable feeling of inadequacy that he hated but was unable to rationalise away. A self-analysis had revealed a latent desire to be one of them, which was not exactly astounding. But the truth was that had he been granted a genie's wish he would not have chosen that calling. He honestly felt that he was in the far better job but he still could not explain why he continued to feel that twinge of envy.

'It's good to see you again,' Seaton said, leading Stratton through the hall that was practically empty compared with its usual daytime bustle. The majority of the people around were night-shift cleaners. 'You got any other baggage?'

'No,' Stratton said, shouldering his pack.

'Julie, my wife, has made some food. She won't be up by the time we get home, though. You'll see her and the kids in the morning.'

'I never thought of you as married,' Stratton said.

'Thirteen years.' Seaton sounded neither regretful nor proud.

'Long time.'

'Yep.'

They headed out of the terminal to the short-term car park where Seaton's car was waiting practically alone in the concrete-pillared cavern. A few minutes later they were driving along the George Washington Memorial Parkway that followed the south bank of the Potomac as it curved north-west.

Stratton decided not to mention his request for help

in making contact with the FBI. He'd leave it to Seaton to broach the subject. There was no point in pushing him. He would either play ball or not, depending on his own concerns – which he'd had ample time to contemplate.

The airport was a good ten minutes behind them when, neither men having said a word since leaving the terminal, Stratton felt Seaton glance at him.

'Well, it sure is a small world,' Seaton said. 'How true is that in our business?'

Stratton could only wonder what he was referring to.

'Never ceases to amaze me how everything is connected to everything else if you examine it long enough,' Seaton went on. 'Ever hear the name Skender before – Daut Skender?'

'That a person?' Stratton asked dryly, assuming that it was.

'A man. That job you did in Kazakhstan – if you'd been involved at ops level you'd have heard his name.'

Stratton glanced at Seaton, wondering why he had mentioned that assignment.

'Lit my eyes up when I saw his name on the FBI report,' Seaton continued. 'He's Albanian Mafia, hence the connection to your Almaty adventure – they were the crew ferrying the heroin through the mountains. Skender is a very big fish in a very big pond of organised crime. The Albanians don't get as much airtime as the Russian and Italian Mafias mainly because of their political position but also because no one knows who most of the bosses are. Skender is the head of one of fifteen clans that have ruled Albania for centuries. They got big, and they stay big, by working with everyone: Italian N'dranheta, Comorra, Stidda and the Russian Solsentskya mob. When the FBI finally broke up the pizza connection all the Eastern European mobs moved in to fill the void, in America as well as Italy. But it was easier for the Albanians to take over because of their traditional ties with the Sicilian Mafia. They're into every kind of smuggling you can imagine, including heroin and arms. Skender was big in the early 1990s but his stock went through the roof after the Kosovo conflict thanks to the US and UK governments. Before the war we got the IMF to impose economic sanctions that caused Albania's economy to collapse, putting us in a prime position to 'save' them. Skender was one of the organisers of the Kosovo Liberation Army against Milosevic. We trained and equipped the KLA and then handed them the bulk of the rebuilding contracts after our bombers levelled the place. Skender used those projects to launder millions of his illegal dollars and in a few short months he became a legitimate billionaire. By the end of the decade he was, or at least we suspect he was, running Europe's most powerful heroin cartel. You're probably wondering what the hell this has got to do with Sally.'

Stratton didn't want to interrupt, expecting Seaton to get to the point eventually. All he had been briefed about the Almaty job was that the trade route was used by Islamic terrorist organisations moving components of WMDs, weapons of mass destruction, into the West. Interestingly, the boxes found on Mohammad Al-Forouf's train in Iraq had been identical in appearance to those that Stratton had photographed in

Almaty and had had traces of heroin as well as explosives in them. But there'd been no sign of WMDs.

'Skender has lived most of his life in Albania,' Seaton went on, 'where he has extensive interests in chrome, copper, nickel and platinum as well as an abundance of as yet untapped oil deposits. The guy is one of the most important characters in that part of the world and not just because of his wealth and connections. He has something else, something far more important that we want. He knows the real bad guys. I'm talking Bin Laden, Zakarwy, Usef, Moamar. He can get to them. Hence our very "special" relationship with him. Guess where he lives?'

'I have no idea where this is going but would Los Angeles be too wild a guess?' Stratton asked.

'Got to connect to Sally somehow,' Seaton replied with a nod. 'Skender moved his base of operations to LA from New York a year ago and is currently in the process of centralising his western economic empire on the Pacific Rim, we think in readiness for a move into Asia and south and central America. You'll see it more clearly if you know the background. This next part is my conjecture after I'd read the FBI file and added to it what little I know from the Almaty operation. I believe the FBI has something on Skender – although they wouldn't tell us if they did. It looks like they waited until he'd set up his West Coast operation and secured a couple billion dollars in US and foreign banks that we have some control over before they moved in on him. He hasn't left the country in more than nine months, which is unusual, but neither has the FBI charged him with any crimes. Yet all the signs indicate that they're exerting some kind of pressure on him. If the Feds aren't moving in it's because they're getting something out of it. At a guess I'd say they were pushing for his al-Qaeda connections. They don't need to physically tie him down because if he runs they'll seize his assets, and not just in the US. The FBI are pretty well entrenched in Eastern Europe now and have a lot of influence. US control of much of the world market has many advantages. Sally was killed by two of Skender's soldiers. Open up that glove compartment.'

Stratton opened the compartment in front of him to reveal an inch-thick manila envelope.

'Inside the envelope,' Seaton said.

Stratton removed the envelope and took out its contents: a file containing dozens of photocopied pages.

'What you have there is the long version of what I've just told you. Go to the first tab.'

Stratton held the tab and flicked over a quarter of the file to reveal a photograph of a grisly-looking man in his late thirties.

'Read the guy's name,' Seaton asked.

'Ardian Cano.'

'There were two guys involved in Sally's death. He's one of them. Let me give you another little bit of background. A characteristic of the Albanian crime families – and a major reason why they remain so powerful – is the way they stand together, especially in a crisis. No one gets in unless they're family, and God help anyone who tries to come between them. They're famous for their brutality, chopping up their enemies into pieces – including those enemies' women and children. You cross them and your family could end up being savagely punished. In Albania entire villages have been executed because of a single dispute. It's effective and people think twice about screwing with these guys. Go to the next page.'

Stratton turned the page to reveal a picture of another man, equally brutal-looking. 'Leka Bufi,' he said, reading the name on the top.

'Bufi is Ardian Cano's partner,' Seaton explained, 'and the other guy involved in Sally's murder. Both men were in the KLA together under another guy I'll come to in a minute. The CIA has files on them because we also happened to train them. Skender used the Kosovo war to settle a lot of territorial disputes, which is how he gained control over many of the clans – those two characters came out of Kosovo with a lot of blood on their hands. Both Ardian and Leka are lowlifes, small fry and not related to Skender who might well have thrown them to the wolves for killing Sally but for one reason. Ardian just happens to have a family connection close to Skender. Next page.'

Stratton flicked between Bufi and Cano, embedding their images in his memory before turning the page to a photo of another man. 'Ivor Vleshek.'

'So his papers say. Claims to be Russian, a Muscovite and Skender's right-hand henchman – which is interesting, considering Skender's penchant for nepotism. So why does Skender have a non-Albanian that close to the family? We're pretty certain that Vleshek's real name is Dren Cano, Ardian Cano's younger brother. Ardian and Leka were under Dren Cano's command while in the KLA. Dren was more intelligent than his older brother and much more ruthless. So bad, in fact, that he was wanted by the war crimes tribunal. Shortly after the end of the war Dren went missing, which was no surprise. The few pre-war pictures we have of him are too poor to match. If that *is* Dren Cano then it goes a long way to explaining why Ardian and Leka have not been arrested for killing Sally.'

'The FBI has Ardian Cano and Leka Bufi down as suspects?'

'They were identified by a Korean shopkeeper who witnessed the killing. The shopkeeper's son was almost killed by Ardian same afternoon. The son's a small-time pusher who owed Ardian some money. Can you see how the picture is coming together?'

'You're suggesting Ardian and Leka are not being charged with Sally's murder because of a special relationship that Skender has with the FBI? You've got to be joking.'

'No, I don't think that. It's one more thing they'll have against his organisation. What I am saying is that it might be a question of timing. There is another problem, of course. No witness will testify against Skender's people in court. That Korean shopkeeper spilled the names but he won't say anything under oath.'

Stratton looked unmoved but deep inside he was stunned.

'At the end of the day it's going to be like any other crime,' Seaton said. 'Their guilt has to be proven.'

Stratton looked up as a sign passed indicating that Langley Fork Park was next right. Langley was the CIA's vast operational headquarters. They carried straight on through the junction. Stratton went back to the file and turned the page.

The next photograph was of a man much older than the others, in his early sixties and clean-shaven. He had a large head with long, straggly hair combed back and looked every bit as hard as the younger men.

'That's Skender,' Seaton said.

Stratton studied the photograph for only a moment before going back to the two men who interested him most. A minute later he shut the file and put it back inside the manila envelope.

Traffic was light as they joined the brightly lit Interstate 495. After less than a mile Seaton took an exit onto a highway and a short distance later turned along a minor road. He pulled sharply into the driveway of a large, two-storey house before killing the engine and turning off the lights.

'Home sweet home,' Seaton said, opening his door.

They climbed out and Stratton grabbed his pack off the back seat, the manila envelope still in his hand.

The front garden was manicured and amply stocked with a variety of plant life. Lights were on downstairs while the top floor was in darkness.

'Let's go around back,' Seaton said, leading the way. 'See what we have to eat. I'm hungry. You?'

'I could eat something,' Stratton said, more out of politeness than genuine hunger.

Seaton unlocked the back door and stepped into a modern, tidy, well-appointed kitchen. 'Want a beer?' he asked.

'Sure,' Stratton said, putting down his pack and placing the file on top of it. He didn't particularly fancy one but was fighting against a growing realisation of his lack of sociability.

Seaton took a couple of bottles from the fridge, popped them with an opener, handed one to Stratton and offered up the neck of his. 'Sorry we're not getting together under better circumstances,' he said.

Stratton tapped Seaton's bottle with his own and they both took a swig.

'Let's see what the old gal has knocked up, as you guys say,' Seaton said as he opened the oven. Lifting out a pot with a pair of oven gloves on his hands he removed the lid and looked inside. 'Hmm. She's not the best cook in the world,' he said, keeping his voice low. 'But she has a couple dishes she's worked on over the years that are pretty good. She wouldn't dare attempt anything new with guests.'

Seaton put the pot on a breakfast table, took a couple of plates from a cupboard and dug some cutlery out of a drawer. 'Sit down. Make yourself at home.'

Stratton sat at the table as Seaton spooned what looked like a stew onto the plates. It smelled good and Stratton suddenly felt properly hungry.

'You got family?' Seaton asked.

'No,' Stratton replied.

'You live alone?'

'Yes.' Stratton didn't particularly want to talk about his personal life but he knew that it would help to create a more relaxed atmosphere with Seaton. 'My parents died when I was young. I was an only child.'

'Never been married?'

'No.'

'Not even close?'

'Once – maybe. Looking back, I think I was kidding myself. Not her, though, just me. She was a lot smarter.'

'Sounds like that was some years back?'

'Yeah. Family life and this job mix like oil and water; for me at least.'

'You have to work at it, that's for sure. We've had some rough rides but the kids changed everything. You take fewer risks when you've got a kid, let me tell you. And coming home means a helluva lot more.'

Stratton's thoughts went to Josh and Jack – and to Sally. His only significant experience of a family.

'You go to state or private school, whatever it is you call it in the UK?' Seaton asked.

'What we'd call a state school – in London,' Stratton replied, taking a mouthful of the stew. 'Like most guys I joined up soon as I left school, in my case to get away from the city.'

'You don't like cities?'

'I don't like crowds.'

'I'm a country boy myself. Upstate New York. Ever been there?'

'Nope. Haven't been to very many places in the States. Mostly Norfolk, Virginia.'

'Navy SEALs?'

Stratton nodded as he took another mouthful of food.

'I almost joined the SEALs.'

'You were in the navy?'

'No.'

Stratton thought that was strange since, as he understood it, you had to be a member of the US Navy to join the SEALs. Seaton picked up on his curious look.

'I went to Chicago University,' Seaton explained. 'Got an MBA in Mideast studies and joined the Rangers. Did two years as an LT when I had an urge to be a Navy SEAL. I was about to transfer over to the navy when I got the call to join the agency. I'm telling the story kinda back to front but – well, I had an uncle who was a CIA deputy in Cuba at the time. We got drunk together at my father's wake, while I was in the Rangers, and I told him I wanted to be a CIA agent. I only half meant it – kinda sorta. The SEALs were my first choice but the truth was anything that was, you know, special would do. I didn't know much about special forces or the CIA. Next thing I know my CO calls me into his office and tells me I'm not joining the navy and I'm off to Camp Peary to do CIA selection. Fifteen years later, here I am.'

Seaton went back to his meal. 'Well, so much for how we end up doing what we end up doing,' he said, struggling to be philosophical.

Something was obviously bothering him and Stratton decided to leave it alone.

'I was surprised that the Albanian syndicates would still want to have anything serious to do with Islamic terrorists,' Seaton went on as if eager to change the subject. 'But I guess they have to keep their trade routes moving and al-Qaeda, or whatever you want to call them, do have a lot of control over product. This whole business of trying to nail the syndicates and put them out of business is bullshit, though. It's expensive, takes up a lot of manpower, and soon as you put one group away another moves in to take its place. You want my opinion, it would be best to leave them where they are and work on controlling them.'

'Maybe that's what the FBI is doing with Skender,' Stratton said.

'Hail to them if it's true.'

'So you agree with letting the syndicates get away with crimes, then?' Stratton asked dryly.

'Okay. I ran into that one but you know I don't want anyone to get away with Sally's murder. Look at it objectively for a moment if you can. Don't let your anger cloud the reality. Truth is, everyone's allowed to get away with something now and then.'

Stratton nodded while trying to control a rising feeling of combined anger and helplessness. All this talk of criminal giants and mega-injustices was making him feel insignificant. He took a long swig of his beer.

'Of course, the goal must be to eventually eradicate these criminals,' Seaton went on. 'But you've got to do it at the source, control the way they make and secure their wealth so that no matter who steps in to take their place the squeeze remains.'

'Sounds great, but it's not likely to happen by tomorrow, right?'

'Nope,' Seaton said. 'But it evolves . . . Our biggest fight at the moment is against Islamic fundamentalists but the mechanisms that we are putting in place against them work against the syndicates too.'

Stratton nodded, hiding his true feelings. Seaton was on the side of the FBI as far as Skender was concerned, although Stratton did not doubt his sincerity regarding retribution for Sally's murder. Stratton was only looking at it from a personal point of view but he could see it no other way.

Seaton got to his feet. 'Well, I'm gonna hit the sack,' he said, stifling a yawn. 'You know where the beer is and the TV's in the lounge. Your room is at the top of the stairs, straight across the hall.'

'I don't mind crashing on the couch,' Stratton said, feeling awkward about being a house guest.

'Julie will. Bed's made up and ready to jump in. Shower's at the end of the hall. See you in the morning,' Seaton said as he walked out of the room. Then he paused in the doorway and looked back at Stratton. 'What I said about controlling people like Skender – I didn't mean they should get away with murder. Those freaks who killed Sally should fry.'

As Seaton made his way upstairs Stratton found himself unsure about the man's sincerity. He felt alone in his desire to see justice done in its most basic form. He got to his feet, picked up the file and his pack and made his way through the house and up the stairs. He was tired, having slept little since arriving in the States. But there was far too much on his mind and the more he thought about things the more daunting it all appeared. Dealing with the rules for getting Josh home was going to be difficult enough but pressurising the FBI into prosecuting Sally's killers felt beyond him. The more Stratton thought about the legal processes, the more he was tempted by the darker solutions, such as kidnapping Josh and killing Sally's murderers. Due diligence was beyond him but cold-blooded execution was not. If Jack could speak he'd beg Stratton to tear those two creeps apart: the world could only be a better place without them.

After a couple of hours spent lying on the bed and

reading through the file Stratton nodded off. But he awoke a few hours later because of the combination of jet lag and strange surroundings. Before he could get back to sleep he found himself speculating about how to deal with the two Albanians if he chose to – physically, not legally. It would not be the first action of its kind for Stratton although it would be the first time he had planned such a thing outside the remit of British military intelligence. The important difference was not lost on him: he would be operating without the support of his government so he'd be out in the cold and alone if anything went wrong. But that safety net had always been largely a psychological one because in just about every operation of its kind that he'd been part of in the past he would have been killed if he'd been caught.

Stratton kept pushing the idea out of his head, believing it to be bravado, but it returned each time demanding further examination. He eventually decided to humour the demons for one reason, namely that the best way to dump a plan was to prove that it couldn't work. He began by breaking it down into phases: target assessment and vulnerabilities, methods and options, feasibility studies, equipment procurement, and evacuation plan. But he could neither dismiss nor approve any scheme due to lack of the one thing that was the key to any operation: information. He went back to the file. But it did not have sufficient detail and Stratton slowly dozed off again with it open on his chest.

Chapter 10

When Stratton finally fell asleep for the second time it seemed like only minutes later that a knock on the bedroom door woke him up again. As he sat up tiredly it opened and Seaton stepped into the room wearing running shorts, T-shirt and trainers.

'Want to go for a run?' he asked.

Stratton rubbed his face in an effort to push the sleep away. 'Sure,' he said, not entirely meaning it. It was practically instinctive for an SF operative to say yes to such an offer, especially when it came from a foreign host in a similar profession.

'You got any kit with you?' Seaton asked.

'Yeah. Give me five minutes.'

'Great. The boys want to meet you. They're fans of British special forces and,' lowering his voice, 'I've told them some stories about you, maybe a little polished in places, but you know what kids are like.'

Stratton forced a smile which disappeared as Seaton stepped forward and picked the file up off the floor. 'See you in a couple minutes,' he said as he left the room with the file tucked under one arm.

As Seaton closed the door behind him Stratton dangled his legs over the side of the bed and breathed a sigh. He wasn't quite sure how he felt about Seaton taking the file: it seemed a little like withdrawing a gift. But perhaps he was being oversensitive. The file wasn't his to keep anyway and he put thoughts of it out of his head.

Five minutes later Stratton walked down the stairs in running gear to see the front door open and Seaton outside stretching his legs. He was talking with two boys, both of them on BMX-type bicycles and wearing helmets, as well as knee and shin pads.

'Hi,' Stratton said as he stepped outside. The two boys immediately went serious and looked up at him in some kind of awe.

'This is Bobby,' Seaton said, introducing the older boy. Stratton shook his hand.

'Pleased to meet you, Bobby.'

'And your namesake, John.'

'John,' Stratton said as he shook the youngster's hand.

'They're gonna come with us, see if they can keep up with us old-timers. But we're going to give you guys a run for your money,' Seaton challenged them.

'You're on, dad,' Bobby said. Both boys were grinning. 'Which way you going?' he asked as he pointed his bike up the path. His younger brother followed suit.

'Ah, well, that's the catch,' Seaton said. 'We get to choose the route as and when and you've got to see if you can hang on in there.'

'No cheatin' and goin' over fences this time,' the smaller boy piped up.

'Okay. No fences,' Seaton said, winking at Stratton. 'You ready?'

'Whenever,' Stratton replied, getting a quick stretch in.

'Let's go.'

They set off down the sidewalk towards a large patch of woodland in the distance. Seaton led them across a main road empty of traffic and onto a wide earth track, moving at an easy pace. Stratton felt cold and a little stiff at first but soon warmed up and came alongside Seaton as they entered the wood. The boys pedalled along behind, hot on their heels, watching their father like young hawks as if at any moment he might attempt to make a break for it.

Stratton was feeling in good shape, having managed to get a fair bit of running in since returning from Iraq and he moved easily along. Within a mile he felt completely awake and warmed up. The two boys cruised happily behind, their little legs going like the clappers with seemingly limitless energy. Stratton wondered if Seaton's earlier wink indicated that he had some sort of surprise in store for them. Then, as if he'd read Stratton's thoughts, Seaton picked up the pace and suddenly darted off the track onto a narrow, muddy footpath. Stratton moved up a gear behind him, as did the boys.

The path narrowed even more as it moved out of the wood and threaded through a large patch of dense bushes. Yards before it went back into the wood Seaton bounded up a steep bank and into the trees where the ground foliage was sparse with no defined path.

The boys had trouble peddling up the bank and John had to dismount to push his bike with his brother's help. But they quickly remounted at the top and were soon closing in.

Seaton did not relax his pace and Stratton began to wonder who he was challenging – Stratton or the boys. Whatever, Stratton felt he was up for it and with several gears still in reserve he pushed up onto Seaton's heels.

The ground dropped away suddenly to reveal a large puddle that could not be circumnavigated without diverting through large bushes and Seaton ploughed into it. The water was only a few inches deep but the soft muddy bottom dropped the level to just below their knees and their feet were covered in a thick black sludge when they emerged on the other side.

Stratton glanced back to see the boys enter the mud pit, keeping as close to the edge as possible. It immediately slowed them but perseverance pulled them through. Once again they shot up to speed and closed the gap.

Seaton took a second to check on his boys. Then, as if disappointed that he had not yet lost them, he abruptly changed direction again and speeded up.

The ground rose up a steep incline to where the trees gave way to a thick heather-like shrub and they pressed on across a large patch of open ground before descending into the wood once more. The sun had failed to break through the heavy cloud and it began to look dark enough for rain. But at this stage of the run it might have been welcome as Stratton was beginning to sweat from the humidity.

The boys had suffered a little with the lumpy under-growth and, unable to find a rhythm, started to drop further back. Seaton was aware of this and put on another spurt.

A stream some twelve feet wide appeared across their front with a steep bank on the far side. Seaton did not slow as he leaped in up to his hips and waded through the fast-moving water. Stratton was halfway across when Seaton scrambled up the other side and pushed off at the run without looking back. When Stratton made the top of the bank he paused to look back and see the boys sliding to a halt at the edge of the stream. Bobby looked up at him, frowning. Stratton shrugged and sped off in pursuit of Seaton.

Seaton had put some distance between him and Stratton and kept the pace up across a stretch of open ground towards a line of trees. It was now obvious to Stratton that he was the focus of the race since Seaton must have been aware that his boys had stopped as he pushed on into the trees. Stratton accelerated after the other man and kept up the pace until he was at his heels again, lowering his hands in an effort to relax his shoulders and control his breathing whose rate had markedly increased. They were pounding along at a fair trot and Stratton began to wonder how much more Seaton had left in him. The man was obviously a regular runner and both were playing a game of who would break first, though Stratton was aware that Seaton's main advantage was his knowledge of the terrain.

They hit a muddy path used by horses and Seaton kept up the pressure along it until they hit a dryer patch where it opened up as it dropped down a steep incline. Stratton put on a spurt to come alongside

Seaton but as the path began to narrow again Seaton elbowed him hard in the side in a bid to take the lead. Stratton's hackles immediately rose as he almost tripped, unsure whether or not it had been an accident.

The dip bottomed out and the path widened again. It looked straight now for a good half-mile or so. Stratton moved alongside Seaton to let him know that he was up to the pace and Seaton responded by increasing it still more. Stratton kept up with him, moving up into what he felt was probably his last gear short of an all-out and very limited sprint, doubting that he could keep up with Seaton if he increased the pace any more.

Seaton in turn, was digging as deep into his heart and lungs as he could but he knew that if Stratton pushed on ahead one step more he would not be able to stay up with him. His motivation for the race was anger and frustration but with himself, not with Stratton. The night before, talking with Stratton in the kitchen, had been the first time he'd lied to anyone about his military career and how he'd got into the CIA and he was not sure why he had done so. In the past, when the subject had come up, he'd simply avoided the details, which was only to be expected of him and befitted his clandestine aura.

Why Seaton had felt the need to build up his image in Stratton's eyes was something that he could not understand at the time. Lying in bed later that night, unable to sleep because of it, he had finally had to accept that it was because Stratton intimidated him. Stratton made Seaton's own perceived shortcomings more obvious and appeared to do with ease what

Seaton had failed at with every effort. Normally, Seaton was confident, often ebullient and even inclined to act superior about who he was, what he did for a living and for his country. In many ways there was no reason for him to feel otherwise for he occupied an important and privileged position. But his importance became invisible as far as he was concerned when in the company of men like Stratton. He knew it was ridiculous but he could not help it because the feeling couldn't be dismissed as entirely psychological.

Seaton had gone to the Rangers but he had never actually joined them as he had said, and that had been after, not before attending a SEAL selection or BUDS (Basic Underwater Demolition). The biggest lie – by omission, that was – was that he had failed the selection during Hell Week, the most distressing and painful five and a half days that took place three weeks into the course. After limited sleep, endless beastings and constant berating from the SEAL directing staff Seaton began to complain of a gut problem. He was invited by the duty corman to step down from the course and start another at a later date, which was standard practice for a candidate suffering from any malady. But the thought of having to go through it all again only filled Seaton with dread. The stomach disorder had been a fabrication and he had hoped that as an officer he might somehow slide through. But it didn't work like that in the SEALs.

Faced with no other way out Seaton went to the 'drop area', a decision he was to regret eternally, and rang the infamous ship's bell that announced to all who heard it that the student whose hand gripped the white toggle had quit. For weeks after, Seaton stuck to his story of a painful gut and even managed to gain some sympathy from friends when a doctor recommended rest and medication. But what Seaton had failed to comprehend at the time, although he did some years later, was that no matter what the physical dilemma, no one ever gave up, and to actually ring the bell in order to quit was regarded by some as a more cowardly option than suicide – which would have been cowardly enough.

By leaving the navy and joining the army Seaton hoped that there would be little chance of meeting anyone who knew of his failure. Then, as if he had forgotten why he had quit the SEAL selection, he signed up for the Rangers, the toughest US army unit by reputation. It appeared that Seaton had the mettle to attempt such rigorous selection courses but not enough to see them through. It was at this point, before the course had begun, that Seaton's father had died and at the wake he'd got drunk with his uncle, a CIA department deputy in Cuba who subsequently organised an interview with the Agency based on Seaton's proclaimed ambitions. Although Seaton had never started the Rangers course he was technically seconded to the unit when he got the call to attend CIA selection – hence the grounds for the second untruth he'd told: that he'd been a Ranger lieutenant.

During Seaton's entry phase into the CIA his uncle had managed to hide all reference to his nephew's failed BUDS selection, believing that he'd had a legitimate reason to quit and that it would be unfair to have his reputation tainted simply because of a medical disorder. Seaton now focused his ambition on joining the CIA's Clandestine Service for which he had adequate qualifications, what with his Mideast MBA as well as his military background.

Unfortunately, problems arose from Seaton's polygraph test and he was suspended from the course pending investigation. The queries stemmed from a series of questions presented by the polygraph interrogation officer about any attempts that Seaton might have made to join a secret organisation other than the CIA. The officer was ignorant of Seaton's failed SEAL selection and when Seaton gave a negative response the polygraph reacted unfavourably. Once again, it took his uncle's intervention to smooth things out and after resitting the test and completing the course Seaton was eventually accepted into the Agency but on a probationary level only. However, within six months he had proved himself, all was seemingly forgotten, and he was given his first NOC (Non-Official Cover) posting in Iran.

And that was where Seaton's past failures, psychological or otherwise, should have been forgotten, after he'd succeeded in gaining an enviable position in a top-secret government organisation. But the ghosts apparently remained. It seemed that Seaton had never truly disposed of his latent desire to be a front-line field operative of Stratton's stature. This might have been because he had failed to recognise the special drives of such an animal, drives that he himself did not possess in sufficient intensity.

Seaton exacerbated his dilemma that morning by first painting Stratton as a hero to his sons – who were indeed greatly impressed – and then by deciding that his only means of establishing his superiority was to challenge the man. None of these actions were planned and were symptomatic of a deeper problem. Seaton never understood the difference between not being good enough and not fitting in, something that Stratton would have explained to him if he had asked.

Seaton suddenly tried to bump Stratton off the path and headed up a steep incline. But since Stratton was on the inside and kept his footing he was in a position to gain the summit first. Seaton realised his situation and lashed out with an arm, in desperation more than malice, a blow that Stratton only just managed to block. As he kept up his pace Seaton took another swing, catching Stratton on the ear.

Stratton saw red and retaliated viciously, catching Seaton on the side of the face with the back of his fist. The blow stung and Seaton's blood rose as he made a grab for Stratton's shirt.

Stratton tried to wrench Seaton's hand away as they reached the crest together, both near exhaustion, spattered with mud and breathing fiercely. Stratton let loose with his fist, connecting with Seaton's jaw with enough force to make him lose his balance and drop to the ground.

'What's your problem?' Stratton yelled, nearly out of breath.

Seaton scrambled to his feet, breathing fiercely, his fists clenched as though he was itching for a fight. '*Mine?*' he shouted. 'It's *yours* I'm worried about.'

'What are you talking about?' Stratton asked, confused by Seaton's hostility and waiting for his next attack.

'I know why you came here,' Seaton said, spitting mud from his bloody mouth. 'You want to punish those two goons who killed Sally – and you want me to get you the information to do it.'

'That's not why I came here!' Stratton said.

'Bullshit.'

Stratton was growing angrier at Seaton's sudden madness.

'Do you deny that's what you plan to do?' Seaton persisted.

'I've made no plans of that kind.'

'Then you're making them now.'

Stratton couldn't fathom where this was coming from – or going to. If Seaton was that worried all he needed to do was warn the FBI. It had to be something more. 'You don't think they deserve to die for what they did, do you?' Stratton asked, testing him.

'That's not your job.'

'No one else seems to want to do it,' Stratton replied.

'Why did you come here?' Seaton asked.

'To find out if the Feds were going to do anything about Sally's murderers.'

'And now that you know they're not?'

'Is that true?' Stratton asked, wondering what else Seaton knew.

'I didn't give you the whole file, but yes, that's true – for the time being, at least.'

Stratton was beginning to dislike Seaton. 'Tell me something,' he asked. 'If it had been Julie they'd killed, right in front of your boys, how would you feel?'

'That's not what this is about.'

'It's *exactly* what it's about,' Stratton said. 'Let me

make it easier for you. If it'd happened in another country, Kosovo for instance, Julie murdered by the KLA just for being on the wrong road at the wrong time, would you've had second thoughts about tearing them apart?'

Seaton didn't say anything. Some of the wind had been taken out of his sails.

'Jack and Sally were the closest I've had to family for as long as I can remember. Their kid is in a child-protection centre at this very minute, wondering what the hell just happened to his life. Now, I don't know what the hell I want to do or what I'm supposed to do. Maybe I came here because I thought *you* might know – but all I found was some psychotic arsehole who seems to be even more confused about life than I am right now. Let's just forget the whole thing.'

Stratton stepped back and started to walk away.

'Why didn't you ask me for my help?' Seaton shouted.

Stratton stopped and looked back at him.

'You don't think I'm good enough, do you?' Seaton said.

Stratton suddenly saw something in Seaton that he had not expected to find, though he had seen it many times in others. Bizarre as it might seem, Seaton was trying to prove himself. It was not uncommon when working with non-SF to find them trying to prove themselves, sometimes in odd ways, or acting in what they assumed was an SF manner. But Seaton was an established CIA operative, an enviable position for most, yet he was displaying classic signs of resentful inferiority.

'You're not in a position to help me,' Stratton said, avoiding the real issue.

'What does that mean?'

'You have a family, for one thing,' Stratton said. 'Anyway, when I have the choice I work alone.'

'What if I was to tell you that I think those Albanians should pay?' Seaton said.

'I'd say that makes little difference since I don't know if I should or could do anything about it.'

'So why don't you ask me for my help?'

'You don't get it, do you, Seaton? This belongs to no one but me. If you want to help, I don't want anyone to know.'

Seaton looked confused but at least he was no longer taking it personally – or at least Stratton hoped not. Whatever was happening here, Stratton wanted to keep Seaton on his side. Part of the job, after all, was making allies.

'Let's just forget this visit ever happened, okay?' Stratton said. He then turned away and broke into a jog along the track, leaving Seaton to watch him go.

When Stratton was out of sight he checked through the trees to find the sun which had been at their backs on leaving the house. Following it should eventually bring him back to the main road that they had initially crossed and then it was either left or right to Seaton's street.

Stratton soon emerged from the wood onto the highway and found the house shortly after. The boys were out the back, hosing down their bikes as he took off his shoes and socks and went into the house. He could hear someone in the lounge, caught a glimpse of Seaton's wife and went up the stairs to avoid her. Within ten minutes he had showered and got dressed. Without saying goodbye to anyone he headed out of the house and up the road. Within half a mile a taxi appeared. Thirty-five minutes later he was stepping into the airport departure lounge and heading for check-in.

The next flight to Los Angeles was in an hour and a half. Stratton made his way to the gate, took a seat in the waiting area and tried to relax. But his thoughts would not allow him a second's rest: Josh and the problem of getting him back home, Vicky and his hopes of making her into an ally, and Jack's ghost sitting behind him wondering what Stratton was going to do about the two Albanian thugs – all these concerns threatened to overwhelm him.

The time dragged by and eventually the gate came to life with the arrival of airline staff. This was followed shortly by an announcement for all Los Angeles-bound passengers to proceed to the gate and board the plane.

Stratton waited for the last few people to head down the tunnel towards the entrance to the plane, which he could see outside through the large plate-glass windows. As he stood and picked up his bag he saw Seaton, dressed in a tracksuit, his face still smudged with dirt, heading towards him, carrying a manila envelope.

They stared at each other. Seaton stopped in front of him, a smear of dried blood still on the side of his mouth where he had wiped it.

'I've been called a few things in my life but never a hypocrite,' Seaton said.

He held the manila envelope out to Stratton. 'It's the complete file, Ardian and Leka's details and the latest FBI report. If you decide to do something you're probably gonna have to forget Leka. He's in a Santa Monica lock-up awaiting arraignment for beating up his girlfriend a couple of nights ago. He did it in public and she's still in hospital. The police are pressing the charges and he's going to go down for it.'

Stratton took the envelope.

'When you're done with the file, burn it,' Seaton urged.

The last call for Stratton's flight blared over the speaker system. Stratton and Seaton stood in awkward silence for a moment.

'Would you promise me one thing?' Seaton asked.

Stratton looked at him, unsure if the CIA agent was stable or not.

'Try the peaceful way first. Give the law a chance.'

'Look, I – er – I don't think I'm going to do anything—'

'I know,' Seaton interrupted. 'I'm just asking that if you do . . . whatever you do, try the legal route first.'

Stratton shrugged, feeling most uncomfortable talking this way with Seaton now that he had lost confidence in the man.

Seaton held out a baggage stub with the usual computer printout of numbers against the flight details. 'Something for you. It's already on the plane – we have a special relationship with the security here. You wouldn't have gotten it on board on your own.'

Stratton could only wonder what 'it' was.

'There are four numbers written on the back. You'll know what they mean. When you see it you'll wonder why the hell I gave it to you – I'm not even sure myself. Maybe I want you to know that I'm on your side. Maybe I just want to impress you. I don't know. I was there too when Jack died, remember that. It was my op. Maybe I owe him . . . Christ, will you get the hell outta here before I change my mind.'

Stratton looked into Seaton's strangely sad eyes a moment before walking away.

Seaton watched until Stratton disappeared down the tunnel. Then the CIA man headed across the hall, looking a little lost.

Five and a half hours later Stratton stood in the baggage hall of LAX, staring at the conveyor belt as suitcases and holdalls dropped out through a hatch to move slowly around the moving oval track. He had no idea what he was looking for and expected to have to wait until all the luggage had been claimed before he could compare the stub to its other half on the last remaining bag. Then a briefcase made of heavy-duty black plastic popped from the hatch and he knew that it was his.

Stratton watched the briefcase slide down the delivery ramp and onto the conveyor belt where it made its way past expectant passengers towards him. No one else reached for it and as it came alongside he picked it up and inspected the tag. The numbers matched. He shouldered his pack casually and headed towards the exit. A security officer checked the tag against his stub and waved him through the double doors which led directly outside and onto the four-lane one-way ring road that connected all the terminals of LAX. Within a few minutes he was in a taxi and heading out of the airport. The traffic was light as he passed through Marina Del Rey to the beach road and north towards Santa Monica.

When Stratton arrived inside his rented apartment he dropped his pack, placed the case on the dining table, went into the kitchen and filled the kettle. He put it on, dropped two Lipton tea bags in a mug and looked back at the case as the water came to the boil. The single clasp that secured the case required a four-digit combination to open it – the numbers written on the baggage stub, no doubt.

The kettle automatically clicked off as the water boiled. He filled the cup, poured in some milk from a carton in the fridge, stirred the liquid for a moment and then sipped it. The tea was hopeless, a combination of cheap leaves and vitamin D milk, he decided.

Stratton walked to the table and placed the mug on it. Then he tilted the case onto its rear edge, rolled the combination numbers to correspond with those on the stub and pressed the release catch. It flicked open and he lowered the case so that it rested flat on the table's surface again.

He raised the lid to reveal, as he'd suspected, an explosives specialist's travel pack, similar to the SBS type he had used at Josh's birthday party. It was filled with a variety of miniature detonators, along with fuses, cortex, tools and plastic explosives. Seaton knew that Stratton would prefer the indirect method: explosives allowed an assassin to distance himself from the

162

target whereas using a gun required a direct line of sight.

Stratton closed the case and took his mug to the window where he looked out across the city. One thing that niggled at him was his promise to try and resolve the situation by peaceful means first. That might require a level of exposure which, if things did not go well, might make the task of concealing his part in the administration of any other type of justice more difficult.

Stratton's thoughts drifted to Josh and he suddenly felt uneasy. But after deciding to take things one step at a time and abort if at any stage he felt the risk was too high, he felt a little better. There was nothing to be gained by ending up in a US jail for the rest of his life – or worse – simply to avenge Sally. Jack would not expect that of him. But if the Albanians were otherwise going to get away with Sally's death and Stratton could make them pay and – of course – get away with it, that would indeed be sweet and just. By close of play the following day he would know.

Chapter 11

Josh was kneeling on the floor in a corner of the child-protection centre playroom, reaching expectantly into a plastic shopping bag. Stratton was beside him. Josh pulled out a Game Boy, then a model fighter aircraft. Although he was pleased with the presents there was only a hint of his usual excitement as he unwrapped them.

'Thanks, Stratton,' he said softly.

George was watching with envy from across the room. Even though he wanted to move closer to get a better look at the new toys he held himself back.

Stratton reached into the bag, removed a gift, and looked over at the other boy. 'This is for you, George.'

George's eyes lit up. He stumbled as he pushed off from a standing start to run the short distance across the room before braking hard on the shiny linoleum floor. He took the package and examined the contents inside the transparent container to find an assortment of small plastic soldiers in various fighting positions. 'Wow! Targets!' he exclaimed, pulling open the wrapping as he knelt down and poured them onto the floor.

Josh's interest was aroused. He shuffled closer to

George and placed the fighter aircraft beside the soldiers. 'This is their air force,' he explained. The two boys immediately began sorting out the men and discussing how they could best be utilised in a battle that would also include George's helicopter.

Stratton stood up, smiling. He suddenly sensed that someone was looking at him. It was Vicky Whitaker, standing in the doorway and wearing a smile of her own.

'You got a minute?' she asked quietly, as if not to disturb the boys.

'I'll see you later,' Stratton said to Josh, ruffling his hair.

Josh immediately stopped playing and got to his feet. 'When?' he asked, somewhat demandingly.

'Tomorrow.'

'Can't you come back later today?'

'I don't know.'

Josh looked down in disappointment.

'Maybe Miss Whitaker will let me take you out for a meal,' Stratton said.

George was the first to look at Stratton, his eyes wide with hope.

'And George too, of course.'

Both boys then looked at Miss Whitaker as if she was their mother.

'Can we, Vicky – I mean, Miss Whitaker?' George pleaded.

Her smile disappeared and she folded her arms across her chest, giving the boys a disapproving look.

Stratton shrugged innocently, looking as hopeful as the youngsters.

'That's a very big maybe,' she said. 'And by that I mean probably not.'

'Maybe means yes,' George almost whispered to Josh and Stratton with an air of experience. 'Vicky's a real softy.'

'Don't you believe it,' Vicky warned.

Stratton winked at the boys. 'Let me see what I can do,' he said quietly to them before walking towards Vicky Whitaker. She gave him a stern look as he walked past her and left the room.

She followed him into the corridor, closing the door behind her. 'You shouldn't get their hopes up like that,' she said in a matronly manner.

'Hope is just about all those boys have while they're in here.'

'*Trust* is the single most important element of the relationship we try and build with these kids. George could be moved to a foster home any day now. Don't promise them things that you can't deliver.'

Stratton humbly took another ticking-off. 'You're right, as usual. I'm sorry.'

And, as usual, Vicky was completely disarmed by his sincerity. She wondered what it was about this man of whom she knew so little that made her feel she could depend on him. He was without doubt unusual – and also mysterious, it seemed. 'Josh has quite an imagination,' she said, heading down the corridor.

'Don't all kids?' Stratton asked, falling in alongside her.

'He talks about you all the time.'

Stratton thought he could see what was coming.

'Now that you mention it, though, he does have quite an overactive imagination when it comes to playing soldiers.'

'He says you're a secret soldier and a spy for the British Government.'

'That's the last top secret I tell him,' Stratton said, feigning flippancy.

'On your form, under employer, you put British MoD. What's that?'

'Ministry of Defence.'

'So you *do* work for the government?'

'Yes.'

'Are you a soldier?'

'Yes.'

'Fifteen years, you put on the form.'

'That's right.'

'Why does he call you a "secret" soldier?'

'Well, it's kind of a game we play. Whenever I visited his mum and dad after being away he would ask where I'd been and I'd tell him some tall story. It became something of a tradition between us.'

'So you're not really who he thinks you are.'

'What does that mean?'

'I mean in terms of work – you don't do the job that he thinks you do.'

'Is that important?'

'I suppose not.'

'Is this a trust thing?' Stratton asked, a touch of cynicism in his voice.

Vicky sighed, annoyed with herself. 'I'm sorry. I need to lighten up a little. That was a poor attempt to stick my nose into your personal life – it's nothing personal.'

'I understand.'

'I hope you do. We've had some apparently very nice people arrive here to take responsibility for children, people who've turned out to be not so nice after all.'

'You don't need to explain. What do you want to know?'

'Well . . . nothing, really,' Vicky said, unsure where she was going with the questioning. 'Being military could be useful as far as securing guardianship is concerned. There'll be no missing years on your records, for instance, and plenty of people to vouch for you.'

Stratton had thought about calling someone in British military intelligence. But he had a feeling that trying to light a fire under the Californian social and welfare services would not be any easier for someone from that organisation if it did not involve operational necessity. He decided to leave that particular avenue alone unless he ran into a serious problem. 'Will it really take very long?' he asked.

'Myers could be more efficient but I can push him only so far before he gets all petulant. Then he'll dig his heels in and become deliberately obstructive. To be blunt, he's a jerk.'

'Say it how you feel,' Stratton said.

Vicky grinned, then averted her gaze as if embarrassed.

She suddenly looked like a girl and not an officious bureaucrat, albeit one with a warm and generous heart.

'I shouldn't talk about him like that. It's not professional.'

'Sometimes it's good to express how you feel.'

'But not to strangers,' Vicky said, turning serious again as she remembered something. 'The one area where Myers has been efficient was in locating a temporary foster home for Josh. That's because one of his main tasks is moving kids out of here as soon as possible. It's pretty quiet around here right now but it can turn into a zoo overnight, believe me. Four months ago we had over a hundred children crammed in here and we're only officially equipped for fifty. They don't just come from disrupted families. We get a lot of young illegal immigrants and you'd be surprised at the number of kids we have to take back from foster parents.'

'How do you get to qualify as a foster parent?'

'Horrifyingly easily, unfortunately. The state pays good money to foster parents but with a lot of them that's all they're in it for. There've been cases where we've inadvertently placed children in worse places than we originally got them from. You wouldn't qualify so don't go down that road if you're thinking about it. For one, you have to be a resident citizen.'

'How soon could he be relocated?'

'A week maybe. I won't know exactly until we're closer to a date.'

'Will you know who'll be fostering him or where he'll be living?'

'Yes. But that information is confidential. Look, I'm on your side, John. Or, to be precise, I'm on Josh's. I can see how much he loves you and how much you care for him. There's no greater qualification than that in my view. I'll fight for that any day of the week, but I don't make the rules.'

Stratton nodded his appreciation. 'I wish you did,' he said checking his watch and aiming towards the door. 'Well, thanks again, Miss Whitaker.'

'You can call me Vicky if you want. I'm not quite the stuffed shirt I look – okay, I am, but I don't like to be.'

Her comment brought smiles to both their faces.

'I don't see a stuffed shirt,' Stratton said, looking her in the eye.

At face value the comment seemed open to interpretation. But Stratton's sincere expression ensured that it conveyed only the most respectful appreciation.

'See you soon,' he said, offering his hand. Vicky took it and he held hers for a second before shaking it. It was small and soft, and the touch felt good, immediately demonstrating to Stratton his need for female company. But he quickly pushed all thought of that aside, this being neither the time nor the place for a romance.

Vicky watched him walk away until he was through the door. Then, as she turned to head for her office, she caught Dorothy looking at her from behind her reception desk and wearing a broad, suggestive smile. Vicky immediately adopted an air of prim decorum, marched to her office, and let its door close behind her.

Chapter 12

Stratton passed through the electronic security check at the entrance of the Santa Monica Court Administration building that was in the same block as the police department. After being thoroughly checked by a security officer he headed into the lobby and consulted a room directory on the wall. The place was bustling, thanks to a broad spectrum of Santa Monica life milling in and out: police, lawyers, plaintiffs, defendants, the underprivileged and the well-heeled.

The district attorney's office was on the second floor. Stratton walked to the stairs halfway along the corridor from the front door and paused on the first step, wondering what he actually expected to achieve with this visit. His intentions were to speak to the DA personally and lobby to have the two thugs responsible for Sally's death investigated. Though he did not know the procedures for making such a request he could guess at some of the problems he would encounter. The DA would inevitably ask him to reveal how he came to know the identities of the two men and for obvious reasons he could not tell them the source. Nor could he involve the Korean shopkeeper since that would place a death sentence on the man's head.

Ideally, Stratton needed a prosecutor who'd be interested in an FBI cover-up. But that was too much to hope for and would be impossibly complicated, requiring all kinds of proof that he could not offer. But he had at least to try. Between one step and the next another problem popped into his head: his own exposure. If, for argument's sake, he did decide to take action against the thugs himself, showing his face in the public prosecutor's office would not be the wisest thing to do.

Stratton stayed where he was for a moment to think his strategy through once again. Then a commotion at the building entrance took him out of his thoughts. He looked up to see half a dozen uniformed policemen, several openly carrying Heckler & Koch MP5K sub-machine guns held across their chests, and a couple of plain-clothes officers march in. They were escorting a middle-aged Latino man with intense features and wild black hair whose hands were cuffed behind his back.

'Stand aside, please,' the lead officers called out as they pushed their way none too gently through the jostling crowd.

At the same time the stairwell above Stratton was suddenly packed with half a dozen Slavic-looking men in a range of dress from colourful Hawaiian shirts and jeans to expensive suits. They were heading down from the floor above. The two groups were on a collision course.

The men on the stairs stopped, mainly because their

passage was suddenly blocked by a couple of armed policemen but also due to the reaction of the Latino prisoner whose demeanour suddenly became violent as he saw them. He started to shout in a mixture of Spanish and English, directing his vituperation at the group on the stairs.

'You *pindeho* piece a' shit, Skender!' he yelled. 'I'm gonna tear your fucken' heart out, you *muher*! You hear me? Skender!'

The police immediately grabbed him. At the mention of Skender's name Stratton's stare flashed to the group on the stairs.

The cops divided their attentions between the Latino prisoner and the Slavic-looking bunch, clearly threatening instant violence should either side try anything.

'Rot in jail, Colombo,' one of the men on the stairs called out. 'You won't have a living relative left by the time you get out – if you ever do, you spic fuck.'

Stratton recognised the man in the smart suit as Ivor Vleshek who, as Seaton had explained the CIA suspected, was really Dren Cano, Ardian's brother. He looked exactly like his photograph: his murderous eyes were unmistakable.

The abuse enraged the Latino prisoner who made a violent attempt to break through his police cordon to get at the Slavic group. They automatically shifted their weight forward in response. But the police held both sides apart and dragged Colombo past the stairs and along the hallway.

Stratton scanned the faces above him and identified Skender at the back. The man was dressed in an immaculate coat and had a cravat around his neck tucked into a silk shirt. He looked like a warlike Visigoth stuffed into expensive modern clothes. He also looked as old as he was, in his early sixties, his complexion rugged. But his long dark hair and the fire in his eyes indicated a strength that was a long way from fading away into age.

Skender stared unblinkingly at the still-yelling prisoner, his eyes filled with malice, until Colombo disappeared out of sight and earshot along with his dark blue shield of law enforcers.

Stratton could not see Ardian among the group and his stare focused on Skender again as if he was compelled to look at him. The group exuded an unmistakable malevolence as tangible as the drab, solid walls of the stairway.

As the corridor emptied, Skender's lead bodyguards, large and fearsome-looking, continued on their way down the stairs. Stratton moved to the wall to let them pass. This was not enough for the lead bodyguard who reached out a hand to push him down.

'Get outta the way,' the thug said as he took hold of Stratton's jacket at the shoulder.

The blood quickly rose in Stratton and he held his position. The bodyguard grimaced at the insolence and responded by putting more weight behind his shove. But he was unprepared for the reaction that this provoked. Stratton stepped back to make the bodyguard straighten his arm while at the same time taking hold of the bruiser's wrist. As the bodyguard overreached, Stratton twisted his wrist with sudden force, jerking the arm forward and then slamming the palm of his other hand up against the elbow joint, almost breaking it. The bodyguard yelped as his knees automatically gave out and he dropped the last step, his two hundred and fifty pounds flattening his face against the concrete floor. His lips split open.

Two more bodyguards instantly grabbed Stratton who released the first one's wrist and went limp as the others slammed him back against the wall, their hands reaching inside his jacket to frisk him. He could not take them all on and had no intention of trying. Though it had not been the wisest course of action to take down the first bodyguard he had been unable to help himself. The sight of these men, knowing of their callous contempt for others as well as their brutal history, had filled him with hatred.

'He's clean,' one of the thugs said. Cano stepped close, their noses inches apart as the rest of the group headed down the corridor.

'Cano!' a man's voice called out from the hall. 'Take your wolves and join the rest of your pack.' The man spoke with some authority. He was in plain clothes and was one of the party escorting the Latino prisoner. Judging by his age, bearing and authoritative voice, he was a senior officer of some kind.

Cano ignored the man who closed in, not intimidated by the group.

'Move on,' the man said, a more threatening tone entering his voice 'Now – or I'll personally charge you with disturbing the peace,' he added.

'How you doing, Agent Hobart?' Cano said.

'I won't ask again,' Hobart said. He was an intelligent-looking Anglo-Saxon with greying hair. In his late forties, he had a degree of refinement about him.

'He assaulted one of my men,' Cano growled coldly as the bodyguard got painfully to his feet, holding his sore elbow, blood trickling down his chin.

'Looked like self-defence to me,' Hobart said. 'What do you think, Hendrickson?'

A younger man, also in plain clothes, stepped in behind his boss. 'That's exactly how it was, sir.'

Cano's face broke into a thin smile. Then he stepped back and nodded to his men. They released Stratton. 'One a' these days, Hobart . . .'

'Cano,' a strange-sounding, gravelly voice interrupted. It was Skender, who was standing with the rest of his people at the entrance. His gaze moved from Cano to Hobart, and he smiled slightly and nodded. Hobart did not respond.

Cano stared into Stratton's eyes long enough to relay an instant hatred. Then, like a well-trained Rottweiler, he turned around and joined the rest of the group as they left the building.

Seconds later the hall was practically empty.

'Who are you?' Hobart asked Stratton none too politely.

'I was on my way to see the DA—'

'Then get going,' Hobart said, interrupting Stratton. The lawman walked away with Hendrickson. 'Damn it! Why wasn't I told that Skender was going to be here today?' he demanded.

Stratton remained on the steps for a moment to adjust his clothes and loosen the tension in his neck. So that was Cano and Skender, he mused. They were indeed a fearsome group and he was confident that had the incident taken place in a less public place it might have had a different ending for him. It served as a warning to respect the dangers they represented.

He headed up the steps to the next floor where the DA's office was signposted at the end of the corridor. After waiting half an hour he was eventually told by a secretary who showed little interest in what he had to say to come back the following day. She added that he should bring a lawyer with him.

Stratton walked back down the stairs feeling sure that he would achieve nothing unless he could fund some massive legal representation privately. He stepped out into the bright sunlight and headed away from the court buildings.

As he tried to think of other peaceful ways of resolving the situation he found himself leaning more and more towards walking away from the whole thing. But as soon as he contemplated the possibility voices in his head hounded him, accusing him of deserting his friends. He fought back by telling himself that he was not yet abandoning them. Stratton felt he was going mad as his mind was dragged first one way then the other, loyalty pitted against common sense, duty towards friends against self-preservation.

As he crossed the road he knew that he was on the verge of turning his back on Jack and Sally. He was unaware of the black Mercedes stretch limousine with dark-tinted windows that drove slowly out of the police department parking lot and pulled onto the main road behind him.

Stratton cut down Second Street, passing a McDonald's on his left. Feeling hungry, he decided that right then junk food seemed okay to him. The famous fast-food establishment was quiet inside and after ordering a hamburger, some fries and a soda he considered eating the meal in the restaurant. But after a quick scan of the other customers, namely two overweight families and their children on one side scarfing down a feast that would sustain a small village in the Sudan for several days and a filthy bum eating like a pig on the other, he elected to eat while he walked. A stroll along the front might help to clear his head, he thought, and he headed for the entrance.

As Stratton walked outside two large men in Hawaiian shirts stepped from either side of the door and followed him. He glanced over his shoulder and slowed to face them, recognising them as two of Skender's bodyguards from the courthouse. He prepared himself for an attack.

But instead of moving in on him they stopped at a safe distance, eyeing him warily. They had seen the ease with which he had taken down their friend and although they felt confident in their ability to crush him they were cautious.

'The boss vants to speak to you,' one of them grunted in a heavy accent, jutting his chin past Stratton.

Stratton looked over his shoulder at the black stretch limousine, the only vehicle on the far side of the large car park. His mind raced as he considered various evasive-action options. This was obviously to do with the bodyguard he had felled since Skender and his men could not possibly know of his interest in Sally's killers.

'What does he want?' Stratton asked.

'You should ask him,' the thug said, taking a step forward.

'Maybe some other time,' Stratton said as he stepped back and headed off across the car park. Another thug appeared in front of him and he stopped to look around. Another goon was behind him and a fifth, a fat one, climbed out of the limousine and put his hand inside his jacket as if he had a weapon concealed there. Stratton reviewed his options which were limited to making a run for it.

The original pair closed in and halted a yard away from him. 'You can do this the easy way or the hard way,' the first thug said, pulling back his jacket to reveal a semi-automatic pistol in his belt. 'Don't matter to me. Boss didn't say you had to walk to the car yourself.'

Stratton wondered if these people were genuinely fearless of using guns in public but he was not curious enough to find out.

'You can eat your lunch in the car,' the thug said.

Stratton accepted that the situation was out of his hands, for the time being at least. He faced the limousine and walked towards it.

He reached the vehicle where the fat thug standing outside it looked him up and down before beckoning him closer. Stratton took another step forward.

'Raise your arms,' the man ordered.

Stratton obeyed, holding his meal in one hand and the drink in the other while the man frisked the length of his body, including his ankles. When he stood up he held out his hand. 'I'll take the meal.'

'That's what this is all about? You want my lunch?'

The man smiled thinly. 'The meal,' he said.

Stratton handed it to him.

'Get in the car,' the fat man said as he shuffled aside.

Stratton glanced around at the others who had closed in. He leaned down and stepped inside the limousine.

The fat thug holding his food tossed it to an even fatter one who looked inside the paper bag while following the others towards a white sedan parked on the street.

The limo interior was spacious, with seats on three sides and a drinks cabinet by the door. Stratton chose the back seat where he faced Cano who sat leaning forward, his fingers clasped together, looking at him solemnly. A glass partition behind Cano separated the passenger cabin from the driver's compartment where a man sat in the passenger seat beside the driver. The fat thug who had greeted Stratton outside climbed in, closed the door behind him, and sat on the long seat between the two other men. Stratton had for some reason expected to find Skender inside but with his absence and the demonic Cano in his place the situation seemed even darker.

'This is very nice,' Stratton said, looking around. 'My first limousine.'

'You search him well, Klodi?' Cano asked his ape.

'Yeah, I did, Mr Vleshek.'

Cano turned around to tap on the glass partition. A few seconds later the vehicle pulled smoothly out of the car park and headed south in the direction of Venice Beach.

'You look like a confident guy,' Cano said in precise

English though the Slav accent was strong. His voice was slow and calculating as if Cano was trying to sound as articulate as possible.

Stratton studied the man who, despite the expensive suit and finely trimmed black hair and goatee, was typical of the Albanian KLA types he had known in Kosovo. Stratton had spent several months, on and off, in various parts of the province, mainly in Pristina, its capital, and in the town of Podujevo in the north-east on the main route out of Kosovo for the retreating Serbian army and refugees. Like most of the other operatives with whom he had served in Kosovo, he had initially considered the Albanians borderline okay, understanding their hatred for the Serbs. During the early days it had seemed that all they wanted was to be rid of a people who had tried to wipe them off the face of the Earth, although throughout history it had been a two-way, see-saw fight, one side as bad as the other.

As the war progressed and the Serbian army left Kosovo, forced out by NATO, the dark heart of the Albanian psyche showed itself. Pockets of Serb civilians such as farmers remained, some of whom stubbornly maintained their right to stay while others were unable to escape because they didn't have transport or were too old, too young or too feeble to make the long journey to Serbia and then re-establish themselves there. The Albanian hatred for them was totally relentless. What had begun as an amicable partnership between NATO and the KLA to oust the Serbian army from Kosovo turned into an internal security situation where the UN and NATO-led K-For were the police and the KLA became the delinquents. On more than one occasion Stratton had crossed swords with them and blood had been spilled but always the KLA – they were not sufficiently well trained or equipped to take on the British military and were certainly not skilled enough to take on special forces.

Stratton had seen the results of Serbian and Albanian atrocities and he reckoned that there was not much to choose between the two as far as brutality was concerned. But due to the area he operated in it had been the ruthlessness and savagery of the Albanians, the KLA, that he had witnessed more often. Looking at Cano reminded him of so many KLA members he had seen: that same brooding, sometimes vacant but usually hate-filled look.

'What am I doing here?' Stratton asked, glancing at Klodi who was staring ahead between them and breathing heavily in the way that overweight people sometimes do.

Cano studied Stratton, looking as if he could not make his mind up about something. 'Where you from?' he asked. 'You don't sound American.'

'I'm English.'

'Ah, English,' Cano said, an unmistakable sneer twisting his face as his thoughts transported him to another very different time and place that was still so much a part of his every living fibre. 'You're the first Englishman I've spoken to in a long time.'

Stratton could see the contempt in Cano's eyes and wondered if it was reserved just for Englishmen. According to Seaton's file Cano had been a mid-ranking officer of the KLA, heavily involved in 'cleansing' Kosovo of Serbians. Graphic images of mutilated men, women and children flashed across Stratton's memory and he wondered how many of those atrocities had been ordered or even carried out by this man.

Despite the many horrors of war that Stratton had seen in his lifetime the sight of women and children butchered by hand had always filled him with immeasurable disgust and hatred for those who did it. Many of the scenes he had witnessed in Kosovo bore evidence that the perpetrators had not just executed but had had fun doing it. A method he had often come across, one he had first seen in Afghanistan and peculiar (so he'd thought) to the Hazara tribe, was the driving of a large nail into a person's brain, often through the centre of the forehead so that the killer could look the victim in the eye as the spike was hammered home.

In one particular village in the south of Kosovo that Stratton and his team had happened across, not a living soul remained, a common enough occurrence. But on this occasion all the village's men and women, old and young alike, were found dead in a barn, shot through the head or with their throats slit. An even more sickening sight was that of the babies, a dozen or so, nailed through their heads to the barn door.

Stratton had been consumed with an urge to kill those responsible if he ever learned who they were. Now that he was sitting opposite a man wanted for such atrocities there was a rekindling of that loathing and repugnance, though he tried not to let it show.

Strangely, as he stared into Cano's eyes, they seemed to mirror his own.

Cano had not been to England but he hated the English more than any other nationality outside the Balkans – though that had not always been the case. His was a private hate, one of many. He had been brought up on hate and a lust for revenge. Hate had been a staple part of his educational diet from the day he could understand the concept: as he grew to manhood it had grown with him.

Cano had been born into a vicious conflict that went back hundreds of years. His teachers, neighbours, friends and family made sure that he and all the other youngsters in the community understood why they should fight and kill for their heritage. The Serbians' historic entitlement to Kosovo went as far back as the fourteenth century but the Albanians claimed to be descendants of an ancient tribe that had occupied the land before the time of Christ.

The Muslim Albanians profited from a 500-year Turkish occupation insofar as the Ottomans kicked the Christian Serbs out, but just before the First World War the Balkan states united to drive the invaders away and the Serbian army marched back into Kosovo. During the Great War the Albanians managed to kick them out again, only to be reoccupied by the end of it.

The Second World War saw Kosovo taken over by the Axis powers and the Serbs driven out once again. When Tito came along with plans to unite the Balkans, in order to enlist Albanian support he promised them Kosovo. But that had been a lie and once again the

Kosovar Albanians found themselves fighting to govern their homeland.

Two decades later Cano was born. During his youth the Albanian struggle to retain Kosovo had been conducted mostly by political means and at one point had looked like succeeding. Then one Slobodan Milosevic arrived on the scene and practically overnight had stripped the Kosovar Albanians of their autonomy.

The Albanian leadership tried to conduct a peaceful resistance against Milosevic but Cano, now a young man full of strength and vigour, along with many others sought to oppose him with violence. Thus was born the Kosovo Liberation Army in which Cano built his reputation for bloody and merciless cruelty. When the West became involved he welcomed their political and material support: for the first time in his life he truly believed that the day might come when the Kosovar Albanians would see their land returned fully to their control. But when the Serbian army was driven from Kosovo Cano and his colleagues became suspicious about the true intentions of the West.

When NATO began bussing back into Kosovo Serbians who could prove their rightful claims to land the Kosovar Albanians reacted violently. Acting on orders from on high, Cano had been one of many young leaders encouraged to organise operations designed to dissuade the Serbs from returning, a task he embraced with unnatural enthusiasm. His lust for blood was insatiable and no Serb, no matter what their age, gender or political leaning, was safe while they remained in Kosovo.

Cano gained experience in the use of explosives. It became his preferred method of attacking his enemy, and it was after one such deadly ambush that he ran foul of a small group of British SAS troopers. This encounter left him with scars both mental and physical, and another private hate for him to nurture.

Cano was very particular about his explosive ambushes: he went to great lengths to calculate the maximum death and destruction that he could inflict. His preferred locations were busy roads with earth banks in which large holes could be dug and filled with ordnance such as artillery shells and mines. There were plenty of those in Kosovo. An electrical detonator was then attached to a camouflaged command wire that trailed to a point of concealment where Cano and his men could safely hide while simultaneously observing the ambush location. All they needed to do then was wait for a convoy to pass by. Cano tried to avoid hitting NATO vehicles – not that he cared about killing their soldiers. However, some NATO outfits made an effort to find the perpetrators of such ambushes whereas killing just Serbs seemed to provoke little reaction.

One particular afternoon, on seeing a convoy of NATO-protected cars, lorries, tractors and vans winding its way along a valley road towards his ambush spot, Cano selected for destruction several tarp-covered old military trucks in the centre of the column. They were, of course, filled with civilians.

The detonation ripped through the vehicles, shredding their canvas coverings and the occupants. On paper the action did not appear uncommonly spectacular since the report simply described an explosion that killed seven, including two children, and wounded twenty-four. For the survivors who had to deal with the carnage it was horrifying beyond belief. More than a dozen of the wounded died within days of the report, and though none of the NATO escort had been physically hurt, several were later sent home suffering from psychological trauma.

Most of the seriously injured were women and children – faces torn off, burst eyes, numerous amputations – and then there were those who had lost their minds. Few sights are more disturbing than a mother holding the shattered body of her child, so utterly bereft that her life has lost all meaning.

Six men from G Squadron 22 SAS, all carrying heavy backpacks and webbing laden with ordnance and equipment, happened to be in the area and arrived at the scene twenty minutes after hearing the explosion. They quickly set about helping the wounded while the team commander, a sergeant, made a security sweep.

It was not long before he found the detonation wire and traced it to the command site in a clump of bushes on the crest of a hill a couple of hundred metres away. The troop's operational directive was to set up an observation position by dawn the following day in an area several miles away. Since they had ample time, and to a man were appalled by the attack, they agreed to spend the daylight they had left carrying out a follow-up on the off chance of finding the killers.

The tracks from the command post headed across soft, moist ground towards a wood on a crest that overlooked the next valley. It was estimated that there were no more than seven or eight different sets of boot prints. Shortly before last light the team emerged from a wood on the flat valley floor to see the tracks leading towards a small hamlet of half a dozen assorted brick and wooden buildings a quarter of a mile away. The ground was open for several miles beyond, with no sign of life. Having calculated that the team was little more than ten minutes or so behind their quarry, the SAS men thought it was fair to assume the ambushers had stopped in the hamlet.

The SAS troopers spread out as they crossed the open field, weapons ready in their hands, fingers on the guns' trigger guards, safety catches off. NATO troops had been ambushed in the past by KLA units – wrongly identified as such, according to the Albanians afterwards – and the troopers were not about to get caught unawares. They traversed a fence and a ditch before closing in again on one of the nearest buildings, a dilapidated breeze-block structure. They went to ground to listen and observe, the first procedure on arrival at a target, and remained still, as if they were part of the landscape, not making a sound.

Five minutes later a man walked out of the largest building in the centre of the hamlet, a barn or warehouse with a rotting wooden roof, and stood in the open to urinate. He glanced around as he did his business but not with any great interest, unaware that several pairs of eyes were watching him through telescopic rifle sights. The man's military fatigues were old and in need of a wash and the shoulder flashes immediately gave him away as a member of the KLA.

He was joined by a similarly dressed man from the other side of the hamlet who was carrying firewood. As they went back into the barn-style building the SAS sergeant signalled his team to close in on the structure from two sides. As they reached the corners of the wall where the door through which the men had entered was situated they could hear voices coming from inside.

There was no sentry outside, indicating the group's lack of professionalism as well as their confidence that they had not been followed. The door was the only entrance to the building: there was no other escape route except for a window at the rear which was high in the wall and more of a vent and source of light than anything else. No one would have time to get through it, anyway.

The troopers removed their large packs, left them in two piles back from the building's corners, moved forward to gather either side of the door and, after a brief test to check that it was unlocked, on the sergeant's nod pushed the door open and walked in. They quickly cleared the doorway so as not to be silhouetted in it and spread out along the interior wall their mixture of M203 (M16s with under-slung grenade launchers) and M3 assault rifles levelled as the last man turned to cover the outside just in case an unexpected visitor arrived.

The KLA fighters, seven of them, all men, were sitting around in various states of relaxation and undress, most with their boots off, obviously planning on staying the night, while a couple were lighting a fire in the centre of the dirt floor. Cano was in a far corner, leaning back against a bare breeze-block wall and lighting a slender cheroot when his dark-eyed gaze shot towards the door as it opened.

The Albanians faced the unwelcome intruders, a couple of the KLA men reaching automatically for their weapons. Then they suddenly froze as they realised that these soldiers were NATO – and not run-of-the-mill squaddies, either. This group had a battle-honed maturity about them and a confidence to match. More dangerous even than that, something about their postures and expressions conveyed a willingness to open fire at the slightest provocation.

'Go ahead,' said the tall, powerfully built red-headed sergeant, a man whose experience in SAS matters spanned some fifteen years, from Central and South America in the late 1980s and the first Gulf War in the early 1990s to various minor operations since in the Middle East and Africa. 'This sodding country may be lawless but that works both ways – and no one's gonna miss you fuckers for a second.'

The Albanians stayed still. Although only a couple of them understood what the English north-countryman with his strong accent had said they all seemed to have got the gist of it.

The sergeant was aware that his assessment of the legal aspect of the conflict was not entirely accurate. If he carried out his threat the result would, if discovered, be denounced as a British atrocity. But he was confident that the Albanians would apply their own brand of common sense to the statement and believe every word of it.

'Who's the leader here?' the sergeant asked.

Cano was far smarter than the rest of his men: he actually understood the legal basis of the NATO occupation. But the sergeant had assessed him accurately insofar as Cano had no respect for any law and trusted no one who said they did. He got slowly to his feet, watching the sergeant, wondering what kind of man he was and if murder was something that came easily to him. Cano had spoken hardly a word of English before NATO had arrived in his country but as the first American F16s screamed across his skies he had started to learn. He realised that it would be a wise Albanian who at this point in history knew the tongue of the most recent invaders, the language of the richest and most powerful country in the world.

Cano had guessed that these men, though, were British rather than American even before the leader had spoken. Furthermore, their unusually long hair and several days of facial growth, plus their webbing and weapons indicated that they were special forces. He himself had been trained by American special forces and knew the difference. He had seen men like these on the roads and in the countryside when they had usually been carrying large packs. It was known that they often patrolled for days, sometimes weeks, in all weathers, doing what he had no idea, although of late he had suspected that they were spying on KLA activities. Now he knew for sure and cursed himself for not being more vigilant when he and his men had escaped from the ambush site.

'I am in charge,' Cano answered in broken English as those of his men who had been sitting got to their feet. They were all strong and hard-looking. Had this been a bare-fist fight they might have given the SAS a run for their money. But that was never going to happen.

The red-headed sergeant let his gaze fall on Cano. He did not look pleased to see him. 'Come 'ere,' he growled.

Cano did not lack courage and took his time taking the first step, maintaining his own sneer of contempt as he walked towards the soldier who was a head taller than him. Cano stopped in front of the muzzle of the sergeant's rifle and stared him in the eye.

The sergeant knew that these were a tough and arrogant people who did not shy away from a fight easily. But at his level of soldiering much more than brute force was required of a man if he was to earn another's respect and the sergeant had none for these types. 'You blow away those people on the road a couple miles north of here?' he asked accusingly.

Cano knew there was no point in lying, certain that the soldiers had followed his group to the hamlet. 'It was us who fought the enemy, yes,' he announced proudly, as if this Englishman had no right to challenge his authority.

'Enemy?' the sergeant said with disgust. 'Did you identify your target before you pressed the button, laddy? Did you see the women and children you maimed and killed, you bastard?'

For Cano to admit that he had to the English who evaluated everyone else by their own holier-than-thou criteria and who could never begin to understand the true nature of the struggle between Albanian and Serb would only invite bitter judgement. But to deny it

192

would compromise Cano's dignity and self-esteem and he was not prepared to suffer that no matter what these foreigners intended. 'They were Serbs,' he said, spitting out the name as if it was dirt in his mouth.

The sergeant's disgust deepened. 'You piece of shit,' he muttered, shouldering his weapon. 'Turn around.'

Cano did not obey, unsure how far the man was prepared to go. He kept his gaze fixed on the English soldier's face.

'I said turn around,' the SAS sergeant repeated, an unmistakable threat in his grim expression.

The barrel of the gun in the hands of the trooper beside the sergeant drifted towards Cano's chest. Unwilling to trust his judgement of their likely tolerance any further, Cano obeyed. The sergeant's hands landed hard on Cano's shoulders as he faced his men and for a second Cano thought he was about to get a beating. Then the hands moved down his body as they searched him. They paused at a bulky side pocket, reached inside, and removed a ball of white malleable matter the size of a small fist. A quick sniff revealed the substance's identity and the sergeant spun Cano around to face him again.

'What's this?' the sergeant asked.

'You know what it is,' Cano said.

'Good quality,' the sergeant said, squeezing it and inspecting the light oily residue it left on his skin. 'C4?'

'PE4,' Cano said, aware of the irony that he had used the British and not the American military variety of plastic explosive to carry out the ambush.

The sergeant didn't care how this KLA shit had got

hold of British explosives. That wasn't what this was about. 'You like this stuff, don't you?' he asked, holding it in front of Cano's face as if he was about to shove it into his mouth.

Cano did not waver.

The sergeant checked inside Cano's bulging breast pocket and removed a small coil of fuse wire. 'Regular Guy Fawkes, ain't we?' he said with a grin that had danger written all over it. 'Eat it,' he said.

Cano looked at the explosive, then back up at the sergeant, refusal written across his face.

'I said eat it,' the sergeant growled, pushing it closer to Cano's face.

Cano did not show the man any weakness and maintained his resolve.

'You don't eat it, I'll shove it up your arse and detonate it,' the sergeant said, tossing the ball of explosive slowly up and down in his hand.

Cano did not relent.

The sergeant handed his gun to the trooper beside him and swiftly grabbed the lapels of Cano's jacket, lifting him slightly as he swept his feet out from under him. Cano dropped heavily on his side as he landed on the floor. Several of the Albanians took a step forward but froze again as the SAS troopers' fingers tightened menacingly on their weapons' triggers.

The sergeant knelt down, his knee landing solidly on Cano's chest, and pushed the plastic explosive against his mouth. 'Eat it, you fuck,' he growled. But still Cano would not obey. 'Eat it,' the sergeant repeated, brutally pushing the explosives against Cano's lips, trying to force them apart but without success.

The sergeant stopped to reconsider. 'Fine,' he said, sighing. 'We'll go for the other option, then.'

The sergeant rolled Cano onto his front. Then the SAS man removed a long slender knife from a sheath on his belt, pulled up Cano's jacket, grabbed the waist of his trousers, inserted the knife between it and Cano's skin, and cut through the fabric with ease, tearing the trousers and underpants open all the way to the crotch to expose Cano's white buttocks. The Albanians watched motionless as their leader was humiliated but few had the desire and none the loyalty to intervene. Most of them were conscripts who had been practically press-ganged, or at best strongly coerced, into joining the KLA on pain of violent punishment for themselves and their families if they did not. So any allegiance to Cano was largely superficial.

The sergeant held up the ball of plastic explosive and looked at one of his lads. 'This ain't gonna fit,' he said. 'I'll 'ave to make the hole bigger.' And with that he knelt heavily on Cano's spine, took hold of one of his arms and twisted it across his back. Then he stuck the end of the blade between Cano's arse cheeks and pushed it into his rectum for several inches.

Cano jerked in spasm as the blade cut into him. He let out a yell, unable to control himself. The sergeant pressed down harder on Cano while twisting the arm further up between his shoulder blades. The weapons in the hands of the other SAS men remained firmly aimed at Cano's mates.

The sergeant withdrew the bloody knife and wiped it on Cano's back. 'Right, then,' he said in a business-like manner. 'Let's see if it fits now.'

He rolled the plastic back and forth over his thigh until it resembled a phallic shape and shoved the end between Cano's cheeks, pressing it firmly into his bleeding anus. Cano shuddered but did not make another loud sound or effort to roll over, as if allowing the man to do his worst.

'Won't go all the way in. Bit of a tight-arse, are we? Never mind. We'll just have to make the hole bigger.'

But instead of using his knife the sergeant left the explosive in place, half its length sticking from between Cano's buttocks. Then he took the fuse wire, placed one end into the detonator and crimped it with his teeth. Next, he pressed the det into the plastic and searched one of his own breast pockets. A second later he produced a lighter, struck it, and held up the flame, pausing to look at the faces of the Albanians whose expressions ranged from mystified to horrified. His own men even glanced between themselves, wondering if it was their leader's intention actually to light the fuse. Everyone in the room was surprised when he really did touch the flame to the end of the fuse. It crackled into life, hissing as it burned, giving off a thin wisp of smoke.

The sergeant got to his feet, put the knife back in its sheath and took his firearm back, looking at the KLA members with contempt. The fuse was a couple of feet long and, depending on its quality, the flame would take about a minute to reach the detonator.

Cano was tense and shaking in sweaty agony, still refusing to make any move.

The two groups faced each other, the sergeant standing, smiling broadly as he waited until the fuse was halfway consumed before nodding to his men to head out.

Seconds later only the sergeant remained in the doorway. 'Shit's gonna fly any second now, lads,' he said.

And so it appeared that the sergeant had not been bluffing, though all of his men would later say that they believed he was right up until the moment he lit the fuse. The Albanians had also doubted his seriousness but were now convinced that their leader was about to have his backside blown off. They moved back, a couple of them dropping to the ground and covering their faces, except for one who could not bear it any longer. As the fuse burned down to an inch from the detonator he lunged forward, grabbed it, pulled it from the charge and threw it into a corner where a few seconds later it exploded with a loud crack.

The SAS sergeant burst into laughter. 'I wondered how long you pricks would leave it before someone saved his arse.' He stopped laughing and his threatening scowl returned. 'Anyone sticks their head outside this door in the next hour will get a bullet through it . . . And you,' he said, looking down at Cano. 'I ever see your face again I'm going to slit your throat open like a goat's.'

A second later he was gone.

Cano reached behind him with a shaking hand, removed the bloody lump of explosive and rolled onto his back, keeping his legs straight, gritting his teeth in an effort to ride the stinging pain. It was the humiliation that hurt more than the wound: he silently vowed the same throat-slitting threat against the English soldier as the sergeant had made to him and could only pray that one day he would meet him again in more favourable circumstances.

Cano's men let him be, knowing better than to try and help him – they knew they would only get abuse or worse for their troubles. It was more than a week before Cano was walking normally and a couple more before he could pass solids in the toilet without pain.

Several months later, as Cano was preparing for an ambush beside his old haunt, the Pristina-Podujevo road, he received word that the West was planning to set up a war-crimes tribunal for Albanians as well as Serbs. He learned that his name had made it to a list of persons wanted in connection with ethnic cleansing. Obviously he needed to leave Kosovo if he was to avoid imprisonment so he accepted the unexpected assistance of a distant member of his family and made his way into Albania.

A few days later the same family member invited Cano to meet the man who had given him the original warning as well as helping him to get out of Kosovo. (The money necessary for his escape had been channelled via the distant relative.) The man was Skender, whom Cano had never met although he had heard of him. His reputation for brutality as well as for generosity to his family was legendary. Shortly after submitting his curriculum vitae, most of which Skender was in any case familiar with, Cano was enlisted into the vast crime organisation.

There was plenty of work for a man of Cano's skills. Although he had expected to operate from Albania,

Skender had bigger plans for him. Two months after arriving in Albania Cano was sent to Turkey to 'cleanse' a section of Skender's trade route that was having minor problems with local bandits. Eleven months later and after more than five hundred suspected bandits and members of their families had simply disappeared he was moved on to Russia where, to his complete surprise, he was given a new identity – or an old one, depending on how you looked at things: it had once belonged to a vacuum-cleaner salesman who no longer needed it after he mysteriously disappeared.

Skender had already earmarked Cano for his forthcoming Pacific Rim operation and a year later he arrived in America, travelling as 'Ivor Vleshek'. It had been remarkably easy getting a visa to travel to America. All that was required was payment to a crooked judge in Russia, of whom there were plenty, to provide a detailed profile and an affidavit for the visa application. It was practically impossible for the FBI to investigate the information over the head of a senior Russian official and, as in so many cases, the Feds had little choice but to grant the request.

Two years after leaving Kosovo, Cano, or Vleshek, was a legal resident in the US and as long as he remained gainfully employed as a 'Specialist Interpreter for Albanian/American Businesses Opportunities' he could stay in the country indefinitely. Within three months Cano married an American woman whom he met only once and two years later, a year before the woman met with a fatal car accident while driving under the influence of alcohol, he received his Green

Card along with an application form with which to apply for full citizenship after three more years of residence.

Cano stared at Stratton as the memory of the day when he'd been defiled back in Kosovo lingered. He hoped that such a bizarre coincidence was possible and that this was one of the men who'd humiliated him, though as far as his memory served there was no resemblance. The man was old enough to have been one of the SAS men and certainly looked as if he could once have been a soldier. But even Cano was aware that he was clutching wildly at straws. It was of no real consequence anyway since Cano didn't need an excuse to be brutal and the man was, after all, English.

'You ever been to the Balkans?' Cano asked anyway.

'Where?' Stratton answered.

Cano gave it up. 'What are you doing here?' he asked, sitting back.

'I'm on holiday.'

Cano took a cigarette packet from his pocket, removed one and offered the pack to Stratton.

'No, thanks.'

Cano put the cigarette in his mouth and the packet back in his pocket. 'Why'd you come to LA for a holiday?'

'I've never been here before.'

Cano lit his cigarette with a gold lighter and blew a long line of smoke into the passenger cabin.

'You here alone?'

'Yes.'

'You always go on holiday alone?'

'Sometimes,' Stratton said, glancing at Klodi and the lump in his jacket that revealed where his pistol was.

'You a fag?'

'You got something against gays?'

Cano shrugged. 'I just wondered. There's a lot of fags in this city. A single man comes here on holiday, you gotta figure, the guy must be a fag.'

If Cano was trying to wind Stratton up he obviously had little experience of the English who were the wind-up masters of the world. 'Well, don't knock it unless you've tried it is what I always say.'

Cano looked for an insult in Stratton's expression but could not see one. 'What's your name?' he asked as he drew on the cigarette.

'John Stratton.'

'You can prove that? You got ID?'

'Why do I need ID? You want to tell me what this is about?'

'You're not in a position to demand anything,' Cano said. 'Show me some ID.'

Stratton was waiting for a moment that he could use to his advantage. What that might mean he had no idea and he would only know when the moment presented itself. Until then he would play along. As he reached into his shirt's breast pocket Klodi moved surprisingly fast for a fat man, grabbed his hand and reached into the pocket. He pulled out a passport and handed it to Cano.

Cano opened it, compared the photo to Stratton in the flesh, then flicked through the pages. 'You don't travel too much.'

'That's a new passport,' Stratton told him. He'd been through more than a dozen since working for the intelligence services.

Cano kept hold of the passport and stared intently at Stratton once more. 'What do you do for work?'

'I'm a diver.'

'See, Klodi?' Cano sneered, looking at his thug. 'Aren't divers all gay?'

Klodi, who looked as if he had the IQ of a fish, nodded in solemn agreement.

'A deep-sea diver,' Stratton emphasised. 'Oil platforms.'

Cano was uninterested. 'What were you doing at the DA's office?'

'I was curious about maybe getting a job here and I wanted to see what I had to do to get a visa.'

'That's Immigration, not the DA's office.'

'That right? Maybe you could give me some advice.'

Cano did not appreciate Stratton's attitude: his dislike for the Englishman was increasing by the second. He took a puff of his cigarette, put it out in the ashtray on the drinks cabinet and removed a large, shiny bone-handled knife from a sheath inside his jacket.

Stratton's gaze flicked to the blade. He watched as Cano put the tip on the carpeted floor and, balancing the knife in the vertical, spun it while he thought.

Stratton could feel the seconds ticking closer to the moment when he would have to do something. His heart was starting to beat a little faster and his breathing grew shallower as his body began to pump adrenalin through him in preparation for something that he knew he had to do. Precisely what and how, though, he could not decide since the choices were so limited. It was his habit from years as an undercover operative, where overreaction was ill-advised, to wait for the enemy's move that signalled their intent and then initiate his own – but this was fast becoming a case for him to act first. His body tensed as his senses screamed a warning that the two villains were about to do something.

'You ever had a knife shoved up your ass?' Cano asked, his stare following the edge of the blade.

Stratton sprang forward, slamming Klodi in the throat with the side of his hand while at the same time kicking the knife out of Cano's grip. As Cano made a grab for him Stratton brought his elbow across, catching him in the side of the head. Klodi quickly recovered and rolled his weight forward to grab Stratton and take a swing at him. The heavy blow caught Stratton in the gut while Cano followed it with a punch to his face. As Klodi laid into Stratton Cano scrambled for the knife. Stratton twisted to avoid a savage haymaker and Klodi's powerful fist plunged into the drinks cabinet, shattering bottles and glasses.

The front passenger looked back to see the fracas as did the driver who received a warning slap from the passenger to keep his eyes on the road. The glass partition opened and the passenger got onto his knees and leaned in through the narrow opening in an attempt to get involved. But he was too big to squeeze in very far and Stratton stayed just out of his reach.

Stratton made a lunge for Cano who was reaching for the knife, the single most dangerous item in the fight. He put his weight onto the man's back while grabbing the door handle and pushing it open against the wind. The limousine was passing through Venice on the beach road, shops and buildings on either side, the sidewalks crowded with pedestrians.

Meanwhile, Klodi grabbed Stratton's hair from behind in an effort to yank him back as Stratton took hold of Cano's arm above the hand that now held the knife. Stratton jabbed his elbow back, catching Klodi in the jaw and almost breaking it. But this gave Cano the opportunity to take a firmer hold of the knife. As Stratton lunged forward once again and threw Cano back onto the seat the front passenger was able to land a blow on Stratton's head. Still unsatisfied with his contribution to the fight he reached into his jacket and pulled out his pistol.

The driver glanced back for a few seconds. When he looked forward again the vehicle in front had stopped at the end of a line of cars halted by a traffic light. He slammed on the brakes, sending the passenger backwards into the dash, winding him. At the same time his head thumped heavily against the windscreen, causing him to drop his pistol.

Blood trickled down Stratton's face into one of his eyes from a cut on his head. But things were far too serious now for him to care about it. As the limousine pulled away with the flow of traffic Klodi grabbed Stratton from behind and flung him to the floor against the open door. Cano stabbed down at him with the knife but Stratton managed to twist himself around and grab the hand that held it. Cano straightened his arms and pushed down in an effort to shove the tip of the blade into Stratton's chest as his head and shoulders were forced outside, the door pressing against him – if it hit anything he would be crushed.

The driver saw the open door in his wing mirror and, unable to tell who was actually hanging out of it, did his best to prevent it hitting anything, which meant moving into the centre of the road and forcing oncoming vehicles to swerve out of his way. The passenger had managed to get back onto his seat, his back aching and head thumping. He searched the floor for his gun.

Klodi leaned past his boss to punch Stratton as best he could in the crowded doorway while Cano pushed the knife closer to Stratton's chest. Stratton was in a precarious position and needed a dramatic change of tactic, otherwise he'd be lost. Instead of trying to force Cano back he suddenly pulled him down onto him while guiding the knife over and past himself. The action was successful to a degree, bringing Cano halfway out of the door. In a sudden panic-induced effort not to fall out Cano made a grab for the door frame, which resulted in the knife dropping from his hand and bouncing out of the vehicle to clatter along the street.

Stratton's major concern now was not to lose his head, literally, as it moved further out of the car door. But then it occurred to Stratton that it was the only direction to go and so he yanked even harder while twisting his body. Both men, now facing each other, hit the road with their shoulders. Klodi immediately grabbed his boss in an effort to stop him falling out and they drove on down the road through the crowded street, attracting the attention of everyone they passed.

The thugs in the trailing white sedan had seen the door open from the start but were unable to determine what – apart from an obvious struggle – was going on. When the limousine had paused because of the traffic lights one of them had started to climb out but had quickly jumped back in when the limo pulled away again. When they realised that it was the Englishman hanging out of the doorway they moved closer and directly behind, ready to run him over if he was ejected. But then Cano suddenly joined him.

Stratton's leather jacket was wearing out fast at the shoulder as he bounced along and kicked out violently to release his feet, one of which was trapped under Klodi's bulk. He placed his free foot against Klodi's face and, with a supreme effort, pushed back with all his strength. He flew out of the limousine and bounced and rolled to the kerb where the following sedan swerved in an effort to run him over, missing him by inches.

It was not yet over for Cano who was doing all he could to stop himself from following Stratton. Then Klodi recovered in time to plant a hand on the door frame and yank his boss inside, throwing him hard against the opposite door and almost knocking him senseless. It was at that moment that the limousine driver swerved to avoid an oncoming lorry and the open door hit the back of a parked car, slamming it shut with such force that it closed savagely on Klodi's fingers. Whereupon Klodi let out a howl that could be heard for a considerable distance despite being muffled inside the vehicle.

'Stop!' Cano yelled at the driver above the screaming.

The limousine braked instantly, swerving slightly as it screeched to a halt. Cano pushed on the door to try and open it, not to release his employee but in a manic effort to get outside and pursue Stratton. He quickly gave up, found the button for the sunroof and pushed on it violently as if the added force might speed up the electric motor.

The sedan came to a stop behind the limo and the men peeled from it as Cano clambered out onto the limo roof, dropped down onto the boot and ran up the street.

Cano, along with his men, reached the place where Stratton had ejected. They searched between the parked cars and inside shops all the way back to the corner of the intersection that they had driven through. The right turn entered a quiet residential area and the left was a broad, dead-end street leading to the beach with a bustling market at the end packed with small stalls and hundreds of shoppers.

'Shall we go look for him?' one of Cano's men asked.

Cano ignored him as he walked out into the street to get a better look. Beyond the market was a line of tall palm trees marking the start of the beach. But there was no sign of the Englishman. Cano then looked down at his feet to see his knife. He picked it up, inspected the blade and then noticed the blood trickling from a large graze on his hand. It began to sting as if seeing it had activated the pain. But Cano ignored it as he slid the knife back into its sheath under his jacket and inspected his shoulder where the jacket was ripped away to expose more bleeding flesh. Anger flashed through his heart at the thought of the man escaping him and he vowed to kill him if he ever saw him again. Only twice in his adult life had he received any kind of a beating that he had not avenged and both had been from an Englishman.

Cano walked back to the limousine, followed by his men, to find the driver and passenger struggling to pull open the door. Klodi was in tears on the other side of it.

'It won't budge,' the passenger said, giving up. 'It's stuck real good.'

They all looked to see four swollen fingers sticking out from the door seam.

'That's gotta hurt,' one of the thugs said with under-stated sincerity.

'Tell him to shut up,' Cano said coldly as he walked to the white sedan, leaving the others to figure out how to free their colleague.

Chapter 13

Stratton stood in the bath under the gushing shower rose, hands planted in front of him against the white-tiled wall. The warm water running down his body turned red as it streamed from his feet and down the plughole.

He had been lucky. His body was badly grazed from the fall, and he had a cut on his head. His jacket was shredded in places where it had saved him from more severe injury, especially to his shoulder where the leather had given way to his shirt and then to skin at the last moment before he'd ejected from the car. His head throbbed from the pounding he had received. His cheeks were bruised, his lips cut, his nose cracked, and the skin was gone from his knuckles where he had punched out wildly. His elbows and knees were swollen but miraculously no bones appeared to have been broken, though he suspected he'd sustained a couple of cracked ribs. They sent out sharp pains if he took a deep breath or coughed to clear the blood that had trickled down his throat from a wound in his mouth.

Stratton needed a chemist or a drugstore. But, like a wounded animal, all he could think about was finding somewhere safe to crawl into and hide. He must have looked pretty horrific as he staggered along the board-walk judging by the way that people, wearing looks of disgust, moved aside to let him pass.

Stratton had managed to get to his feet almost as soon as he had rolled to a stop against the kerb and had run into the busy market by the beach. But after several hundred yards, checking back to see that he was not being pursued, he had slowed to a painful walk. It took half an hour to reach the Santa Monica Pier where he crossed the Pacific Coast Highway, using a footbridge. Then he climbed a steep flight of zigzag-ging steps cut into the cliff to reach the park on top. His apartment building was opposite.

He crossed Ocean Avenue, dodging between the slow-moving cars, and walked into the courtyard. His keys were still in his tattered pocket. The sole person he met was an old lady who waited for the elevator beside him. She only glanced at him and acted quite naturally as they entered the elevator together, as if the sight of a badly beaten man was not an unusual one in this city.

Stratton had left his tattered clothes on the floor of the living room before he underwent the painful but necessary process of washing the dirt and grit from his wounds. The stinging caused by the soap and water gradually subsided as he got used to it. He turned off the taps, stepped out of the shower and gently patted his body with a towel, which was soon stained in blood. A coating of antibacterial cream would have been ideal but for now all he wanted to do was lie down and rest.

Stratton eased into an armchair and tried to relax. But he could not set aside the day's events. On the contrary, now that he had time to collect his thoughts the true horror of the situation came into focus. That Albanian bastard had tried to kill him, but for what? Felling one of his overzealous thugs at the DA's office? Stratton considered the possibility it was he who had overreacted by attacking Cano. The man might only have intended to threaten him, not actually harm him. Whatever the truth, all he could think of at that moment was revenge. He wanted to kill Cano so badly that he could see himself doing it. Something intrinsic in the man, not just his murderous history, projected an image of pure evil.

Stratton's gaze fell on the file on the table a few feet away. He sat forward slowly, dealing with the pain, picked up the papers and sat back again. He flicked through the pages to a section containing names, addresses and contact numbers, reached for his mobile phone, dialled a number and put the phone to his bruised ear. He had one more thing to do before he took a long, hard look at the situation and came to a final decision.

Someone picked up the phone at the other end. 'Hello,' a gravelly voice said.

'Skender?' Stratton asked.

Skender was in the palatial living room of an enormous modern luxurious house. A huge plate-glass window took up an entire wall and revealed a view of an opulent marble swimming pool with a tennis court and gardens beyond, all set against a backdrop of the city of Los Angeles sprawling away into the distance far below. The décor and every piece of furniture cried grandeur. The centre of the room was a sunken square lined by broad, comfortable couches, one of them occupied by a beautiful girl no more than twenty years old. She wore a virtually transparent gold-lace dress that could be described as modest only in the amount of material that had been needed to make it. Another girl of similar age was standing by the pool, drying her slender, tanned and naked body – she'd just climbed out of the water.

Skender was wearing an unbuttoned shirt that revealed a strong grey-haired chest. Despite his age, he looked as if he could still bench-press his own weight. A wide, strong neck had a vivid scar across its front where his throat had once been slit. The wound, which was the cause of his deep gravelly voice, looked old.

'Who is this?' Skender asked, as he eyed the girl standing outside. She turned her back on him to raise a foot onto a sunlounger before bending over to dry her leg.

'A life for a life,' Stratton said.

Skender suddenly forgot about what he was planning to do to the Russian girl who had arrived with her friend a short while ago. He gave the caller his full attention. He could hear the serious intent in the voice clearly enough and although he had no clue about the caller's identity nor about what lay behind the cryptic comment, the subject was death. This was a commodity that Skender had dealt in all his life and which he took seriously.

'Some lives are worth more than others,' Skender

212

said calmly, taking a cigarette from a silver box on a polished olive-wood side table. The girl on the couch immediately got to her feet, glided over to him and picked up a heavy gold oyster lighter from the table. She lit it and held the flame to the cigarette's tip.

'Ardian Cano and Leka Bufi killed an innocent woman. Turn them over to the police or I'll make them pay,' Stratton said softly.

Skender drew deeply on the cigarette and blew out smoke as the girl walked around him. She dragged her hand across his chest and around his back before returning to her post on the couch.

'This woman. Was she blood or love?' Skender asked coolly. His gaze moved to the patio door as it opened and the naked beauty walked in, the towel draped around her neck falling either side of her breasts.

Stratton didn't answer.

'I know how you feel,' Skender said as he watched the nude girl brush past him and sit beside the one in the gold-lace dress. 'Seven years ago my wife and son were shot dead in my own house. To this day I do not know who did it.'

'What would you do if you found out?' Stratton asked.

'I would take them apart – slowly, piece by piece, with a pair of pliers or some tool like that,' Skender replied as he watched the naked girl wrap her arms around her friend's neck and put her tongue inside her mouth. Her friend responded by running her hand down the naked girl's body from her breasts to her buttocks. Then, as her friend's slender fingers slid between her parted thighs, the nude young woman glanced at Skender and smiled provocatively. Skender watched impassively, his thoughts focused entirely on how the caller had got hold of a number that was known by only a handful of people in the whole world. 'But that is my problem and your problem is your own,' he added.

'That's not enough,' Stratton said. 'What's your answer?' He felt as though he'd been given it. But because of the serious nature of his likely response he needed it made clearer.

'You just had it.'

'I won't ask again.'

'I'm pleased to hear that,' Skender said and replaced the phone in its cradle. He stared ahead as he considered the call. The threat might require his attention if it was genuine. But since he planned to do nothing it was now the caller's move, so he would forget about it until that move was made. As he dismissed the conversation from his thoughts his eyes refocused on the naked girl who was lying back on the couch now while the other girl pleasured her with her tongue.

Skender walked over and sat beside them to get a closer look. The naked girl reached out to caress Skender's leg but he took hold of her hand in mid-air and pushed it away. 'No – if there's one thing I cannot tolerate it's affection.'

Stratton lowered his mobile phone and contemplated the brief conversation. What stuck in his mind most about it was not so much what Skender had said but what he, Stratton, had. He'd threatened to retaliate if Skender refused to comply with his wishes, and

Skender had indeed refused. The gauntlet had gone down and so the question was, did Stratton really mean to revenge Sally? Was that what he had wanted to do all along but had refused to acknowledge? The whole thing was absurd in so many ways: he had made a threat without a plan to back it up and the rule was, if a plan didn't look like it could work perfectly, abandon it. Problem was, Stratton hadn't even made one. He realised that he really had only one way to go: he had to devise a plan and decide on its feasibility. Basically, if it looked like he could get away with it completely he would go ahead.

Stratton flicked through the file and stopped at the report on Leka where it indicated that the Albanian was incarcerated at the Santa Monica court awaiting arraignment on the twenty-first. Stratton checked the date on his watch to confirm that it was now the eighteenth, which did not give his battered body very long to heal. The report also indicated the law firm representing Leka and detailed their scheduled meetings. A feasible way of gaining entry to the lock-up facility came to Stratton almost immediately. The main problem was how to deal with a target who was inside a jail and probably the other side of bars when there was no way of getting weapons into the building.

As Stratton stared at several coins on the table an idea began to germinate. He reached for the largest coin, a quarter, put down the file, got stiffly to his feet, and went to the table where he sat down carefully in front of the explosives box, all the while gingerly nursing his aching ribcage.

He opened the container, removed the pack of SX

– a concentrated RDX compound with almost twice the explosive power of PE4 or C4 – and peeled away a portion that resembled a slice of processed cheese. He removed the plastic wrapping, laid it flat on the table and, using the small graphic knife from the kit, sliced off a length and began to roll it into a ball. It was similar to plasticine: the more he manipulated it in his hands the warmer it got and the easier it was to mould. When it was soft Stratton pressed it against one side of the quarter and shaped it into a small conical pyramid in the centre of the coin. Then he laid it on the table to evaluate it.

The packet of chewing gum that he'd bought from the Korean shop was on the table. He removed one of the strips, slid off the paper and unwrapped the silver foil. He placed the stick of gum on the sheet of remaining SX, traced around the edge with the knife, cut away a strip the exact size of the gum and wrapped it carefully in the silver foil. Then he slid it into the paper sheath and placed it back in the packet.

The plan was workable, Stratton decided, but it needed a test run. The key elements were that he should not be seen or, more importantly, recognised and should leave nothing like fingerprints or DNA behind.

Stratton remembered seeing a *Yellow Pages* in the entrance cupboard. He got up, found the directory and took it to the couch where he sat back and thumbed through it. Just as he found a shop in Santa Monica that claimed to have the widest range of Hallowe'en and other costumes on the West Side he was suddenly overcome by a need to sleep. The day had caught up with him and he decided to work on the rest of the plan later. The urge to remain on the couch was strong but he wanted to lie flat. He put down the directory, pushed himself up, moved into the bedroom and lowered himself slowly onto the bed, his grazes stinging where the scabs that had already formed cracked with every move. He rested his head on the pillow, pulled the bloodstained towel over him and closed his eyes. Ideally he would have liked to rest for a week and recover fully but he did not have the time. There was a lot to do, most of all where Josh was concerned.

As Stratton closed his eyes the plan took shape in his mind. He realised that he was enjoying this part of the process. Preparing an operation, especially one that he was going to carry out alone, was satisfying. But before he could get properly into it Cano's face appeared in front of him and Stratton's eyes jerked open. Realising that the image was not real, he closed his eyes once more, forcing himself to relax so that he could fall asleep.

At that moment Stratton wanted Cano at his mercy more than anything else. He was certain, should his wish be granted, that mercy would be the last thing he'd show the bastard.

Chapter 14

Stratton stood in front of the court buildings. He was wearing a tan jacket, ironed trousers and polished brown shoes. His hair was dyed blond and had a parting for the first time in probably more than a decade. Heavy spectacles partly covered his bruised eyes, a false *hombre* moustache more or less concealed the wounds on his lips and a goatee – or as much of one as he had been able to grow in the three days since his beating – completed the disguise. He carried a small laptop case. As he adjusted his colourful tie he headed for the entrance of the Santa Monica District courthouse and the security checkpoint where half a dozen people were waiting to be processed.

Stratton joined the queue and watched as two security guards took their time checking each person thoroughly. After passing through a standard frame detector the contents of each person's baggage were checked and before entering the building another electronic sensor was run up and down the lengths of their bodies. Stratton passed through the frame without triggering an alarm and his laptop case was opened to reveal some pens and paperwork. He raised his hands, wincing as his cracked ribs complained. The hand-held sensor swept over his body, beeping at his trouser-belt buckle – the noise was ignored – and again alongside his jacket pocket. He produced some small change which satisfied the security guard who allowed him through.

Stratton stepped into the cavernous crowded hall and paused to look around. The courthouse interior was an L-shaped configuration with half a dozen doors staggered either side of the longer wing. The broader, shorter wing housed the entrances to three court-rooms that appeared to be in full swing with spec-tators and legal representatives milling in and out through the large double doors.

A police officer was crossing the lobby and Stratton moved to intercept him. 'Excuse me, officer,' he said in a southern accent. He wore a broad, innocent smile.

The officer glanced at him without slowing.

'Where are the detainees awaiting arraignment kept?' Stratton asked, moving to keep pace with him.

'That door at the end,' the officer said, pointing as he headed down the longer wing.

'Thank you,' Stratton said, stopping as the officer disappeared into the crowd. Stratton had rehearsed his American accents all morning while getting ready in his apartment and more loudly as he'd walked to the courthouse, trying to select one that was suitable. He eventually went for the Southern accent simply because, although it sounded almost ridiculous to him and far too exaggereated, he could hang on to it better than any of the others.

Stratton looked towards the door indicated by the cop. It was at the far end of the lobby, past the courtroom entrances. A guard was standing in front of it – obstacle number two.

Stratton was happy with the plan so far and decided to take it to the next stage, once he'd had a moment to compose himself and rethink his dialogue. As he moved through the crowd and approached the guard he put his broad smile back on. 'Hi,' he said. 'I'm here to see Leka Bufi – he's a prisoner awaiting arraignment.'

'You his attorney?'

'One of them. I'm from Myers and Carrington,' Stratton said, quoting the company's name from the file. But the officer didn't seem interested in the information.

'Raise your hands, please, sir,' the officer asked.

'Oh,' Stratton said, acting surprised and maintaining his nerdy act. He held out his arms as if he was being crucified and a pain shot across his chest. He tried to disguise his wincing.

The guard noticed it and was also curious about Stratton's bruises.

Stratton widened his grin. 'I was having a fight and a game of hockey broke out,' he said.

The officer ignored the weak attempt at humour as he ran a metal detector over Stratton's body. It beeped at his buckle which was, as before, ignored and again when it detected the change in his pocket.

Stratton hurriedly took the money out to show the officer who checked the pocket again before running the detector over his case. Satisfied, he pushed a button and the door buzzed.

'You can go through, sir,' the officer said.

Stratton nodded his thanks and as he reached for

the handle the door opened. A man in a suit and carrying an expensive leather briefcase pushed through.

'Excuse me,' the man said, almost bumping into Stratton as he hurried across the hall and into one of the courtrooms.

Stratton walked through the door and as it closed behind him he paused to look at the only way ahead: a flight of stairs going down. He followed them to the first landing where a woman with an armful of files and a pen gripped in her teeth made her way up past him. Then he carried on to the bottom and found himself facing a door with a small security window set in it.

He peered through the little window to see a long, clinical-looking hallway with four or five cubicles to a side. There was no sign of life. He turned the handle to find the door locked. On the wall was a button beneath a rectangular patch, evidence that a sign had once existed there. He pushed the button. A buzzer sounded inside and he waited a moment before hitting it again. He watched patiently through the glass but there was no movement and the only sound was the muffled tread of foot traffic in the court-house above. His finger was hovering over the button once again when a door opened at the far end of the hallway and a hatless police officer walked along it towards him.

Stratton stepped away from the window. A key turned in the lock and a second later the door opened. He faced the officer who looked at him dryly, a clip-board in his hand.

Stratton beamed his nerdy smile once again. 'Hi,' he said.

The officer just looked at him.

'I'm Jud Bailey, assistant to Aaron Myers,' he continued in his Southern accent, which all of a sudden sounded to him like a Scouser's. The officer did not appear to notice.

'Who do you represent, sir?' the officer asked as he checked his clipboard.

'Leka Bufi.'

'What was your name again?'

'Jud Bailey.'

'You're half an hour early,' the officer said.

'I must be eager, I guess. Okay if I wait?'

'I can't let you see your client without your attorney.'

'That's okay,' Stratton said. 'I gotta buncha paperwork to do anyhows.'

'You can wait over there,' the officer said, indicating a couple of lightweight plastic chairs against a wall in a small alcove. A water dispenser was the only other furnishing.

'Thanks,' Stratton said, stepping into the alcove as the officer locked the door behind him and placed the key, which was on a chain, in his pocket. 'Where is he?' Stratton asked.

'Who, sir?'

'Mister Bufi?'

'I'm not sure if he's come up yet, sir. They'll put him in one of the booths when one's free.'

'Thanks again,' Stratton said, beaming as he headed for one of the plastic chairs and sat on it. 'You have yourself a good day.'

The officer walked away without replying and Stratton wondered if he'd been a little over the top with the accent. He heard the officer walk down the corridor and pass through the door at the end. A muffled sound seemed to rise gradually from the floor: he realised it was the noise of voices from some of the cubicles.

Stratton got up and leaned around the corner. The corridor was empty.

He sat back down, put his case on the seat beside him, took his packet of chewing gum from a pocket, removed a stick, unwrapped it, put it in his mouth and started to chew it. A door opened and closed somewhere and then it went quiet again but for the muffled conversations.

Obstacle three dealt with, Stratton thought to himself. All he needed to do now was locate Leka. But this was supposed to be only a test run: there was no point in attempting the next phase now unless he was going to go through with it. He'd gone far enough for the day and it was time to call the guard. But there was one slight snag. If he did decide to return the following day – the last opportunity he'd have, in fact – there might be a problem since he had given the legal assistant's name to the officer. If the real guy turned up after Stratton left, Stratton might not be able to return.

That was no small problem, Stratton decided, and one that he should have anticipated. But he'd been too keen to test his plan. The truth was that few plans got to be tested in this way and deep down Stratton was still struggling against the notion of carrying it out for real. He was torn between thinking it was the right thing to do and the cautious inclination not to take pointless risks just to satisfy a need for revenge.

Stratton decided to carry on with the test and see where it led. The chances were that it would prove to be impossible anyway. He shut off the disputing voices in his head, opened his briefcase, removed a file, stepped into the corridor dividing the cubicles and walked slowly along it.

As he drew level with the first two cubicles he paused to look inside through their security-glass windows set in the walls. All the cubicles were the same design: there were two heavy metal doors, one to the corridor, the other no doubt leading to the cells, a small table and two lightweight plastic chairs either side of it. These first cubicles were empty. Stratton tapped the window which was, he reckoned, some thirty millimetres thick and doubtless bullet-proof.

He carried on walking, pretending to read the file, and glanced into the next cubicle where two men were seated at the table opposite each other. The one facing him was dressed in a business suit, the other, small and red-haired, was wearing an orange one-piece prisoner overall. The guy in the suit glanced up at Stratton who moved on.

The opposite cubicle was also occupied by a lawyer and a prisoner who did not resemble Bufi either.

The next cubicle was empty. The one opposite contained a female prisoner and a lawyer.

The second-to-last cubicle was also empty but as Stratton was about to pass it the inside door opened and a prisoner was led in. Stratton saw that it was

Bufi. An officer stood in the doorway, indicating for him to sit in the far chair. The officer glanced up at Stratton who went back to pretending to read his file and carried on out of view.

A moment later Stratton heard the cubicle door close and he turned around, walked back and stopped outside the window to look into the room again. Bufi was seated with his back to the glass.

Stratton studied the man who was large and ape-like. In that moment all he could see was him beating Sally with his powerful hands. It was obvious there would never be a time better than this to kill the man – Stratton had seconds to make a decision. He decided that fate had put him in this position and that he could not pass the chance by.

He checked quickly to see that no one was looking from any of the other cubicles, stepped away from the glass and put the file on the floor. Then he removed the pack of gum from his pocket, shook out the remaining stick and unwrapped it. He rolled it around quickly in his hands until it was soft and then fashioned it into a small conical pyramid. He selected a quarter from his change, pushed the SX carefully onto one of its faces, took the chewing gum from his mouth, stuck it to the other side of the coin and pushed it against the glass directly behind Bufi's head which was only inches away.

Stratton quickly turned his belt buckle over to reveal a small length of metal, no bigger than half a matchstick and held in place by gum. As he removed it a tail of black string attached to one end uncoiled: he carefully pushed the end no more than a couple of millimetres into the top of the conical pyramid.

He made another quick sweep of the cubicles as he took out a folding packet of matches, tore one from the strip and checked Bufi – he had not moved. This was it, the moment of no return. The hell with it, Stratton decided and struck the match.

As it burst into flame a loud buzzer sounded. Stratton looked up to see a lawyer inside one of the cubicles standing at the door to the corridor. Stratton shook the match out and headed back down the corridor to the seating area as the officer entered from the door at the opposite end. Stratton barely made it around the corner as the officer headed for the cubicle. The sound of a key turning in a lock was followed by voices as the lawyer thanked the officer.

Stratton could only pray that neither man saw the quarter stuck to the glass. Then he remembered his file on the floor. A second later the officer and lawyer arrived at the main door, which the officer then unlocked. The lawyer passed through and as the officer closed the door and locked it again he glanced at Stratton who smiled pathetically.

The officer walked away and Stratton listened intently, waiting for his footsteps to pause. But they continued to the end of the corridor and passed through the door there which clanged as it shut. Then there was silence.

Stratton got to his feet and looked round the corner to see the quarter and file where he had left them. He prepared another match as he approached. Bufi had not moved but as Stratton was about to strike the match the Albanian turned to look at him. He could not see the matches in Stratton's hand below the level of the window and if he noticed the quarter stuck to the glass he did not react to it, more interested in Stratton who was staring at him.

Stratton smiled. Bufi gave him a chilling look before turning his back on him again.

Stratton lost his smile and struck the match. Back at the point of no return, he mused. From here on the plan was in its weakest phase: it relied on several factors that were hopeful rather than probable. The choice was a simple enough one: quit now or get the hell on with it. He chose to follow his heart and get on with it but felt suddenly and uncharacteristically nervous. His stomach began to churn. It was strange but he reckoned he knew why. Working against an enemy of his country was, after all, his job and the support he had from his government under such circumstances gave him the confidence he needed. But on this mission he was truly on his own − especially if he was caught.

Then Stratton looked at the man who had slaughtered Sally. He remembered her voice on the phone followed by her screams and then the sound of Josh crying. He touched the match's flame to the bottom of the length of black string, which immediately ignited. He extinguished the match, picked the file off the floor and hurried back to the seating area.

The explosion was surprisingly loud for such a small piece of plastic, accentuated by the flat surfaces and confined space. Seconds later an alarm bell sounded as smoke began to drift along the corridor.

Stratton dropped to the floor as the sound of buzzers joined the alarm bell. The lawyers and defendants in the cubicles wanted out. The door beside Stratton opened and an officer stepped in, holding his gun.

'What the fuck,' he exclaimed as he looked around.

Stratton sat up, feigning shock and fear as another officer ran up to him.

'What happened, Joe?' one of the lawyers shouted above the noise of the alarms.

'Don't know,' came the reply.

'I heard a gun,' Stratton called out. 'In one of the cubicles.'

'You hurt?' the first officer asked him.

'No.'

The buzzers continued to sound and were joined by the noise of banging on the cubicle doors, adding to the confusion.

'Stay there. Don't move,' one of the officers said to Stratton as they made their way along the corridor and into the smoke.

Stratton didn't waste a second. He got to his feet and slipped through the door, closing it behind him. The guard's key was still in the lock so he turned it and left it in place. One of the officers saw the door close and called out as he hurried to it, yanking hard on the doorknob as he looked through the small window in time to see Stratton race up the stairs. He grabbed his radio.

Stratton made it to the top of the stairs at full speed. As he reached the door he slowed down and pushed calmly through it.

Most of the people in the crowded hall were listening to the alarm bells and asking those close by what was going on. The entire courthouse appeared to have come to a standstill after the explosion except for those officers who were running about listening to radios and trying to ascertain what was happening.

Stratton pushed through the crowd towards the front door where he saw several officers gathering. He paused to consider an alternative escape plan but could not think of one other than the obvious. 'Fire!' he called out. 'There's a fire below!'

It had the immediate desired effect. The crowd made a general move that soon became a panicky surge towards the entrance. Officers, as confused as everyone else, were pushed aside by those wanting to flee until one of them picked up a radio message. He called for his partners to close the doors and not let anyone out.

The officers' concerted effort to push the large double doors shut only served to fuel the panic among those trying to get out. They shoved against the officers even harder.

Stratton got to the doors and added his weight to the would-be escapers. Along with a handful of others, he managed to squeeze outside just before the officers succeeded in closing the doors. He kept on going and crossed the parking lot briskly while removing his false moustache and glasses. A moment later he was heading down the street towards a large mall two blocks from the beach between the courthouse and his apartment building, leaving the pandemonium behind him.

Inside the mall entrance all was calm with no one remotely aware of what had happened a block away. Stratton dumped the removable parts of his disguise in a trash bin before casually making his way to another entrance and across the street to his apartment building.

It was a bright sunny day and Stratton's heart rate was almost back to normal by the time he rounded the corner onto Santa Monica Boulevard where the blue-grey sea glistened beyond the palm trees that ran along the top of the cliff. He was confident that he had made a clean escape. Next would come the wait to determine the success or otherwise of his mission. With a regular mission it was not unusual to have to wait hours and sometimes days to learn the outcome of an attack: quite often it required satellite surveillance or other forms of high-tech intelligence to ascertain damage. In this case Stratton would use the best intelligence source of any criminal or terrorist organisation and that was the media. In his experience the media was generally a very poor source of accurate information since they were more concerned with drama. But in this case he felt that he could rely on them.

All in all, Stratton felt good about the little operation and could not help thinking now about finishing the job and going after Ardian. It seemed that now he had started he should finish. The internal voices of caution returned but he was tiring of them. They were right, of course, but so were the others. Besides, what was particularly sweet about killing Ardian was that he was the brother of the prick who had tried to kill Stratton in the limousine.

It was well worth carrying out a feasibility study, Stratton reckoned. If it looked good, there'd be another test run.

Chapter 15

Hobart arrived at the main entrance of the Santa Monica District courthouse as the sun was setting behind him. He walked towards the door at the far end of the courtroom lobby where a couple of police officers stood guard. He knew his way around, having made several recent visits to the building. As he approached the door he flipped open his FBI badge and clipped it to the breast pocket of his jacket. The officers were already inspecting the badge as he walked towards them and stood aside to let him through.

He walked down the steps and paused in the doorway of the interview room to observe the activity. A camera flashed inside a cubicle somewhere towards the end while several officers in plain clothes were inspecting the area and taking samples.

'Is it okay to walk through here yet?' Hobart asked no one in particular.

One of the officers looked up, saw the badge, and waved him in. 'Walk down the centre and keep clear of that area,' the man said, indicating the seating alcove.

Hobart obeyed the instructions and stopped outside a cubicle inside which were two more officers. One was examining the far wall, which was spattered with dark bloodstains, while the other stood still, looking at the floor while holding his chin and apparently contemplating something. Hobart had been an FBI agent for nearly twenty years and had long since learned that time spent patiently studying people and crime scenes before talking to anyone or touching anything was often productive.

Hobart's early working years had primarily been devoted to the eastern seaboard of the USA, mostly New York and Washington DC, followed by nine years in Eastern Europe, specifically the Balkans. He'd spent the last eighteen months in Los Angeles, the FBI's single most heavily populated territory. He had worked so long for the massive bureaucratic machine that his youthful eagerness, zeal and keen response to the dramatic had become dulled. He had hoped, too, by this stage in his career to be further up the promotional ladder. Too many disappointments, more than anything else with the organisation's unhealthy indulgence in politics, had dampened much of the fervour which had originally inspired him in his chosen vocation. But he was not a burn-out and had lost none of his enthusiasm for the purity of the job. A fire of some kind still smouldered somewhere deep inside him, fuelled by hostility towards the enemies of his country. He often suspected that much of what he had left was a kind of patriotic mania or anger. Not the best reason to get up each morning and go to work.

Hobart was something of a dormant volcano and it was that aspect of his character that made him memorable to others, the impression he gave that he was about to erupt at any moment. What kept him on an even keel was the belief against all the odds that there was someone somewhere on top of this wasteful, misguided heap of bureaucracy who actually knew what they were doing and had a plan for a saner and more logical solution to the madness of the world.

Hobart's wife, a former journalist for the *Washington Post*, always accused him of naivety when it came to his work, usually when she was drunk – which, fortunately, was not often. Her most damaging rhetoric, however, came when she was sober. She had written several accusatory articles about the FBI, exposing incompetence, misinterpretation of intelligence and inappropriate use of funds. Although her exposés were, in the great scheme of things, a small cry in the dark, she was as irritating as a paper cut to Hobart's superiors, sufficiently so for them to include an unwritten condition to his offer of promotion to the LA office: she would have to quit her job on the *Post* and accompany him to the West Coast. To Hobart's surprise, she agreed without much of a fight. It seemed that he wasn't the only one in the family who had grown cynical about their contribution to world enlightenment.

Hobart was robust, though. He applied this quality to his own shortcomings when he recognised them, or when they were pointed out to him by his wife. But it was things over which he had no control that frustrated him most and contributed more than anything else to his private cynicism. Most of these things were politicians.

It was during Hobart's tour of duty in the Balkans that the greatest blow to his confidence regarding US foreign policy, specifically on Kosovo, had been dealt.

But even though he felt isolated in his views – enough not to air them with fellow agents, at least – he still wanted to believe there was an intelligent game plan in place. When the Los Angeles posting came along he was content to put aside his private concerns, expecting to be preoccupied with more routine FBI work – until he arrived in his new office and was briefed on his chief assignment and told why, in fact, he had been on the shortlist for the job.

All Hobart's troubling thoughts returned with a vengeance when he realised that, despite being on the other side of the world now, he was going to be drawn even deeper into the gut of his old East European problem. But had he been told that he would soon find himself in such a dark place that he would tear down the pillar principles on which his entire professional life had been built and light a fuse that would start a war against one of the most powerful crime lords in America, he would not have believed it.

'What happened?' Hobart asked.

Both scene-of-crime officers looked up at the three white letters of his badge boldly emblazoned on a black background and then at Hobart himself. He was used to every kind of response from fellow law-enforcers who were not directly connected with the Bureau. The expressions on the faces of the two cops in front of him conveyed the most common reaction: 'What's the goddamned FBI doing here?'

'A detainee got whacked,' the officer who had been contemplating the universe offered while the other went back to picking at the brick wall with a small tool.

'I know that much,' Hobart said. 'Leka Bufi. What happened?'

'Not exactly sure yet. Bufi was sitting in the chair here, his back to the window, and he got it through the head. One hell of a gun, if that's what it was. This bullet-proof glass is good against any pistol and most assault rifles.'

'It'll stop high-velocity up to 7.62 long,' the forensics officer said to the wall.

'You saying someone got a gun in here?' Hobart asked, inspecting the glass. The hole was large, the size of a tennis ball, and surrounded by a thick black scorch mark.

'We're considering everything at the moment,' the first officer said. 'Mind if I ask what the FBI is doing here?'

'Bufi was a name on my case file.'

'Albanian Mafia?'

Hobart ignored him as he looked at the body outline draped over the table and the dried blood on the floor and wall.

'Took most of his head clean off,' the officer added.

'Got it,' the forensics officer said with satisfaction as he yanked something small out of the wall and inspected it. 'If that was a gun it sure fired a strange kind of bullet.'

He carried the object in a pair of tweezers and placed it on a plastic evidence bag on the table. They all took a close look at the small, twisted, charred piece of metal the size of a fingernail.

'Looks like there's a pattern along one of the edges,' the forensics officer said, holding a magnifying glass over it. 'A coin, maybe,' he added, glancing at his buddy who gave him a surprised look.

Hobart straightened to study the walls and windows of the corridor once again. He was interested in the bit of metal but would wait until the lab report to find out precisely what it was. There was a concentration of pockmarks in the wall and door directly opposite the cubicle, suggesting some kind of back-blast effect from whatever had gone through the window. Hobart had had a lot of experience with explosives, particularly in Kosovo, and had seen many bodies shredded by bits of flying metal from mortars, grenades, artillery shells, mines and booby-traps and such like. He had never seen anything quite like this before, though. If he had to choose a word to describe how it stood out from other examples he had seen, that word would have to be 'precision'. This had been an IED of some kind, he was sure of that, and it had been small, clean and exact.

Hobart looked back at the two officers who were still examining the piece of metal. 'Sergeant – or is it Lieutenant?'

'Sergeant Doves,' the first officer said.

'I want every piece of debris collected up – every bit of cloth, metal, glass, everything – and placed inside its own evidence bag and sent to the FBI office on Wilshire.'

Doves looked around at the countless bits covering the floor, some of it stuck to the soles of his own shoes. 'You gonna be sending down one of your teams?' he asked hopefully but not expecting much. Resentment was his underlying response to the request since it meant that he was effectively working for the Feds.

'Not if you do a good enough job, sergeant,' Hobart said, looking directly at both men, making his point clear, before walking away.

Chapter 16

Stratton leaned against the concrete barrier that skirted the top of Santa Monica's cliffs a hundred feet above the Pacific Coast Highway, a road that stretched, with some interruptions, from Panama to Alaska. He was pretending to read a newspaper while at the same time keeping an eye on all movement into I Cugini, an Italian restaurant on a corner just south of his apartment building. It had a broad, exposed entrance with quiet sidewalks and most of the clientele arrived by car. After drivers and passengers had alighted the vehicles were whisked away by red-waistcoated valets to an underground parking lot beneath the large, modern shopping complex of which the restaurant was a small part.

This was the fourth day in a row that Stratton had occupied the same spot in the busy park during the lunchtime hour to observe everyone who went into the place. Seaton's file had listed two of Ardian Cano's favourite daytime food stops, the other being a Japanese restaurant in Beverly Hills. I Cugini was certainly the most convenient for Stratton, being literally a stone's throw from his apartment building. Had it not been for a hotel next door he would have been able to watch the restaurant entrance from the comfort of his living room.

It was nearing the end of the lunch period and still there had been no sight of the Albanian. Stratton was beginning to have doubts about this method of finding him. The file described Ardian as passionate about his food and a creature of habit and listed several of his night-time hangouts where he was often joined by colleagues as well as by his brother Ivor – or Dren. Stratton preferred not to run into that crowd again unless it was on his own terms and placed his hopes on the Italian restaurant.

The newspapers had revealed sufficient detail to confirm that Bufi was dead. The police were not prepared to discuss the cause other than saying that a projectile had entered his head. The media turned this into a grenade attack, based on advice from their so-called experts. The papers went on to describe Bufi's crime-syndicate dealings and the beating-up of his girlfriend, stating how he was a generally unsympathetic character that the world was better off without. Typically, the media dramatised it further by speculating that it had been a contract killing commissioned by rival mobsters.

Stratton had considered tracking Ardian from outside one of his nightspots to one of the three places where he was thought to be living: with a girlfriend, with a colleague, and – the third and most likely location – his brother's house in the plush residential area immediately north of Sunset Plaza. Stratton decided to give the Italian restaurant another couple of days before reviewing the matter since it was too convenient for his apartment – and also for visiting Josh who was little more than a mile away. The boy continued to weigh heavily on Stratton's mind since the child's immediate future remained unclear. Still, according to Vicky there were signs of stirrings from the UK side.

Vicky and Josh had been visibly shocked by Stratton's bruised face, which looked even worse two days later. But he managed to satisfy their curiosity with a tall story of a bar brawl between him and two short but stocky Irishmen who had taken a dislike to him for being English, though it had to be said that they'd been a little drunk at the time and Stratton had not been very polite on first meeting them, distracted by all that had happened.

Vicky was sceptical at first. But by the time Stratton had added the finishing touches to his elaborate tale, colouring it with historical 'facts' to help explain the Irishmen's ill feeling, she was so absorbed in the stories that went back as far as the Roman Conquest that she couldn't begin to imagine what else could have happened to him. He created a happy ending by explaining how, being typical, big-hearted Irishmen, after the fight was over with no clear winner they'd returned to the bar and bought each other a couple of rounds. All Josh wanted was to be reassured that the other guys had come off worse than Stratton. He was not disappointed with the descriptions of their injuries – out of earshot of Vicky, of course.

The one bit of bad news concerning Josh, which Vicky asked Stratton not to share with the boy, was that even though it looked as if he would be flown back to the UK sometime soon, possibly in the next two weeks, he might have to move to a temporary foster home until that day because of the child-protection centre being overcrowded. The trouble with that was that it would be more difficult for Stratton to see Josh since the visits were essentially a privilege bestowed upon him by Vicky and because he was not a relative that privilege would not transfer with Josh to the foster family. Stratton decided to deal with that when the time came but at least for the time being things seemed to be moving ahead.

Another problem was Sally's body. The FBI were dragging their feet – deliberately, it would appear – in processing the paperwork needed to release it to be shipped back to England. But still Stratton remained optimistic, hoping it could all be sorted out around the same time and sooner rather than later.

Then, as if the gods had heard Stratton's other plea, a sedan pulled up outside the restaurant and a man who matched the file's photograph and description of Ardian lifted his large frame out of the passenger seat and onto the sidewalk. He had a brief exchange with the Mexican valet as if they knew each other. Then he walked up the short flight of steps with the driver and in through the restaurant entrance.

Stratton was certain enough that it was Ardian to carry on until he could confirm it, leaving himself ample scope to abort if it was not. He folded the news-paper as he headed across the park to the intersection and then along the sidewalk to his apartment building.

As Stratton entered the elevator he checked his watch. Three minutes had passed since Ardian's arrival. He pushed all the what-if scenarios he had gone through out of his mind as he stepped inside his apartment, pulling off his sweatshirt and heading for the bathroom where his disguise was waiting. For this little operation he had selected a ginger goatee, dark glasses, and a colourful tie to go with his white business shirt. He opened a jar of hair gel, scooped out a liberal amount and rubbed it into his hair, pushing it back to give himself a slick look, washed his hands and tied his tie. A small amount of glue applied to the goatee stuck it neatly to his chin and after a quick check in the mirror he went to the living-room table to collect a small Gucci shopping bag that he had picked up in the mall.

A moment later Stratton opened his apartment door a crack to check that no one was about. Then he hurried along the corridor to the emergency exit, down the stairs and onto the street. It took less than a minute to reach the front of the restaurant and eleven minutes after leaving the park he stood in front of the little reception desk where a sign asked patrons to wait to be seated.

The restaurant was quite large and tastefully decorated in a classic Italian country style with a patio and seating for around sixty people. There was no sign of Ardian at the two occupied tables that Stratton could see from the entrance. He stepped further into the restaurant to look around a large pillar draped in an imitation grapevine. He saw the back of a man seated at the end of a table tucked into a corner. He took another step forward to see two other men, then stepped back as he sensed a figure walking towards him from the kitchens. It was a pretty young woman, colourfully dressed and wearing a broad smile which Stratton returned as she approached.

'Are you here for lunch, sir?' she asked sweetly.

'Are you still serving?' he asked in a Scottish accent. After the struggle he'd had trying to sound American he had decided to go for something more manageable. The city of Santa Monica had one of the largest single populations of expatriate Brits in the world: few Americans who lived and worked there were surprised to hear any of the multitude of UK accents.

'We serve all day,' she assured him. 'Is there just one?'

'I'm alone, yes,' he said.

'Inside or outside?' she asked.

'Outside would be nice.'

The girl picked up a menu. 'This way,' she said as she walked into the restaurant. Stratton followed, glancing at the table in the corner where four men were seated, all Slav-looking, the one at the end facing him being the one whom he thought was Ardian. Stratton stared at him and just as he moved out of sight the man looked up at him. All the file pictures of Ardian were full-face and they matched what Stratton now saw in the flesh. He even detected a resemblance to the Albanian's younger brother that was not so obvious in the photographs.

The hostess breezed onto the patio that was surrounded by several sizes of clay pot brimming with a variety of plants – a slice of Tuscany in California – and led Stratton to a table under a white sunshade at the back. He chose to sit with his back to the sea and from where he could see the edge of Ardian's table though none of the men at it.

'Can I get you anything to drink?' the hostess asked, her indelible smile sparkling even more brightly in the sunshine.

'A bottle of water would be nice,' Stratton replied.

'Still or sparkling?'

'Sparkling.'

'We have Pellegrino if that's okay?'

'Fine,' he said.

The young woman handed him the menu. 'Someone will be along in a moment to take your order,' she said as she turned and walked away back into the relative darkness of the restaurant. A minute later a Latino boy arrived with a small basket of fresh bread and breadsticks with a knob of butter and a spoonful of blended olives in two small porcelain jars. He laid them quietly on the table and walked back to his station in a corner where he continued to clean a large espresso machine.

There were only two other people sharing the patio with Stratton, a couple at a table on the far side who were deep in conversation. Stratton placed his Gucci carrier bag on the seat beside him and picked up the menu, glancing occasionally at the Albanian's table.

Stratton had checked the place over the evening before his first stake-out, taking a drink at the bar while watching people at the tables. He'd come up with a simple enough idea for killing Ardian – though it was perhaps a bit gruesome. It did, however, rely heavily on an unwitting character to play a major role, someone whom he had not yet met. But as the double doors from the restaurant opened he looked up to see that very person walking towards him. She was wearing a classic interpretation of the uniform of an Italian waiter: black trousers, a crisp, white shirt and colourful tie, and a white apron, tied at her waist, that reached almost to her shoes. She was short and ample in build with a busy head of dyed red hair and her practised smile appeared as she closed in, holding a small green bottle and a glass.

'Hi, there,' she exclaimed, her eyes wide as if he had just magically appeared. 'And how is your day going so far?'

'Fine,' Stratton replied with equal enthusiasm, as if they knew each other. 'How's yours been?'

'Great,' she said a pitch higher while displaying two perfect rows of large white teeth. 'Have you had a chance to look at the menu?' she asked as she unscrewed the bottle-top and half filled the glass that already had ice and a wedge of lime in it with the fizzy water.

'Yes. I'd like a bowl of spaghetti bolognese.'

'Sure,' she beamed. 'Not a problem. Anything else?'

'That'll be fine, thanks. Have you worked here long?' he asked.

'I've been here about a month. I'm from out of town – Oklahoma. I came here six weeks ago, got a great apartment only twenty blocks from the beach and this is the first place I applied for a job and they asked me to start the next day. I was so jazzed. It's so perfect here.'

'You're an actress, right?'

'Yes! How'd you guess?'

'You look like one,' Stratton said, radiating flattery. You could throw a stone anywhere in Los Angeles and hit a wannabe thespian. They arrived in Tinsel Town by the thousands every year from all over America and the world, looking for stardom, but only a handful ever succeeded in scraping even a meagre living from it.

'Thanks,' the waitress said, practically bursting with joy at having her talents recognised. 'Are you in the business?' she asked.

'No. Nothing as glamorous, I'm afraid. I'm an accountant – for the company that owns this restaurant, actually.' The night of his reconnaissance Stratton had read the blurb at the front door that described the chain of restaurants dotted around the city, all owned by one corporation. 'I'm quite new, too. I'm gradually doing the rounds of the restaurants, you know, getting to know them.'

'Oh. Shall I tell the manager you're here?'

'Do me a favour and keep it to yourself until I've finished my meal,' Stratton said, lowering his voice. 'I'll pop into the office once I'm done. I want a quiet lunch.'

'Gotcha,' she said, tapping the side of her nose and winking. 'I'll go put your order in.'

As the waitress walked away back into the restaurant she was beckoned by someone at Ardian's table. Stratton watched as she walked over to them, replying to whatever she'd been asked. A hand reached out to pat her bottom but she sidestepped to avoid it and from that point on appeared to have difficulty maintaining her smile. A moment later she nodded and, looking flushed, walked over to a computer console where she typed in her orders, pausing a moment to compose herself as if she had been through a small trauma.

Stratton snapped off a piece of breadstick, dipped it in the olive paste and ate it while a distant siren broke through the sound of the beach traffic. Seconds later a police car speeded down the boulevard and off into the distance.

Stratton picked up the Gucci carrier bag, placed it on his lap and opened it. Inside was a plastic resealable sandwich bag containing what looked like spaghetti soaked in a light transparent oil. Inside another clear wrapping was a tiny white plastic moulding the size and shape of a thimble. The waitress came back onto the patio, carrying a tray. He closed the top of the Gucci bag as she placed a bowl of spaghetti bolognese and a small dish of freshly grated parmesan cheese in front of him. Then she held out a large wooden pepper grinder.

'Black pepper?' she offered as she aimed it over his meal.

'No, that'll be fine, thanks.'

'Can I get you anything else?' she asked.

'I'm good.'

'Great. Let me know if you need anything.' She beamed again as she picked up the empty tray, turned on her heel and walked away.

Stratton opened the carrier bag, took out the sandwich bags and carefully opened the seal on the one containing the spaghetti, which was in fact SX cortex or detonation cord in a light machine oil. The oil played an important part in giving malleability to the plastic explosives. Stratton opened the smaller bag and removed the plastic component. Then he took one of the lengths of cortex, dabbed its end with his napkin to remove the oil and pushed it into a hole in the plastic component that was designed to grip it. He then scooped the bolognese sauce onto a side plate, forked some of the spaghetti into the Gucci bag, replaced it with the spaghetti-like cortex, mixed that with the remaining warm spaghetti to blend it in and slipped the small plastic device underneath to conceal it. Then he poured the bolognese sauce back on top. After tidying it up, cleaning the rim of the bowl with his napkin and sprinkling a little parmesan on top it looked as neat as when it had first been placed on the table.

Stratton looked for the waitress. She was near the entrance, talking to the hostess. He raised a hand. The hostess noticed him and nudged the waitress who headed towards him as he put the sandwich bags into the small carrier bag which he then folded and pushed into a trouser pocket.

'Is everything okay?' the waitress asked as she entered the patio.

'I haven't even tasted it yet. I wanted to ask you something. Do you know those gentlemen at that table in there?'

She glanced over to where the Albanians were sitting and her smile waned. 'Those guys? I don't know them but they're regulars,' she said, as if regretting that was a fact.

'One of them is a Mister Cano – Ardian Cano.'

'Yeah, he's in here at least twice a week.'

'He's a bit of a handful, isn't he?'

'That's an understatement,' she said. 'They've got a lotta hands, though. He a friend of yours? Because if he is I'd like you to ask him and his friends not to be so rude—'

'He's no friend of mine,' Stratton said. 'In fact, he was down at the Water Grill the other day,' he went on, naming one of the chain of restaurants downtown. 'He implied that some of the food was not up to scratch, notably the bolognese sauce.'

'He never said anything to any of us, as far as I know,' the waitress said, looking bemused.

'It wasn't a formal complaint,' Stratton said, making light of it. 'It was just something he said in passing. Anyway, I'd like you to do me a favour. Would you give this dish to Mr Cano, tell him it's with the compliments of the house and that we would very much like his expert opinion on it. You see, I think he perhaps had a one-off bad dish that day and this way we can get a first-hand comment from him. What do you think?'

'Sure.' She shrugged. 'Personally I think he's a pig and wouldn't know bolognese from dog food. But you're the boss.'

'I'm not anyone's boss – I'm just following orders.'

'Whatever.' She smiled. 'I'll give it to him.'

'Thanks,' he said as she picked the dish off the table.

'But if he touches my butt I'm gonna pour it over his head.'

'Not this time,' Stratton said in a pleading manner. 'Just this once be nice – if he touches you I promise he'll never do it again.'

'Sure?' she asked.

'I give you my word,' Stratton said with undiluted sincerity.

'You got it,' she said and walked into the restaurant, carrying the dish.

Stratton quickly wiped everything that he had touched, the glass, dishes and cutlery. Then he stood and walked around the table.

The waitress placed the bowl on the table as she explained to Ardian what Stratton had asked her to.

Stratton took a device the size of a matchbox from his pocket and pushed a button on its face: a tiny red LED light flickered. As he walked through the doors into the restaurant he pushed the button a second time and the LED light turned green. He put his hand with the device in it in his pocket and glanced over at Ardian who was looking between the bowl and the waitress as she answered a question. Stratton slowed to a crawl as Ardian looked down.

Stratton's thumb lightly touched the button on the device but he was unable to initiate the process yet. There was enough SX in the bowl for the blast to cause Ardian serious injury but the waitress was too close. Explosives had two distinctive, destructive characteristics: blast, which was a combination of shock wave and rapidly expanding gases that disrupted tissue; and shrapnel, which was low-velocity matter. The cortex was purely blast but since it sat in a china bowl there was a high risk of shrapnel.

Stratton pretended to be looking at the various Italian country murals that covered the walls while continually glancing at Ardian who now moved the bowl towards one of his friends. The man leaned down to sniff it and they all laughed at something one of them said which appeared to disgust the waitress. Ardian reached for the bread bowl, took a roll, pushed it into his large mouth and chewed greedily as he talked. The bowl of spaghetti travelled to another of the men who dipped a fork into the sauce and inspected the texture before tasting it. The bowl was then pushed back to Ardian who pulled it under his face for another close sniff. Stratton's finger stayed poised on the button: the waitress was still too close to escape possible injury.

Stratton's peripheral vision suddenly caught movement at the restaurant entrance. But he fought not to look because the waitress had stepped back and the ideal moment to detonate the device seemed to be at hand. Then Ardian's face broke into a broad grin and he stood up. Stratton looked towards the entrance to see Dren Cano walking in with Klodi who was wearing a heavy cast around his hand. The brothers greeted each other with a hug and held each other's hands as they stood and talked.

Stratton turned his back on them, suddenly concerned that his disguise would not stand up to any level of scrutiny. He decided to get out of the restaurant as soon as possible but his problem was how to retrieve the device. Chairs were dragged over from nearby tables and the men talked loudly as Stratton moved along the wall towards the entrance, feigning interest in the various bits of artwork until he came to an antique cabinet with glass-panelled doors. He could see the men in the reflection. Cano was seated beside his brother, ordering drinks from the waitress.

As Stratton was about to carry on moving to the exit he was stopped by a sudden change of mind. He shifted position to improve his view in the poor reflection to gauge Ardian's proximity to the bowl which was in front of him again – and now there was the added bonus of his brother being close by. Stratton could still not see clearly enough and he wanted to turn around to get a better look. But the waitress was still taking the men's orders and so he waited, fingering the button on the device and ensuring that his departure route was clear. When he looked back into the reflection he saw Klodi looking directly at him.

One of Klodi's compadres was trying to involve him in a conversation, unaware of Klodi's sudden interest until the man got to his feet.

Stratton looked at Ardian's reflection to see that he had a fork in his hand and was about to dip it into the spaghetti, still talking with his brother. Klodi stepped to one side to get a better look at the man with his back to him who looked vaguely familiar.

Stratton had only seconds to decide whether to get out of the restaurant right away or risk another fight with Cano that he might not survive this time. His gaze flashed to Ardian who was now dipping the fork into the bowl. Then he saw Klodi say something to his friend and they both looked at Stratton with interest. Klodi took a step towards Stratton as Ardian dug the fork into the spaghetti and twirled it around, mixing it into the sauce. He pulled the bowl beneath his chin, lowered his head and drew the luscious, writhing bundle up to his mouth.

'Hey! You!' Klodi called out to Stratton as he took another step towards him.

The overburdened fork approached Ardian's mouth. It opened like a grouper's and the dripping pasta was pushed inside, tendrils of spaghetti hanging down, still connected to the rest of the meal in the bowl. His teeth came down onto the *al dente* mass and then froze in mid-bite as his taste buds detected something unusual. His gaze dropped to the bowl where he noticed something else that was unusual. The fork dipped back into the remaining pasta where it retrieved and raised the tiny plastic device with the single strand of spaghetti hanging from it.

Stratton turned from the cabinet as the waitress passed him. He headed for the entrance, intent now on getting out fast.

'Hey, you! Klodi called out again, moving to intercept him.

Stratton's finger hit the button on the device as he walked out of view of the table and the hostess's 'Goodbye, have a great day' was cut short. The explosion was like an enormously loud clap, singularly sharp and high-pitched. It was immediately followed by the noise of smashing glass, a tremor as the building shook slightly, a short, echoing rumble that brought down the ornate ceiling light onto the table and finally a piercing scream from the waitress.

Ardian's body remained in position for several seconds after the explosion, surrounded by a light wisp of smoke, his head completely gone along with the hand that had been holding the fork. Blood spurted in a weak fountain as rapidly decreasing pressure in the arteries at either side of his windpipe pumped it down over his chest and back and onto the floor.

Cano was lying on his side, holding his face with bloody hands. Everyone had been struck by bits of Ardian and spaghetti bolognese though it was difficult to tell the difference. Only a row of front lower teeth attached to a piece of jaw on the table was recognisably human debris. For several seconds the other men remained frozen in shock.

When Cano lowered his hands, blood was dribbling from cuts all over his face and in particular from one of his eyes where a piece of white china was sticking out. Ardian's torso fell forward with a heavy thump to cover a large, almost perfectly symmetrical hole in the table where the bowl had been. The compression of his chest and stomach against the edge of the table caused a spurt of blood and mucus to shoot from his severed neck onto one of his colleague's laps.

Cano was in a great deal of pain and sat perfectly still as he opened his good eye wide enough to look at what was left of his brother. For a moment he remained in shock, his ears ringing loudly while he took in what had happened and brought himself under control. He also had to deal with the intense stinging in his wounded eye.

Klodi was the first to recover since he had not been facing the blast. As he glanced around at the mess he removed something wet that had struck him on the neck and discovered that it was a top lip with a bit of nose attached. He flicked it away in disgust and made his way to the entrance where the hostess was crawling around on the floor, throwing up and crying at the same time. Klodi stepped over her and reached for the door where the valets were cautiously looking through, opened it and shuffled down the steps and onto the sidewalk. Half a dozen or so people were in the street, all of whom had stopped to look towards the restaurant but Klodi could see no sign of the man he was certain was the one who had fought him in the limo.

Stratton was already in the park and taking the long way back to his apartment while he removed his goatee and dark glasses and carried out a post-operation analysis, searching his memory for any way that he might have left obvious clues. All in all he felt the hit had been a success. He now needed to put it behind him and concentrate on the final stage of his mission, which was to get Josh and his mother's body home. He had completed the revenge phase but he felt a hint of concern about being discovered. He would pay a heavy price for the murders if he was caught and if he did end up in jail the question of whether it had all really been worth it would haunt him.

As Stratton entered his apartment and closed the door sirens on vehicles coming to a stop close by drifted in through the windows. He considered quitting the apartment and finding somewhere else to stay. On the other hand, if the police connected him to either of the incidents before he finished what he had to do they would find him no matter where he lived. He thought about the prospect of going on the run for the rest of his life and considered the many places around the world where he could lose himself. Africa sprang to mind, where he could do mercenary work, or the Far East where he could bounty-hunt pirates for local police forces. There were actually, plenty of countries where he could hide while earning an okay living but he shook the thoughts from his head, growing irritated with himself. He sat back on the small sofa to take the weight off his feet, a jabbing pain shooting through his ribs to remind him of his injury. He would have liked to go to sleep there and then but he had to get over to the child-protection centre and see Josh. Stratton pulled himself off the couch before he got any more comfortable and went into the bedroom to wash and change.

Chapter 17

Hobart sat in his office on the eleventh floor of the big grey Federal building on Wilshire Boulevard. The road ran east from Santa Monica's cliffs three miles away and across the entire city. The FBI's California headquarters was situated in Westwood, LA's secondary business centre that was crammed with towering glass office blocks overlooking a vast university campus.

It was mid-morning and Hobart was coming to the end of a pile of e-mails, a hundred and fifty-three in total, which was not an unusual number on most days of the week. He made a point of reading them every morning even on his days off and on holiday simply because they would pile up relentlessly if he didn't. About half of them were intelligence reports and minutes of meetings from all over the world that his rank gave him access to, the rest concerned FBI matters in California.

The fifth e-mail on that morning's list was from the forensics department two floors down and had been sent to Hobart late the night before. The subject heading referred to the case of Leka Bufi who had been killed in the Santa Monica courthouse and there was a sub-reference to Ardian Cano's explosive demise in the Italian restaurant several days later. But instead of attaching the laboratory report as usual the e-mail was empty apart from a line requesting Hobart to make a personal visit to the lab at his earliest convenience.

Like everyone else in his team, as soon as Hobart had heard that Ardian had been killed with an explosive charge he had assumed that the two murders were syndicate-related. Both men were lowlife runners for Skender but had also been involved in extracurricular criminal activity that included drug trafficking and prostitution. There was, of course, one other connection between the two men that was known only by Hobart, his assistants and a handful of senior Bureau persons and that was their role in the murder of an Englishwoman in Venice. But that only served to confuse any theories Hobart had about the double assassination and he dismissed it as a coincidence.

Hobart had considered the possibility that Skender was behind the executions since his employees' link to the death of the Englishwoman as well as their private business were serious disciplinary matters that the Albanian gang-lord would have a serious sort of punishment for. However, the glaringly obvious reasons against Skender being involved in the deaths were that he did not need to go to such sophisticated lengths to get rid of two of his own men – they would simply have disappeared – and such an overt action would only complicate further the special relationship he enjoyed with the FBI. Hobart's thoughts went to his filing cabinet that contained several highly confidential files, one of them concerning the murder of Sally Penton and containing practically conclusive evidence of Ardian and Leka's involvement in it. The file could now be declassified since the perpetrators were deceased but Hobart decided that he would leave it where it was for the time being, along with several others that recorded a variety of crimes connected with the Albanians. One day Hobart hoped to connect Skender with them, a day he looked forward to with great enthusiasm.

It seemed that never a week went by without something happening to stir up the greatest problem of Hobart's career to date: the views he held regarding Skender's special deal with the United States Government, views that were distinctly contrary to those of the most senior people in the Bureau. Due to the seriousness of the issue Hobart had not mentioned to anyone except his wife that he was livid with the deal that the Bureau had made with Skender. It was a complicated arrangement but in essence Skender was providing the Bureau with high-grade evidence that would put away some of the biggest brokers of organised crime worldwide. But more importantly he had made a promise to point the finger at some of the top members of al-Qaeda, something he had not yet delivered on. All this was in exchange for some very generous concessions on his past crimes.

Only a few years ago, prior to 9/11, the best deal that Skender could have hoped for would have been some degree of immunity from prosecution but most likely he would just have got a reduced jail sentence and been put out of business. But 9/11 had changed everything and whoever helped to bring in big-name terrorists was now in a very strong position no matter who they were. Hobart did not agree that a criminal should enjoy such a high degree of immunity, regardless of what they provided in return, and certainly not Skender whom he did not trust and knew better than anyone else in the Bureau did. But the FBI mandarins thought differently.

Hobart was left with little enthusiasm for finding whoever was behind the killings of the two Albanians since Skender was not a suspect. Add to the mix the fact that Ardian and Leka had both been members of the KLA whose atrocious activities Hobart was only too familiar with and he frankly found it very hard to assign precious agent time and taxpayers' money to investigate it further. The fact was that the world was better off without the pair and although as a professional he could never condone the murders and was supposed to make all attempts to bring the killers to justice his conscience was not pressing him very hard.

All that aside, Hobart did have an urge to head downstairs right away and find out what the mystery e-mail was about. Its author, the forensics officer investigating the case, was an old friend who obviously had something interesting as well as secretive to say since he chose not to write it. However, Hobart had a few more e-mails to take care of, experience having taught him that since there would no doubt be another fifty or so by late afternoon he should clear them when he had the chance or end the day at his computer, which was something he loathed.

An hour later, as Hobart finished reading the last e-mail and pushed his chair back on its wheels another two popped up onto the screen. He ignored them.

They were daily situation reports from one of the Asian Pacific offices whose staff were just arriving at work and they could wait. He fastened the top button of his heavily starched white shirt as he stood up and drew his tie neatly to his throat as he headed for the door. A minute later he was jogging down the emergency stairs, avoiding the lifts as he usually did in a vain attempt to get some exercise. He opened the door onto the ninth floor and headed along the corridor to Forensic Department C, the smallest of the building's forensic cells but the most specialised.

Hobart pushed through the door into the laboratory that was the size of a volleyball court. Half of it was divided into small cubicles, each with its own special piece of electronic equipment. He paused to look around. There were four technicians busy at work in various parts of the lab and he spotted the one he had come to see in a cubicle on the other side of the room.

Hobart walked over and knocked on the glass door where a rotund balding man in his fifties was busy examining something through an electronic microscope. 'Phil?' Hobart said just softly enough for him to hear.

Phil turned to see who it was, immediately stopped what he was doing, put on a pair of spectacles, got up from his stool and opened the door.

'Hi, Nate,' Phil said as he stepped out of the cubicle. Hobart's Christian name was Nathan, though few people below his rank even knew he had a first name. Phil checked his watch. 'I was expecting to see you earlier.'

'You know how it is. So how's your day going?' Hobart asked with an uncommon degree of warmth that he reserved for his handful of friends. He had known Phil for over fifteen years, having worked with him in New York and then in Kosovo. There were few in the Bureau with whom Hobart mixed socially and even fewer he would describe as close but Phil was one of them. Having been in the job about the same length of time and having worked in many of the same theatres of operation they shared a similar cynicism and political leaning. Like Hobart, there were few people Phil would share his personal views with.

The big difference between them was that, unlike Hobart, Phil had lost all optimism for the future, believed the world was going downhill fast and had long since ceased to expect any positive change, believing that he could not make an iota of difference no matter how hard he tried. His one saving grace was his genius for forensics. Phil was one of the best if not *the* best in the FBI and over the years he had provided crucial evidence in many a challenging case. As Phil often said, if the job hadn't also been a damned good hobby he would have quit it years ago. Hobart, among others, was happy to see him stick around.

'It's been worth coming into work the past few days,' Phil said in a low voice that he always reserved for negative comments about the job, even when they were alone. Being old school he was permanently afflicted with the paranoid belief that the walls literally had ears. Add to that his long-standing hatred of the CIA for personal reasons and the inference took on a more sinister meaning – he believed that the CIA spied on everyone including the FBI. Hobart himself wasn't infected with that level of paranoia – although he too had little time for the CIA – and dismissed it as part of Phil's particular brand of eccentricity.

'The Bufi-Cano hit?' Hobart asked. 'Your report was interesting mainly because of its economy of detail, namely you said nothing.'

'I didn't e-mail the report because I wanted to talk to you about it first,' Phil said, his voice remaining low. 'Let's go for a walk.'

Hobart shrugged his okay. He had nothing too pressing at that moment and, even though Phil was eccentric, he wasn't known for being melodramatic.

Hobart walked to the door and went outside into the empty corridor. Phil followed and Hobart turned to face him, folding his arms across his chest, ready to hear what his friend had to say. An agent left an office down the corridor and walked towards them.

'Let's go outside,' Phil said as the agent passed them to enter another office.

Whatever Phil had to say was obviously too sensitive to reveal in the hallway and although this was turning into more of a chore than Hobart had anticipated he knew better than to argue with Phil's paranoia. If he wanted to hear what Phil had to say he was going to have to go through the pantomime. Hobart sighed inwardly and headed for the emergency exit.

'I'll meet you down in the lobby if you're going to take the stairs. I don't do exercise.'

Hobart stopped before opening the door to the emergency stairs, turned on his heel and headed down the corridor alongside Phil to the elevators.

A couple of minutes later they were walking out of the front of the building, past the complex array of security sensors and the armed guards checking all who entered. They stepped through the glass doors into the bright warm sunlight, the air filled with the noise and fumes from the crowded six-lane boulevard a stone's throw away.

Phil did not say a word as he led Hobart around the side of the building, into the vast parking lot and across to an area that had few cars and was empty of people. He stopped at a location that he deemed suitable for his revelation, looked all around to check that no one was paying any special attention to them, and faced Hobart.

'We've got something pretty interesting here, Nate,' Phil said calmly.

'I guess,' Hobart replied, glancing around the parking lot.

'*Dark* interesting,' Phil emphasised.

'Dark?' Hobart asked.

'Can you level with me? I'm talking about Bufi and Cano.'

'Level with you?'

'Will you stop repeating everything I say? I'm being deadly serious here.'

'Phil, I'm always serious and I don't know what you're talking about. Level with you about what?'

'Okay. I'll get to the point,' Phil said, then paused to stare into Hobart's eyes and double-check something.

'You sure there's nothing you can't tell me about those guys and why they were hit?'

'Nothing I *can't* tell you?'

'Yeah. Can't. I ain't asking you what it is. I'm just asking you if there is something. If you can't tell me just say so.'

'Come on, Phil. If there's ever anything I can't tell you about anything then I can't say if I can or I can't, can I?'

Phil studied his old friend for a moment. 'They were both former KLA, am I right?'

'Yeah. They were ex-KLA. So what?'

'And there's nothing about them that's special, no red flags, no involvement in anything against the government, our government – just tell me that much.' Phil jumped in as Hobart was about to answer. 'I wanna know if they were involved in anything against our government. It's an important question.'

'As far as I know they had nothing to do with anything against our government,' Hobart said with an audible sigh. Phil was not privy to the connection between the two Albanians and the killing of the Englishwoman since it was highly confidential and Hobart would not tell him. But otherwise he could see no reason for Phil's heightened concern.

'Okay,' Phil said, lowering his shoulders in a vain effort to relax his neck while taking another quick look around. 'There's no doubt that Bufi and Cano were killed by the same people or the same organisation,' Phil stated.

Hobart nodded. That seemed obvious enough.

'Question is who, right?'

Hobart nodded again. Phil was dragging this out like some kind of soap-opera sleuth but Hobart remained outwardly patient. He knew that Phil would eventually get to his point and the quickest way was to let him do it in his own time.

'Nate. Those guys weren't taken out by any ordinary hitter. In both cases the method was ingenious but there's a lot more to it than that. I'm talking about the explosive material used. It was identical in each case. It was an RDX-governed compound with a tetryl booster and some of the most purified nitrates I've come across. It was plastic explosive, like C4, but twice as concentrated. The closest match I found on file was super-cyclo-tetryl-trimethylene-trinitramine 7, an experimental military compound that NASA refined for their ejection-escape capsules, but this stuff is a grade higher than that. My point is, you can't get this stuff on the street. There are probably only a handful of countries sophisticated enough to manufacture such a compound. It's highly specialised. And something else. Explosives are measured by the speed at which they burn. Basic C4 is around 24,000 feet per second, for instance. You need a detonator of similar power to ignite it, or if not, you need a primer to cover the middle ground between the explosive speed of the det and that of the actual explosive material. An ordinary C4 detonator would not have been powerful enough to initiate that type of SX. It would have just blown it away like it was cake. The detonator used to initiate those hits was of the same high-grade material but not only that, they were micro dets. Micro-super-X dets. You hear what I'm saying, Nate?'

'I hear what you're saying,' Hobart said.

'A micro-SX det is Star Wars, Nate. The people who use that kind of explosive get a government pay cheque and work out of an office that's a long elevator ride underground.'

Hobart did not outwardly respond but Phil had his full attention. The revelation was more than just fascinating. Hobart did not for a second doubt Phil's evaluation of the specialised explosive and its non-availability on the street. The inference was the explosive was either given by a person in government to someone to use or was used by a person who themself had direct access to it – and that, as Phil was saying, implied that the hit was carried out by a government organisation. But then, when the quality of the targets was considered there was an instant erosion of that notion's credibility since Ardian and Leka were essentially nobodies.

'Are you sure about this?' Hobart asked. 'I mean, I'm not questioning your analysis of the explosive, but what about its availability? What about the Chinese, or the Russians? If they have this stuff then it's possible it could have found its way into the marketplace.'

Phil was shaking his head in frustration well before Hobart had finished his sentence. 'That would be like Microsoft's latest software leaking onto the street. Yeah, there's a million-to-one chance that it's possible, but there's something else that throws up a red flag here. The technique. The hitter used it to perfection, like he had training. It was surgery, Nate. That coin through the back of Bufi's head was genius. Ask yourself this. In all your years in the business, how many IED hits worldwide have you even heard of anywhere near as sophisticated as this? I haven't, and I'm in the goddamned business.'

Hobart was slowly becoming convinced and with that came a growing anger. The question, then, was not *if* Leka and Ardian could be a target of a government agency but *why*? And if it was true, someone from government, his own or someone else's, had made a hit on his turf. Skender and his organisation were exclusively Hobart's to control and monitor and anyone, no matter who they were, from the President down, had to go through him about anything to do with the Albanian syndicate in Los Angeles.

If there was one thing that really pissed Hobart off it was the blatant flouting of protocol and the circumvention of government-ordained authority. It was a primary corruption of the system that was unprecedented in the US. If he could do anything to prevent it happening he would do so in a heartbeat, even if it meant taking those responsible to the Senate and exposing them publicly, no matter who they were. This sort of subversion tore into the very principles of governing authority that the country was built on. If Phil was right, and Hobart found him all too convincing, Hobart would get to the bottom of this if it took all the resources he had at his disposal. This was not just a double homicide: it was an invasion of his case and therefore personal. The Bufi-Cano file had just found itself reclassified and at the very top of his list.

Hobart took his cellphone from his pocket, punched in a number and put it to his ear.

The phone rang in an office on the same floor as Hobart's, two doors along the corridor, and was picked up by his young assistant. 'Agent Hendrickson,' he said as he held the phone with his chin and continued tapping the keys of his computer keyboard.

'It's Hobart.'

'Sir,' Hendrickson said, stopping almost immediately and taking hold of the handset.

'What are you doing right now?'

'The Chaves case, sir.'

'Give it to Mendez or Stefanowitz. I want you on the Bufi-Cano murders.'

'The Bufi—' Hendrickson started to say with some surprise. This month's cases were already outnumbering last month's with a week to go and only yesterday morning Hobart had told the office to put the Englishwoman murder case on the bottom of the pile and keep putting it there until its hair started falling out.

'That's what I said,' Hobart reiterated. 'I want you to crawl all over it. You're looking for anything that doesn't fit.'

'Like what, sir?'

'Well, that's the thing about something that doesn't fit, Hendrickson. You'll know it when you see it.'

'I'm on it, sir,' Hendrickson said, but Hobart didn't hear him. His phone was already closed and dangling in his hand by his side. He looked at Phil, only because the man was staring at him. Hobart's mind was still racing through the consequences of a government agency being responsible for the killings. At that moment it didn't matter which one.

'This is bad, isn't it?' Phil said.

Hobart didn't answer.

'I mean, this is *real* bad. This kind of stuff went on all the time in the seventies and eighties, but not now.'

'I don't need to tell you not to say anything about this to anyone, do I?'

'You kidding? I may be an old conspiracy theorist but I've watched all the movies and I know what happens to the first guy with the hot info. Tell you the truth, I didn't sleep a wink last night.'

'This isn't a movie, Phil. No one's coming after you.'

'What about when the report goes out? I'm supposed to send a copy to New York and another to the pool.'

'Give me a hard copy. Don't email it to anyone yet. Label the pool copy confidential then post it onto the site empty.'

'But that's going to throw up a flag. These people will be waiting for the report.'

'Refer all enquiries to my office. And take it easy. It's past you now. It's in the system. Okay? Like I said, no one's coming after you.'

Phil nodded and visibly calmed down. 'You're right,' he said. Hobart was making perfect sense as usual. 'I guess I got a little wound up when for a while there I was the only person who knew. I'm okay now. What are you going to do?'

'You're going to have to forget it and leave it with me, okay?' Hobart said in a fatherly manner.

'I'm already there,' Phil said, allowing a smile of relief to grow on his face. 'I'll wait and read about it in the papers.'

'You do that,' Hobart said, knowing that it might never get that far. Like any bad news, if it could be kept in-house that was as far as it would go. His only concern about Phil was that the man was in the winter of his career in a business he believed to be corrupt and there was that distant possibility that he might decide to do something that he'd consider heroic while he still had the chance. As Hobart stared at Phil he decided that was probably unfair of him and he patted his old friend on the shoulder.

'Come on,' Hobart said. 'Let's go back and see this report.' They headed across the parking lot towards the building while Phil began to explain the various chemical make-ups of different types of plastic explosive and how it affected their performance and dictated their different uses. Hobart tried to listen with some interest but his mind kept flicking to the new problem at hand. This case was now possibly one of the most important he'd handled in recent years.

Chapter 18

A shiny black stretch limousine slowly pulled off the road and onto an uneven patch of sun-baked mud on the edge of a large bustling construction site. It came to a stop outside a chain-link security fence and a grey Cadillac sedan pulled alongside it. Three dark-skinned Caucasian Neanderthals in expensive suits climbed out of the sedan with muscle-bound slowness and spread out around the limo, checking in all directions, hands hovering close to pistols and sub-machine guns hidden inside their jackets. One of them nodded to the passenger in the front of the limo and he climbed out and opened one of the rear doors.

Skender eased out of the spacious interior, buttoning up the jacket of an immaculate cream suit, the collar of his shirt turned down outside it in a style that would provoke feelings of nostalgia in any who enjoyed the fashions of the 1970s. He walked over the hard ground in his patent-leather shoes and in through the security gate, followed by two of his men. The security guard, a redneck type who had never seen proper military service, saluted Skender and bid him good afternoon as he passed his sentry box. Skender ignored him and walked several yards onto the site before stopping to look up, a smile growing on his craggy face.

'It's beautiful,' he said to his thugs without looking at them, not that he was addressing them in particular but he wanted to say it to someone. 'I love watching it grow day by day.'

Skender was gaping at a huge new office building near completion, a startling design emulating ancient Egyptian pyramids. Shimmering plates of dark green glass locked into copper-sheathed steel frames covered all four steeply sloping sides from the second floor to the sixteenth. The seventeenth or top floor was also glass but was gold in colour. Two smaller pyramids were located at opposite corners of the site, creating an overall impression like a typical picture postcard of Giza. The ground around the building was paved in Italian marble that continued out several metres from the base of the building, with towering newly planted palms springing from it in places.

To some critics the edifice verged on the kitsch but it was eye-catching nevertheless. Hundreds of workers were busy operating cranes, earth-movers and dumper trucks as the exterior cosmetics – landscaping, lighting and pathways – were well under way. Lorries ferried their loads in and out through the main entrance where kerbstones were being laid in preparation for the tarmac fill that would connect the lavish drive to Washington Boulevard that ran along one side. The site took up an entire block in Culver City, a modern development of Los Angeles a couple of miles from Beverly Hills and occupied by the likes of Sony and MGM studios, fine restaurants and expensive art shops.

The business premises were interspersed with middle-class residential buildings.

Skender traced the steep, imposing façade with his eyes from the pinnacle down to a magnificent main entrance of bronze-coloured glass and copper and steel supports. As his gaze rested on a pair of massive eleventh-century wooden doors twenty feet high and with heavily inlaid carvings, an import from India to maintain the impression of the ancient shrouded in the modern, Dren Cano stepped through them and into the pillared portico.

Skender headed off through the site towards Cano, followed by his men. 'Is it gonna be ready in time?' he shouted to an engineer who was perusing a stack of plans laid out on a table.

The engineer looked around and immediately grinned with forced enthusiasm on seeing who had posed the question. 'Hey there, Mister Skender. You betcha it's gonna be on time.'

Skender smiled thinly as he continued on without a pause, confident of the answer before he had heard it. Before the first bulldozer had moved in to demolish the old houses and apartment blocks that had previously occupied the site every contractor, supplier and union involved had been subtly warned that it would be most unwise if there were to be any sudden price hikes, cancellations or delays of any nature for any reason, including Acts of God such as weather or accidents. Similarly gilded threats as well as lavish gifts were bestowed upon certain members of the city authority to persuade against any unforeseen problems with the various planning permissions that would be required.

Only one company failed to heed the warnings, one of the two cement suppliers contracted to deliver the thousands of tons of concrete required. It was an oversight on their part: apparently they had not researched the client thoroughly enough to take the threats seriously. When one morning the cement trucks did not arrive due to a reprioritisation by the company concerned in favour of another client across town Skender's retribution was swift and decisive. The company's owner happened to be on holiday in Hawaii at the time with his wife and two sons. The morning following the non-delivery they were all found in their rooms with their legs broken and the arms of the owner himself painfully fractured above the elbows as a bonus. Rumours spread swiftly among the work-force with some help from Skender's people and there were no further obstructions to the site's progress. In fact the general cordiality of the contractors and workers increased to a sycophantic level. When, after three weeks, construction was a day and a half ahead of schedule Skender rewarded every worker with a thousand-dollar bonus that sealed their devotion to the task.

Skender stepped onto the marble-floored concourse in front of the cathedral-like entrance and stopped to scrutinise the intricate inside roofing of the portico.

Cano looked like hell: his left eye was covered by a silk patch and there were stitches all over his face. He had lost the use of the eye, which had been removed, and he was waiting for the plastic surgery on the tattered eyelid to heal before having a false eye put in. Words could not describe the hatred he felt in his heart for the person who had killed his brother and done this to him. It was greater than any he had experienced in his life and was so strong that when he thought of Stratton – Klodi had told Cano of his sighting of Stratton at the restaurant – when the memory of the man's image loomed in front of him, Cano's facial expression physically changed and he looked as if he were growling or about to snarl.

Skender had told his senior security manager to take a few weeks off to rest and to heal his body as well as soothe his heart, aching for the loss of his brother. Cano refused. There was only one thing that could come even close to dulling his pain and that was to see – literally – Stratton's head on a plate.

'They're waiting for you in the penthouse,' Cano said sombrely.

'Good,' Skender said without looking at him. He wore an expression of approval at everything he saw until his gaze fell on several workers huddled around a square hole in the centre of the white marble concourse. Skender glanced at the main doors to the building, then back at the hole in the ground, gauging the distance and positioning of it. With the look of approval gone from his face, he headed towards the group.

'Hey! What are you guys doing?' he growled as he approached the workers.

They looked around and straightened immediately on seeing who it was.

'This is where the statue's gonna go, Mr Skender,' the foreman said, somewhat nervously, wondering why Skender was looking so pissed off.

'The hell it is,' Skender growled.

'We're going exactly by the plans, sir,' an engineer said, suddenly checking the papers in his hands, fearing he had got it wrong.

'I don't give a damn what the plans say. I want it here,' Skender said as he turned around and paced closer towards the entrance until he stood squarely fifty feet in front of the doors. 'Here,' he repeated as he faced them, feet wide apart and hands outstretched as if doing an impersonation of Moses parting the Dead Sea. 'Like this. You got that?!'

The foreman hurried over to Skender, pulled a spray can from a pouch, and scurried around him, spraying a thin red line on the marble.

Skender lowered his hands, looked at the square drawn around him and nodded. 'It arrives today?' he asked although it sounded more like a statement of fact.

The foreman looked instantly worried again. 'No, sir. It'll be in place by the opening ceremony. I assure you.'

Skender looked at him coldly, decidedly unsatisfied with the answer.

'They're pouring the mould by the end of the week,' the foreman hurriedly added. 'I'm told it looks pretty damn good, Mr Skender.'

'I want it in place no later than the day before the opening ceremony. You understand me?'

'It'll be in, sir.'

Skender studied the man for a few seconds before a thin smile grew on his lips. It had far more sinister qualities than the unsmiling look.

Skender disconnected from the foreman who was

277

only too relieved and headed towards the main entrance, Cano alongside him. As they reached the doors Skender paused to look at his head of security. 'Don't be so down, Dren,' he said, using Cano's real name which he sometimes did but only when they were outside and there was no one within earshot. 'We will find who killed your brother.'

Whenever Skender addressed Cano by his real name Cano never took it as a sign of affection since he knew that the man did not possess a scrap of any such. He saw the usage as a subtle reminder of who he really was and that Skender had control of his life. On the day when Cano had joined the ranks and given Skender the Besa – a solemn pledge to keep one's word on pain of death – Skender had warned him that he would pay the ultimate price for any form of disobedience.

Skender had a special punishment for those in his employ who crossed him. The technique varied but the purpose was always the same: to keep the victim alive for as long as possible but in a condition of utter agony. This might mean amputating as much of the person as possible, cauterising each removal or applying a tourniquet and adding salt to the wounds. Another method was to direct a blowtorch onto various body parts at intervals, while another involved injecting into the bloodstream various chemicals that caused unimaginable headaches and burning pains throughout the body, reviving the victim if their heart ceased to beat due to the pain or the chemical poisoning. The methods were limited only by the imagination of the torturer.

And just in case anyone hoped to escape such an end by killing the master himself it was well known that Skender had deposited a large sum of money with a family of infamous assassins, ironically Croatians rather than Albanians, who would carry out such executions of any persons found responsible for Skender's death, even if it was an accident. The sum was considerable and apparently allowed for the execution of up to twenty persons so that if, say, only one person was involved in the incident, the other nineteen slots would be filled by that person's most immediate family members. The assassins were entirely reliable since they had many such contracts with powerful underworld figures and it would not be good for their business to leave an obligation unfulfilled. The bottom line was that Skender was a deadly man to cross – in any direction.

Cano had not been promoted to the position of Skender's head of security just because he was as ruthless as he was intelligent. Cano also displayed qualities of initiative whereas other subordinates were afraid to make any decision without first clearing it with the master. Allowing a level of free thinking from an individual within the ranks had its dangers but Skender appreciated its advantages and in any case Cano had proved his loyalty as well as an intuitive understanding of Skender's methods over the years. It was the greatest single display of trust that Skender had bestowed on any individual but he was aware that such traumatic events as losing an eye and a brother in one afternoon and then to have the killer walk free might put a strain on Cano's single-minded dedication to Skender. He would wait and see how things developed.

'I think we have already found him,' Cano said.

'You have him?' Skender asked curiously. A small warning bell went off in his head.

'No,' Cano said. 'Not yet.'

Skender could not have cared less about the death of Cano's brother or the loss of his eye. He was more concerned with the possible wider consequences of the recent deaths. He was confident of the position he had carved out for himself with the Federal government by turning in some old enemies, providing carefully selected snippets of information on some weapons-supply networks used by terrorists and dangling a big carrot in front of them with the promise of delivering up an al-Qaeda leader. But the stupid killing of the Englishwoman and then the deaths of Bufi and Ardian were problems he could do without.

If Ardian had not been Dren's brother Skender would have had him and his moronic sidekick Bufi executed after they had killed the Englishwoman. It would have been a lesson to others. But if he had killed Ardian he would have had to kill Cano too since he would then have become an enemy. Skender had made that one concession to Cano but he would not allow another. Cano was possibly signing his own death warrant by pursuing his brother's killer. Skender wondered if Cano understood that. Or was his anger and depression so great that he could think of nothing else but retribution?

'You say you only *think* you know who was responsible?' Skender asked.

'Yes, but I will make sure.'

'And do you think you know who he works for?'

'I think he is working alone.'

'Alone?'

'You have seen him. At the district attorney's office in Santa Monica. He was the man at the bottom of the stairs who attacked Vlen.'

Skender shook his head as if he did not remember although he had a vague image of the man in his head.

'He was in the restaurant when Ardian was killed,' Cano went on. 'He ran off seconds before the explosion. He's an Englishman. A secretary in the DA's office remembered an Englishman asking about an Englishwoman's death in Venice a week ago. And one of our cops, Draper, down at the Santa Monica Police Department, described the same guy asking about the case.'

Skender remembered the Englishman who had telephoned him. 'This cop, Draper, he told this Englishman it was Ardian and Leka?'

'No. He told him nothing.'

'Then how'd he find out?'

'I don't know.'

Skender thought on that for a moment as he stared into Cano's eyes. The Englishman had no doubt got Skender's phone number from the same source who had given him the names. That had to be a pretty high-up source. 'Why do you think he isn't connected to anyone?'

'This was a revenge killing.'

'How would he know it was your brother who killed that Englishwoman if he's not connected with someone who would know?'

281

'I've no idea. But he ain't business. He don't even live in this country. He came over because the Englishwoman was killed and the next thing is Bufi gets taken out and then my brother.'

'And so he just happens to find out and marches into the Santa Monica courts, through a dozen cops, kills Bufi in his cell, escapes, then kills your brother right in front of you — and you think he's just an ordinary guy.'

'Okay, so maybe he's got talent. My point is, he's not connected to us. This wasn't about business. Look, boss, I know how sensitive things are right now. I'm not about to do anything stupid. Let me find out who he is, then I'll come to you with what I've got.'

'You know where he is?'

'No, but I have an idea how to find out. I want this guy, boss. I've never asked you for anything before, but I'm asking now. It's the Kanun of our *fis*. It's the Kanun.'

Skender walked away and stood looking into space while Cano watched him. Skender's immediate impulse was to have Cano killed as soon as possible and end it there. But deep down he knew only too well the meaning of retribution for wrongs committed against one's family. The Kanun was a set of norms that constituted the Albanian syndicate's common law, a code that had been in place for centuries and was used by all the *fis* or tribes. It was the blood-bond that held the Albanians together and made them so much more dangerously different from other nationalities in the same business. Skender could not ignore it for it was in his own blood.

Strangely, while listening to Cano, especially the part about his new nemesis being an Englishman, Skender had been reminded of his own youth, for it was a man from that country who had been responsible for the destruction of his entire family. Skender was from the Geg tribe who occupied the mountainous regions of Northern Albania. Unlike most of his current peers, Skender's family had not been linked to crime but were strongly political. They'd been followers of Zog, the ousted King of the Albanians.

When Mussolini invaded Albania in 1939 the King had fled to England. Geg chieftains, one of whom was Skender's father, organised an anti-communist royalist group and in 1952, a few years after Skender was born, the King, whose son Skender was named after, joined a plot organised by the US and Britain to help the loyalists overthrow the Albanian communist government that had by then taken power.

Hundreds of Albanian émigrés and refugees were recruited, many by Skender's father, and infiltrated back into Albania for the coming fight. However, the plot was revealed to the communists by the infamous British double agent Kim Philby. Practically every Albanian infiltrator and many of the Geg tribe, including Skender's parents, were brutally murdered.

Skender was barely six years old on the morning when the killers came to his village. There had been no warning. No one was to escape death, no matter what their sex or age. Skender remembered waking up to the noise of screams and gunfire. He climbed out of the bed he shared with his older brother and two sisters and ran to the window to see what was happening. The first sight he saw was the woman who lived across the road being dragged outside with her three children after her husband had already been shot. Skender watched in horror as they were killed by a combination of rifle fire and sword thrusts.

Seconds later the front door to his own house was kicked open and more gunfire erupted. They killed Skender's mother first and as his father rushed out of the back room with his gun raised he was cut down by a volley of fire from several government soldiers. Then came the sound of someone running up the stairs. Skender reacted instinctively. He jumped up onto the windowsill and pulled himself over it. As he hung on to the window frame the bedroom door burst open and shots rang out. A bullet smashed through the window and Skender let go to land hard on the small roof along the front of the house before rolling off and hitting the dirt road.

A soldier immediately saw the little boy but instead of shooting he raised his sword and ran at him. Skender scrambled to his feet and sprinted around the side of the building with all the strength he could muster. The soldier followed but Skender knew his own backyard and, being a fraction of his pursuer's size, was able to dart through a hole in a wooden fence as the sword swung down. He rolled down the steep slope in between the houses. Skender was free from that pursuer but there were many more soldiers in the village and the sound of wholesale slaughter had risen to a frenzy.

Skender continued to run, not knowing where to go other than downhill since it gave him the greatest speed. He paused between two buildings to consider his options. The sounds of screams and shooting surrounded him and all he could think of was continuing on to the bottom of the village, across the road and into the river.

A bullet hit a wall inches away from Skender, painfully splattering his cheek with plaster. He looked up to see a soldier aiming a rifle at him from a window. The next bullet hit the ground between his feet and he was off running again, ducking between houses and sheds, pushing through flimsy fences that corralled various livestock and on until he reached a road. He ran across it without a glance in either direction. As he leaped up onto a bank on the other side a hand grabbed him by the neck, twisted him round as if he was a doll, and raised him off the ground.

Skender could barely breathe. His vision blurred but he could see the huge grinning face of the communist soldier, a monster of a man with bad teeth and a beard. Skender pulled at the man's gnarled fingers and kicked out with his shoeless feet in a vain effort to release himself. But the man just grinned, even as he removed a knife from its sheath and drew it slowly across Skender's throat, cutting deeply into it. The man then walked a few yards, holding the boy at his side like a dead chicken, and unceremoniously threw him into the swiftly flowing river that was full and freezing at that time of year. Skender plunged beneath the surface and was dragged and rolled along the gravel bed. He fought to reach the light and when he broke through to air he took in great gulps, unaware that much of it – as well as some water –

was coming in through the slit in his throat. He had to fight not only to stay on the surface but also to keep his throat clear enough to take in precious air. He slammed into a boulder and managed to grab hold. Then, with a supreme effort, he pulled himself up onto it. While he gulped in air he could still feel fluid going down his throat and as he violently coughed and retched he could see that it was blood, not water. He gripped the wound and scrambled across some other boulders to the river bank, keeping a tight hold of his throat. He ran through a wood, not knowing where he was heading. Like a frightened, wounded animal he was desperate to find a cave or a hole to burrow into and hide.

Skender must have covered half a mile or so, stopping every now and then to cough up blood that had trickled into his lungs. As he pushed on through a clump of bushes he was suddenly grabbed, pulled to the ground and held down by his shoulders. When he looked into the eyes of his attacker he saw that the man was not in uniform and that the people with him were villagers like himself. They were two families with several children and they all looked as frightened as him.

Skender then started to choke uncontrollably and on seeing the blood gushing out of the slit in the boy's throat the man quickly turned him over. Skender had been lucky. When the communist soldier had held him up to kill him he had pushed Skender's head as far back as it could go, thereby forcing the carotid arteries behind the front of his windpipe. When the knife had been drawn across his neck the windpipe had been cut but the blade had not penetrated deeply enough to sever the two arteries either side. Had Skender's head been bent forward he would have died in seconds.

As soon as Skender had recovered from his choking fit the man got him to his feet with warnings that they all had to get going. He forced Skender to keep his chin firmly pressed against his chest. One of the women placed a strip of cloth around his neck and after a while the bleeding subsided. Skender could now breathe without spitting up blood every few seconds.

For several days he remained with the family as they made their way through the mountains, holding on to the person in front of him while keeping his chin pressed against his chest to keep the wound closed. Eating the soup they gave him was almost intolerable – every swallow caused a searing pain – but he forced himself to eat, aware that it was a matter of pain or death. Skender did not say a word the whole time, unable to speak. It was not until they reached a small farm within sight of Lake Shkodra on the western coast that he was taken to a professional healer.

It was weeks before Skender could utter any kind of sound and more than half a year before he could form words again and talk loudly enough to be understood. People said his croaky little voice had a charm to it but that was only while he was young. As it began to break in his early teens it became deeper and more ominous, befitting the image of a man who'd clearly once had his throat slit.

The man who had helped him that day brought him into his family's drug-trafficking business and

Skender began his working life as a courier. As the business grew and became more sophisticated Skender displayed a high degree of intelligence and ingenuity and was given a greater control of operations. Then he came up with the idea of opening a travel agency as a cover for the movement of drugs, illegal immigrants, prostitutes and arms into Italy and the rest of Europe. This increased his power still more. By his late thirties Skender had offices in Milan and Paris, two of the main gateways into Europe.

With the death of his new father on Skender's fortieth birthday he assumed control of a vast territory. By the mid-1980s the growth of his empire was being seriously impeded by his inability to launder the vast pile of cash and other undeclarable assets that he had amassed, thus preventing further investment. But then came the war in Kosovo.

Having taken control of many aspects of the KLA's operations against the Serbs, Skender immediately saw a further opportunity when the Americans got involved. He set up shop as a building contractor and when the rebuilding of Kosovo and Serbia began, financed by America, he spent his drug money on local workers and building materials and deposited the legitimate payments for his construction work in banks all over Europe and America. It was amazingly simple and he became a legitimate dollar billionaire practically overnight.

Despite being Muslim, a leader of an army as demonic and brutal as any SS outfit of World War Two and rumoured to have ties with the likes of Osama Bin Laden's international terrorist network Skender's overt anti-communism and pro-Americanism were credentials enough for him to be embraced by the Clinton administration. But better-informed critics warned that Skender was more like a phoenix rising from the ashes – and not necessarily on the side of the West.

By the time that Skender was ready to build a legitimate operation in the United States and leave his ongoing and expanding crime organisation in Albania in the care of a syndicate of Bajraks or families that he had control over, he had gained huge US governmental support and made personal friends with a dozen senators and high-ranking officials in the administration. His plans remained largely unhindered with the arrival of the Bush administration but his prospects took a turn for the worse after 9/11 due to his terrorist connections.

By that time Skender had invested a great deal in the US and he might have continued to operate just below the radar had an investigation into his Bajrak partners back in Albania not revealed a direct link with Bin Laden's weapons-supply network in the period leading up to the Twin Towers strike. There was evidence to suggest that Skender's narcotics-trafficking routes had continued to be used by the terrorist leader. Furthermore, Bin Laden was receiving funding for his activities directly from Albanian sources connected with Skender. At one point it looked as if Skender's goose had been well and truly cooked.

However, the man was not without a string or two to his bow and the survival instincts that had saved his life when he'd been a boy were as strong as ever.

In the final analysis it was an American government that had given Skender the power he currently enjoyed. If necessary he could produce damning evidence of American financing and training of personnel who later became key players in the international terrorist arena. But that was not enough to keep him out of jail since the new administration, although not squeaky-clean itself, would not be overly concerned about any exposé of their predecessors' dodgy foreign policies.

Skender had to offer something substantial to keep the wolves at bay and he was quick to respond. He promised to provide information that would allow the Americans to monitor terrorist supply lines – and he indicated that he might be able to give them something even bigger. He suggested that he could one day deliver Bin Laden himself. This was a daring ploy but it had the desired effect and gave him time to reorganise. The fact was that he could indeed be very useful in delivering Bin Laden to the Americans and they believed as much. But that would also pitch Skender from the frying pan into the fire, not just because of the danger from the Islamic militants under Bin Laden's control but also because of the vast number of anti-westerners among his own people in Albania.

The Americans understood that as well and were willing to give Skender the space to manoeuvre, but they would not sit back and allow him to dictate the schedule entirely. Serious problems in Iraq, Afghanistan and other parts of the world meant that they were anxious to see some worthwhile results from this special relationship. Time was running out for Skender:

short of the big prize, no matter what he gave the Americans they would always want more. They would hound him until he delivered on his promise, with the clear-cut understanding that if Osama Bin Laden died in the interim Skender would be expected to deliver the terrorist leader's replacement.

To add to these troubles, Skender had been warned that all his current and future activities within the US had to be legitimate and above board. Regardless of any help he provided against international terrorism his deal was not a licence to run a crime syndicate. He was given a period of grace to get his business affairs in order and its end point was now in sight. That was why matters like the extracurricular activities of his employees and the murder of the Englishwoman were counter-productive for Skender's plans. The transition from criminal activity to legitimate ditto was bound to have its problems.

Ultimately, Skender wanted to be rid of all ties to his countrymen. But the harsh truth was that he would always need their protection and the only way he could maintain that was to rule as an Albanian clansman. There was no way around it. He would have to let Cano have his revenge if he was to maintain stability within the ranks. It was the Kanun.

Skender faced Cano and stared at him for a moment. 'I want you to be sure of everything before you make a move on this man – do you understand?'

'Don't worry.'

Skender drew closer to Cano so that his face filled his subordinate's vision. 'Don't worry? Is that what you

291

just said to me? Don't you *ever* tell me what to do again, ever.'

Skender walked off through the doors.

Cano cursed himself for being so stupid. The comment had been a slip of the tongue but it had been the wrong time to make such a mistake. It was also a reminder that working for Skender was like riding a wild tiger – if he should ever lose his grip he would fall off and be torn apart. Cano had no illusions about his place in the operation and no ambitions to be anything more than what he already was to Skender. He could never take the reins. He was and would always be an outsider. Had things gone better for him in Kosovo perhaps he could have had his own Bajrak but that was now nothing more than a nostalgic dream. He often wondered when his usefulness would end and if he should flee before then and hope to find a place to hide. But Skender would be relentless: he would set the world against Cano who would be hunted down, for his crimes in Kosovo as well as for his betrayal of Skender. He was in limbo and as powerless as those condemned to dwell in that place of myth. But that was a concern for another time. Right now Cano was in a position of control and he also had a mission: to avenge his brother's murder.

Cano walked inside the building and followed Skender into one of several elevators, took a key-card from his pocket and slipped it into a slot. The doors closed. Seconds later the high-speed elevator accelerated between floors and came to a smooth stop at the top of the building.

The doors opened and the two men stepped out

onto a floor where workmen were laying cables and decorating surfaces. Skender and Cano walked along a curved corridor that was green glass on one side, revealing a large boardroom. Seated in luxury chairs were several men in expensive suits, most of them as old as Skender.

'Gentlemen.' Skender beamed as he walked through the glass doors that slid open automatically as he approached. 'Thank you for coming to my new offices.'

The men got to their feet out of politeness but nothing else. It was clear that they were powerful men in their own right, a meeting of old lions who still possessed the sharpest of teeth and claws. They were a group of wealthy bankers and investors, all legitimate and all seeking to become even richer. In the centre of the room was a table with a large model of a modern residential and business community at the edge of a lake. Skender's secretary was waiting for him and handed him a file while Cano pushed a button on the glass door. It slid closed, leaving him outside in the corridor and cut off from the meeting. 'Okay, guys,' he said to the construction workers in the corridor. 'Time for a smoke break.'

The men immediately downed their tools and headed for the emergency stairwell without a word or a second glance back. As the last man filed through the exit door Cano locked it from the inside and stood alone in the silent corridor. He watched a moment while the men surrounded the model on the table, Skender's lips moving but not a sound penetrating the glass. Then Cano walked into a small kitchen by the exit, closed the door behind him and removed his mobile phone from a pocket. He punched in a number and held it to his ear as it chirped a couple of times before someone picked up at the other end.

'Valon. What we talked about this morning – go ahead. Call me as soon as you have anything.'

Cano ended the call and pocketed the phone. Then he reached inside a pocket and removed a bottle of pills. His hand started to shake as he undid the top. His eye socket, which had been pulsating painfully for the past hour or so, had suddenly become excruciating. He popped the painkillers into his mouth, filled a plastic cup from the water dispenser and washed them down. As he stared at his battered face in the small mirror on the wall his expression changed to a snarl as the image of the man he hated most in the world overlaid his own.

Chapter 19

Stratton stood on a corner a block from the child-protection centre, looking toward its entrance. He checked his watch. He'd been there nearly fifteen minutes and had begun to wonder if a hiccup in the plan had developed, although that was not the reason he felt restless – he'd been feeling that way practically all day. And since he'd arrived at the centre he'd had one of those strange tingles in the back of his neck, a nudge from his senses to tell him that someone was watching him. But the street was empty of any other life. He put it down to a general feeling of stress, a reaction to the murders that he had carried out.

The sound of a gate clanging shut cut through the silence and he watched Vicky, George and Josh heading down the sidewalk towards him.

When Josh saw Stratton he ran to him. They hugged each other tightly. George caught up and stopped beside them, looking envious at the affection that Josh was receiving.

'How's it going, George?' Stratton asked as he ruffled the other boy's hair.

'I'm okay,' came the reply.

Stratton looked up as Vicky approached. 'Thanks,' he said to her.

She smiled, although it was obvious that she was nervous. 'Can we get away from here?' she said, looking over her shoulder. 'If Myers catches us I'm toast.'

Stratton led the way across the road. Within minutes they were in a taxi heading across town.

McDonald's had been voted, by the boys of course, as the eatery of choice and Vicky directed the driver to one such establishment on Venice Boulevard.

Traffic was light and they arrived at the location within ten minutes, all alighting while Stratton paid the fare. As they faced the famous fast-food restaurant their faces fell at the sight of boarding over the doors and windows and a sign across the front in large letters announcing that it was 'closed for renovations'.

'Damn,' Vicky muttered. 'It's closed.'

'Bummer,' George sighed.

'Now what?' she said, racking her brains for another location.

'Can't we just go to another?' George asked.

Josh held on to Stratton's hand, happy just to be out of the centre with him.

'What do you think?' Stratton asked.

'I can't think of anywhere close by,' Vicky said, looking a little frustrated. 'We'll have to get another cab, I guess.'

Stratton looked across the road where a large army-surplus shop occupied the corner, a broad banner across its front stating *WE DO WAR!*

'You guys got your soldiers with you?' he asked.

The boys dug into their pockets to produce a small

tank, an armoured car and a couple of dozen troops. Josh also had his little wooden camel.

'Why don't you go over to the park? I'll be back in a minute.'

Vicky glanced at Stratton and he winked at her.

'Okay,' she sighed. Although she was confident that Stratton had a solution to the problem she could not imagine what it might be. 'Come on.'

She took the boys' hands and headed down the street towards the patch of green that boasted a couple of mature trees. Stratton crossed the road and stepped into the store, ducking through a colourful collection of sleeping bags and rucksacks dangling on display in the entrance. Inside was an Aladdin's cave of camping and military paraphernalia. Ten minutes later he emerged with a bulging plastic bag.

Stratton joined the gang who had secured one of the two benches in the small park. Vicky sat patiently while the boys conducted a special forces assault at one end of the bench. Josh was firmly in command of the attacking forces and explained to his enemy commander that he couldn't shoot Josh's men scaling the bench legs because they did not have them in their sights below the cliff edge. George insisted that he had special guns that allowed him to shoot around corners – he'd read about them in a magazine somewhere.

They stopped the battle as soon as Stratton arrived and watched expectantly as he removed the contents of the bag. Vicky was equally curious, noting the slogan on the carrier bag which was the same as that on the banner across the front of the shop.

Stratton took out several heavy-duty plastic packages,

what looked at first glance like a regular can of food but with unusual markings and a ring at either end, and some bottles of Coke and water. He laid them out on the bench.

'What's that?' Josh asked.

'Lunch,' Stratton replied as he examined one of the packs. 'MREs. Meals ready to eat. Army food.'

'Wow!' George exclaimed. 'Real army food?'

'Soldiers' food for soldiers. Jambalaya or meat loaf in gravy?' he asked.

'What's jambalaya?' George asked.

'You're about to find out,' Stratton said, handing him the pack. He gave the meat loaf to Josh. 'Open up the bags and I'll show you how to prepare the meal.'

They pulled the packages open with some difficulty to reveal in each one two slender cardboard containers, a flat plastic bag with a green filament insert at the bottom, a brown plastic spoon and a clear packet containing an assortment of accessories. These included chewing gum, a flat pack of toilet paper, a tiny bottle of Tabasco sauce, and a wrap of wind-proof matches.

'I'll take those for now,' Vicky said, swiftly relieving the boys of their accessory bags. She'd spotted the gum and the matches.

'Okay, watch carefully,' Stratton said as he took George's package and one of the plastic bags with the green inserts, opened a bottle of water and poured a small amount into the bag. He then removed a silver foil bag from each of the cardboard containers – one labelled rice, the other jambalaya – and inserted them snugly into the bag with water in it. Then he folded the end over to form a seal.

'What are you doing?' Josh asked.

'Feel the bag,' Stratton said, holding it out to him.

Josh gripped the bag and immediately pulled his hand away. 'Wow! It's hot!'

'That's how soldiers heat up their meals in the field.'

George felt the bag and snatched his hand away too, yelping with surprise.

Josh took the meat-loaf package and copied what Stratton had done while George gingerly took hold of the top of his bag.

'In five minutes the foil bags'll be as hot as the outside one.'

George studied his bag, fascinated by the tiny bubbles that fizzled up from the bottom of it as the chemical reaction between the water and the green filament continued.

'Not too much water,' Stratton advised as Josh poured some into his bag. 'That's enough. Now put in your meat loaf and vegetables.'

Josh complied and the boys sat back, giving each other cheesy grins and staring at their bags as if they were television screens.

Vicky picked up the odd-looking can and examined it. 'Minced beef and vegetables,' she said, reading the label. 'This our lunch?'

'I haven't seen one of those in years,' Stratton said. 'It's a self-heating can. Same principle as the bags but a different method. See the ring on the bottom?'

Vicky turned it over to reveal a ring at the end of a piece of string whose other end disappeared inside the can.

'Pull it,' Stratton said.

Vicky tugged at it but it wouldn't budge.

'Harder,' he urged.

Vicky yanked harder on the string. It gave way as a small rod slid out. The can began to hiss. Vicky gasped and dropped it onto the bench.

'It's not a bomb,' Stratton said, grinning as he placed the can in the upright position. 'There's a small thermal element running up through the centre. Wait until it stops hissing, then pull back the ring on the top and enjoy.' With that, he took a plastic spoon from the carrier bag and offered it to her.

She took it with underwhelming enthusiasm, forced a smile and watched her lunch as it hissed away on the bench.

Stratton reached back into the bag and took out a couple of protein bars.

'You're not having an army meal?' Vicky asked.

'I've had enough MREs to last me a lifetime.'

Vicky gave him a suspicious look, then carried on watching her can as the hissing reached a climax before at last petering out.

'Go ahead,' Stratton said. 'It's ready.'

Vicky gingerly picked up the can that was now quite hot and, wrapping the empty carrier bag around it to protect her hand from the heat, took hold of the ring on the top. She pulled it back to reveal a dark brown stew-like substance. 'Hmm,' she said sarcastically. 'Yummy.'

Stratton grinned. 'Go ahead. Try it.'

'It looks like dog food.'

'Where's your sense of adventure?'

'If I was adventurous I'd have been an astronaut.'

Nevertheless, Vicky took a firm hold of her spoon and gingerly dipped it into the slush as if the can contained a mash of maggots. She scooped out a spoonful and held it up to inspect it. She looked away to see the others watching her: Stratton grinning and the boys chuckling as if she was about to eat a worm.

She put it to her lips. Then, deciding that she was being pathetic, she placed it in her mouth and chewed. She nodded as if it tasted okay, although her expression indicated otherwise. 'Not bad,' she said. 'And our guys go to war on this stuff?'

'Not any more. The MREs are new but that's got to be from the Korean War. Nineteen fifty-two or thenabouts, I reckon.'

Vicky's reaction was immediate and involuntary. She spat the food several metres away and grabbed the bottle of water to wash out her mouth as the three boys burst into laughter. She pulled open one of the accessory bags and took out some toilet paper. 'Apt,' she mumbled as she wiped her mouth and exhaled as she looked at the grinning faces.

'Am I just here to entertain you three?' she asked, acting seriously before a genuine grin formed on her face. 'To be honest, it wasn't that bad – but I'll pass on the rest if that's okay.'

Stratton offered her one of the protein bars, which she took.

'Can we eat ours now?' George asked.

'Sure,' Stratton said.

The boys opened the heating bags and carefully removed the foil packets of food. Stratton helped

George open his and dig out a spoonful. The boy put it in his mouth. 'It's good,' George said, digging out another spoonful by himself.

Josh tasted his and agreed with George. The boys went right back to their game while they ate.

'Can we go for a walk?' Vicky asked Stratton.

'Sure,' he said getting to his feet.

Stratton unwrapped his protein bar and took a bite out of it as they strolled around the edge of the park. Vicky unwrapped hers but started to speak before eating any.

'I have some good news for you, though you don't deserve any after trying to poison me.'

'You're a good sport.'

She smiled at the compliment, remembering how she used to be and how much her job had changed her over the years. But she pushed the self-pity aside, not wanting to spoil her afternoon. 'Josh's move back to the UK is almost finalised,' she announced. 'He could be out of here in three or four days.'

Stratton was pleased to hear it. 'Will I be able to take him back?'

'Technically, no. He'll be escorted onto the aircraft and the airline staff will look after him during the flight until he's met by a social worker at the other end. But I don't see why you shouldn't be on the same flight – I'll let you know the details as soon as I get them.'

'Thanks.'

Vicky smiled at him but couldn't hold the expression for long. Something sad inside was tugging at her.

Stratton noticed but didn't want to ask what was

bothering her, suspecting that he knew. 'Would you like to have dinner with me?' he asked.

Her smile returned. 'Sure. I'd like that very much.'

'So would I,' he said.

Vicky looked at Stratton softly and for a second he felt like a kid on his first date. It was a nice feeling although at the same time rather awkward. It seemed silly to think of the young woman and himself in any kind of a relationship but it was impossible not to toy with the idea. He was a man, after all, and she was attractive, intelligent, fun and easy to be with. Still, there was no way he would be able to come back to this town again, not for years, if ever.

He wondered what it would be like to be with Vicky in England. But as soon as the notion occurred it crumbled under the weight of reasons why it would never work. It was difficult enough to have a relationship with a local girl who had friends and family and probably a job to occupy her while he was away. But it would be selfish, maybe even cruel to bring home someone from a foreign land and expect them to wait around while he disappeared for weeks and often months at a time. Besides, Vicky was married to her job anyway. Still, undeniably, there was something very pleasant about being with her. For one thing, he seemed to be able to forget his troubles when they were together. 'Oh, Vicky,' he sighed out loud, not meaning to.

'What?' she asked.

'Nothing – I was just thinking how very nice it is to know you.'

'I was thinking the same thing.'

Stratton took her hand in a spontaneous gesture and kissed it. 'Good,' he said. 'Why don't we just forget all the problems we have at the moment, and the world's too for that matter, and just – well, I don't know. Forget them.'

'You know something, John Stratton? If there was anyone who could do that for me it would be you.'

They drew an inch closer together, brushed shoulders and carried on walking, enjoying each other's company. But in the back of Stratton's mind he was aware of a certain vulnerability that affection for a woman exposed him to. The feeling of endangerment had been bad enough where Josh was concerned but it was worse now. The uneasy premonition of earlier that morning was suddenly stronger than ever.

Valon Duka sat in the back of his nondescript blue van, watching Stratton and Vicky through a pair of binoculars from two hundred metres down the street. He had watched the child-protection centre for several hours that morning as instructed by Cano before the man who matched the description he'd been given had arrived on foot.

Duka was a surveillance expert, having learned his trade while serving ten years in the Sigurimi, the communist Albanian secret police. Now he worked for the syndicate both as an instructor and an operative on the higher-priority tasks. He was in his fifties, smoked close to three packs of cigarettes a day and drank vodka heavily at night. But when it came to his job he was a devoted professional.

Duka's techniques were old-school, using little in

the way of sophisticated modern technology beyond high-powered optics and, occasionally, listening devices. His stocks-in-trade were patience and thoroughness and his speciality was tailing. He was famous for achieving by himself what others using entire teams could not. His motto was 'Distance, distance, distance' and he preached endlessly to his students that the further one could get from one's target without losing contact the better. But the further back one kept the more easily one lost sight of one's prey. That was where Duka's particular genius lay: it was what separated him from others in his profession.

Duka had the uncanny ability to 'feel' where an out-of-sight target had gone, as well as the confidence and patience to persist even when it appeared to everyone else that he had made the wrong choice. His comrades back in the Sigurimi used to say that he could see through walls. When asked how he did it he said he could not explain, describing it as lucky, though in truth he did not know if that was so. It was an extra sense, like the sense of knowing when you are being watched.

The target this day had been easy enough though Duka could feel that the man had a kind of natural awareness that would not be obvious to an ordinary watcher. It served as a warning to Duka to be doubly cautious with him. But under these circumstance, even if the target had had no doubt that he was being followed Duka would have been very difficult to detect. The city was busy but not too busy, and American towns were the easiest of all to conduct surveillance in because nearly all of them were designed on the Roman grid system with all roads, or most at least, straight and heading north-south or east-west. This meant that the target did not need always to be followed directly and could be tailed along parallel routes. Two adults and two children together made it easier.

The move back from the park to the child-protection centre was even simpler since it quickly became obvious to Duka that the man and his companions were returning to the start location. He moved ahead of them along a parallel street and was already watching the centre from four blocks away before they arrived. After the man had left the woman and children where he had met them it was easy to keep him in sight while he walked down the street looking for a taxi. After that it was a straight run to the beach while keeping half a dozen vehicles between them. The final task was to house him and then watch the location for some time to establish it was indeed the target's home.

Duka knew nothing about the man he was following nor did he care. His mission that day was to obtain an address for the target and nothing else. He watched his man enter the building and a few minutes later saw a figure on the fourth floor heading along a corridor. He did not need to identify the apartment number. That would have been an unwise move during the first tailing of a new target and besides, Duka knew how Cano operated. As long as he had the building pinpointed there were many ways of finding out what else he needed to know.

As the sun set beyond the ocean, Duka left his

position leaning against the rails that lined the cliffs of the Santa Monica park opposite the pink towers. He walked to a small car park across the road where he had left his van. Once inside the vehicle he called Cano to give him the coded details of the day. Then he started the engine, pulled out into the traffic and headed for that first shot of fermented grain that would be waiting for him in his favourite watering hole downtown.

Chapter 20

Hobart was sitting back in his office chair, having read the last of his emails for that day. He was thinking about the Leka-Ardian killings as he had done pretty much continuously since hearing Phil's forensic revelations.

The main problem that Hobart was having was his inability to decide where to begin searching for clues to the identity of those behind the murders. Phil had given him a list of probable users of the explosive material, with NSA organisations at the top – an enormous investigative task on its own. Then there were the CIA, the DIA, several other intelligence groups that had anti-terrorist units, and half a dozen or so special forces groups that also used the stuff. Add to that the red tape he would have to wade through just to *talk* to any of those highly confidential, secret and top-secret organisations and the task became painful even to contemplate: Hobart would not be able to delegate much of the liaison work to his assistant due to the seriousness of the matter.

And then, of course, whoever the guilty party was could hog-tie any investigation with an arsenal of delaying devices, pleading national security and the like. Frankly, the odds against finding something and then being able to prove it were incalculable. What Hobart needed was a big fat clue to fall right out of the sky and land on his desk. Since he didn't believe in miracles he was pretty stumped.

Hobart got to his feet and looked out over the city as the last light faded. He hated this time of day. As if the stress of the job wasn't enough, he had to leave the office and join that mess of slow-moving traffic for at least an hour before he could pull out of it and into his quiet little backstreet in Van Nuys in the valley. If he was a drinking man he would wait out the worst of the traffic in one of the many bars up the street that would be filled with like-minded people at that time of day. But he wasn't.

A buzzer sounded and a voice came over a small intercom beside Hobart's computer monitor. 'Sir?' It was Hendrickson.

Hobart turned back to his desk and pushed a button on the intercom. 'Yes.'

'Do you have a minute to come look at something?'

'What's it about?'

'What you asked me to do, sir. I found something that doesn't fit.'

Hobart didn't reply. He walked out of his office, down the corridor, and into the agent pool a couple of doors away.

'What is it?' Hobart said as he stopped beside Hendrickson's desk by the window. Hendrickson was staring at his computer monitor. He sat up straight and started tapping on the keyboard, bringing up several windows.

'Well, sir. I've been going over Leka Bufi and Ardian Cano's careers and, well, there's really nothing—'

'You know I hate long introductions, Hendrickson. You're a talented researcher, which is why you work for me. But can you edit it a little.'

'Yes, sir. Sorry, sir. The most recent incident that connects the two is the Sally Penton murder – which we believe was coincidence, a wrong-place-wrong-time scenario. But since we're looking for the *un*obvious . . . Turns out her husband was British special forces. Our people in London were pretty helpful with information about him and sent me this one page.'

Something stirred in Hobart and he leaned on the desk to look at Jack Penton's photograph on the monitor. He had not briefed Hendrickson on Phil's forensics report yet and so the mention of special forces had hooked him.

'I thought I was onto something until I found out that he died on active service in Iraq nearly a month ago. I continued digging through his wife's – widow's – file and noticed that she made a phone call on her cellphone just before she died. It was to a UK cellphone in Austria – a man called John Stratton. I went back to my people in London and they just got back to me. All access to Stratton is denied. When they enquired further they were directed to the Brit Ministry of Defence where they ran into a wall. He's SIS, sir. The British Secret Intelligence Service.'

Hobart pondered the information for a moment

until he could mentally taste it. 'Get London to push harder. At least find out where he is.'

'He's here, sir. Or at least he was. He arrived in town the day after Sally Penton was killed.'

Hobart stood up and exhaled softly. He knew better than to jump to conclusions but despite the rule of never pinning the crime on the first person whom the hat fits something deep inside him was shouting that this was his man. Hobart's immediate feeling was relief that at least it wasn't an American outfit behind the killings. Suddenly it didn't seem like such a serious matter. It was bad in many ways – a Brit SIS operative carrying out a personal revenge operation on US soil – but it wasn't as big a deal as it had seemed that morning. He was hoping that the Brit was guilty and that it was not too good to be true.

'Okay,' Hobart said, getting down to business and sounding more like his old self than he had for a long time. 'Airports, car-hire companies, hotels, credit cards and cash machines. Let's find out if he's still in this country. And if he is, let's haul him in.'

Hobart then thought about something that Phil had said to him which now impressed him with its appropriateness. 'A long elevator ride underground,' he said softly.

'What was that, sir?' his assistant asked.

'Good work, Hendrickson. You've earned your weekend off.'

Hendrickson wanted to say something sarcastic but accepted the compliment with a smile. 'Do you want me to get onto it now, sir?'

'No. Give it to Gomez. You get on home.'

Hobart walked out of the office and back along the corridor to pick up his jacket and head home. He was feeling altogether better about things and the drive might not be so stressful after all. As he stepped into the office another thought gave him pause. He had planned to visit Skender in the morning to discuss a few things and wondered if he should warn him that there was an outside chance the person who had targeted Leka and Ardian might want revenge against him too. The possibility was a long shot since Skender had had nothing to do with the woman's death but Hobart's job was about covering every angle. On the other hand, he couldn't help smiling at the thought of this Stratton guy bumping off Skender. But, much as he hated the Albanian, at the end of the day he had a job to do and if it meant keeping that piece of scum alive then so be it. He would get across to Skender's office first thing in the morning.

As Hobart pulled his jacket on a couple more things suddenly niggled him. First, where had this Brit got the explosives from? He couldn't have known he was going to avenge Sally Penton's murder before he arrived in LA since he didn't know the details of her death. That meant he'd got the explosives while in the US. Second, where had he got the information about Leka and Ardian since the cops hadn't given it to him? If this Stratton guy was SIS he was well connected and the answers to both questions could well point in some intriguing directions. Stratton had to have a relationship with someone in US intelligence or the military. That could be interesting.

Hobart was in the doorway of his office when yet

another thought stopped him in his tracks. If he was going to warn Skender he should do it sooner rather than later.

He went back to his desk, flicked through a Rolodex and dialled a number on his phone. A second later it picked up. 'Is Skender there?' Hobart said.

'Who is this, please?' a female voice asked.

'Hobart. FBI.'

'One minute, please.'

Hobart looked out of his window while he waited with the phone to his ear. The traffic had not abated in the slightest.

'I'm afraid Mr Skender is busy at the moment,' the female voice said.

'Is that right,' Hobart said and put the phone down. Everything about the Albanian annoyed Hobart at the best of times but having him ignore a call from the Bureau made the FBI man's blood pressure rise.

He walked into the corridor, slamming the door of his office behind him. Five minutes later he was driving out of the car park, through the backstreets and towards Culver City. Traffic was heavy even on the smaller side streets but half an hour later Hobart arrived outside Skender's new building. It was floodlit so that workers could carry on throughout the night. He walked past the sentry box, ignoring calls from the perplexed security guard to show him some ID, and strode across the marble concourse and in through the entrance.

Cano was in the lobby, talking with a couple of his apes, as Hobart walked in followed by the security guard.

'Take me up to your boss,' Hobart ordered Cano.

'He just walked right on in, Mr Vleshek,' the security guard whined. 'Wouldn't show me no ID or nothin'.'

'Go back to your gate,' Cano said to the security guard, his stare fixed contemptuously on Hobart. 'Mr Skender expecting you?'

'I don't give a damn,' Hobart said looking around the lobby as if Cano himself was of little importance. 'Look, if he prefers he can come down to my office. Tonight, that is. And that's not a request, it's a demand.'

Cano smirked as if Hobart's demand was meaningless.

'Don't fuck around with me, Vleshek. Your boss is the one with friends in high places. No one said anything about you and I don't like you.'

Cano maintained his look of contempt as he pulled a phone from his pocket and punched in a number. The call was picked up after a few seconds. 'Hobart's here – in the lobby.'

There was a pause while he listened.

'He's acting pretty tough today,' Cano answered. Then he said 'Okay,' taking the phone away from his ear and pointing towards an open elevator. Hobart walked towards it and stepped inside, followed by Cano who placed a key-card in a slot and hit the penthouse button. Seconds later they were ascending fast.

They stood in silence together for a few seconds. Then Hobart glanced at Cano. 'How's the eye?' he asked.

Cano did not answer because he realised that Hobart had said it for no other reason than to poke fun at him.

Hobart knew that it was a childish comment but he enjoyed making it nonetheless. The fact was that these people had him over a barrel as long as his orders from on high were to treat them with kid gloves. He found it extremely frustrating.

The top-floor doors opened and Hobart followed Cano into the curved corridor, past the conference room behind its glass wall and on to a pair of large, elaborate doors. Cano pushed through them without knocking to reveal Skender wearing a white silk shirt open to his chest, white slacks and white leather loafers and seated in an armchair beside a large ornate oak desk as he perused a file. He took off a pair of reading glasses as he looked up and smiled as Hobart stopped in the centre of the room, facing him, Cano remaining by the doors.

'Well, General Hobart. The only honest Fed on the West Coast. So what do you think of my new building?'

Hobart looked around the room, nodding as if impressed. Two of the walls displayed a pair of modern and no doubt expensive abstract paintings and what appeared to be pieces of ancient pottery on stands were dotted around among the mixture of modern and antique furnishings. The ceiling's planes were angular, forming a point at one side of the room, the pinnacle of the pyramid. It was different.

'Interesting,' Hobart said. 'Who was the architect? Frank Lloyd Wrong?'

Skender grinned. 'Did you know, this is the first major construction of its size in this city to be built on time and under budget?'

'Yeah – I heard what happened to contractors who didn't turn up on time.'

'I don't know what you're talking about. Do you, Ivor?'

Cano shook his head slowly.

'Opening ceremony's in a week,' Skender continued. 'And you and Mrs Hobart are invited.'

'Can't wait. Are Mr and Mrs Bin Laden invited too?'

'I'm full of surprises, Hobart. You never know.'

'Save your horse crap for the people who eat it. This isn't a social call. I'm here to tell you that your time's running out. You'd better start shaking that tree of yours a little harder. Those two traffickers you turned over to us, Bavero and Puta, were your meal ticket for last month. I want someone new and bigger for this month. And don't worry. Unlike those prick friends of yours in the administration I'm not expecting you to hand over Bin Laden. We both know you probably have more chance of delivering the Man in the Moon. While I remember, here's a to-do item for you to slip under a fridge magnet. I want something by the end of this week or the opening ceremony is about all you'll ever see of this place. I'll give you a lead. Over a ton of heroin hit the East Coast last month, ferried in by mules from Sicily. That's an Albanian trade route. I want to close it down. That'll buy you next month's freedom. And you should know that I'm going to keep on your back either until you're all dried up or until your friends tear you apart to stop themselves ending up on your list. And another thing. The amnesty honeymoon's over. The next employee of yours who steps out of line I'm putting them in chains. Have I made myself clear?'

Skender looked totally unperturbed as he picked a speck of fluff from his shirt, got to his feet and placed the file on his desk. He put his hands in his pockets and strolled over to Hobart, stopping a few feet in front of him. He stifled a yawn as he removed his glasses and rubbed his eyes. 'Sorry. You were sending me to sleep.'

Skender put his glasses in his pocket and took a long look at Hobart. 'You don't live in the real world, Hobart. You think you do but you don't. You know, we have this little bird in Albania, lives in the mountains, a bit like your road runner. It's like a little chicken but it ain't good to eat. But this little bird makes a lot of noise all the time. It walks around screaming and screeching like it's in charge of everything. It thinks it's more important than it is. People usually leave it alone because it's kind of funny, the way it struts around. But if one comes into your house and starts squawking, which they sometimes do, well, that can be too much and there's only one way to shut them up.'

'Is that supposed to be a threat?'

'It's just a story, Hobart. A little slice of life in Albania. It's the way we live. We'll never change. But you're too stupid to see that.'

'I like it when people think I'm stupid. It feels so much better when I'm waving goodbye to them as they walk down that dark tunnel to the cell at the end of it.' Hobart started to walk away, then thought of something else. 'Oh, one more small thing. The guy

317

who killed Leka Bufi and Ardian Cano. He may be coming after you. I'm not telling you out of any concern for you. It's just that *I* want to be the one who puts you away, not him. Do I need your card to go down in the elevator?' he asked Cano.

Cano shook his head.

'I'll see myself out,' Hobart said as he walked on, pausing in the doorway to look around the room. 'I wonder what we'll do with this building when you're gone – it'll become state property, you know.' Hobart smiled and headed along the corridor to the elevator.

Skender gave a long sigh and shook his head. 'He's annoying, isn't he?' he said as he went back to his desk, sat behind it and stared at the ceiling in thought. 'Did you find out anything more about this Englishman – what was his name?'

'Stratton. We have the building he lives in. An apartment block in Santa Monica.'

'How would you do it?'

'Bring in a team from out of town. There'll be no connection to us.'

Skender pondered it further as he looked at Cano. 'You can have him. Just make sure it's clean.'

Cano nodded and left the room.

Skender swivelled in his chair to face the glass window. His life had been about staying one step ahead. The fact that he was still alive was proof of that for in his game to lose meant to die. Hobart and the FBI could not even begin to match the nemeses he'd faced down in his sixty years but neither could they be ignored. Skender wasn't worried about ending up in any jail. He would leave the USA long before that became even a remote possibility. But he enjoyed his life in America, his home in the hills overlooking the city, his new office building and his plans to create a legitimate empire. He needed time and would find another little fish to throw to them. The Sicilian connection was out of the question since he controlled that himself but there were other things he could offer.

One thing was for sure: Skender would not allow Hobart or the Feds to dictate to him. They would accept what he gave them and in his own good time, not theirs. Meanwhile he would cultivate his contacts among the higher echelons of American bureaucracy. Those were the ones who would one day tell the Bureau that Skender had done enough and proved himself worthy to join their community. Money was everything and if you could not buy the Hobarts of this world or the people above them you kept going higher still until you found someone you *could* buy. It was as simple as that and it was why Skender could sleep peacefully at night.

Skender picked up the file. It contained a collection of art catalogues from his interior designers and with only a couple more days left to put in his order he continued looking through it. The building would not be completely finished for the opening ceremony next week but it would look as if it was. There were a handful of minor technical problems but the construction and decorating would be completed. Skender was pleased with the way things were going. The invitation list was impressive and many of the bigger names including the governor, the mayor and three senators had already RSVP'd. He turned the page to a Botticelli with an asking price of six figures. To Skender it looked like cheap porn but the designer thought it would look good in the lobby so he ticked the 'yes' box.

Hobart walked out of the building and across the concourse towards his car. Outwardly he looked his normal serious self but inside he was angry. While listening to himself spouting off in Skender's office he had realised what it was that he hated most about the man. Skender was bullet-proof as far as the Bureau was concerned. He could keep feeding them crap for years and get away with it. As long as he kept giving them something with the ultimate promise of one day delivering big he could keep Hobart off his back for God only knew how long. Hobart knew he would not get the support for any threats he made and would be told to cool it if he tried.

It was times like this, cases like this that made Hobart want to quit. Maybe Phil was right, but Hobart couldn't give in to the temptation. His wife had given up. That was why she had been happy to quit the column in the *Washington Post* and come out to LA. Recently she had taken to leaving around the house articles describing properties and lifestyles in the Carolinas. The money they could get for the house in the Valley would buy them a small mansion in that part of the country. He would have no problems getting a job as a security adviser to some corporation on the East Coast. His wife had given him thirty good years and deserved it and the truth was that he also owed it to himself. He was burning out. He decided he was going to pour himself a small whiskey when he got home and take a look at those articles.

Just the thought of it made Hobart feel a bit better and that, sadly, was a bad sign. The problem if he resigned now would be his conscience. He would have to convince himself that he was leaving the Bureau because it was the right time to do so and not running away because he had failed. What he needed was one last success. But he knew that the only kind of success that would do the trick was the impossible one of putting Skender away.

As Hobart climbed into his car he paused to grimace and shake his head. The day had not ended well after all and he told himself that he should've gone home from his office and quit while he was ahead.

Chapter 21

Stratton and Vicky were seated at a small table in the back of an elegant bistro on Main Street, Venice. A waiter was filling two white china cups in front of them with coffee.

'Thank you,' Vicky said as he left. 'Cream?' she asked Stratton as she picked up the little jug.

'Thanks,' Stratton said and she poured some into both cups. 'I read somewhere that most of the population of California weren't born here. You one of those?'

'No. I was born three hours north of here in a small town called Caliente, a few miles from Bakersfield. My roots are Cornish.'

'As in Cornwall, England?'

'Yep. Caliente used to be a mining town. Great, great, great-whatever grandfather Whitaker was a miner. He came over in the 1800s – the Gold Rush after the tin and copper ran out in Cornwall. Caliente's local store still sells Cornish pasties. I lived near an old abandoned mine. I used to explore it all the time as a kid, until my dad found out.'

'So you were adventurous when you were a kid?'

'Until I learned fear, I guess. My dad started telling me all kinds of horror stories about mine accidents until I couldn't bear to go inside one again. And now I sit at a desk. Isn't your work sometimes dangerous?'

'Sometimes.'

'After two hours you know everything there is to know about me, which is pretty sad when you come to think about it. All I know about you is that you were orphaned when you were six years old and ended up in an orphanage. Then you joined the military when you were eighteen. That's not fair.'

'You don't want to hear the whole story on our first date, do you?'

'No, but maybe a little more. I like hearing about how you grew up and what you do.' Vicky smiled. 'How about some war stories, then?'

'I can't think of anything more boring than a guy telling a girl war stories to try and impress her.'

'You haven't tried to impress me at all – which is nice. Something tells me there's a whole lot about you that's impressive, though. You can tell me one little war story if you want.'

'You shouldn't talk about your own combat exploits. It's not dignified.'

'You never tell your war experiences to anyone?'

'Not to people who aren't in the business.'

'Go on. Please. Just a little one. You know, my life is pretty boring to say the least and I've never met a real soldier before, not one like you.'

Stratton played with his cup while he thought. Then he gave an audible sigh. 'You want to hear a war story, do you?'

'Yes,' Vicky said, sitting up and preparing herself to be entertained.

'Okay – a story to glorify war. You heard of a place called Northern Ireland?'

'I've heard of Ireland, obviously. Didn't you guys have some problems over there a few years ago?'

'Some. Well, one day I was in Belfast railway station – Belfast is the capital city of Northern Ireland. It was during the rush hour and, much like any main-line station you can imagine, it was pretty crowded. People were getting on and off trains while hundreds of others watched the boards showing departure times, destinations, platforms, cancellations – that sort of stuff.

'In the middle of the station was a lone British soldier on guard duty, wearing his camouflage outfit and carrying a rifle over his shoulder. He wasn't really being a soldier right then, more like playing the part of a police officer. He was eighteen years old, fresh from his basic training, and he'd been in Ireland all of three weeks. He was a nice young lad, hadn't achieved much in school, never made the school soccer team despite playing his heart out at every game, but he wanted to make something of himself and so he joined the army. He was the kind of kid that bullies would pick on in school and he hoped that the army would toughen him up. Not that he wanted to be a soldier all his life, he didn't really know what he wanted, but he felt it was the best start that he could give himself, considering his limited opportunities.

'His mum thought the army was a good choice but she didn't want him to go to Northern Ireland because of the troubles. The way the news told it there were bombs going off every minute and terrorists sniping at soldiers all over the place – which was an exaggeration, though the place had its dangers for sure. Anyway, off he went to Ireland and found his first post as a sentinel in Belfast railway station.

'That afternoon, as he was standing around and looking forward to his break in an hour or so, a couple of mothers with pushchairs and toddlers were heading across the station and when they saw the soldier they began to abuse him. They were Catholics and he represented the British occupiers who'd been murdering their kind for centuries. Their children were being brought up to hate the British and, well, if the young English soldier had been asked to explain why, he would have been pushed to answer. He didn't really know what the conflict was about in truth but he was a soldier and it was his job to obey orders. He'd been excited initially about going to Northern Ireland but that soon wore off after he got there.

'Anyway, the mothers could see that he was just a boy and nervous at that and started telling him to get out of their country. Then one of them spat at him, which was immediately copied by one of the children and another child ran up to him and kicked him in the leg. The soldier wasn't sure how to handle the situation since he'd never been told what to do in such circumstances and so he just stood there and took the abuse.

'Suddenly a shout rang out somewhere in the station close by. It was a single loud cry from a man in the crowd. The soldier never saw him nor made out what he shouted. Then he saw an object bouncing along the station floor towards him. It was a hand grenade, no bigger than a tennis ball. He'd used them once in training and since then he'd never seen another. But he knew instantly what it was.

'The grenade rolled to a stop a few feet away from the young soldier, right in front of the children and their mothers. Time slowed to a crawl for him as he watched the evil device hissing on the ground, the children looking at it, frightened, though they did not know why. They were fixed to the spot as if in a trance. The mothers knew what it was all right and moved to grab their children. But it was obvious to the soldier that they would never get out of the way in time. He probably never knew what made him do it – an instinct, perhaps. You see, he was a good man with no malice in his heart and far too young to be a cynic. He dived past the children and threw himself onto the grenade as it went off.

'I arrived a few seconds after the explosion and saw the boy lying there, face down, unmoving, smoke drifting out from beneath him. The two mothers were holding their frightened children and staring at the soldier in stunned silence. Then one of them got to her knees and crawled to the body and reached out to it. She shook the boy and said something, then crept closer and remained on her knees by his side and began to cry. She lowered her head and started to shake the dead boy while chanting something. I walked closer as soldiers came running across the station concourse and I could hear that she was asking him to forgive her. She kept saying it over and over again: Forgive me. Dear God. Forgive me. She was the last person he had seen alive and she had spat at him, and then he had saved her children's lives and at that moment it was beyond her comprehension . . . They gave the boy's mother a medal, I think.'

Vicky was trying to fight back a tear. But she failed and touched her eyes with her napkin.

Stratton took a sip of his coffee and stared at his cup after replacing it in its saucer.

'I'll never ask you to tell me a war story again,' Vicky said. 'I'm sorry. I didn't realise what you were trying to say.'

'I didn't mean to upset you,' he said.

'I think you did, but I deserved it.'

They sat in silence for a while before leaving the restaurant and catching a taxi back to Santa Monica. Stratton had asked the cab to take Vicky home first but she insisted on dropping him off since he lived on the way. When the cab pulled up outside Stratton's apartment block she climbed out with him.

'You sure about this?' he asked as the taxi pulled away.

Vicky looked over her shoulder. 'Too late. Taxi's gone. I'd like to come up if that's okay – unless you don't want me to.'

Stratton smiled and put his arm around her. They walked into the building.

Across the road, in the darkness beyond the palm trees in the park, a man who was watching them pulled a cellphone from his pocket and brought up a number.

The call was answered by a man in the back of a saloon car parked in the alleyway behind Stratton's apartment building. He listened for a moment, disconnected the call and dialled a number. 'He just arrived with some chick,' he said in a Chicago accent to two men in the front.

On the roof of a three-storey building behind the apartment block a man squatting behind a row of air-conditioning units answered his cellphone. Then he crouched lower and concentrated on the windows of Stratton's apartment across the alley and a floor higher than him.

The elevator arrived on the fourth floor and Stratton and Vicky stepped out of it. There was no one else around and as they walked towards his door Vicky stopped to enjoy the view from the corridor window.

'This is beautiful,' she said. 'You can see all the way up the coast to Malibu. Do you have this view from your apartment?'

'No,' he said, coming alongside her and taking in the view himself.

The moon was up, half of it at least, its white light bathing the sea between the tall palms. Vicky moved close to Stratton and looked up at him. He faced her and moved his lips to meet hers. They kissed gently, her hand coming up to touch his face.

Their breathing quickened. Stratton moved back and held Vicky's hand as he retrieved his key from his pocket with his free hand and led her towards his door. As he reached it he let go of Vicky and gripped the doorknob while inserting the key into the lock. He stopped before turning it. Some kind of soapy film was smeared on the doorknob. He put his hand to his nose and smelled it. Marzipan. He tensed as every one of his senses screamed to full alert. There was only one thing he knew that smelled of marzipan – besides marzipan itself – and that was plastic explosive.

'What is it?' Vicky asked.

Stratton shot a glance up and down the empty corridor, then took hold of her hand again. 'Come with me,' he said softly as he led her quickly back down the corridor.

She could sense the tension in him. 'John, what is it? Are you going to tell me?'

'Just stay there,' Stratton said as he steered her around the corner to the small alcove in front of the elevators where there was also an emergency-exit door. Beside it was a small table with a pot of plastic plants and an ashtray on it. Stratton took his notebook from his pocket, tore out part of a sheet, wiped his hand, went to the small table and, keeping his back to Vicky, undid the fly of his trousers and peed into the ashtray. She leaned a little to try and look past him, wondering what on earth he was doing.

Stratton dipped the paper in the urine, shook off the excess liquid, took a lighter from his pocket, lit it and held the flame under the paper. As the paper began to turn purple it crackled, giving off tiny sparks. Stratton dropped it in the urine and went back to look at the door. The small test had proved his suspicions correct. Someone who had handled plastic explosives had been in his apartment.

Stratton's immediate fear was for Vicky but he couldn't let her go until he knew precisely where the focus of the attack was. Someone wanted to kill him and he had to assume that they were professionals and had a back-up plan – which meant that

Vicky was in danger whether or not the apartment was the target.

He opened the fire-exit door carefully and looked up and down the dingy, poorly lit metal and concrete stairwell. There was no sign of life and he came back to Vicky's side.

'Stay here. If I tell you to go I want you to take those stairs down to the bottom and then get away from the building as fast as you can.'

'What's wrong? You're scaring me.'

'Please, Vicky. Trust me.'

She looked at him strangely but there was nothing else that Stratton could say. 'Just stay here and don't move,' he said, holding her shoulders firmly. Then he released her and walked back down the corridor to his apartment.

He took out his key, placed it in the lock, turned the handle slowly and pushed open the door just enough to allow his fingers inside. He ran his hand along the top of the door, down the edge and along the bottom. If there was a trigger, whoever laid it would have had to be able to set it and remove their hand before closing the door. Stratton could feel nothing unusual and so he opened the door carefully and looked around the immediate area. He dropped to his knees and crept inside, all the time scanning for anything out of place. There were several types of improvised explosive devices or IEDs that could be used in a situation like this. Mechanical triggers could be either a 'push', activated by pushing something like a door against it, a 'pull' such as a trip wire, a pressure-activated mechanism set off by, for example, stepping on something, or a pressure-release contrivance detonated by lifting a weight off the device. Another type was a command-detonation charge such as a radio-controlled unit.

Stratton moved carefully through the room, keeping low in the darkness. The moonlight shone through the windows, which helped a little. But he did not want to turn on the lights in case a bomb was wired to the electricity or was light-sensitive. Also, someone could be outside, waiting for a sign that the apartment was occupied.

The living room and adjoining kitchen appeared to be clear as far as he could tell from his position on the floor. He kept on his hands and knees as he headed towards the bedroom and bathroom. As he reached his bedroom door he immediately noticed that the counterpane on the bed was not as neatly spread as he had left it. He lowered his face to the floor. He could not see underneath the bed since the counterpane touched the carpet on all sides so he crawled forward and slowly raised an edge to reveal a box set squarely beneath the bed frame. It was sealed, had no protrusions and in its location was unlikely to have a mechanical switch since he was clearly not expected to find, let alone touch it.

Stratton moved a little closer, stretched out a hand, gently took hold of the box and slid it out from under the bed. It was a shoebox with no lid and inside was a large cube of white plastic explosive wired to a battery and a cellphone. There was a good pound and a half of the stuff, Stratton estimated, enough to completely gut the room and shred anyone inside. It was a classic terrorist device of moderate sophistication, intended to detonate when the cellphone was called. It told him a little about its creator insofar as it had been handmade in a garage rather than mass-produced in a factory.

Stratton disconnected one of the wires from the detonator, thereby rendering the device safe, and took a moment to consider his options. 'Who?' and 'Why?' were the burning questions. The most obvious links were with the two Albanians he had killed. How their colleagues had found him was the next question. He had slipped up somewhere – seriously.

Thinking about the cellphone Stratton realised it was highly likely that someone was watching the apartment, waiting to dial the number and detonate the device. Stratton had obviously not been seen entering the apartment itself, suggesting that the bomber was outside somewhere and watching the windows for the lights to go on or some other sign of life inside.

Stratton crept around the bed to the window and raised himself sufficiently to see over the sill. It was not a good enough position and he moved to the edge of the window, got to his feet and stood back. A brief scan of the nearby rooftops through the blinds revealed a man doing a bad job of concealing himself behind a row of air-conditioning units and looking in Stratton's direction. The man then put something to his ear, a cellphone perhaps, and moved to the parapet to look below.

Stratton pulled a chair over to the window and climbed onto it, enabling him to see down into the alleyway. Halfway along it, towards Santa Monica

Boulevard, he saw a car with a man standing outside it with his hand to his ear, the rear door open beside him.

The man climbed back inside the saloon and closed the door. 'Guy ain't in his room yet,' he said to the two men in the front.

'Maybe they're makin' out in the corridor,' said the front passenger.

'They could be startin' on the living-room floor in the dark. Ain't you guys got any imagination? They'll get to the bedroom soon enough,' suggested the driver.

The older guy in the back sighed and laid his head back. 'I hope he don't take all night. I got reservations at the Tropicana.'

Stratton stepped down off the chair and considered his options. His most urgent need was to get away from the apartment building and find somewhere to hide for a couple more days. But he could not decide if he should do anything about the would-be assailants first. There was a certain logic in going on the offensive since he might destroy some of those who were after him, thus reducing the extent of any future threat. And if Cano was in the car and Stratton got rid of him the impetus of the vendetta might lessen when the driving force behind it was dead. The next question was what did he have to lose by trying. The answer to that was clearly nothing and it was therefore a risk worth taking. Still, the clock was ticking and he had to make a decision quickly. The pros: Cano had tried to kill him and Vicky and would try again.

Offing the bastard was a matter of survival, plain and simple. The cons: there weren't any – he'd killed two Albanians already and a couple more wouldn't make a whole lot of difference.

Stratton kept low as he moved around the bed with the bomb, grabbed a towel from the bathroom and, half-crawling through the living room, returned to the front door and stepped back into the corridor, silently closing the door behind him.

As he walked towards the elevators he wrapped the box in the towel. Vicky was waiting where he had left her. Before she could utter a word he took her by the arm and led her back along the corridor, past his apartment and towards the fire exit at the end.

'Are you going to tell me what all this is about?' she asked, sounding a little annoyed.

'No. I can't Vicky. It's better you don't know,' Stratton said as he took her hand. Together they raced down the stairs.

Stratton paused at the bottom, opened the door slightly and looked out. If someone was still watching the lighted entrance the chances were that they would not see the darkened emergency-exit door open further down the street. It was a chance that he had to take.

'Go left and keep walking. I'll catch you up in a few seconds. Go.'

Stratton practically pushed Vicky out through the door and she immediately started to walk away. He found an empty beer can by the stairs and placed it carefully against the bottom of the door frame. Then he stepped outside, letting the door shut against the can, and hurried down the street.

He caught Vicky up before she reached the corner and walked around it with her before stopping her with a gentle pressure on her arm. 'You keep walking up this street and catch the first taxi you see. Please don't ask me anything now. I'll call you at the centre tomorrow, okay?'

She studied him for a moment, not afraid any more but deeply concerned. She glanced at the bundle under his arm, then looked into his eyes again. 'Okay,' she finally said. 'You'll call me tomorrow?'

'First thing,' he said.

Vicky looked very disappointed as she lowered her gaze and walked away from him up the street.

Stratton watched her get twenty yards ahead before following. As she crossed the road she hailed a taxi and he turned the corner towards Santa Monica Boulevard. He looked back to see her climb in and as it pulled away he broke into a jog.

Less than a minute later Stratton was standing on the corner at the end of the alleyway, looking at the back of the sedan parked twenty yards away. Pedestrians walked past him on the busy boulevard, no one taking any notice of him. He uncovered the box and attached the wire he had disconnected. He looked up to check that the man on the roof was not visible, then moved quickly at the crouch into the darkened alley along the wall, dropping to his knees as he reached the car. He quickly pushed the bundle underneath it, scurried back to the busy boulevard and broke into a run, back around the block the way he had come. He slowed to a fast walk as he approached the emergency exit of the apartment building. He stepped inside, kicked away the beer can and ran up the stairs, not stopping until he reached his door.

Stratton stepped inside, paused to take a few deep breaths and turned on the light.

He removed his jacket, dropped it onto the back of a chair and went into his bedroom. He turned on the light and drew the curtains.

The cellphone on the seat beside the man in the back of the saloon rang and he picked it up, listened a moment then lowered it as he cut off the caller. He dialled a number. 'About time,' he said. 'Hope he's gettin' laid. Nothin' like going out with a bang is what I always say.' He punched in the last number then hit the call button.

The explosion rattled Stratton's windows. He looked round the side of the bedroom curtain to see the car in flames, its rear end practically destroyed by the detonating fuel tank.

Stratton dug his pack out of the wardrobe, crammed all his clothes into it, hurried into the bathroom to collect his washing stuff and went back into the living room. He pulled on his jacket, took the CIA explosives pack out of one of the kitchen cabinets and jammed it into his bag, which he now zipped up. Then he left the apartment. He hurried along the corridor back to the emergency stairwell, took the stairs several at a time and stepped out onto the street.

Stratton walked past the entrance to the alleyway where a crowd had gathered to stare at the burning car, and along Second Street where he searched for a taxi. His plan was to find a cheap hotel in another part of town, wait for Josh's release and then get the hell out of the country. But one thing was worrying him. Whoever had tried to hit him might know about Josh and possibly about Vicky too. That was a major cause of concern and one for which he had no immediate solution. One possibility was to kidnap Josh from the centre but that option was a minefield. Another was to go to Vicky, except that he did not know where she lived and had no home or cellphone number for her.

A cab pulled over. As Stratton climbed in he had a terrible feeling that things might be falling apart for him.

Chapter 22

Stratton awoke the following morning in a seedy hotel that had been recommended by the taxi driver. It was in Mar Vista, midway between west and central LA. The area appeared to have more Hispanics and blacks than whites in it, judging by the characters on the street. When Stratton had asked the driver about going further east the man had said that he wouldn't like to speculate on Stratton's survival prospects, seeing as he was way too white to be going any further east in that part of town.

The hotel room, which smelled of tobacco smoke, was basic to say the least. It had a TV, en-suite shower, a cigarette-burned carpet with matching sideboard and the added feature of a vibrating bed – five minutes per quarter, according to the slot machine bolted to the wall above the side table. Stratton slept fitfully and awoke early. After taking a shower he checked the local news station on the TV and heard a report of the exploding car in Santa Monica. It was described as possibly a gang-related fuel-tank sabotage but the report gave no other details.

Stratton had planned to be at the child-protection centre for eight-thirty a.m. but could not find a taxi until he had walked a mile towards the beach. As the cab approached the centre he leaned forward in the back seat to look through the windscreen at a street that was unusually busy. Several of the vehicles were police cars.

The cab stopped on the corner and Stratton jumped out, paid the driver and hurried to the entrance. But as he was about to open the gate a police officer stopped him.

'Excuse me, sir,' the officer said, barring his way. 'Do you have business here?'

'Not exactly,' Stratton said, playing it cautious while at the same time growing increasingly concerned.

'Then you'll have wait back over there,' the officer said, pointing down the sidewalk.

'What's happened?' Stratton asked.

'I can't say, sir. Now you'll have to step back, please.'

Stratton looked towards the building entrance to see Vicky walking out of the building while talking to a police officer. He moved along the fence, hoping to catch her eye, willing her to look his way. She stopped at the top of the steps and as the officer wrote something in his notebook she looked up and froze as her gaze met Stratton's. The officer asked her another question and she had to look away from Stratton while she answered. Then she stared back at him, this time with a strange look in her eyes. The officer said something else to her to which she nodded. Then he walked away.

Vicky paused uncertainly before heading along the narrow path towards the gate, past the officer on guard and down the sidewalk towards Stratton. As she approached he started to speak. But she cut him off, her voice quiet yet harsh. 'I need to talk to you,' she said, moving ahead of him and around the corner before stopping and turning to face him. She looked fraught and strung out, her gaze roving everywhere before settling on him.

'Just tell me one thing first,' Stratton said, grabbing her shoulder. 'Is Josh okay?'

Vicky brusquely shook his hands away, an expression of horror and suspicion on her face. 'This morning as Dorothy was arriving two men walked in behind her and asked to see him,' she said, keeping her voice low. 'They said they were police officers and wanted to ask him some questions. They showed her their badges. I wasn't here yet, nor was Myers. Dorothy should have waited for one of us but she went and got Josh anyway and they grabbed him.'

Shortly after she had begun speaking Stratton's hands had gone to the sides of his head. He closed his eyes, knowing what was coming.

'They punched Dorothy to the floor when she tried to stop them and then they left. The security guard was just arriving and they beat him up on the porch and took his gun. No one saw the car they got into or where they went.'

Stratton could not quite control himself yet. He walked past Vicky, his fists clenched tightly. When his eyes opened they looked wild but he could say nothing, his mind in turmoil.

'The police asked me to tell them everything about Josh,' Vicky went on. 'I told them about you. I . . . I thought you might have had something to do with it. After last night – I didn't know what to think. I saw the news this morning – the car that exploded outside your apartment building. It happened just after I left. You had something to do with that, didn't you? Don't lie to me, John. I know you did.'

Stratton didn't react to her, as if she was no longer there, his mind already focusing on other things: formulating, calculating, planning, seething, hating.

'Stratton!' Vicky shouted. 'I'm asking you a question. You know what this is all about, don't you?'

Stratton looked away, shaking his head, not in denial of her question but in disbelief at this turn of events. All he could think of was how miserably he had failed the people he loved, not only Josh but his mother and father too. Josh had been taken out of revenge for what Stratton had done. He, John Stratton of the SIS and SBS, should have seen it coming: in a way he had but he'd been too slow to act. He should have gone to the centre last night and taken Josh away himself. But he had been complacent, worried about repercussions that would have been nothing compared to those that would now result from Josh being kidnapped by Skender's people – it had to be them for there was no one else to suspect. Stratton had gambled with Josh's life. The little boy had trusted him, innocently placed all his hopes in the one person he had left in the world who could help him – and Stratton had betrayed him with sheer incompetence.

'John! Talk to me, for God's sake!'

Stratton finally looked up into Vicky's tormented eyes. 'It's me they want,' he said.

'Who are "they"?' she asked, getting frustrated.

'The people who tried to kill me, – us, in fact –
last night. You would have died too.'

Vicky didn't understand. There was too much information and too little clarification. 'Why did they take
Josh?'

Stratton was afraid to answer the question. Any
answer would sound pathetic. 'Revenge,' was all he
could say.

'For what?' she insisted.

'They killed Josh's mother so I killed them. It's quite
simple, really,' he said, getting angry himself. 'It's probably the stupidest thing I've ever done in my life,' he
added.

Vicky still did not know what to make of it but
Stratton's pain and feelings of guilt were obvious. 'Why
didn't you come to me, tell me? I might have been
able to help.'

Maybe she was right. Maybe she could have helped
him get Josh away if she had really understood the
situation. But that was hindsight and Stratton doubted
that she would have felt able to aid him last night. It
didn't matter now.

'We have to tell the police,' Vicky said.

'That won't help him.'

'That's ridiculous. If the police know who took him
they can get him back.'

'The people who took him don't care about the
police. They *own* the police.'

'I can't believe that,' she said.

'Listen to me,' Stratton snapped at her. 'They are
Muslim Albanians and will never admit to kidnapping
him. They want me and when they have me they'll

kill Josh too. They have no hearts, no pity, no code other than never giving way to anything other than death. It's how they've lived for hundreds of years and nothing will change that. Do you understand?'

Tears rolled down Vicky's face as the truth of what he'd said hit home. Some of the tears were for Josh but some were for herself. She had dreamed about this man she thought might be the shining knight in her sad, lonely life and who was going to take her away from all this, and now it was over. He was an enigma and she realised that she had known no more about him the night before – when she had been prepared to give herself to him – than she did now. She began to wonder if he was actually something dark and terrible. There was evidence of that in his eyes, sure enough. Now they were filled with malevolence of an intensity that she had never seen before.

Vicky did not realise that she had stepped back from Stratton in reaction to a sudden pang of fear, for Josh as well as for herself. 'Who are you?' she asked softly.

It was as if he could read her thoughts. 'I'm sorry for you,' Stratton said. He stepped away from her, his thoughts on the police around the corner, wondering whether she would tell them that he was there. 'I'm Josh's only chance,' he told her, hoping that she would believe it, then, disturbingly, doubting it himself.

Vicky remained where she was, transfixed as he walked away.

When Stratton was out of sight she lowered her eyes as she felt something inside her crumble away, perhaps her last vestige of hope. Her life's experiences so far had shown her more than anything else what a rotten world this was. The original idea of devoting herself to healing the lost souls of children had been intended to give some purpose to her life. But after so many years all she was left with were mostly stories of sadness and broken hearts, and instead of building her own sense of self-worth she had become as much a victim as those in her charge. Perhaps that was why she sympathised with their plight as much as she did: she often felt less like a healing angel and more like the inept leader of a hopelessly lost flock.

Vicky's hands came up to her face and she began to cry like a baby.

Chapter 23

Hobart stood at the bedroom window of Stratton's former Santa Monica apartment, looking down onto the alley where he could see a large scorch mark surrounding a sizeable scoop in the tarmac. During the immediate follow-up investigation the police had found the apartment manager beaten and tied up in his room. When they took the tape from his mouth he immediately started ranting about how two men had arrived in the early evening, enquiring about accommodation. Then they'd suddenly taken him at gunpoint to his room and asked about an Englishman named Stratton. As soon as he had provided a key to the apartment they'd tied him up.

When Stratton's name hit the police communications network it was automatically filtered out to Hobart's department as per his request. The occupants of the blown-up sedan had been identified as Chicago hoods and Hobart surmised that Skender had found the identity of Leka and Ardian's killer and attempted his own revenge.

Hobart was impressed as well as disturbed with the Albanians' intelligence-acquisition network that had located Stratton quicker than the FBI had been able to. Skender had obviously brought in outside hitters to cover his involvement but Hobart wondered if the man knew precisely who he was up against. This Stratton guy was obviously skilled, judging by the hits in the court cells and the restaurant, but this counter-hit, whatever it was that he had done exactly, displayed an alertness and initiative under pressure that were, frankly, outstanding. The Chicago goons had obviously come for Stratton and somehow he had turned the tables on them.

One thing that continued to niggle Hobart was Skender's reasoning behind this attempt on Stratton. Hobart was well aware of the Albanian propensity for revenge but Ardian and Leka were not related to Skender. On top of that Skender must have been angry with the two idiots for stepping out of line in the first place. Going one step further, Skender might even have appreciated Stratton taking revenge for Sally's murder although that was a speculation beyond Hobart's knowledge of Albanian redemption protocol. Hobart found it too hard to accept that Skender would risk his special relationship with the Feds for those two idiots. If he was forced to, he would have to put it down simply to the arrogance of the man.

Whatever the answer, Hobart was now faced with a double duty: to find Stratton to protect him from the Albanians – and them from him.

An FBI forensics officer stepped into the room. He was wearing a thin pair of rubber gloves. 'Okay to do in here now, sir?'

Hobart walked out of the bedroom. He paused in the living room where another forensics officer was at work, brushing the dust off the small dining table and sweeping it into a plastic bag.

Hobart was standing in the apartment's main doorway when the elevator doors opened. He looked up to see Hendrickson step out and walk down the corridor towards him.

'Sir,' Hendrickson said before he reached the door. Hobart could tell from his pensive look that the young man had something urgent to reveal.

Hobart wore his usual dry expression as he walked out into the corridor and waited for his eager young assistant.

'Sir. Sally Penton had a son. He was with her when she was killed.'

Hobart flashed him an angry look. 'You're telling me this now?'

'I'm sorry, sir, but I didn't see the relevance of it at the time.'

'*Relevance*? Stratton killed the boy's mother's killers. The son was nothing *but* relevant!' Hobart exclaimed.

'I was on my way over to the child-protection centre today to interview him and—'

'Don't tell me. Stratton's taken him,' Hobart said, reckoning immediately that Stratton would want to protect the boy from Skender.

'I don't think so, sir. Stratton's working alone here – at least, we think he is. The kid was abducted by two men this morning, neither of whom matched Stratton's description. In fact, a witness who was beaten by the men knew Stratton and swears that neither was him.'

Hobart flashed Hendrickson another look as a new set of implications pelted his brain.

'Stratton's been in contact with the kid nearly every day since he's been in LA,' Hendrickson went on. 'The boy was due to fly out of here in a couple days back to the UK.'

Hobart looked out of the window at the clear blue sea beyond the palm trees. But he saw only his thoughts. 'So, what do you deduce from all of this, Hendrickson?'

'Deduce, sir?'

'Yes. To deduce. To draw a logical conclusion from something already known or assumed by a process of reasoning. It's what we're supposed to do for a living, goddamn it.'

'Well . . . Skender's people killed Stratton's best friend's wife—'

'What?' Hobart interrupted.

'Yes, sir,' Hendrickson said, feeling like a schoolboy who had forgotten to hand in his homework. 'I only found that out from our people in London before I left the office this morning. Stratton is or was in Brit special forces.'

'Wait up a minute,' Hobart interrupted again. 'Stratton's a civilian now?'

'No, sir. He works for the British government, that's a certainty. It's just that it's unclear who he belongs to, the SBS – Special Boat Service – or SIS. Jack Penton was also in the SBS – they're like the SAS but they also do seaborne operations. Penton and Stratton were on an op together in Iraq a month ago when Penton was killed. Stratton is also Josh's godfather, Josh being the kid's name. But Stratton isn't on the special forces books, like he's been moved. All enquiries to the SBS about him are deferred to the Brits' Ministry of Defence. That's why it's been difficult to get anything on him.'

Hobart readjusted his thoughts. 'Go on with your deduction.'

'Okay,' Hendrickson said, looking into space as if this was a quiz. 'So . . . Stratton revenged Sally Penton's murder because of his relationship with the family. One of Skender's people then decided to avenge the deaths of Bufi and Cano—'

'Why'd you say one of Skender's people and not Skender himself?' Hobart interrupted again.

'Because Skender's not related to either of the men. He himself should have had them punished but he didn't for some reason. I think Skender is less of an Albanian today than he was before he came here. He wants to stay in the States so he's trying to adapt his m.o.'

Hobart nodded. Hendrickson's reasoning was crude but interesting. Hobart himself hadn't gone so far as to suspect someone else in Skender's organisation but it was undeniably worth considering. 'Go on,' he said.

'Well, maybe Skender but most likely someone else orders a hit on Stratton which backfires and so the kid is abducted.'

Hendrickson stopped there and Hobart looked up to see he was not about to continue. 'Why?'

'To get at Stratton, swap him maybe, I don't know. I doubt whether the kid will survive those guys.'

'And the possible repercussions? What now?'

'Now . . . now I think the faecal matter could hit the air-oscillator. This Stratton guy is no pushover.

He's showed that he's capable of taking on Skender's people and winning. But not like the David and Goliath concept. More like a small guerrilla group taking on a professional army. He has advantages in being alone and being able to move freely. I don't know what his skills are other than explosives but the guy kicks ass. The score is five to one if you count the kid. I think Stratton's gonna go for them.'

Hobart found himself broadly agreeing. 'So what do we do now?'

'Look for Stratton.'

'Of course. But should we give Skender protection?'

'Not for me to say, sir.'

'Off the record. What would you do?'

'I don't want to say even off the record, sir.'

Hobart knew that like everyone else on the team Hendrickson would like to see Skender and his people burn in hell. The thought of protecting the mobster was anathema. But Hobart had a job to do. How to achieve that was another problem. Skender would refuse any overt protection and if he suspected even a covert operation to protect him he'd accuse the Bureau of spying on him, which was against their special agreement.

Hobart decided to deal with that later. Right now he had to find Stratton. He would also put a team on the abduction but he knew that there was little chance of finding this kid Josh if the Albanians had him. Hobart needed more information on Stratton. A photograph would be a great start. The Brits would eventually help, once they accepted that their man was involved in a civilian homicide. But depending on how high up the ladder Stratton was they would want to get involved too. That could take time.

Then Hobart had a thought. The Brits worked hand in hand with the Americans in Iraq and in other matters too. There was therefore a good chance that Stratton had worked with American intelligence at some time and if so there would be a file on him somewhere in the USA. Then Hobart's thoughts went back to the explosives that Stratton had acquired while in the US and suddenly the chance that he had once associated with US intelligence became more than just a possibility.

'Sir?' Hendrickson asked, taking Hobart out of his thoughts.

'What?'

'What do you think, sir?'

'About what?'

'My deduction.'

'I think it was pretty good, Hendrickson. I want you to put out an APB to every US intelligence and special forces unit in this country.'

'What's an APB, sir?'

'Don't you watch old cop movies, Hendrickson? An all-points bulletin. Keep it simple. No information or mention of the homicides. All you need is a response to a British military operative named John Stratton. Cover everyone, and I mean everyone including the Salvation Army and the Boy Scouts. And make sure it's in yellow,' he said, referring to the high-lighting of the text that everyone who read it would know meant highest priority.

'Yes, sir,' Hendrickson said.

'Now,' Hobart said.

Hendrickson nodded and turned away.

'Hendrickson,' Hobart called out. 'I was joking about the Salvation Army and Boy Scouts.'

'I know, sir,' Hendrickson said. He hurried to the elevators only to discover that they were both on the top floor. He moved to the emergency stairs.

Hobart glanced back at the apartment. He did not expect to find anything in there that would lead to Stratton's discovery so he headed for the elevator and pushed the call button. He considered Stratton's likely options from this point on, assuming that the guy would expect the cops to be looking for him now. He'd probably go strictly cash, withdrawing as much as he could each day from various ATM machines. He'd also move to a low-profile and cheap local hotel. The main question was, how might Stratton go about getting Skender to hand over the kid? The obvious method would be to offer up in exchange something that Skender valued more than the kid – or more than Stratton, in fact. That would probably be Skender himself.

The elevator arrived and Hobart stepped inside, lost in thought. He had to assume for now that Stratton had more explosives – they appeared to be his preferred weapon. Skender would need to be convinced that Stratton could take him out, perhaps with a demonstration of some kind. That was what Hobart would do. But there he stopped himself, suddenly seeing the futility of trying to put himself in this Brit's shoes when he and Hobart were completely different animals. Hobart could never have conceived hits like

352

those in the court cells or the restaurant, for instance. Those had been conceived by the mind of a person greatly experienced in that world, which made Hobart wonder what kind of an SIS operative Stratton was. In the CIA, for instance, there were two categories of front-line field agents: one was intelligence gatherer, the other direct-action operative and some, the best of them, could play either part. Hobart was convinced of one thing. He was probably going to need an adviser, someone who could shed some light on Stratton's options. The question was, where would he find such an operator?

The elevator doors opened and Hobart stepped out into the lobby and through to the alleyway where his car was parked. His plan for the time being would be to carry on with the search routine and hope either that they got lucky or that Stratton got sloppy. But it looked as if it was anyway going to be a case of waiting for the man's next move. That wasn't an unusual situation in Hobart's line of work but there was another reason why he would not rush to shift heaven and earth to find the Brit agent. The real victim in all this now was the kid: Hobart had to admit, though he would never say as much to anyone else, that Stratton might well be the boy's only chance.

Chapter 24

Stratton, wearing a baseball jacket and cap, watched Skender's new building complex from inside a small office-block entranceway across the street. For almost an hour he had studied the place from every angle, circling the block and observing the comings and goings of workers, especially Skender's security team. Skender himself had arrived a few minutes after Stratton had begun his surveillance, turning up in his cavalcade surrounded by bodyguards like some visiting state dignitary, and Cano had come out of the building with yet more guards to escort his boss inside.

The surrounding security fence had been removed and the landscaping, a complex design of lawns, flower beds, trees and fountains, was almost complete. The entire block was ringed by new steel street lamps with added spotlights on top of each one to illuminate the building at night. The finishing touches to the curving drive that led from the boulevard to the entrance were being made. A crane was slowly positioning a large crate in the centre of the concourse, directly in front of the ornate entrance – some kind of statue, Stratton suspected – while a handful of helmeted engineers carefully supervised its touchdown, inch by inch.

The place was very much a fortress, with guards covering every entry point including a barrier to the underground parking. Adding up all the men Stratton had seen on duty on the first-floor balconies, at various windows and emergency exits, the main entrance, the garage and doing roving patrols – plus another dozen to allow for those he could not see – there were around fifty. Then, working on the assumption that they did three eight-hour shifts per day the total came to a hundred and fifty. Assuming one shift was on standby or stand-down inside the premises Stratton felt that a fair estimate of security manpower would be about a hundred men at any one time. Quite the small army.

Stratton reviewed his objectives in order of priority once again in the hope that doing so would help to inspire a so far uninspired plan. The final outcome obviously had to be getting Josh back to England alive. To achieve that Skender had to believe that his own life was at stake if he did not hand over Josh. To convince the Albanian of that was the hard part. A demonstration of intent could be useful but Stratton had no time to waste and he might get only one shot. Another option was to find something that Skender valued as much as his own life but unless Stratton could figure out what that was, or even if there was such a thing, he was still at the starting block. Meeting Skender face to face was an option but reaching him and then getting away after looked like too much of a risk.

Stratton told himself to step back and take a completely new look at matters. In the meantime he decided to use another essential tool in any operation of this nature: psy-ops.

A payphone hung on the wall of the lobby and Stratton walked over to it. He took his notebook from a pocket, flicked to a page of names and numbers, inserted some coins into the slot and dialled a number.

Cano was in the small kitchen on the top floor of Skender's business centre pouring himself a coffee when his cellphone rang. He took it out of his pocket, hit the receive button and put it to his ear. 'Yeah.'

'Vleshek? This is Stratton.'

Cano was about to pour some milk into the cup and paused. 'How'd you get this number?'

'I'm full of surprises. I know a lot about you, for instance. Your real name is Dren Cano.'

Cano put down the carton of milk. He struggled to contain his shock at hearing his real name on the lips of another man besides his boss for the first time in ten years.

'I could give that information to the police and you'd end up in a cell in the Hague waiting for your war-crimes trial, but I'm not going to,' Stratton went on. 'I'll tell you what the deal is, Cano. You hand the boy over to the police or take him back to the child-protection centre and I'll leave you alive. If you don't it's war.'

'That right? You need an army to go to war.'

'I work alone. The kind of war I have in mind, you're already outnumbered.'

Cano closed the kitchen door and kept his voice low although the anger in it was plain to hear. 'Now you listen to me, you piece a' shit. You can take your threats and shove 'em up your ass. I'll tell you what the deal is. Your life for the kid's. It's as simple as that. I'm gonna give you a couple days to get your things in order, say your goodbyes, and then you call me. If I don't hear from you, you can say goodbye to the boy. I'll personally slit his throat and sell his organs. And that bitch you were with the other night – I'll fuck her too. There's no negotiation. Oh, and one more thing. If anything happens to me, the kid dies anyway. The next time I hear from you, you better be letting me know where I can send the boys to pick you up. Now get lost.'

Cano disconnected from the call and screwed his solitary eye shut. The empty socket of the lost one was beginning to throb beneath its silk patch. He reached for his painkillers and popped several in his mouth. But Cano had worries apart from his physical pain. The first was what would happen if the Englishman did not take the deal. The hits on Bufi and Cano's brother had been the best that Cano had ever seen and the guy had escaped his clutches twice now. Hobart was looking for Stratton, which might play in Cano's favour but the bottom line was that Cano wanted Stratton dead. Cano held the ace, of course – the kid – but he had no plan. What bothered him was that Stratton had to make the next move and Cano strongly doubted that he would simply hand himself over. Nor did Cano know if Stratton was willing to sacrifice himself or even the boy to get even.

Cano wondered if he should approach Skender with the problem. But there were greater dangers for Cano in that direction, the most obvious one being that

Skender did not know that Cano had kidnapped the boy and would be none too pleased if he found out. Cano remained hopeful that he could wind up this business without Skender discovering what his henchman had done.

Cano was treading a fine line and was feeling dangerously rattled.

Stratton replaced the phone and walked back to the window to look up at the top of the pyramid. He did not know whether he had gotten to Cano and he was not entirely confident that he had. But at least it set the goalposts firmly in place, for now at least. Stratton either turned himself in, whereupon both he and Josh would be executed and possibly Vicky too, or he went on the offensive. With the police now probably looking for him and with no idea yet what he was going to do this was beginning to look like an impossible task. But that was because he didn't know enough about his enemy. The more he could learn, the better the chances were of finding a chink in Skender's armour.

As Stratton stepped out of the building, pulling his baseball cap low over his eyes, he saw a man walking from one of the site contractors' portable cabins on the edge of the square as a crane moved into position, getting ready to lift it onto the back of a truck. The man, who was wearing a shiny white hard hat, was carrying several large tubes and rolls of paper. He placed them inside a car parked on the street and went back to the portable cabin.

Stratton didn't waste a second. He crossed the road, went to the car and looked inside. As he suspected, the rolls of paper were construction blueprints. After a quick glance to make sure that the man had gone back into the cabin, Stratton opened the car door, removed them and walked briskly away without looking back.

Chapter 25

Vicky walked down the pathway from the child-protection centre entrance, out of the gate and along the empty street towards her car around the corner. As she approached it, reaching for the lock with the key, she stopped and looked up. Standing across the road watching her was Stratton.

Vicky was a little shocked. She'd expected never to see him again and did not know what to say or how to react. Then she looked down, ignoring him, and opened her car door.

'Vicky – I need to talk to you,' Stratton said as he crossed the road.

She stopped and watched him walk around the back of her car and step onto the sidewalk to face her. 'I spent two hours with the FBI today. You're wanted for two murders,' she said.

'Those were the men who killed Sally.'

'My God,' Vicky said, putting a hand to her brow. 'Despite all that has happened I somehow hoped they were wrong. How stupid does that make me? Three men died in that car you blew up. Did you know that?'

'They came to kill me.'

'You've got it all figured out, haven't you? You're

crazy, John. You're certifiable. We have a process of law in this country.'

'Not for everyone. If you knew the whole story you'd understand.'

'I don't think so, John. There is no way I am ever going to condone murder, even for revenge. Josh's kidnapping is your fault, John.'

'I know.'

Vicky could see Stratton's pain and was unable to stop a sudden feeling of sympathy for him.

'Now I have to put it right,' he said.

'How are you going to do that?'

'Give them what they want.'

'You?'

'Yes.'

'Go to the FBI, John. There has to be a way to work this out.'

'You don't know these people. They want their revenge and they'll have it one way or another. If I go to the Feds I'm out of it. I'll get locked up. They'll never let Josh go, anyway. They'll kill him even if they have me. It's a mess, Vicky. I came here to tell you I'm sorry for everything – for you, for Josh, maybe for us too.'

Vicky thought she had dealt with this after their last meeting. But her emotions welled up and she was unable to beat them back.

'We won't see each other again,' Stratton said. 'It hurts me to say that.'

She blinked hard to stop the tears.

'Bye,' Stratton said before turning away and walking up the street.

'John!' she called out, a part of her wanting him to come back and talk to her. But deep down she knew that it was futile. He needed help, which was what she was supposed to be good at, but this was beyond anything she had ever experienced before. She had been ready to give herself to him, something that was so very difficult for her to do. Stratton had released something in her. A desire she had not felt for anyone in a long time. She had even daydreamed of going back to England with him, fantasised about waking up with him in his home. It seemed obvious that Stratton would adopt Josh and she would play the role of the boy's mother. It was an idyllic prospect: an instant family, a man, a son, a purpose – and then suddenly it was all shattered.

Vicky watched Stratton walk away until he disappeared around a corner. Then she climbed into her car and, unable to drive for the moment, sat there feeling a terrible sorrow for Stratton, for Josh and for herself.

Chapter 26

Stratton heard Vicky call his name but chose not to respond. Any further conversation with her would have been pointless and, frankly, painful. He liked her, more than he'd imagined he could have when they'd first met, but if their worlds had been far apart that day they were out of sight of each other now.

He walked around the corner and crossed the road to an old workhorse of a GM pick-up truck parked in the quiet residential street. The grey paintwork was chipped in places, revealing patches of rust and its original fire-engine red. Storage cabinets ran along both sides with rails on top connected by crossbars for ladders. Stratton had seen it advertised in a local newspaper. Its previous owner was an old independent roofing contractor in Mar Vista who'd been happy to announce that he had finally given up hauling all the crap around himself after getting wise to subcontracting and buying himself a used but newer and smaller Toyota pick-up. From now on the only thing that he was going to haul up ladders and onto roofs was his own ass to inspect the work of others.

Stratton climbed in, put the key in the ignition and turned it. The heavy old petrol engine cranked over a couple of times before gunning noisily to life. The old man had said that she might sometimes sound as if she'd died in the night but apart from the occasional hangover she was a reliable old gal.

Stratton pulled the heavy door shut and wiggled the loose column gear change until the needle lined up with the 'D' and the vehicle shunted into drive. He released the brake, pressed the accelerator pedal slowly down and the truck jerked forward with surprising power. The wheel turned easily, aided by the power steering and he steered the pick-up out of the parking space, straightened it up in the centre of the narrow road and accelerated noisily between the cars parked on either side.

He turned onto Fourteenth Street heading south and five minutes later was driving east on Highway 10 that joined the 405 North within a couple of miles. On the springy bench seat beside him were the rolls of construction blueprints for Skender's building, a couple of yellow-page directories and a sheet of notes: names and addresses of shops and warehouses and a long shopping list. Next stop was Bakersfield, 150 miles north of LA. From there, after acquiring the items on his list, Stratton was going to head for a small town called Twin Oaks just beyond Caliente where Vicky had been born and an operations base that he had found on the Internet thanks to something she had told him over dinner.

He had a plan, or at least a broad outline of one, that was going to need a lot of work to turn into reality. It was risky and it was big – and it was the only way he was going to get Skender's attention.

There was one aspect of it that Stratton chose not to think about in too great detail and that was the high risk to him personally. It was a two-part plan, each with several phases, the final one of which he would only implement if it looked as if he had failed to save Josh. He'd examined thoroughly the two choices he had – to go for it or to run – and had chosen the first simply because he knew that he could not spend the rest of his life with the guilt of having failed Jack and his family.

The freeways had not been very congested although the pick-up had struggled to climb the steep and winding southern slope of the Grape Vine, a hilly region of the San Andreas Fault that ran north of LA. Three hours later Stratton was pulling into a massive industrial and commercial complex on the east side of Bakersfield that was filled with manufactured-goods and materials outlets of almost every kind.

First stop was a hardware superstore where he bought a ten-gallon drum of quarter-inch ball-bearings, a tarpaulin big enough to cover the inside of the pick-up, four ten-gallon industrial cooking pots, the largest glass bowl he could find, a gas burner and gas bottle, several wooden serving spoons, a large sieve, a thousand-foot reel of thin cord, a packet of heavy-duty freezer bags, several rolls of masking tape, a couple of hundred feet of fine wire and thirty-two plastic sandwich boxes the size of house bricks.

Stratton's next visit was to an outdoor-adventure store where he bought every camping-fuel stick or hexamine tablet they had in stock, which amounted to around seventy pounds in weight. It was short of the amount he needed but after locating every similar store in the city and clearing them of their stock he had about enough. The next place was hard to find and Stratton drove around the complex for almost ten minutes before he saw a sign advertising Alan's Chemicals.

He pulled into the building's forecourt, shut down the engine, stepped out of the truck's cab and climbed onto the back to make sure that the tarp was neatly covering everything that he had bought so far. Then he jumped down and headed for the reception building, a small prefabricated add-on to the front of an old hangar-like warehouse.

A customer at the counter was being served and Stratton walked over to a small messy table covered in powdered milk and sugar where a coffee pot was brewing beside a sign inviting customers to help themselves.

An old guy in dirty overalls stepped out from the back and adjusted his spectacles on his nose to focus on Stratton. 'Can I help you, mister?' he called out.

'Yeah,' Stratton said, walking over to the counter while stirring his plastic cup of coffee.

'What is it you need?' the old guy said, wiping his hands on an oily rag.

'You have ninety-per-cent nitric acid?' Stratton asked.

'Just a second,' the oldster said as he punched several keys on a dirty computer keyboard and scrutinised the old monitor screen to check that he had brought up the correct page. 'I know we got it, I just gotta get an invoice set up fer yer. How much do you need?' he asked, satisfied.

'Twenty gallons.'

'Not a problem,' the storeman said as he hit the keys and consulted his monitor again to make sure that he'd put in the correct order.

'Ethyl alcohol?'

'Yep.'

'Five gallons?'

'Five gallons,' the other man repeated as he typed it in.

'You sell mercury metal?'

'How much you need?'

'What's it cost?'

'I can sell you a pound for eight hunnerd dollars.'

Stratton had hoped it would be cheaper. He needed four times that amount and didn't have enough money. 'Just curious,' he said. 'That'll do it.'

'Trade or charge?'

'Cash okay?'

'Cash is always okay,' the old man said as he punched several more keys and an aged dot-matrix printer at the other end of the desk came to life and started to spew out a page. 'Lotta acid. What you makin' there?'

'Gotta couple of boilers to strip,' Stratton said with a smile.

'That'll do the trick, I guess,' the storeman said as he tore the page from the printer roll and placed it in front of Stratton.

Stratton read it as he pulled a wedge of crisp new dollars from a pocket and counted out the bills. The old guy checked the amount, placed the cash in the till and gave Stratton his change.

'That your truck?' the storeman asked.

'Yep.'

'See you outside in five minutes.'

Stratton left the reception building, walked to his vehicle and consulted a map to commit the next stage of his journey to memory. A couple of minutes later he heard the small tug and trailer drive out through the hangar entrance and looked up to see the old man at the wheel. Stratton walked to the rear of the pick-up as the storeman pulled to a stop alongside and shut off the engine.

'Hope you don't mind me not helpin' you load this stuff,' the old man said as Stratton took hold of one of the large bottles. 'Truth is I'm too goddamned old.'

'That's okay,' Stratton said. 'I need the exercise.'

'Gonna be a cool night, I think,' the storeman said as Stratton placed the last container onto the back of his pick-up, pushed it forward and then climbed onto the truck's bed to secure the load. As he moved across the bed he accidentally caught the tarp in his foot, pulling it enough to expose some of his previous load which the old man caught sight of as Stratton straightened it out.

'So where you from?' the old man asked. 'English if I had to guess. We get a few a' them around here.'

'That's right,' Stratton answered as he jumped down, lifted up the heavy tailgate, slammed it home and placed the securing pins in either side. 'Well, gotta get going,' he said as he headed for the cab. 'Oh. Where can I get some dry ice around here?'

'Pete's refrigeration. Down that way,' the old guy said, nodding in the direction.

'Thanks. You take care now,' Stratton said as he climbed into his cab.

'You too,' the storeman said as he boarded his tug, started the engine, took a look at the registration number under the pick-up's tailgate and headed away.

He stopped at the hangar doors as Stratton turned out of the lot and onto the main road. The old man switched off the engine, climbed off the tug's seat and walked into the reception block. He picked up a pen beside an order book and scribbled down Stratton's registration number, pausing halfway through to think. Then he crossed it out, started again, studied it some more and shook his head. 'Damn it all,' he muttered, cursing his memory.

He dug a notebook from a pocket, found a number, picked up the phone, dialled and waited. He looked out of the window but Stratton was well gone.

'Hank. It's Joe, down at Alan's Chemicals. I got something you might be interested in. You guys sent us a letter some time back about letting the cops know about people buying suspicious combinations of chemicals and stuff. Well, maybe I got one for yer. Had a guy just bought some nitric acid, a lot of it, and in the back of his truck he had a whole bunch a' fire tablets. Fire tablets are made out of a chemical called HMT – hexa-methylene-tetramine. Mouthful, ain't it? When I was in the service I was in EOD so I know a little about explosives. You mix nitric with that stuff and you got somethin' that'll go bang, I know that much. The guy was also lookin' fer mercury metal. Now you mix mercury and nitric and you end up with that stuff kids use in cap guns. Course, you gotta know what you're doin'. Yeah, he's gone. Left a couple minutes ago in an old grey GM pick-up. I didn't get the licence complete – RJ479P, I think. English guy. Paid cash, too. Sure, I'll be here till five if you wanna send someone down. Not a problem.'

Joe put the phone down and took another look at the registration number. 'Boiler stripper, my ass,' he mumbled.

Stratton made two more stops in the industrial complex to buy a large block of dry ice, a flashlight, a couple of petrol lights, a twenty-foot reel of small-gauge plastic piping, twenty gallons of water, a thermometer and a large tin of glue. Then he got back onto the highway and headed east out of Bakersfield.

Half an hour later he stopped in the town of Arvin, inhabited totally – or so it appeared – by Mexicans, to fill up his fuel tank and purchase a couple of days' supply of food. From there it was an easy climb north-east up the foothills of the Sierra Nevada mountains and into the folding hills that hid the small town of Caliente.

As Stratton drove through the sparsely populated settlement he tried to imagine Vicky living there as a little girl. Apart from the occasional modern car the sleepy, arid place looked like an old turn-of-the-century western movie set. There was one liquor store, one general store, a bar, a post office and a railway depot, all well spaced along a broad stretch of road, the only sign of life being a couple of dogs and an old man sitting on a chair outside the depot.

The farming appeared to be strictly arable, the countryside hilly, rocky, parched and dotted with Californian oak trees, a smaller, brittle, less majestic version of its splendid European cousin. Past the town a newly metalled road followed a broad, winding creek that cut deep into the hills, its sides steep and rocky. Where they could get a foothold, pine and oak trees grew.

Twin Oaks, a few miles further on, was even more sparsely settled than Caliente. Stratton consulted his map as he passed a collection of houses that looked abandoned and then a bar set back from the road with a couple of pick-ups parked outside. He had to slow for several cows meandering along the road, then, a mile beyond the last house, he reached a distinct hairpin bend where a dirt track headed towards higher ground and woodland half a mile away. He turned off the metalled road and followed the track to a fork at the entrance to the wood, glanced at the map and took the right-hand route. A couple of hundred yards later he stopped in front of an old wooden gate that barred his way.

Stratton climbed out to inspect the gate where the wood crowded in on both sides. A bleached wooden sign with barely readable letters and fixed at a jaunty angle to one of the gateposts warned of an abandoned mine ahead and stated that entry was not permitted. A rusty chain looped around a post was all that secured the gate and he unravelled the links, picked up the end and pulled it open.

He drove the truck a few yards past the gate, climbed out, closed it, replaced the chain, and drove on. The wood remained close on both sides and a couple of hundred yards around a gradual bend the track gave way to a large open space tightly packed with derelict old wooden constructions of various sizes.

As Stratton drove slowly in among the buildings he spotted a barn with one of its double doors lying on the ground and what appeared to be rusting machinery of some description inside. The structure had enough room for the pick-up and he eased it in. When he shut off the engine a near-total silence descended.

Stratton pulled the high-powered flashlight from its box, climbed out of the cab and stepped into the sunshine. The air was warm and dry.

He took a walk around, his footsteps clearly audible as his boots crunched on the soft sandy soil. He inspected each building in turn. Most were completely empty with unreliable-looking floors, some had the odd piece of furniture and machinery and one shed contained dozens of rusting spades, picks, hammers and boxes of heavy spike nails. The mine had been closed for a hundred and thirty years, according to the Internet site, abandoned when the cost of extracting the gold had exceeded the value of the yield. There was apparently still a fair amount of the precious metal to be had but it would only become a viable operation again when it reached $1,000 an ounce at today's money value which was apparently unlikely.

Stratton finally came to the towering wooden derrick that supported aloft the massive wheels that the trolley drag cables looped over before disappearing into the winch house. Near the foot of the derrick was the main entrance shaft itself. A thick metal pipe ran out of the mine into another building close by that contained a couple of rusting water pumps. Flooding had apparently been a problem at the mine's lower depths and the water had had to be pumped out twenty-four hours a day.

He felt the heavy, sturdy timbers surrounding the entrance that was a good ten feet square and, turning on the flashlight, he walked inside, checking the ceiling and supports as he made his way cautiously down the gradual incline. It became noticeably cooler and only slightly narrower and three hundred feet inside the passage suddenly opened out into a low-ceilinged cavern which was a meeting point for three other tunnels. The ground was level at this junction, the tunnels leading off it steeper than the entrance shaft. Stratton checked the supports that surrounded and held up the centre of the cavern and decided that this would be a good place to set up the 'kitchen'.

A distinct odour had gradually increased in strength the deeper he got and he remembered that one of the mine's problems was rotting timber supports at the lower levels – below the water table – which produced dangerous gases. Just as he wondered if he should have added a canary to his shopping list there was a sound behind him and he quickly aimed the flashlight, catching a small ground squirrel in the beam. It was standing on its hind legs, its nose twitching as it inspected this uncommon visitor. The animal was a sign that the gas was not at a serious concentration and confirmed an assumption that the beams in the water-logged sections far below had probably long since rotted and given off all their gases.

Stratton dug a cracker out of his pocket from a packet he had been munching on during the drive and tossed it near the squirrel. The miners had always fed the rats to encourage them to stay close by – a dead rat indicated the possibility of bad air. The cracker landed just in front of the squirrel, spooking it, and it took off up the shaft.

Stratton made a final and more thorough inspection of the cavern ceiling before trudging back up the entrance shaft and back out into the sunlight. An hour later he had hauled most of the equipment off the truck and down into the mine that was now illuminated by the petrol lamps. In that time the sun had dropped below the trees but he cracked on, setting up the kitchen for the first recipe.

After putting on goggles and a pair of thick rubber gloves he picked up the heavy chunk of dry ice wrapped in a cloth, placed it in one of the large pots and put another pot in on top of it. He then carefully poured nitric acid into the top pot until it was half full, hung the glass thermometer on the side and put the lid on the pot. The liquid needed to chill to near zero before he could start and he set about crumbling up all the hexamine blocks until he had a couple of bin bags filled with fine chunks of the stuff. A couple of hours later the acid was cool enough and he started to add the hexamine to it slowly, making sure that the temperature did not get too high.

When the acid was saturated with a third of the HMT Stratton gave it a long, steady stir and let it stand for twenty minutes while he quarter-filled the third pot with water. He then began to ladle the white slushy substance from the acid into the water and every now and then used the sieve to scoop out the now cleaner particles from the water, placing them into the fourth, still empty pot. He continued this process until all the solids had been strained from the acid and he was left with a white mulch that he mixed with more water to remove as much of the acid as possible. The final phase of this part of the process was to sieve out the mulch once again and place it on the stretched-out tarpaulin to dry.

When Stratton had finished he estimated that it would take another two batches to process the rest of the hexamine. Due to the limited life of the dry ice he cracked straight on with it.

By early morning the tarpaulin was covered in the flaky white powder which, when dry, would become one of the most powerful high-explosive materials ever invented. It was known as RDX. The compound was fairly stable, although if a heavy enough piece of ceiling were to fall on it the explosion would probably be felt in Bakersfield. But considering that the ceiling had remained intact for the last hundred and thirty years Stratton felt the odds were in his favour.

He poured the used acid down one of the shafts, dumped the remaining ice, turned off the lamps and headed out of the mine. The acid fumes had gradually been getting to him and he needed to rest as well as let the air quality in the mine get back to what it had been. He climbed onto the front bench of the pick-up that was long and comfortable enough to suit his needs and within minutes was fast asleep.

Six hours later Stratton was awake again. After a quick bite he headed back into the mine with the thirty-two plastic sandwich boxes.

He lit the lamps, inspected the RDX to find that

it was almost dry and set about removing the sand-wich boxes from their cartons and taking off all their lids. Using a wooden spoon he half-filled each box with RDX. When all thirty-two were done he scooped the remaining explosive into a couple of bin bags and put them in a far corner for later.

Next, he opened the drum of ball-bearings and carefully spooned them into the sandwich boxes on top of the RDX, filling each container to the top, an average of two hundred balls in each, he estimated. Then he closed the lids tightly and stacked them to one side.

The sandwich boxes constituted the first phase of Stratton's operation, although they were not quite complete. He stared at them, contemplating how much more work he had to do. For the first time since leaving LA he wondered if he was completely crazy and then reminded himself of his options. Fight or run. That was enough to get him back in focus and concentrate on the next task, which was to run a test of the RDX. Stratton had made this type of explosive on his special forces demolitions course but just in small amounts. It looked, smelled and felt right but there was only one way to make sure.

Only a little was needed but nevertheless he could not risk exploding it in the open and attracting attention — secrecy had been one of the main reasons for choosing this location in the first place. However, there were obvious risks with detonating even the smallest quantity inside the mine. The beams might be solid but he had no idea how unstable the rock above them was.

To reduce the risk of bringing down the roof in

the kitchen Stratton constructed the test apparatus several hundred feet along one of the passages that led deeper into the mine. It was a simple device: a sledgehammer suspended from a beam on the end of a long piece of string looped through a bent nail, the head a couple of feet above a metal plate on the ground. The string led back up the shaft to what he considered to be a safe distance and, to test the tackle, he released the string, allowing the hammer to fall onto the plate. He returned with a piece of RDX no bigger than a pea, re-rigged the hammer, and placed the explosive compound on the metal sheet precisely where the hammer had struck. Satisfied that everything was in position he turned on the flashlight to light his way back up the tunnel when he saw the ground squirrel standing in front of him in its beam.

'I'd head back up the tunnel if I were you, mate.'

The squirrel looked at him, twitching its nose, and as Stratton moved towards it the little animal scampered back up the shaft.

Stratton reached the safe point, only to find the squirrel waiting there for him. 'If you're going to stick around you might want to put your fingers in your ears,' he advised.

The squirrel got up onto its hind legs as if in response and watched him.

'Don't say I didn't warn you,' Stratton said as he took a last look around, shone his flashlight back up the shaft towards the entrance just in case he had to leg it, looked back at the taut string disappearing in the other direction around a slight bend, and released it. A second later there was a terrific boom, the noise accentuated by the confinement of the shaft. Dust fell from the ceiling and he moved several paces back, ready to run. But the rumble of falling earth soon subsided and complete silence descended once again.

Stratton checked every surface of the shaft with his torch as he carefully walked back down it. Dust filled the air as he approached the test site but all the supports appeared to be solidly in place and the ceiling had held. He found the hammer lying several feet from the impact point, its wooden handle broken, and although the metal plate was in its original position it had a serious dent in the centre of it.

'Not bad at all,' Stratton said as he inspected the underside of the plate. Then he looked back up the shaft, wondering what had become of the ground squirrel.

Chapter 27

Ten miles from Twin Oaks on a remote hillside a small solar-powered analogue seismograph picked up the tremor and automatically transmitted it through its antenna, using the Southern California Seismic Network. It was relayed to the central computer facility in the seismology laboratory on the Caltech campus in Pasadena, Los Angeles. Here the data was instantly converted into a digital format so that computers could read, process and store it.

A technician responded to a data-arrival signal and isolated it for examination. The graph displayed an unusual peak and, using the vector capabilities formed by two other seismographs that had also picked up the tremor, he plotted the location.

A colleague working on the other side of the room who had also heard the data alarm looked up from his computer monitor. 'What was it?' he asked.

'It wasn't a fault tremor – it's a mile from the nearest fault line. Looks like it was an explosion, same as the peaks from Lanser's quarry but nowhere near it.'

'Where was it?'

'Twin Oaks, near Caliente.'

'That's way out in the boonies. Maybe someone's

liquor still blew up,' the other guy said with a chuckle.

'I guess,' the first technician agreed. He saved the data and went back to his work.

Stratton set about preparing what he needed for the next phase, which was the construction of the detonators. But he was missing one essential ingredient that he would have to get later that evening. He spent the next few hours cutting the narrow plastic pipe into three-inch lengths and then sat down to study the construction blueprints of Skender's building.

A large part of the special forces explosives course that he had attended had been dedicated to studying structures and identifying their weaknesses and fulcrums, points where the minimum amount of explosive would have the greatest effect. Stratton was encouraged to discover that Skender's architect had used a great deal of suspension in his design: much of the building's support relied on a huge pillar that ran up its centre like a tent pole. Had the designer used a wigwam construction where the building was supported by its sides it would have made his job more complicated because the primary stress locations would have been more spread out and difficult to reach on the outside shell of the pyramid. As it was, the primary supports hinged off the central pillar, making it sturdier against earthquakes and relying heavily on a system of centralised strength.

The rest of Stratton's explosives course had dealt with the manufacture of a range of volatile compounds, the different uses of low (gunpowder, for example) and high explosives, various types of booby traps, and mathematical formulas for calculating the precise amount of explosives required to cut steel and concrete, as well as the best shape into which a charge should be formed for maximum effect. In the old days saboteurs had used the more simple formula of 'P for plenty' but with the development of plastic explosives scientists and mathematicians began to take a greater interest in the subject. Plastic explosives, which were basically RDX mixed with plasticisers, were not only pliable but very stable compared to TNT. They could be cut with a knife for precision work, could literally be thrown around and even set light to, be it only in small quantities at a time. But they could be detonated with a hammer blow.

The most important factor in the creation of precise cutting formulas, as far as special forces were concerned, was that exact amounts of explosives could be calculated for given jobs, allowing saboteurs to carry less and blow up larger and more complex targets. Such as steel girder bridges: in the old days large – and hence heavy – amounts of the more unstable TNT were placed against main supports to blow them to smithereens. But it had required large teams to carry the stuff into enemy territory whereas relatively small amounts of PE4, or C4, and even less Super-X, precisely shaped and placed to cut specific girders, could do the same job.

Each time Stratton studied the plans for Skender's pyramid he saw more and more possibilities and his familiarity with the building increased.

As darkness descended Stratton decided to make a move since it would take a good hour or so to get to his destination and a hot fast-food meal on the way sounded appealing. He climbed into the truck and backed out of the barn. An hour and a half later he arrived at a large town called Simi Valley north of LA, pulled into a side road and killed the engine. He took one of the bottles of nitric acid off the seat, placed it in his backpack, climbed out and walked up the road.

The bars were still open and traffic was light and although he was the only pedestrian in sight it wasn't an ungodly hour to be walking through a neighbourhood.

He turned a corner onto a street where houses lined one side and a large warehouse behind a chain fence occupied the other. A large floodlit sign on the side of the building declared that it was the Avion Corporation. Below it another sign warned of security alarms and armed response. Avion's advertisement in the yellow pages described it as the largest model-kit warehouse in California, specialising in model aircraft and spare parts. The street was intermittently lit where the houses were but beyond them it was relatively dark.

Stratton stopped in the darkest patch and checked around. Then he quickly scaled the fence, dropped over the other side and moved into the shadows.

After waiting for several minutes to watch the road and the houses for any sign of movement he made his way along the edge of the warehouse to a collection of dumpsters against its side. Another quick scan around showed that the coast was clear. He climbed onto a dumpster, reached for the edge of the roof and pulled himself up. It was as difficult as he had anticipated with the weight on his back but after a struggle he got a leg up on the gutter and hauled himself onto the gently sloping roof.

Stratton kept on his belly to avoid being silhouetted, removed his pack and the bottle of acid inside and pulled on the rubber gloves. The outer layer of the roof was made of bitumen sheeting and using his knife he cut out a man-size square to expose the next layer, which was made of a heavy-duty composite. A weakness of most commercial premises was the roof since security companies usually only fitted the doors and windows with alarms. Motion detectors inside were also generally unpopular in warehouses because most such buildings had rodents of some sort in them and the animals could knock things off shelves. Also, birds often wandered inside, and that rendered the cheaper systems useless, sometimes for weeks until the creature eventually escaped or died. But since ordinary burglars rarely gained entry through the roof because of the degree of difficulty it was not a major issue.

Stratton unscrewed the bottle cap and carefully began to pour the powerful acid onto the composite. It reacted immediately and within a few seconds he was able to poke through the softened material with his knife to form the same size of hole as he had cut in the bitumen. Below the composite lay thick fibre insulation and the remaining acid quickly ate through it and through the thin ceiling sheeting below that.

Stratton pushed the eroded mess through into the warehouse, took out his small flashlight and shone it inside. He was directly above a stack of shelving, which was not a coincidence. The advertisement picture of the inside of the warehouse showed it crowded with rows of shelving the length of the building on both sides.

He dropped his pack onto the top shelf and lowered himself through the hole to land beside it. The shelves were sturdy enough to support several tons and he grabbed his pack, let it drop a good twenty feet to the floor and scurried down the supports.

Stratton's flashlight soon located the model-aircraft section and from there a more detailed search produced what he was looking for: a stack of four-channel radio receivers, each the size of a penny. They were advertised at $14.99 apiece. If he'd had enough money he would have bought them but he'd been left a little short after all the other purchases. Two shelves above there were several unopened boxes containing fifty receivers each. Stratton helped himself to two and placed them in his backpack. Further down the aisle was a selection of transmitters and he helped himself to the most expensive one. Next on the list were batteries. These he found two aisles down, along with some wire-strippers and a box of electrical tape. A couple of minutes later he was scaling the shelving back towards the hole in the roof.

The roads were quiet on the way back and as Stratton passed the now familiar Bakersfield industrial estate where he had made purchases the day before he questioned the wisdom of this next burglary at such a late hour. There was no traffic around in the estate so he'd be conspicuous in the old truck and there were bound to be security patrols. He was going to have to take a bit of a walk.

He parked in a residential street across from the estate's perimeter and emptied his backpack. Then he got a pickaxe he had taken from the mine's tool shed and moved across the road and into the estate.

He broke into a jog, keeping close to the buildings and avoiding well-lit areas until he arrived at Alan's Chemicals.

A chain secured the large hangar doors at the front of the warehouse and although it was poorly lit Stratton made his way round to the back to play it as safe as possible. As he slipped into the shadows a pair of headlights slowly rounded a corner and headed up the road towards him. Stratton watched as they drew closer to see that it was a security patrol. The car maintained a slow speed, cruised past and continued up the road and out of sight.

Stratton continued round to the back of the building and to a door with a heavy padlock on it. The place was completely dark and run-down. The rear looked even shabbier than the front, with junk and empty containers strewn all over the place. As soon as he had realised that he could not afford the amount of mercury that he needed, he had looked at the warehouse with a view to breaking into it. Considering the condition it was in, he'd had a hunch that there wouldn't be much in the way of security. An inspection of the rear door showed that it was old and loose and pulled out a good two inches against the padlock, making a functioning alarm pad impossible – any movement such as one caused by a gust of wind would set it off and an alarm company would have insisted that the door would have to be replaced with a sturdy one.

Stratton placed the pick behind the padlock latch and heaved it up. The old wood gave way easily and the entire latch dropped to the ground. Stratton put down the pickaxe, opened the door and quickly checked around the frame for an alarm pad, just in case. But as he'd suspected there was none.

He closed the door behind him and moved quickly, walking past the shelving and searching with his flashlight as he went. Halfway along the first set of untidy shelves he found an open box containing a dozen or so small bottles labelled 'Mercury Metal'. He pocketed half a dozen and was about to head back when he saw a can of latex. It was something that he had considered at the outset and then changed his mind about since it was on the non-essential list. But now that it was here in front of him he took it.

As he reached the back door to leave he saw a couple of emergency gas masks hanging from a hook, something that he had overlooked during the initial procurement stage but which the acid fumes had reminded him of. He helped himself to one.

Once outside, Stratton took a moment to shove everything into his pack. Then he made his way back along the side of the warehouse, retracing his footsteps to the pick-up. Half an hour later he was following the Caliente River once again, heading back to Twin Oaks.

On arrival at the hairpin junction he killed his lights and slowly followed the track by moonlight back to the mine. As he parked back inside the barn he decided to grab a few hours' sleep since, if all went well, he would complete his preparations by late afternoon the following day and be ready to make the move back to LA. Skender's official building opening was scheduled for two days ahead. Stratton aimed to be there to make his contribution to the ceremony.

Chapter 28

Hobart sat in a comfortable leather recliner in the cramped cabin of a six-seat Falcon 10 jet aircraft. One other person shared the chartered flight with him, a businessman seated at the back and working on a laptop computer. Hobart had not exchanged a word with him.

Early that morning Hobart had been awoken by Hendrickson with two pieces of information that had been important enough for him to get out of bed, get authorisation to charter an immediate flight and head to Burbank Airport. The first news was that the CIA had responded to the second APB that the Bureau had sent out regarding one John Stratton who was wanted in connection with two homicides in LA. It was a brief note from a department chief, simply stating that after consulting with the Brits they were available to assist the FBI with their inquiries but with the predictable condition that they needed more information on the case. Hobart was the one who needed information and he knew from his previous experience of working alongside the Central Intelligence Agency on more than one occasion that the best way to get it was to sit down in front of them and lay his cards on the table – some of them, at least.

The Bureau and the Agency had a decades-long history of contempt for each other, something that Hobart regretted because of the obstacles that it created. They generally regarded each other as incompetent bunglers, empire builders and mandate expanders. This often resulted in duplication of effort and failures of communication on both sides, thus damaging attempts at interdepartmental cooperation and threatening national security. The conflict between the two organisations irritated the strongly patriotic Hobart but it seemed to be impossible, given their respective histories, to resolve easily. Even many of his new, young agents who had not yet had dealings with the Agency bore grudges that could only have been handed down from older operatives.

The Bureau itself was going through a period of great disadvantage in the mud-slinging stakes because of the recent and highly damaging criticisms thrown up by the 9/11 Commission Report. Its autopsy of the Bureau left its body parts open to the vultures. Some scathingly vitriolic senatorial arguments about whether it should be left at the helm of national intelligence gathering hadn't helped. One of the FBI's responses, which did nothing to help soothe the conflict, was that it had at least admitted to having major flaws whereas the CIA remained tight-lipped about their own massive shortcomings.

There was also too much dead wood in both communities, too many old agents who would resist any changes because of ingrained suspicion or simply natural stubbornness. To many it seemed that both outfits were as bad as each other and Hobart accepted that if a change for the better was ever to happen it would not be during his time.

The second piece of information that Hendrickson gave Hobart originated from a keyword arrest system that the Bureau had installed in the interstate police-report network program that had been set up a couple of decades earlier to aid in tracking criminals who moved from state to state. Two of the trigger keywords that Hendrickson had fed into the system were 'explosives' and 'Englishman' and both had come up on a single Bakersfield police report.

An initial investigation produced a description of the Englishman that matched those which the FBI already had from various sources including the waitress at the restaurant where Ardian had been killed, the manager of the Santa Monica apartment complex, and a social worker in charge of administration at the child-protection centre where Sally Penton's son had been held. This was enough to convince Hobart that Stratton had stayed in California with the intention of going on the offensive against Skender.

'We'll be landing in Dulles in twenty minutes,' the stewardess said to Hobart, snapping him out of his reverie as he looked out of the window.

'Thanks,' he said and checked the time as she squeezed past his seat to inform the other passenger. Hobart thought about adjusting his watch to local time, which was three hours ahead of West Coast time, but then decided to leave it alone. He wanted to keep his consciousness on a California schedule and besides, this was literally a flying visit. He aimed to be back in LA that night.

Half an hour later Hobart walked through the gate into the arrivals lounge. It was empty except for a man in a suit sitting across the room and reading a magazine. He put it down on seeing Hobart and got to his feet.

Forty minutes later they drove past a sign for CIA Langley and shortly after turned through one of the heavily guarded entrances on the perimeter of the vast complex. They stopped to present their ID cards to an armed sentry. The pole barrier went up after a heavy steel vehicle dam behind it powered slowly into its slot in the road and they drove in, round the back of one of the large office blocks and into an underground car park.

The driver, who had not said a word since asking Hobart for his ID at the airport arrivals gate, led the way into an elevator which ascended to the third floor. Hobart followed him along a pristine corridor to one of a dozen matching doors spread evenly along it. The driver opened the door and stood back for Hobart to enter a room that was windowless and sterile but for a conference table surrounded by half a dozen chairs.

'Can I get you anything: water, coffee?' the driver asked, remaining in the doorway.

'No, thanks,' Hobart replied as he put his briefcase on the table.

'Someone'll be with you in a couple minutes,' the driver said before closing the door.

Hobart removed his jacket, placing it on the back of a chair, straightened his tie and sat down. The room was so quiet and still that he could feel his pulse beating away in his body. It seemed a little fast to him and he thought about how long it had been since his last medical check-up. Then he remembered that it had been on the day of his wife's birthday: the tests had taken longer than he'd expected and he'd almost been late for their celebratory dinner. She had raised a glass to wish them both a long and happy life, a sentiment uncommon for her, and as a result he remembered being suddenly worried since the results from his tests were not yet ready. He'd read more than he should have into the coincidence of the toast. As it had turned out he was as fit as a fiddle but the dinner had been a quiet one because of his concerns.

Hobart put his fingers against his throat and counted the pulse, which appeared to have already slowed. Then, feeling ridiculously self-conscious, he stopped himself. Why was it that the older people got, their fear of death increased? When you're young and with everything to live for you don't think about it. But when you reach an age where statistically you know you should have less years to live than the number you've already been alive for you think about it more often. Death was inevitable.

The thought triggered speculation about Stratton's likely remaining time on earth. The guy was on a suicide mission and surely heading in the old pine-box direction fast. If Skender's people didn't get him the police or the Bureau would. Even if by some miracle he did survive he was looking at a long, long time behind bars, all because he believed he owed it to his buddy, his buddy's wife and their kid. A sad fact of life, thought Hobart, was that if you were born a man of honour and integrity you were bound to run up against authority in the long run: the law sure as heck didn't make allowances for those qualities.

The door opened and three men in suits walked in.

'Bill Weighbridge,' the taller, older, more polished-looking man said, holding out his hand unsmilingly, his stare immediately assessing his FBI counterpart.

Hobart stood, took Weighbridge's hand and shook it. 'Hobart,' he said.

'Sam Belling, Bo Anderson,' Weighbridge continued, introducing his colleagues who took their boss's lead and formally shook Hobart's hand.

Weighbridge sat down a chair away from Hobart and the other two men sat at the other side of the table.

'How was your flight?' Weighbridge asked.

'Fine' Hobart replied, deciding to let the other guy get the ball rolling. It was, after all, his office.

Belling was watching Hobart but Anderson was looking down at his own fingers as if he was uninterested.

Hobart's immediate assessment of Weightbridge was that he was a tough-minded man who in his younger days had been physically hard too. He looked confident, in control and dominating.

'I appreciate the importance attached to this visit,' Weighbridge said. 'And I'm sure you want to get back as soon as you can. So, what have we got here?' he asked, sitting back and looking directly into Hobart's eyes.

'I'll get right to the point. First, though, I'd like to thank you for taking the time to see me at such short notice, and also for your help with what we do regard as a very serious case.' Hobart spoke with a hint of humility but not enough to make it obvious that he was stroking the CIA men's sense of superiority. He was well aware, of course, that they had not yet been of any assistance at all. 'This man, John Stratton,' Hobart went on. 'I've come for two things. First, I need to know everything about him.'

A knock on the door interrupted them. Hobart looked up to see it open and a man step in, glance at the faces around the table and then look as if he might be in the wrong room. It was Seaton.

'Come in,' Weighbridge said and Seaton obeyed, closing the door behind him. 'Take a seat. This is Agent Seaton,' he said to Hobart. 'Hobart is with the FBI in California.'

Seaton nodded a greeting as he sat down. Despite having no idea what this was about he suddenly felt uneasy.

'I've asked Seaton to join us because he knows Stratton better than anyone in the Agency. Wouldn't you say that was about right?' Weighbridge asked, looking at Seaton.

Seaton's heartbeat increased its pace as his temples tightened. He was unable to stop some of his surprise showing on his face, his immediate thoughts concerning the box of explosives and the intelligence file that he had given to Stratton. 'Yeah, I know him – though I wouldn't say I know him well.'

Weighbridge interrupted as Hobart was about to say something. 'Before we get into this, I'd like to say something – set some guidelines, if you like. I'm not about to throw up any obstacles here. You've got a job to do and we've got a responsibility to help, and as far as I'm concerned that's how it's going to be.'

Encouraging, Hobart thought. The man appeared sincere enough. Now let's see if he is.

'However . . .' Weighbridge went on.

And so much for *that*, Hobart thought.

'I don't know this guy Stratton personally,' Weighbridge said. 'Never met him, but on paper he has a value, to the Brits and also to us – he's worked for us on occasion. He has a pretty high-level security classification. Works at the sharp end. You'll understand the Brits' concerns about a guy like that getting sucked into a domestic Stateside entanglement such as this. Personally, I don't give a rat's ass about his future. The guy's broken the law and he's got to pay the price. But I want to ask you, and I mean, I'm *asking* you, to bear that history in mind, whatever happens to him. The Brits don't see him as a security risk but this is not a good time to have this kind of publicity getting kicked around by media hounds.'

'Thank you for being so frank and direct,' Hobart went on, maintaining his air of good-natured humility. 'I'll be equally candid and tell you that this case is connected to one of our most high-level and confidential operations regarding crime syndication in this country. We share equally your misgivings about publicity. The police are involved but in a manpower capacity only. As far as they're concerned we're looking for a crazed English guy who has some knowledge of explosives. If the media does become involved – which is probably inevitable since this began as a police case and leaks from that quarter are impossible to prevent – we shall have a credible explanation ready. I would appreciate any help from you in that area.'

Weighbridge nodded. He liked Hobart's style and felt he could trust him. His attempts at sidestepping the bad blood between the two organisations were obvious but Weighbridge got the impression that on a personal level the man was sincere.

Hobart removed several printed sheets of paper from his briefcase and placed them on the desk, pushing one in front Weighbridge and the rest to the other men. 'That's a detailed history of events so far. Why don't you go ahead and read through them, get up to speed and I'll fill you in on the most recent information that we have.'

The men pulled the papers in front of them and began reading.

Seaton read quickly through the details of the two assassinations, the backfired retaliatory hit in the alleyway and Josh's kidnapping. But what he was looking for in particular were any references to the origins of the explosives. As he reached the last sentence he was relieved to see that there were none. He breathed a little easier.

Hobart waited for Weighbridge to finish before handing out another page. 'That's a list of products which Stratton was known to be in possession of by yesterday evening. I understand that these chemicals could be used to produce a significantly powerful explosive device as well as detonators.'

'And a helluva lot of "products" there are, too,' Anderson said, studying the list.

'How long would you estimate it would take him to put a device that big together?' Hobart asked. He'd already had an answer to that question from Phil but he wanted to get these people involved.

'That would depend on what he was making exactly,' Anderson replied, suddenly taking an interest. 'He could produce maybe eighty to ninety pounds of raw cyclonite or RDX crystals in a single day if he has any experience in production. That's a lot of high explosives. Why's there a question mark against the metal mercury?'

'We know he was looking for some but we don't know if he's been able to get hold of any yet.'

'If he does then he's going for mercury fulminate as a detonator.'

'Is that easy to manufacture?' Hobart asked.

'If he doesn't blow himself up he could produce fulminate in, say, half a day,' Anderson said. 'Then he'd want to test it, of course.'

'Test it?' Hobart asked.

'Sure. Detonators are usually made up of a primary and secondary explosive, the primary being the more powerful charge that's initiated by a secondary, less volatile one. Fulminate is a primary explosive but if handled correctly it can be used without the secondary charge. Depending on how this guy constructs the detonator he'd want to be sure that it's going to ignite the RDX.'

'I'm assuming you have an idea what his target is?' Weighbridge asked.

'I want to stop him before he gets that far,' Hobart said, avoiding the question. He wasn't here to discuss every detail of his case with them, just Stratton and his threat potential. 'What I'd like are some recent photos and a description of Stratton, if that's possible?'

Weighbridge looked at Belling who nodded at him.

'It'll be in your office before you get back,' Weighbridge said.

'One other request,' Hobart said. 'I'd like one of your guys to assist us. Someone who would know how an operator like Stratton might think or react in a given situation. Better still, someone who actually knows him.'

Hobart didn't look at Seaton. But Weighbridge threw a glance in the man's direction and pondered the request for a moment.

'You okay with that?' Weighbridge asked Seaton.

Seaton could only wish that he had some hugely important high-priority task that would stop him going to California with Hobart but he didn't. 'Sure,' he said.

Hobart looked at Seaton and nodded. Then he turned back to Weighbridge.

'Anything else?' Weighbridge asked, looking as if he needed to be somewhere else.

'Not right now,' Hobart said.

Weighbridge got to his feet and Hobart did the same.

'Thanks,' Hobart said, holding out his hand.

Weighbridge gripped it. 'You need anything else, go through Seaton and we'll see what we can do.'

'I appreciate it,' Hobart said.

The men filed out of the room, except for Seaton. Hobart repacked his briefcase and pulled his jacket off the back of his chair.

'When are you heading back to California?' Seaton asked.

'I've got a charter waiting at Dulles.'

'And you want me to go with you right now?'

Hobart paused to look at Seaton, picking up a feeling of deep reluctance radiating from the guy. 'That was the idea,' he said, being ever so nice. 'But if you have things to do, maybe Weighbridge can get me someone else,' he said, knowing what the reply to that would be.

'No, that's fine. I was just checking. I'm gonna need a few things. It's a short detour to my house.'

'Sure,' Hobart said, pulling his jacket on and then extending an open palm towards the door. 'Lead on.'

Half an hour later the two men were pulling away from Seaton's house and heading for Dulles International Airport. Seaton and Hobart sat in the back seat of the sedan, staring out of their respective windows, both deep in thought. Then Hobart took his cellphone from a pocket, dialled a number, put the phone to his ear and waited for it to connect. 'Hendrickson? Hobart. You should be receiving an ID on Stratton within the next few hours. It'll probably come in on my private e-mail. Pull it up but do *not* distribute it. That's for the team's eyes only, you got that? Next. The sightings of Stratton in the Bakersfield area. It's likely he's holed up somewhere isolated. Somewhere he can test an explosive device without raising an alarm. It's also possible that he could be done preparing the explosives by today. That means he could be heading back to Los Angeles any time.

I'm on my way to the airport. I should arrive in Burbank by around six p.m. Okay.'

Hobart pocketed the phone and thought through all the information he had once again, checking that there was nothing he had overlooked. 'When's the last time you saw Stratton?' he asked Seaton.

Seaton glanced at Hobart but saw nothing in his expression that gave anything away. 'We were in Iraq together just over a month ago,' he said.

'Was that where Jack Penton died?'

'Yes.'

'Did you know his wife and kid?'

'Jack's? I met 'em once.'

Hobart glanced at Seaton again as a thought struck him. 'That was the last time you saw Stratton – in Iraq?'

Seaton took a moment to think his answer through. Hobart had repeated the question which suggested that it was more than just idle curiosity on his part. It would not take a senior FBI man long to find out from other sources about a domestic flight that Stratton had recently taken. Nor could Seaton ask his wife and kids to lie about the English special forces guy who had stayed overnight. A lie like that would come back to haunt him and then all the other lies, especially any about the origins of the explosives, would be difficult to cover up. 'No. He came to visit me here, the day after he arrived in LA.'

Hobart stared at the side of Seaton's head for a moment. Then he looked away as several pieces of the puzzle slipped neatly into place. Seaton was the one who had given Stratton the information that he'd needed to hit Leka and Ardian – and Hobart would bet his hat that Seaton had also given him the explosives.

The first thing that came to Hobart's mind was that he now had the CIA over a barrel. But he realised that Weighbridge couldn't have known about Stratton's visit to Seaton or he sure as hell would not have invited the guy to the meeting. Seaton had done it as a personal favour to a friend. It was Seaton who Hobart had over a barrel. The obvious question now was where did Seaton's true loyalties lie: with Stratton or with himself?

'So how good is he?' Hobart asked.

Seaton glanced at him, unsure what he meant exactly.

'With explosives,' Hobart added. 'How good is Stratton?'

Seaton looked back out of the sedan window. 'The best explosives experts are often given the title bomb doctor. They call him the surgeon.'

'Great,' Hobart sighed.

Chapter 29

As Hobart was setting off for Burbank that morning, Stratton was climbing out of the pick-up and heading towards the mine with his newly purloined goods from the night before. The ground squirrel was waiting at the entrance and Stratton, pleased to see that the little guy hadn't been hurt by the blast, stopped to dig a cracker from his pocket. This time the squirrel grabbed it up, took a bite, munched on it for a few seconds and scampered off with it. Stratton tossed a couple more on the ground and headed down the entrance shaft.

The process of preparing the detonators was much more complex than making the RDX. Mercury fulminate was one of the oldest detonation explosives around and theoretically adequate to initiate RDX. But it was much more unstable and great caution was required in its manufacture.

A coat of dust had gathered over everything during the night and after lighting the lamps Stratton set about cleaning the equipment he was going to need. Taking one of the pots, he poured in four gallons of nitric acid. Then he put on the gas mask. When he added the first of four bottles of mercury metal, toxic red fumes immediately floated off the liquid's surface. While the mercury slowly dissolved he placed another of the large pots on the gas heater, put the large glass cooking bowl inside it, poured in enough water around the bowl so that it would sit in the pot without floating, half-filled the bowl with ethyl alcohol and then ignited the burner.

While the alcohol heated, Stratton stirred the acid-mercury mix with a wooden spoon. When the ethyl was warm, he carefully poured the mix into it. Within a few seconds it began to bubble and froth while giving off thick white fumes whose colour changed to red and then back to white again in a short space of time. Solid particles started to form in the liquid and when it stopped bubbling he poured it into the third pot, which contained several gallons of water. Using the sieve, he filtered out the particles, placed them back into the glass bowl that he had cleaned out, added some more ethyl alcohol, poured it all back into the sieve and then ran water through it to clean it. Once the fulminate had fully dried it would be ready for use.

An hour later he had all seventy of the three-inch lengths of narrow plastic pipe lined up, each with one end twisted and heat-sealed and stuck into the ground. Their open ends were uppermost. Next came the laborious task of placing a teaspoonful of fulminate into each. Once that was done Stratton cut the fine wire into six-inch lengths, quickly heated the middle of each length over the gas flame and then stretched it, being careful not to break it. He bent each in two at the thinnest point to form a hairpin, which he then inserted into the end of each pipe so that it was buried in the fulminate. Epoxy glue was then dropped into the end to seal the wire and the fulminate inside. Now all that was required was another test.

Stratton used the same location as for the RDX test of the previous day since it appeared to be in a stable state. He walked down the shaft while unreeling the rest of the length of wire and carrying the detonator and a small piece of RDX. The aim of the test was twofold. He needed to prove that the circuit would explode the fulminate and that the fulminate would in turn detonate the RDX. The problem was that he would not be able to tell if the RDX had blown unless he used a bit more than in the earlier test. The mercury fulminate would, of course, be far less powerful than the RDX alone. Still, a little more RDX than before was required to make sure. He would just have to take the risk that he might bring down the shaft's ceiling.

Stratton moulded the hazelnut-sized piece of RDX around the end of the detonator, attached the wires and walked back to the initiation point. He touched one of the wires to one end of a small battery. Then, after a final check around him, he put the flashlight on the ground between his knees so that he could grab it quickly and touched the other wire to the opposite end of the battery.

The explosion rocked the shaft and when chunks of the rock ceiling began to fall around Stratton he grabbed the flashlight and sprinted away as the tunnel collapsed where he had been crouching. He did not stop until he had reached the main junction. Dust was falling everywhere and for a moment, as he made his way to the exit shaft, he thought that he had over-done it. But as the rumbling ceased so did the apparent imminent threat of a serious collapse. Nevertheless, he decided to go outside for a bit of fresh air and give the old mine a few minutes to settle in case.

Stratton did not need to inspect the detonation point as it was evident that the RDX had exploded. After a bite to eat he went back into the main cavern to find everything covered in yet more dust but other-wise in good shape.

Using the spike tool on his knife he made a hole in the bottom of each sandwich box, pushed a deton-ator through it into the RDX and applied some glue to hold it in place. The final stage was to attach a battery and receiver to one end of each wire – leaving the other end free until the moment of placement – tape it all up into a neat package, and place each device back inside its original cardboard box, making it look completely innocuous. Soon the thirty-two home-made claymore mines were ready to go.

Stratton took another short break in the sunshine before returning to the mine with a hammer and a dozen spike nails which he hammered into several of the wooden supports. The next task was to make a length of explosive cord, which he had never done before. But he understood the theory. Taking the can of latex he poured a good amount into the glass bowl. Then he unreeled a hundred feet or so of the thou-sand-foot reel of string and pushed it into the tacky white liquid. Beyond the latex he placed an open bag of RDX and slowly drew the latex-wet string through it so that the explosive crystals stuck to it. As the string got longer he looped it back and forth from nail to nail, hanging it like a washing line. He placed another hundred feet or so in the bowl along with more latex and repeated the procedure until all the string had been coated and was hanging across the nails to dry.

The final job was to fill two dozen of the freezer bags with all but a couple of pounds of the remaining RDX. Then he moulded them into sausage shapes, made a hole in one end of each, pushed a detonator into it, attached a receiver and taped them all up into separate bundles.

When the string, or explosive cord as it now was, was dry Stratton rolled it back around the reel. Then he was done, as far as the cooking and preparations were concerned. He felt quite good about what he had achieved. He picked up the freezer-bag charges, took them out to the pick-up and checked his watch. It was nearly three p.m. and although he was almost ready to go he decided not to leave the mine until dark. He'd spend what was left of the daylight going over the construction plans once again.

He retrieved the blueprint rolls and file from the cab, sat outside the barn in the sun and went through the engineer's folder that contained details of all the companies involved in the construction of Skender's building. There was still one major part of the plan that he had not yet worked out: how to get into the building to plant the explosives.

Hobart was seated at the back of the Falcon 10 charter aircraft, Seaton across the aisle from him, when the stewardess stepped out of the cockpit holding a phone on the end of a long cord and handed it to him. 'A call for you, Mr Hobart,' she said.

Hobart took the phone and put it to his ear. 'This is Hobart.'

'Sir. Hendrickson here. We have some developments. We just picked up a report off the police net from the SCSN, that's the California Seismic Network operating out of Pasadena. Two small unscheduled explosions were recorded at a location east of Bakersfield.'

Hobart sat forward in his chair. 'When?' he asked.

'One was yesterday at 4:35 p.m., the other a couple of hours ago. The SCSN didn't report the first explosion but when the second occurred in the same location they called it in.'

'Where?'

'An area called Twin Oaks about thirty miles east of Bakersfield. The map shows an abandoned mine at that location.'

'Okay. Listen to me. I want you to get an HRT unit mobile a.s.a.p. towards that location, understood?'

'Yes, sir.'

'I'm gonna land at Bakersfield airport — what's its name?'

'Em — Meadows Field, I think.'

'That's it. Meadows Field. I'll meet you there. And I want a bird in the air but I don't want it over the mine. You got that? And don't forget my vest and my gun.'

Hobart got out of his seat, carrying the phone, and went to the cockpit. A few minutes later he returned to his seat, looking pensive.

407

Seaton was watching him and Hobart felt obliged to include him in the loop.

'We're landing in Bakersfield. Stratton's using an abandoned mine to make his explosives. We're gonna stop your boy before he gets to LA.'

'He's not my boy,' Seaton said. But he read the FBI man's meaning, whether it was deliberate or not. Hobart wasn't a fool and it didn't take a genius to work out that Stratton had arrived in LA knowing nothing about Sally's murderers. Then, after a brief visit to a friend in the CIA, he'd come back to LA and taken them out. 'For what it's worth,' Seaton said, 'I told him not to do it and to take the legal route.'

'*Yeah, but you gave him the explosives anyway,*' Hobart wanted to say. But he chose not to.

'But then there was no legal option, was there?' Seaton went on, as if he had read Hobart's thoughts.

'What would you have done?' Hobart asked.

'If my wife had been murdered by scum who were above the law? Well, tell you the truth, I'd like to say I would have done the same, but I don't honestly know. It takes more than just the will to do something like that. You've got to have the ability. Not sure if I have that. What about you?'

'Me? I sure as hell don't have the ability. The reason I wouldn't is because I'd know there was someone like me who was going to stop me.'

'You don't think Stratton knows that? The way he sees it, he spends most of his adult life doing exactly this kind of work for our side and when he needs help all his supposed colleagues can do is hunt him down so that they can kill him like a dog.'

'Well, maybe he should've asked,' Hobart said. Then he immediately regretted the pointless comment. Hobart had had every intention of putting Leka and Ardian away for the murder one day. But then, Stratton wasn't to know that. 'Anyhow, no one's gonna kill him – if we can help it.'

'Stratton's not planning on spending the rest of his life in a cell, I can tell you that much about him. He's playing for keeps on this one. He owes Josh everything and the kid's gonna collect, one way or another.'

'Whose side are you on, Seaton? Maybe you should tell me now because you're no good to me if you're on his.'

'We both know you've got me over a barrel, Hobart. Don't worry. If it comes down to it, I'll take my thirty pieces of silver,' Seaton said, hating the words as soon as they'd left his lips. But what he'd said was true and there was no point in denying it even to himself. He'd done more than most would have done for Stratton – too much, in fact. Maybe Stratton was in this hole because of what Seaton had done to help him but the guy would have found another way to get even if Seaton had baulked. He would have discovered the truth somehow and come back. That was who he was. And now that Josh was at stake this was more than just another mission. Stratton had more incentive than he'd ever had in his life and he was going to see it through.

Seaton looked out of the window. It was still light, the sun dropping ahead of them. Half an hour later the plane crossed the California state line and the stewardess announced that they would shortly be landing at Meadows Field.

Hendrickson was on the tarmac when the Falcon came to a stop. He told the FBI driver to close on the aircraft as the door opened and the gangway unfolded to the ground.

Hobart was first out and didn't waste a second getting into the car, Seaton climbing into the back beside him.

'An HRT unit is on its way to Twin Oaks,' Hendrickson said as he got in beside the driver and the car pulled away. 'They'll wait for us short of the mine if we don't catch up with them before that,' he continued, glancing over his shoulder at Seaton, wondering who he was and hoping that someone would introduce him.

'The cops?' Hendrickson asked.

'Standing by to put in roadblocks if we need 'em. They have the vehicle description and are looking for an English guy approximately thirty-five years old.'

'Where's the bird?' Hobart asked.

'Should be in the area any time.'

'I want it way on the edge of the area. The chopper's job is pursuit in case he makes a break for it.'

'The pilot's been briefed, sir,' Hendrickson said as he pulled out his notebook and turned on a reading light above him. 'Some other reports that came in during the last hour. Alan's Chemicals, where Stratton bought his nitric acid. They think they're missing several bottles of mercury metal and a two-gallon can of latex solution.'

Hobart looked at Seaton. 'What's he need latex for?'

Seaton shrugged. 'Beats me.'

Hendrickson looked between Seaton and Hobart,

sensing something odd there between them. 'I collated all industrial-related robberies over the last forty-eight hours in a radius of two hundred miles,' Hendrickson continued. 'We got a twelve-ton digger taken from a building site in Rosedale this morning, a bunch of power tools last night from a warehouse in Mojave, but that was by a couple of guys. A model store in Simi Valley reported a hundred receivers and batteries taken last night—'

'What kind of receivers?' Seaton interrupted.

Hendrickson checked his notes. 'High-tech ultra-featherlight four-channel FM forty-megahertz aircraft receivers.'

'You got any ECM?' Seaton asked.

'ECM?' queried Hendrickson.

'Electronic countermeasures,' Seaton explained. 'To block transmissions.'

'No,' Hendrickson said, looking between the two men.

'You might want to think about pulling some in,' Seaton said.

Hendrickson made a note.

'How long before we get to this place?' Hobart asked as the car sped out of the airport.

'We burn gas, we can make it in fifteen minutes,' Hendrickson said confidently.

'You know those funny little flashing lights we sometimes use to let people know we're in a hurry?' Hobart asked. 'Well, turn the fucking things on.'

Hendrickson obeyed instantly, kicking himself for forgetting it.

Chapter 30

As soon as the daylight had begun to fade, Stratton had rolled up the blueprints, put them back into the pick-up's cab and gone into the mine to collect the rest of the charges and carry them to the truck. As he secured the load under the tarpaulin and tied the last slip knot he stopped dead as a faint sound dropped out of the slight breeze above. A second later it was gone.

He climbed down, stepped out of the barn and scanned the night sky. It was filled with stars that seemed unusually bright.

As he stood holding his breath, his senses tingling, the sound came again, as brief and faint as before but unmistakable to his experienced ear.

Stratton stepped further into the open and looked up again, panning slowly around. But he could see nothing to confirm that what he'd heard was almost certainly a distant helicopter. Then it came again, a little louder this time, the faint throb produced by rotors cutting through the air.

He stood still for almost a minute, waiting for it again. But the air was empty now except for the breeze gently toying with the treetops.

If it was a coincidence it didn't matter – a rule of survival in the intelligence business was that there was no such thing. The fact was that Stratton had been in the same location for too long.

He hurried into the mine and down the shaft, knowing what he had to do. He'd been considering his contingency plans since his arrival. Some fulminate remained in the glass bowl and he placed it in the centre of the cavern, grabbed up the reel of explosive cord, tied a knot in the end and carefully placed it in the detonator compound. The remaining RDX was in a corner in a bin liner and he carried it over and lowered it gently on top of the bowl. Then he picked up the gas bottle, leaned it against the RDX and moved the glowing petrol lights alongside it. He picked up the reel and headed slowly back up the shaft, unreeling the cord as he went, ensuring that it remained slack but without any kinks or loops that might negate its function.

When Stratton reached the truck he hung the reel over the driver's wing mirror, climbed into the cab and turned the key in the ignition. But the beast of an engine kicked over once and then died.

'Great,' Stratton muttered as he turned the starter again and stamped on the accelerator. But the truck appeared to have chosen this moment to retire. The smell of petrol wafted from the engine compartment and he cursed himself for flooding it.

He sat back, took a calming breath, left the pedals alone and eased the ignition key around in its slot. 'Come on, old girl,' he said as the starter motor turned over several times without the engine catching. As he let go of the key to give the starter motor another rest the engine suddenly boomed into life, spluttering as a couple of the pistons failed to ignite at first. A gentle pressure on the accelerator increased the revs and as the truck shook with the unbalanced rhythm the idle cylinders suddenly kicked in. The roar grew healthier by the second.

'Attagirl,' Stratton said as he played the accelerator to warm the engine. Then he eased it into reverse and backed out of the barn. He straightened the truck up as the nose faced the track that he could just about make out by the gap through the trees. Keeping his lights off, he eased it into drive and powered slowly forward, his hand out through the window as he unwound the cord. He kept the line slack, being careful not to pull the end out of the charge, and it seemed to take an age to reach the gate. As he closed on it Stratton took his foot off the accelerator and eased the gear lever into neutral so that the truck would roll to a stop without him having to touch the brakes and activate the red tail lights. To bring the truck to a final halt he eased on the handbrake, jumped out, opened the gate, climbed back into the truck and eased it forward.

A few yards past the gate Stratton turned off the road, along a rut that separated the track from the wood, up and over the other side and in among the trees, the lower branches snapping against the sides of the truck. He continued slowly into the wood and when the cord ran off the reel after reaching the end he stopped the truck, using the handbrake again. He turned off the engine.

Stratton climbed out. He walked ahead of the vehicle through the trees until he reached the edge of the wood from where he could see the road several hundred yards away. He watched it, waiting for his night vision to kick in.

As it did, a shape began to grow in clarity on the hairpin bend in the darkness. After a few minutes Stratton had no doubt that it was a large van. Then his heart quickened as the possibility grew that the van and helicopter were part of a net closing in on him. He looked in all directions, not only for signs of other elements of a trap but for a way out. The ground in front of him was rough but all right for the pick-up and he could make the road without using the track if he had to. The problem was what to do then, if he could even get that far, since there were bound to be roadblocks. He had two choices: leave now and abandon the mission or let the noose tighten around his position and then assess the disposition of the enemy and their likely tactics.

A pair of headlights suddenly flashed from the direction of Caliente and a few seconds later they disappeared, extinguished. But he could hear the vehicle's motor and then the black silhouette came into view on the road from Twin Oaks, eventually slowing to a stop behind the van with a brief display of red brake lights. A moment later several dark shapes climbed out from both vehicles and gathered in the gap between them.

'That track leads directly to the mine,' the commander of the HRT unit said to Hobart as they approached each other. The commander was dressed in a one-piece black fire-retardant suit, a Heckler & Koch MP5K sub-machine gun hanging by his side and a pistol in a holster strapped to his right thigh. A chest harness filled with MP5K magazines and a radio with a wire leading to an earpiece completed the ensemble. Behind him the rear doors of the van were open, revealing about two dozen similarly dressed personnel sitting inside.

'How do you want to play this?' Hobart asked as he scanned the distant black wood that hid the precise location of the mine.

'Way I see it, we can do it two ways,' the HRT agent said with a degree of confidence. 'We can debus here and make our way in teams across country to the wood, then head for the mine, cover it from all sides, see what we got and then head in. Other option is to drive up the track, get closer to the mine, debus and move in along the track. The walk-in option is quieter,' he said, looking at the night sky and listening to the still air.

'Unless you get caught up in the wood,' Hobart said, not sounding overly confident. He didn't know the man other than by sight and was never too fond of this military type of operation. Hobart was a Federal agent, by job and by heart, and running around the countryside with a small army made him feel more like some kind of platoon commander. It did not appeal to him.

'We'll do a reconnaissance first, of course,' the commander said, sounding to Hobart more like a soldier than an FBI agent.

'You know exactly where the mine is?' Hobart asked. 'I mean precise distance and bearing?' Hobart knew something about operating in the field from his time in Kosovo, not that he was an expert by any means, but he had on more than one occasion experienced how difficult it was to cross strange country at night.

The HRT commander gave him a hostile look under cover of darkness, feeling annoyed as well as somewhat compromised. Hobart was his boss, sure, but this little shindig was the commander's to plan and organise and he didn't like having his toes stepped on. However, the old hack had a point, he had to admit. 'Not exactly, no. That's why I'd like to do a recon.'

'Recon,' Hobart muttered to himself, beginning to get the feeling that this guy had read too many Nam books. 'Which do you prefer?' Hobart asked. In situations like this the call was usually left up to the HRT commander. But one of Hobart's other problems was handing authority over to subordinates, mainly because he rarely trusted anyone else's decisions but his own.

'Well, since we don't know exactly where the mine *is*,' the HRT commander said. 'I mean, I know it's close but I couldn't point a finger in its exact direction so maybe we should move in along the track. That also covers us if he decides to move out in his truck while we're moving in.'

'Why don't you wait till morning?' Seaton asked. He had been standing quietly in the background but felt the urge to intervene.

The HRT commander looked over at the stranger, wondering who he was.

'Things always go wrong in the dark,' Seaton went on. 'Plus you're giving him a lot of advantages.'

'I've got twenty men in that wagon,' the HRT commander said with some arrogance. 'All professionals and with night vision. We can handle one man no matter how this cake is cut.'

'But isn't this track the only way out?' Seaton asked.

The HRT commander was getting miffed with both these guys trying to tell him his job. 'And what's to stop him just walking out the back? There's a thousand miles of nothin' out there. He could be twenty miles away by morning in any direction.'

'But not with a ninety-pound bomb,' Seaton said. 'I guess you have to ask yourself which is the most important at this stage: the explosives or the man?'

'I want them both,' Hobart said.

'In that case we should head in now,' the HRT commander said.

Hobart wasn't sure about any of the ideas. What Seaton had said sounded like good sense but he didn't like the idea of giving Stratton any more time than he already had. 'Let's head down the track in the vehicles,' Hobart said to the HRT commander. 'Get closer to the mine, see how it feels, then you take it from there.'

'I think that's a good idea,' the commander said with a glance in Seaton's direction before heading for the cab of the van.

Seaton shrugged his indifference and followed Hobart back to the car.

The van started its engine, turned off the road,

creaked down the dip onto the track and slowly headed along it, followed by Hobart's sedan.

Stratton watched them until they were out of sight beyond his stretch of the wood and made his way back, past his truck, to where he could see the gate which he had left open.

A couple of minutes later the large black van moved slowly across his front, closely followed by the sedan. Stratton moved his position to keep them in view when their brake lights suddenly cut through the darkness and both vehicles stopped. Stratton estimated they were just short of the final bend to the mine and a good forty yards beyond the gate.

The back of the van opened quietly and the HRT unit climbed down as the sedan's doors opened and the four people inside stepped out. It was too dark for Stratton to make out any more than a crowd of silhouettes but they appeared to be concentrating their attention towards the mine and not to their rear.

Seaton remained by the front of the car watching the HRT group hold a parliament behind the van, after which the commander broke away and joined Hobart.

'We're gonna move down the track in file in four teams,' the agent said to Hobart in a low voice. 'When we sight the mine we'll break off and take up positions around it. We'll assess the situation from there, see what we've got, and when you give the word we'll move in and take care of this.'

Hobart nodded, though he had a niggling doubt

about something which he put down to the whole military thing.

As the HRT unit moved off around the van and strung themselves out along the track towards the mine Hobart joined Seaton. 'How big a blast is ninety pounds of RDX?' he asked, keeping his voice low. 'I mean, if these guys are around the mine and it goes up, can they get hurt?'

Seaton shrugged. 'Depends where the blast is. If it's in the mine, they could be fine as long as nothing falls on them. If it's on the surface, say, in the vehicle, I wouldn't want to be within five hundred yards of it.'

That was not good, Hobart thought as he looked down the track where he could make out the black silhouettes heading slowly along it.

Stratton watched the line of men move down the track while the other small group from the sedan remained at the vehicles. He headed quietly back towards his pick-up and located the white cord on the ground. He picked it up, dragged it with some care to the truck and gently opened the door so as not to make any noise.

Seaton sighed internally, wondering how this was going to turn out. He walked around the car to look back the way they'd come, his thoughts on where Stratton was at that moment. Seaton expected him to be miles away but if he was at the mine he would know that these guys were coming: their approach was not exactly stealthy.

As he turned to head back to the front of the sedan

and rejoin Hobart his eyes made out a thin grey line on the ground running between the vehicles. Curious as to what it could be he crouched to take a closer look.

Stratton wound the end of the cord a couple of times around the catch inside the pick-up's door frame and looked back through the trees at the silhouettes on the track.

Seaton reached a hand out for the cord, noting that it ran beneath both vehicles. He raised it off the ground a couple of inches, felt the abrasive crystals, released it and put his fingers to his nose. He inhaled the odour that seemed familiar.

'Hobart!' Seaton said as he stood up and moved away from the cord, his stare following it first into the distance towards the mine, then back the other way along the track.

Hobart, Hendrickson and the driver looked round at him, bemused by his raised voice.

'I think you'd better move away from the vehicles,' Seaton said as he closed on Hobart who was practically standing on the cord. Seaton reached out a hand to grab the FBI man's arm.

Stratton pulled open the door as far as it would go, gripped it with both hands and planted his feet to get a solid purchase. Explosives are measured by the speed at which they burn and RDX combusts at around 24,000 feet per second – the speed it would travel if it was stretched out in a line, as it was in this case.

Stratton gathered himself and then swung the door as hard as he could so that it slammed shut, while at the same time turning his back to the cord and ducking away. The blast ripped outwards from the point where the cord had been struck and the door burst back open.

The explosion came out of the wood and down the track like a thunderbolt, tearing beneath both vehicles, rupturing and igniting their fuel tanks at the instant when Seaton grabbed Hobart's shoulder. It shot along the track, swatting the entire HRT unit aside like flies. Less than a second after Stratton slammed the door the mine exploded, rocking the very ground and sending a blast of rubble and dust from the mouth of the entrance shaft like grapeshot from a giant cannon.

Stratton climbed inside the vehicle, started the engine which was still warm and drove forward through the wood all the while holding the door shut since the latch was now broken. He passed out the other side of the wood and across the stretch of rugged open ground towards the road. He kept the speed down while avoiding any large dips or bumps, conscious of the sensitivity of his cargo. Then he mounted the road and sped along it towards Twin Oaks.

As he approached the bar he could see that the lights were on and a dozen or so vehicles were parked in a haphazard manner on the open ground outside.

He slowed as he turned off the road, pulled in tightly alongside a white pick-up slightly smaller than his and stopped. He looked in through the passenger window, saw the key in the ignition and killed his engine. He shuffled across the seat, climbed out of his passenger door, grabbing his gear, and climbed up onto the truck's bed. The white pick-up was empty and as quickly as he could he transferred his load onto it.

A few minutes later Stratton was back on the road in the white pick-up and tearing along as fast as was safe. Caliente was the last bottleneck he had to pass through and from there he had half a dozen choices of roads to the highway and after that a hundred different routes to LA.

As he reached the end of the town he saw a white car parked on the side of the road up ahead and slowed. As he suspected, it was a police patrol car and the state trooper seated behind the steering wheel looked at Stratton as he drove past.

Stratton watched the patrol car in his rear-view mirror, waiting to see if its lights came on. Then it was out of sight.

Stratton knew better than to celebrate prematurely but he had the feeling that for the moment he had slipped the net. But now he knew for sure that the net was indeed there – and closing. He had been lucky so far, there was no doubt about it, and if he was to continue the pursuit of his objective the chances were high that he would fail.

Seaton and Hobart, on the ground beside each other, shuffled away from the heat of the flames from the burning vehicles. Hendrickson's coat was on fire and he rolled over and over, yelling 'Holy shit! Holy shit!' until the flames were out.

None of the HRT crew was seriously hurt, though one had broken an ankle. Another, who had been standing on the cord when it detonated, miraculously only lost the heel of his boot.

Hobart got to his feet as his mind came back into focus. Frustration and anger began to rise in him as he realised that they had walked right into a trap. 'Hendrickson?' he shouted. 'Hendrickson!' he repeated in irritation, looking for his assistant who was beating his smoking clothing and apparently ignoring him.

'Hendrickson!' he shouted again, moving towards him.

Hendrickson looked up, squinting at his boss.

'Call the goddamned cops and tell them to put out their roadblocks! And where's that damned helicopter?'

Hendrickson shook his head and rotated a finger alongside his ear. 'I can't hear a thing,' he shouted. 'Just ringing.'

It was only when Hobart saw Hendrickson's lips moving and could hear hardly anything he was saying that he realised his ears were ringing too.

Chapter 31

Stratton spent the rest of the night in a motel on the outskirts of Los Angeles and early the next morning, after grabbing a bite at a local diner, he made his way into the bustling city. Morning traffic was heavy but by nine a.m. he was parked outside a construction-equipment hire company in Mar Vista, waiting for it to open. He was the first customer to enter the reception office after the man running the desk had drawn up the blinds and turned on the computer. Ten minutes later, on completion of the paperwork, Stratton was directed to an assistant across the yard who explained how to operate the mobile work platform – or cherry-picker, as it was affectionately known – that he had hired for the day. Stratton was happy to leave a credit-card imprint for the final bill because it would not show up on any police trace for at least twenty-four hours, by which time it would all be over. One way or another.

After a brief run-through of the controls, the assistant helped him attach the mobile platform to the back of the pick-up. Minutes later Stratton was making his way through the side streets that led to Culver City.

He came to a final stop just short of an intersection that was at one of the corners of what, according to a brand new sign, was now called Skender Square. He climbed out and walked to the corner to take a look.

The east face of the pyramid shone dazzlingly as it reflected the sun's morning rays, particularly the golden pinnacle that looked as if it was on fire. The concourse bustled with preparations for the forthcoming ceremonies. Colourful banners connected palm trees and street lamps within the square. Several catering trucks were parked near the entrance with dozens of uniformed staff carrying in chairs, tables, linen and endless trays of food and crates of bottles. The back of a flower truck was open with a jungle of flora outside it waiting to be ferried into the building and a van drawing into the crowded drive bore a sign on its side advertising 'Event Productions Fireworks'. In among all this and surrounding the building were dozens of security guards and the ever-present suited thugs watching all. Several of them stood on the first-floor balconies that surrounded the building, from where they could survey the scene.

Stratton walked back to the cab of the pick-up and dug into his pack for the overalls he had bought in the army-surplus store days before. He pulled them on and filled the pockets with long nylon zip-ties. In a side pouch of his pack he dug out bits and pieces of facial disguises from his first day's shopping in LA and put on a pair of glasses. His face was already darkened by several days' growth of facial hair. The last item was his baseball cap which he pulled down low over his forehead before walking around to the back of the pick-up, unhitching the cherry-picker and loading all the sandwich boxes onto the mobile platform itself.

The rig pushed along easily on its four wheels. Stratton waited for a break in the traffic before crossing the intersection to the corner of the square where a metal lamp-post stood, a banner hanging from its top celebrating the opening of LA's newest and most exciting business centre.

The platform was sturdy enough to be raised without stabilisers as long as it was moved directly up and down. Stratton climbed aboard and pushed the up lever. The system, which was electrically operated and would last for hours before it needed recharging, jerked into action as the hydraulic pumps hissed and the platform hummed skywards. He toggled the ascent lever on and off, getting used to the controls.

Stratton took a moment to look at the goings-on from his vantage point. His first observation was that every entrance of the pyramid was guarded by at least three guards and all personnel going into the building – florists, waiters, event staff – were directed to the main entrance only. Here they were searched by hand as well as by metal detector.

Stratton's thoughts had never strayed far from Josh since the day he'd arrived in LA. His heart suddenly began to ache as he wondered where the little boy might be at that moment and how he was being treated. If the Albanians' history was anything to go by they would care little for his well-being and there was no doubt in Stratton's mind that they aimed to kill him eventually – if, heaven forbid, he was not dead already. Josh was insignificant to them and simply a possible means to an end. Life had no value to those animals other than the pain its loss caused others. He doubted that the boy was being kept in the office building since that would be stupid and Skender was anything but that.

Stratton had at one time considered attacking Skender's home, not that he expected Josh to be there either, but had decided against it because the place would be well protected and it would be difficult to guarantee when the man himself would be in. In many ways the office building was an easier target because of its size and the amount of traffic in and out of it. But the main reason for going after it was that it embodied everything Skender was attempting to do in America: his change from drug, arms and human trafficker to legitimate businessman. The edifice was more than a symbol and headquarters of his new empire, it was a homage to himself, to his own vast ego. Most absurdly, it was meant as a snub to the civilised, to those who for centuries had pursued justice, who had fought against wrong for what was plainly right. Stratton was going to hit Skender where he believed it would hurt most and, more importantly, impress upon him that there were lines that he could not cross with impunity, that a single human life had a value, and that, despite a corrupt bureaucratic and judicial system, one man *could* make a difference.

Stratton picked up the first sandwich box, removed it from its cardboard container, attached the loose wire to the battery and then, using a couple of the zip-ties, fastened it securely to the top of the lamp-post. He adjusted it so that the face with the ball-bearings packed beneath it was aimed squarely at the building.

The operation took less than a minute, once he got started. On completion he toggled the descent lever, climbed off the platform as it came to a final stop and pushed the cherry-picker along the street, conveniently cleared of cars for the event, to the next lamp-post.

By the third installation Stratton had the working of the platform down pat and was able to increase the speed of attaching the claymores. It took a little over two hours to arm all thirty-two lamp-posts that surrounded the building. He did this without drawing any attention from the several cop cars that passed. Even a security guard who watched him for several minutes as he prepped the lamp-posts in front of the driveway entrance obviously wasn't suspicious.

On completion of the final claymore installation Stratton crossed the road back to the pick-up and pushed the platform in to the kerb behind it.

The pick-up was a concern to him: he needed to take it somewhere soon and abandon it. But the next phase of the operation weighed heavier on his mind. His original plan had been to get inside the building as a contractor. The file he had taken from the engineer's car revealed that a cable company had yet to wire in an audio/visual system and Stratton had contemplated posing as a technician. But that would have meant making an appointment and there was the risk that if his credentials were checked he could find himself in a trap. Stratton was once more contemplating the prospects of postponing the operation until he could come up with a new idea but more delay meant more suffering for Josh. His anxiety level rose in proportion to his frustration.

A car screeched to a halt behind the platform and Stratton spun around, adrenalin pumping. It was a beat-up old Lincoln town car and the driver's door burst open as a young black guy pulled himself out. He was wearing a red waistcoat, white shirt and black slacks, the same uniform worn by the dozens of staff in attendance at Skender's building. Stratton instantly saw a way through his dilemma.

As the man slammed his car door and hurried towards Stratton to pass him by, Stratton jumped out in front of him with his hands up as if he was a basketball referee stopping play. 'Hey, hey, wait up, wait up,' Stratton said.

'What?' the man said in surprise, adjusting his forward momentum to move around Stratton. 'Outta my way, man. I'm late for work.'

'No, wait. Just one minute. One minute,' Stratton said, shuffling backwards to keep in front of him. 'I'll make it worth your while,' he said in an American twang, not wanting to confuse the issue further by appearing to be a foreigner.

'What's your problem, man?' the black man said, slowing a little. 'I gotta get to work.'

'How much you getting paid for this gig?' Stratton asked, his accent now the Southern slur that he seemed to feel more comfortable with.

'*What?*' the man said, bemused by the question. But the lure of easy money was powerful and even an indirect hint of it could shift a person's focus.

'You're part of the catering staff for this opening

ceremony behind me, right? How much you getting paid?' Stratton asked. 'I'll pay you what you're getting just for telling me.'

The offer, although bizarre, blunted the man's enthusiasm to get away quite so quickly. He took a longer look at Stratton. 'Say what?'

'Tell me how much you're getting paid and I'll pay you the same, right now, right here.'

The temptation then gave way to suspicion since the man had been brought up to know that there was easy money and then there was too-easy money. 'You a crazy motherfucker?'

'I'm not crazy. I'll prove it. How much are you getting paid?'

The man looked Stratton up and down, knowing there was only one way to finish this conversation. 'Hunnerd and fifty bucks.'

'Hundred and fifty?'

'That's what I said. Let's see the money, then,' he said with a contemptuous, doubting smirk.

Stratton reached into his back pocket, took out a wedge of bills, counted a hundred and fifty and handed them to the man who was frankly stunned. 'You sure you ain't crazy?' he asked.

'Not at all,' Stratton said. 'How would you like to earn another five hundred? In fact, make that a thousand.'

'*What?*'

'You heard what I said.'

'What I gotta do, kill some motherfucker?'

'Nope. Nothing illegal. Just a favour.'

'What favour?'

'See that platform? I need you to take it back to the place I hired it from, drop it off, and that's it.'

'Take that back to the hire company?' the black man said, glancing at the platform.

'That's right,' Stratton said, taking the invoice from his pocket and showing the man. 'It's on Venice and Overland.'

'Venice and Overland?' the man said, inspecting the invoice. 'That's a buncha motherfucken' miles from here.'

'I'll give you five hundred dollars now, and when you get there they'll give you my five hundred dollars deposit, which you can keep,' Stratton said, lying about the deposit. But any incentive he could think of to sweeten the deal could only help.

The man was almost hooked but a doubt still lingered. 'I don't get it. Why you gonna give me a thousand dollars to wheel that motherfucker back to the hire company?'

'Okay, I'm gonna tell you, but it's confidential. What's your name?'

'Grant.'

'I'm gonna tell you a secret, Grant, but you gotta promise to keep it to yourself or the deal's off.'

Grant remained confused but the offer of more money had a positive effect. 'Okay.'

'Promise?'

'I promise,' he said, as if he was talking to his kid brother.

'I'm a photographer for *People* magazine. You heard of *People* magazine?'

'Sure.'

'Well, I hired this platform so I could take photos of the celebrities going into the gig, but when I got here I found out they won't let me push it in close enough. So I'm standing here trying to figure out how I'm gonna get in there, and I see you.'

Grant looked at Stratton, then down at his own clothes. 'You wanna get in as a waiter,' he said, figuring it out, a smile growing on his face.

Stratton smiled back. 'You're quick, Grant,' Stratton said. 'And I tell you what. By the time you get back here, you can still turn up for work and get paid for that, too. What do you say?'

'A thousand bucks for pushing that thing a couple a miles,' Grant summarised.

'No. A thousand bucks for the use of your uniform for a couple of hours. Taking that back to the equipment-hire is just doing me a favour.'

Grant beamed. 'Mister. You got yourself a motherfucken' deal. Wait up, though – what am I gonna wear if you got my clothes? I ain't pushin' that motherfucken' thing through this neighbourhood in my underwear.'

'You're gonna wear this,' Stratton said, indicating his overalls.

'That's cool,' Grant said and climbed into his car. As he pulled his clothes off, Stratton unbuttoned his overalls, stepped out of them and tossed them into the car. Grant put them on, climbed out and took a closer look at the platform. 'Motherfucker looks heavy, man.'

'It pushes like a pram. Can I use your car?'

'Say what?'

'I need to get changed.'

'Oh, I get it. Pal, this may look a piece a' shit but it's worth more 'n a thousand bucks, to me at least.'

'I don't want your car. I just want to use it to get changed in and put my gear in. You keep the keys, okay?'

Grant's expression suggested it was okay and nodded. 'Five hunnerd dollars, please,' he said, holding out his hand.

Stratton counted out the money, practically all he had left, and dropped it into Grant's palm. 'Thanks.'

Grant beamed. 'Thank *you*.' He pocketed the money, walked over to the platform, got his weight behind it and pushed it away from the kerb. 'Hey, it do push easy, don' it,' he said as he shoved it down the road. It rolled several yards ahead of him and he hurried to catch it up, then pushed it again, enjoying himself.

Stratton climbed into the car, got out of his clothes and put on the waiter's outfit, which was a little on the tight side. He climbed back out, went to the pick-up, got all his gear and placed it in the boot of the Lincoln. As quickly as he could, he emptied his backpack, went back to the pick-up, loaded the pack with the dozen charges, and hoisted it onto his shoulders. It was heavy and he stooped a little under its weight. He tightened the straps and headed across the road, through the landscape gardening and into the crowd of waiters and caterers unloading the trucks.

Stratton put the pack down by the front wheel of one of the trucks and joined a line of staff collecting items from the back. His mind worked overtime trying to figure out each move as it presented itself. Seeing several catering trolleys to one side he went over to them, took one, and got back in line with it.

A couple of security guards in conversation on the concourse cast an occasional eye over the goings-on around them but seemed more interested in what they had to say to each other. Stratton was soon at the front of the line and as the delivery man reached for a small box Stratton stopped him. 'Give me that big one there. The chickens.'

The man saw the trolley, agreed it was a better option and pushed the heavy box along the truck bed to the edge. Stratton slid it off, balanced it neatly on top of the trolley and pushed it away. Then he stopped as if he had forgotten something and steered the trolley around the truck to where his bag was.

A quick check around showed that he was out of sight of the guards on the concourse and the first-floor balconies. He opened his pack, took out the first charge, opened the box and stuffed it inside one of the cooked chickens. It was too big to fit completely and he turned the chicken so that it sat on the charge, hiding it. Satisfied, Stratton quickly repeated the process until every charge was hidden. He then replaced the lid, dumped his empty pack under the truck, wiped his hands on the side of his pants and pushed the trolley back onto the concourse where he joined the line of staff waiting to be searched at the entrance.

The line shuffled past the large sculpture of a man with its back to Stratton and facing the front doors fifty feet away. Stratton took a look at it as he passed to discover it was a slightly larger than life-size image of Skender wearing a coat that was open and flowing, his arms outstretched like Moses and facing the building as if trying to invoke it to rise up out of the ground. Stratton felt the metal, deciding that it was bronze or something as dense. It was a symbol of Skender's immense ego but it was also something else: Stratton had a perfect use for it.

When it was Stratton's turn to be searched the lid of the box was raised, the chickens inspected without being touched, the metal detector was moved up and down him and after a frisk he was beckoned inside.

As Stratton stepped in through the doors five of Skender's suited thugs were in the lobby. He recognised a couple of them from the McDonald's car park. He pressed his glasses to his face, lowered his head and pushed the trolley under the fabulous chandelier and into a massive ballroom. Islands of tables dotted about the place were gradually being covered in food and drinks of every description.

Stratton paused to take stock and consider his next move. Then he pushed the trolley to an area where rubbish was being collected, picked up a couple of plastic bin bags and, checking around the busy hall to make sure he was not the focus of anyone's attention, reached into the box, removed the first charge from a chicken and put it into a bag. Working quickly, he collected the dozen charges into a couple of bin bags, placed the box of chickens on the table, lifted the bags onto the trolley and placed several boxes of garbage on top of them.

He wheeled the trolley back out into the lobby and stopped beside one of the uniformed security guards at the door. "Scuse me, sir?' he said in his Southern accent. 'Is there somewhere I can dump this garbage?'

The guard looked at him and was about to answer when one of Cano's thugs came over.

'What's he want?' the thug asked. It was one of the goons from the McDonald's car park but he evidently did not recognise Stratton.

'He wants to dump this garbage,' the security guard said.

'I'll take him down,' the thug said. 'Come with me.' Stratton followed him to the elevators and faced them as they waited for one to arrive. Skender's men were all around. Then he heard a familiar voice behind him. Cano had just walked into the lobby to give some orders about securing the floors and to explain where guests, when they arrived in a couple of hours, could and could not go. As an elevator arrived and Stratton, followed by his thug, pushed the trolley inside Cano looked over at them.

'Tony? You going up?' Cano called out, walking towards them.

'Down. Dumping this garbage,' Tony said.

Stratton kept his back to Cano and repositioned one of the bags as if securing it on the trolley better.

'Okay,' Cano said, stopping outside. Tony hit the first-level garage button as Cano glanced at the back of the waiter and the doors closed.

As the elevator descended Stratton moved around to the other side of the trolley. When the lift stopped and the doors opened he pushed it out.

'This way,' Tony said. He led Stratton through the brightly lit concrete car park where a dozen cars occupied a floor designed to take a couple of hundred.

Tony turned a corner to a cage where several dumpsters were lined up and stopped to take a packet of cigarettes from his pocket. 'In there,' he said.

Stratton opened the cage, wheeled the trolley in and threw the top layer of boxes into the dumpster until only his bags remained. Then he glanced at the thug who was lighting his cigarette. 'Can I have one a' them smokes?' he asked.

Tony looked at him as if he were dirt. 'Go fuck yourself,' he said as he exhaled a stream of smoke towards Stratton. 'Get the resta that crap in the dumpster and get going.'

'I can't lift it. My back hurts,' Stratton said, stretching his torso from side to side.

'You put that shit in there or I'll throw you in,' Tony said.

'Give me a hand at least,' Stratton asked.

Tony shook his head with incredulity. 'Goddam faggot,' he said as he approached Stratton and invaded his space. 'Pick it up and dump it or I'll break your fucken' back.' Then Tony looked at Stratton closely. 'Don't I know you from somewhere?' he asked.

'I've done a couple commercials on TV,' Stratton said.

'I don't watch TV. You're the guy at the McDonald's, ain't you?'

'I never seem to get a chance to eat there these days,' Stratton said as he turned to grab the first bag.

Tony reached out to grab Stratton's shoulder. As he did, Stratton swung his body round, one of his hands gripping the fist of the other for extra leverage, and powered his elbow into Tony's jaw, snapping it at the hinge. As the large man fell back and hit the ground Stratton moved swiftly to stand over him and stomped on his throat with the heel of his boot as hard as he could. Tony spasmed as his windpipe collapsed. Stratton brought his heel down several more times until something cracked in Tony's neck and the strength left his body. Tony was still alive – barely – but his breathing was ragged and his limbs quivered. The sound of a car entering the garage down the ramp at the other side of the floor froze Stratton. Its tyres screeched as it turned the corner at the bottom and headed along the length of the garage. Stratton quickly dragged the thug into the cage as the car came to a stop out of sight several rows away. He hid behind one of the dumpsters.

A car door opened and slammed a second later. Footsteps tapped across the shiny concrete floor to where the elevators were. A moment later the elevator doors opened, the footsteps moved inside and the doors closed.

Stratton lifted Tony into a sitting position, gripped him under the arms from behind and heaved him up. Then, grabbing him by the waist, he maintained the upward movement until he could tip the goon over the edge of the dumpster and inside. Stratton looked around for something to throw on top of Tony and saw some pieces of wooden boxes broken down and stacked ready for dumping. He grabbed a plank and was about to place it on top of Tony when something about it caught his attention. It was painted green, with black stencilled letters, and it was familiar in some way.

The stencilled lettering read ER E but was only part of a word or words. Stratton turned over a couple of the other planks and quickly realised that the complete lettering read FLOWER ENGINEERING – the same markings as had been on the boxes placed on Forouf's train in Mosul and carried by the smuggling caravan in Almaty. Had he been investigating Skender's connections to international terrorism the planks might have been an important clue. But now they were irrelevant. He tossed them onto Tony's unconscious body, spread some rubbish over them and closed the dumpster's large rubber lid.

Stratton wheeled the trolley with its load back to the elevator area, pressed the call button and waited. A few seconds later an elevator arrived. He eased the trolley inside and pushed the fourth-floor button. The doors closed.

As the elevator ascended Stratton's silent prayers that it would not stop at the lobby were answered. It accelerated up before quickly slowing as the fourth-floor button glowed and it came to a stop. The doors opened and Stratton looked into the empty curving corridor and pushed the trolley out. The doors closed behind him.

He paused to look around. The design features were familiar to him after the hours of study he had spent on the blueprints but the colours and textures were more 1960s than he had expected. Most of the inside walls were made of frosted green plate glass to give it an open, airy feel and though the floor looked ready to be moved into it was as yet unoccupied.

Stratton moved the trolley along the corridor past

glass office walls that revealed empty rooms. He stopped outside a wooden door, turned the handle and pulled it open. It was a janitor's room and a tight fit but he managed to get the trolley inside. He shut the door.

He quickly put the two bags on the floor, removed four of the charges from one of them, put them on the trolley and opened the door to look outside. The glass wall opposite showed a large room with a massive pillar at its centre. This was the central support, eight yards in diameter, of the entire pyramid.

Stratton pushed the trolley out, up the corridor a few yards, in through the entrance to the large room and towards the pillar. Without a second's hesitation he jumped onto the trolley, stood up carefully so as not to lose his balance, pushed a ceiling tile up, slid it into the ceiling space, picked up the charges two at a time and placed them inside the roof. Then he grabbed hold of a heavy support strut inside and pulled himself up.

Once in, he slid the ceiling tile back into place and looked around, familiarising himself with the layout of the struts and beams that he had studied on paper. He did not need a flashlight since the backs of the ceiling lights illuminated the crawl space, which was riddled with electrical, communication and air-conditioning conduits. Sticking out from the massive central pillar beside him was one of the four main horizontal steel struts that passed through the ceiling space to one of the sides of the pyramid. The vertical strength of the design came from the central pillar, supported by the four sloping sides. Every floor hung from these five main load-bearers.

Stratton had identified the halfway points of the horizontal girders between the central pillar and the sides as the weakest parts of the structure. Theoretically, if they could be cut or even seriously weakened the floor should partially or even completely collapse.

Modern buildings were designed to withstand natural forces like high winds and, especially in California, earthquakes. But unlike the older-fashioned multi-grid structural support system of cubes supporting cubes, they were susceptible to collapse if an unforeseen disaster – such as a bomb – blew away a crucial segment of the structure. A classic modern example had been the Twin Towers of the World Trade Center in New York with a square plan that relied on a four-corner support system with the floors suspended between them. When one or two of the supports were compromised the floors dropped, creating a domino effect of horizontal and vertical collapse.

Skender's building was not quite the same. Being a pyramid, its structure got lighter and stronger towards the top with the four outer sides connecting at the pinnacle. But a similar effect might be achieved in reverse, collapsing the building from the ground up. Stratton was not entirely sure of his theory, which was why he chose to blow three different floors. Still, one thing was certain: if only half the charges did their job then the building would need to be demolished.

He crawled along the ceiling space from minor strut to strut, careful not to disturb any of the ceiling tiles beneath him, until he was halfway along the main horizontal strut. He took one of the charges and shaped it into a pyramid before placing it across one side of the I-beam. The pyramid shape was vital: it was known as a linear cutting charge and had been developed by a scientist named Munro who had proved that such a charge detonated from the outer edge would produce significantly more blast concentrated at the cut point.

There was no shortage of rubbish in the crawl space. Stratton used bits of metal and ceiling tile to hold the charge in place before attaching the detonator and receiver to the battery and making his way back to the central pillar.

He repeated this process with the other three struts within the same crawl space. Then he went back to his start point, carefully removed the ceiling tile, poked his head through to look around, and lowered himself through the hole onto the trolley. He replaced the ceiling tile and jumped down to the floor.

He pushed the trolley back to the janitor's room, left it outside and retrieved the rest of his explosives.

The eighth floor was the next calculated target location. Stratton considered taking the elevator, thinking he might need the trolley, but then decided to reduce the risk of running into anyone by using the emergency stairwell.

He walked back past the elevators to the end of the corridor where there was a heavy fire door with an emergency-exit sign above. He pushed it open: according to the plans the only fire door with an alarm was the one leading into the underground car park. He looked up through the spiralling stairs and banisters to the top. There were faint noises coming from above. They sounded like voices but he could not tell for sure.

Stratton moved quietly up the white-painted concrete stairs. The banister rail was made of simple tube steel. Each floor was clearly numbered, with an emergency light above the number, and as he reached the eighth he stopped at the sound of a cough that echoed from somewhere above. He carefully pulled open the fire door and poked his head inside to see that the floor was basically furnished but still un-occupied.

He stepped into the corridor and made his way along to the central room. The design was similar to the fourth-floor one but obviously the dimensions were much smaller. He headed for the central pillar that was the same size as below and took four charges from the bag, which he then left on the floor with the remaining four charges in it. He climbed onto a desk, pushed a ceiling tile aside, pulled himself up and replaced the tile.

The process of placing the charges took a little less time since the length of the horizontal girders was shorter and he had now practised his technique. Twenty minutes later he was making his way up the fire stairs, again keeping his hands off the banisters and staying away from the centre in case someone was looking into the stairwell.

As Stratton reached the twelfth floor he paused as he heard another cough, still from above, and then what sounded like the rustle of a newspaper. It came again and he carefully peered up, catching sight of a foot on the banister rail as if the person was sitting back in a chair. He calculated it to be on the sixteenth floor, one below the penthouse. No doubt one of Skender's guards was up there.

As he carefully opened the twelfth-floor fire door voices filtered from inside. Since they were not close by and sounded as if the talkers were in a room he lowered himself to his knees and ventured to peer inside. The plate-glass wall allowed him to make out several blurred figures in the larger central room, a half-dozen or so who, since they were not speaking English, he assumed were Skender's thugs. Looking along the corridor and into one of the offices he noticed a camp bed. Further scrutiny of the distorted images of furnishings on the other side of the foggy glass walls suggested that the floor was being used as sleeping quarters for the large guard force that Skender had brought in to secure the building.

The elevators opened and Stratton let the fire door close enough to see through the gap. It was Cano and he let the door close completely.

Cano called out something that Stratton could not understand and a few moments later the voices went silent.

Stratton carefully opened the door to take another look but now the floor appeared to be empty. Then he pushed the door open and stepped inside, letting it close behind him. Being even closer to the top the floor area was smaller still, with space for only half a dozen offices.

He made his way along the curved glass-panelled corridor and stepped into the central room that contained a couple of dozen camp beds surrounding the main pillar. Here the column was tapered, narrowing towards the ceiling. He moved quickly, climbing onto a chair, and within a few seconds was pulling himself up into the ceiling space.

Chapter 32

Cano stepped out of the elevator, followed by half a dozen of his men who dispersed to various posts inside and outside the building. 'Klodi?' he called out.

Klodi, his hand still heavily bandaged, was at the entrance, chomping on a purloined chicken leg which he put into his pocket as his boss called out. He hurried over to him.

'Where's Tony?' Cano asked.

'I dunno,' Klodi said, looking around. 'He was supposed to be on the elevators.'

'That's why I'm asking,' Cano said, becoming irritated.

'Hey,' Klodi called out to one of the uniformed security guards. 'Where's Tony?'

'Tony who?' the Mexican guard asked.

'The big guy. One of our people who was stood at the elevators,' Klodi said.

'Okay,' the guard nodded, remembering him. 'Last time I saw him he was taking out the trash.'

An image suddenly flashed into Cano's head of Tony getting into the elevator with a man in a waiter's uniform who had his back to him.

Cano unclipped a radio from his hip and put it to

his mouth. 'This is Vleshek,' he said into the radio. 'Anyone seen Tony Dosti?'

A moment later a voice broke over the little speaker 'He ain't on the fifteenth.'

'Ain't on the tenth,' another voice said.

'He's in the lobby on the elevators,' another voice said.

Cano gave up and called an elevator.

'Shall I come with you, boss?' Klodi asked.

'Next person leaves their post I'll cut their balls off. Make sure everyone knows that,' Cano said as the doors opened. He walked inside, hit the garage-parking button and the doors closed.

Klodi nodded and turned to see the Mexican guard grinning.

'You think he's joking, ass-wipe? That goes for you guys, too,' Klodi said.

The Mexican lost his grin and Klodi walked back to the main entrance.

Cano stepped out of the elevator into the garage and looked around the concrete vault. He walked to the dumpster cage, which was open, and stopped to take another look in every direction. The only sound was the faint hum from the air-conditioning plant in a room at the other side of the car park. Then a slight noise came from behind him and he turned to scrutinise the dumpsters. The noise came again. At first he thought it was a rodent but as he stepped cautiously into the cage it began to sound more like a moan.

Cano opened the first dumpster and looked inside to find it filled with trash. Then the surface of the garbage moved ever so slightly. Cano reached in a hand and pulled a bag aside to reveal the green-painted wooden planks that had made up boxes which had been used to pack the Albanian artefacts that decorated Skender's penthouse. He lifted one of the planks to expose an extremely ill-looking Tony who was barely hanging onto life.

'Klodi,' Cano shouted into his radio. 'I'm in the garage. Get down here and bring a couple of the guys. Now!'

A few minutes later Klodi and two others were hauling Tony out of the dumpster and onto the concrete floor where he lay prostrate.

'He don't look too good,' Klodi said, kneeling over the man who appeared to be having problems breathing but was still trying to say something. Klodi lowered his ear to Tony's mouth. 'Anyone here speak Italian?' Klodi asked.

Apparently no one did since there was no reply.

Cano was growing impatient and shoved Klodi aside. 'Who did this?' he asked Tony. 'What happened?'

Tony mustered a breath then said something that Cano could not quite understand.

'Say it again,' Cano said, moving his ear closer.

Tony softly repeated the word.

'A waiter?' Cano repeated, not quite understanding.

'English,' Tony struggled to say.

The penny dropped with a clang and Cano stood, raising the radio to his mouth as he moved towards the elevators. 'This is Vleshek. Close all exits. No one gets out of the building. Do you understand? No one!'

★   ★   ★

Stratton stepped through a fire-exit door into an alcove that led directly into the lobby. He paused to observe the frenzied activity around the entrance as several of Cano's men brusquely shoved back people who were coming in as well as those who were on their way out while the goons closed the massive main doors.

The next phase of Stratton's plan required him to get outside but all indications were that the building appeared to be closing down. He quickly scanned around for anything that might provide a clue to getting out and his gaze landed not on the perfect solution but probably the only one. A fire alarm was fixed to the wall beside the fire exit and Stratton whacked it with his elbow, breaking the glass. The building immediately erupted in a cacophony of bells and sirens and he walked into the crowded lobby as event staff emerged from the banqueting hall, wondering what the alarm was about.

'Fire!' Stratton called out. 'Fire! Get out of the building! There's a fire!'

It had the immediate desired effect with a general shift of people towards the main doors. The security guards tried to hold them back. Skender's thugs were overly physical in their own efforts, which only served to increase tension, ignite tempers and fuel the urgency to escape.

Stratton joined the pack, shouting scary warnings above the din of the alarm bells. The mass of people quickly began to reverse the efforts of the guards and Skender's goons to close the doors as Cano stepped from an elevator.

Cano quickly made his way to the side of the crowd, shouting at his men to hold the doors as he pushed his way towards them. As he forced his way to within a few feet of the entrance he noticed someone staring at him from the other side of the mass and suddenly realised it was Stratton.

Cano increased his efforts to push forward, never taking his stare off Stratton while his hand slipped inside his jacket and grabbed his pistol. He ripped it from its holster and struggled to raise it above the heads of those in front of him. As he got it roughly aimed, Stratton ducked out of sight.

Cano pushed even more violently, trampling a woman who had lost her footing in front of him. He ignored her screams as he stood on her in an effort to gain some height so that he could find Stratton.

The mass of bodies squeezed through the main doors as the guards finally gave in to the greater force. Cano surged out with them and onto the concourse where people were flooding away from the building in every direction. Most stopped at what they considered a safe distance to look back and see what the alarm was all about. Cano moved further out, scanning beyond and behind, his gun in his hand, ready to shoot should he catch sight of the person he hated most on this planet. As he came to a stop and turned a full circle, looking far and near, he caught sight of a figure in a waiter's uniform running from the square and down a side street. Although he could not see the man's features clearly enough he knew that it was Stratton. His empty eye socket began to throb.

As Cano continued to look in that direction he

was filled with an intense curiosity to know what the man had been doing in the building and why he'd left.

'Top-floor security, this is Vleshek,' he shouted into his radio. 'Top-floor security!'

A moment later there was a reply.

'Is everything okay?' Cano asked.

'Everything is fine here.'

'Check with all the other guards on that floor. I want to know if there has been anything suspicious in the last hour. *Anything.*'

'Give me a minute. I will check,' the voice said.

It had been about an hour since Tony had been tossed into the dumpster. Stratton had been in the building somewhere, doing something that had taken that amount of time to complete. Perhaps he had been looking for the boy, but that would have been a stupid risk unless he had good reason to suspect that the kid was there. And to search a building that big by himself would have been pointless anyway. Cano could not but respect Stratton's explosives skills and audacity but what the Englishman could possibly have been doing in the building he could not imagine.

'Vleshek?' a voice barked over the radio.

'Yes,' Cano said.

'I've spoken to all the guys and no one's seen or heard nothin' suspicious.'

Cano lowered the radio, his mind churning through possible reasons Stratton could have been there.

'Vleshek?'

'I heard you,' Cano snapped. He made his way back to the main entrance. Anger once again dominated

Cano's emotions as the feeling grew inside him that he did not have the initiative in this fight. He of all people knew the advantages of the small against the mighty. The only thing he had in his favour was time – or, more precisely, knowing that Stratton had little of it.

As Cano entered the lobby, the alarms bells still ringing, he raised his radio to his mouth. 'This is Vleshek. Everyone listen. I want anyone who is not covering an exit to meet me on the second floor, and I mean everyone. And turn those goddamned alarm bells off!'

Chapter 33

A sedan pulled into a side street across from Skender's building and came to a stop alongside the kerb. Inside it Hobart, Seaton, Hendrickson and the driver all sat in silence, looking dishevelled and somewhat fatigued after a night without sleep. They'd spent hours at a medical facility, undergoing checks. Then they'd examined the mine at dawn for any clues or evidence. Having found nothing of value, they'd then learned of the pick-up that had been stolen outside the bar in Twin Oaks and discovered that Stratton's vehicle had been left in its place. They'd decided to head for Los Angeles and Skender's business centre since that was the next logical focus point of the manhunt.

Hobart finally broke the silence with a heavy sigh. 'I'm gonna tell Skender to cancel his opening ceremony,' he said as if he had just made the monumental decision.

Hendrickson, still wearing his singed coat, turned around in the front passenger seat to look at him. 'He's not going to like that, sir.'

'I don't give a damn what he likes,' Hobart said. Then, after considering the comment, he acknowledged the implications of such a decision. 'Call the mayor's office. I think the governor's coming too. Let 'em know we're closing down the building and not to come.'

'Should I say why?' Hendrickson asked.

'Go ahead and tell 'em it's a bomb scare but make sure they understand this is not al-Qaeda or anything like that. Just say we've got a crazy out there with an explosive device.'

'The press'll be here five minutes after I make the call,' Hendrickson said.

'They're gonna know as soon as you call the police chief, the fire department and emergency services. We're gonna need a cordon at least three blocks deep – plus EOD and ECM.'

'We'll have to evacuate every building within the cordon,' Hendrickson said.

'A goddamned nightmare,' Hobart sighed. 'Got anything to add?' he asked Seaton.

Seaton was ignoring him and staring directly ahead.

Hobart looked at him. 'Seaton?'

'There he is,' Seaton said.

Hobart didn't quite understand who Seaton meant – his mind was on so many characters at that second. 'Who?' he asked, looking ahead in the direction where Seaton was staring.

'Stratton.'

Hobart focused through the windscreen on a man in a waiter's outfit walking across their front as Hendrickson spun round in his seat to look.

'That's *him*?' Hobart asked, unable to see a clear resemblance to the picture from the angle he was at.

Hendrickson looked at Hobart, waiting for him to

make the next move. Hobart quickly opened his door and the driver and Hendrickson followed, pulling their guns from their hip holsters.

Hobart put out a hand to keep them behind him. 'No shooting unless I tell you to – is that understood?'

Hobart took the lead and hurried down the centre of the road, a warning tapping anxiously at his brain that this was too easy and something was about to blow up. As he turned the corner Stratton came into full view, walking along, hands empty and swinging by his side, as unthreatening as anyone else in the street.

'Hold it!' Hobart shouted, closing the gap, his gun gripped in both hands, held out in front of him and ready to come up on aim. Hendrickson and the driver adopted similar stances behind and to either side of him.

Stratton heard the voice call out and instantly believed the worst. But he kept walking.

'John Stratton!' Hobart shouted, walking briskly behind him. 'This is the FBI. Stand still or so help me I will shoot you!'

Pedestrians close enough to hear halted as they looked at the three men in the street who were carrying weapons.

Stratton slowed.

'John Stratton, this is your last warning,' Hobart shouted as his pistol came up on aim.

Stratton came to a stop although he did not turn to look. He knew that it had all come to a grinding halt for him and even though he instinctively searched for a clue to a way out there was nothing. He was in the street, cars and people either side and nowhere to run. Suddenly he could see Josh in a dirty corner somewhere, hands tied, desperate and hungry. Stratton was almost filled with the urge to make a run for it, even though he knew that he would never survive. But in many ways it would have been an act of cowardice, taking the easy way out of his guilt for failing Josh. Stratton had never felt such anguish and loss before that moment: it was as if a strange sense of invulnerability that he'd had all his life had suddenly disappeared.

At that moment Grant appeared, walking down the sidewalk and clapping eyes on the very man he had hoped to. 'Hey! You! Motherfucker!' he shouted at Stratton, completely unaware of the guns drawn in the street. 'We need to talk. Yeah, you!'

Grant walked out into the road to confront Stratton. 'Where's my motherfucken' five hunnerd dollars? You lied to me, you motherfucker. I'm talkin' to you, ma—' Grant stopped in mid-sentence as he saw the men behind Stratton with guns aimed at them both. His mouth remained agape as his hands went into the air. 'Holy shit.'

'Keep perfectly still,' Hobart said to Stratton as he came to a stop yards from his back. 'Let's not do anything stupid here. Put your hands up.'

Stratton slowly complied.

'I ain't done nothin' man,' Grant said, quivering. 'I ain't no paparazzi.'

'Move to one side, please, sir,' Hobart said to Grant. 'You stay perfectly still, John.'

Grant stepped to the side, keeping his hands high

as Hobart's driver moved to where he could cover him.

'Now I want you to turn slowly and face me,' Hobart said. 'Nice and easy.'

Stratton did as he was ordered and looked into Hobart's eyes, recognising the man he had seen only once before.

Hobart also recognised Stratton from somewhere and took his time trying to remember. 'Santa Monica courts,' he finally said, mainly to himself, looking forward to interrogating Stratton and filling in the many holes in this case. 'Before I search you, you got anything? Guns? Explosives?'

Stratton shook his head.

'Hendrickson. Give me your gun, then search him.'

Hendrickson handed his gun to Hobart and moved in behind Stratton, a hint of nervousness showing through.

Stratton looked several yards beyond Hobart to see Seaton staring at him. They locked eyes as Hendrickson ran his hands thoroughly over Stratton's body.

'He's clean,' Hendrickson said.

A police car arrived and came to a halt further up the street. Two officers climbed out, guns drawn, and crouched behind their car doors.

'FBI,' Hendrickson called out as he held his badge up for the cops to see.

'Cuff him,' Hobart told Hendrickson who produced a pair of handcuffs.

'Hands behind your back,' Hendrickson said to Stratton.

Stratton obeyed and Hendrickson fitted the cuffs around his wrists and tightened them.

Hobart lowered his gun and closed on Stratton, taking a good look at the man who, up until seconds ago, had been the most dangerous in the state.

'Sir,' Hobart's driver called out.

'What?'

'That's the stolen pick-up.'

Hobart glanced over at it. 'Anything in there we should be worried about?' he asked Stratton.

Stratton shook his head.

'Take a look,' Hobart said to the driver. 'And be careful.'

The agent looked in through the pick-up's windows before he opened the door slowly and peered inside, his confidence growing at seeing nothing that he considered dangerous. He searched under the seats and in the glove compartments. 'Just a bunch of blueprints, sir. No weapons or explosives.'

Hobart eyed Stratton. 'So where is it? I know you have around ninety pounds of pure RDX. Why don't you just make it easier for everyone and tell me where it is?'

Stratton held his gaze.

'Don't tell me it all went up in the mine because I won't believe you,' Hobart said. 'Yeah, I understand you're the strong silent type. Well, that's okay with me. I can play that game too. Officer!' Hobart called out and the two cops came forward. 'I want a lock-up truck here as soon as you can. This guy's going downtown to the Federal jail, a top-security cell, the toughest in the state. We gotta keep him nice and safe while we find his toys. Hendrickson – you go with him, and I don't want him speaking to anyone, you understand. No one. You stay outside his cell until I get there.'

'Yes, sir,' Hendrickson said.

Hobart put his gun back in its holster, feeling a little better about the situation although there were a lot of loose ends to tie up, most of all finding the explosives. But it looked as if the case was at last coming under control.

Stratton had no emotions about Hobart. The man was just doing his job. Stratton was too consumed by his own failure to think about anything else. He'd made a terrible mistake in failing to take account of all the factors lined up against him. He'd developed tunnel vision. He'd seen only Skender and his people.

'You have any idea where little Josh is?' Hobart asked.

Stratton looked into his eyes. 'Only that Skender or Cano has him.'

'Cano?' Hobart said, quizzically. 'Cano's dead. You should know – you killed him.'

'His brother. You know him as Ivor Vleshek.'

A clang reverberated in Hobart's head as another piece of the puzzle dropped into place. Hobart glanced over his shoulder at Seaton and wondered what else the Agency knew that he didn't. When Hobart had arrived in LA and been handed the Skender case file one of the first requests he made was to the CIA for any information they had on the Albanian, knowing that terrorists were using Skender's international smuggling conduits and that the CIA had their own file on him. They'd given him nothing more than he'd already had with an assurance that he would be updated. Lying sons of bitches.

'How do you know the Albanians have the kid?' Hobart asked Stratton, not doubting him but thinking that some proof would be nice.

'Cano wants to trade me for Josh. Listen to me. You lock me up, they'll kill Josh.'

'And your conscience will be clear because that makes it my fault, right?' Hobart suggested.

Anger flashed through Stratton and he leaned towards Hobart, his stare on fire. For a second Hobart was reminded why this man in front of him was considered so dangerous. Hendrickson grabbed Stratton's arms, helped by the two cops, but Stratton had no intention of striking Hobart.

'I take full responsibility for Josh's situation,' Stratton said. 'But right now his life is in your hands. You can play this by the book or you can do something about it.'

'What do you expect me to do? Let you go? Or maybe I can call up Skender and ask him if we can exchange you for the boy?'

'Let me go and I swear I'll come back to you when this is over,' Stratton pleaded.

'Please. I don't have the right to make those kinds of decisions and if I did I'd have to say no. You'd die and God only knows how many others you'd take with you. Put him in the squad car until the van arrives,' Hobart said to Hendrickson. 'And don't leave his side for a second, you understand me?'

461

'Yes, sir,' Hendrickson said as he pulled Stratton away.

Seaton watched as Stratton was placed in the back of the squad car, reflecting on how it had all turned into such a damned mess and was as much his fault as Stratton's. He had felt a pang of guilt when Stratton had looked at him but that slowly disappeared as he watched the Englishman being marched away in handcuffs to a certain future behind bars. The change of feeling had something to do with a loss of respect and Stratton not being as invincible as Seaton had always thought of him: the great John Stratton a failure, handcuffed, captured by an FBI agent, Skender the overall winner and Josh probably never to be seen or heard of again.

Seaton did not feel comfortable about the fact that his own inferiority complex had been soothed somewhat. It was all a mess and he wished that he had been on the other side of the world that day when Stratton had called him at his home.

Hobart looked around at Seaton, wondering what the man was thinking. It was evident from his expression that he had demons of his own to deal with. Seaton had turned in his friend and could not be feeling great about it, especially since, short of a miracle, it pretty much hammered the last nail into the kid's coffin. That was the one thing they were all certain about, that Stratton had been the boy's only hope. Hobart wasn't feeling very good about himself either at that moment. Stratton had been wrong in every conceivable way but so was the way it had ended. Skender and his people were scum, evil bastards who should be paying for their crimes not just against the laws of America but against the whole of humanity. Stratton had only been partially right when he'd said that the rest of this was in Hobart's hands. An innocent young boy was out there somewhere and although Hobart rather than Stratton was now his only chance there was much more than his life at stake.

Hobart reminded himself who he was, what he stood for, and that now was perhaps the time to be counted for the core of those beliefs. He did not outwardly show it but deep inside he was angrier than he had ever been in his life. It was partly because he had never felt such a pawn as he had since he'd been given the Skender case, a tool to be used by those above him. That was not what he had joined up for. He had once believed there was only one way to do anything and that was the right way. He had grown complacent over the years, hoping that one day it would all be put right but by someone else. He'd lived in denial about everything that was wrong with the administration and its selfish motives. But things didn't get put right by doing nothing and waiting for someone else to do them. It took people to make a stand, people like Stratton, and if you were going to close down men like him, well it had better be because you could do the job better.

'You did a good job, Seaton,' Hobart said to him, straightening his back and feeling suddenly determined.

'You need me any more?' Seaton asked, looking like a lost child.

Hobart still wondered what kind of a man Seaton

was, unable to figure him out. Was he a loyal friend doing the right thing, or was he a career man looking to keep his record clean? 'Why don't you stick around?' Hobart decided. 'This show ain't over yet.'

'What more is there?' Seaton asked.

'You forgotten about the kid?' Hobart asked as he walked past him.

Seaton wanted to say that he'd done the job he was sent here to do but he chose to keep his mouth shut. There was no point. He might as well play this one out and keep Hobart happy.

A police lock-up van pulled up. Seaton watched as Stratton was led out of the squad car and into the back of it, along with a police officer. Hendrickson handed his weapon over to one of the officers and climbed inside.

'Hey. What about my waiter suit?' Grant complained as he watched the police officer lock up the back of the van. 'I gotta go to work.'

'Can it,' Hobart's driver said.

Grant gave up with a philosophical sigh. 'So who'd he photograph that everyone's so pissed off about?'

The driver gave him a quizzical look as the lock-up van pulled away.

Chapter 34

Stratton sat chained to a bench that ran the length of the lock-up van as it bumped and creaked along, his hands cuffed in front of him, Hendrickson and a police officer on the bench opposite. He could not believe that it was over, not like this. He had been a move away from holding Skender's building to ransom, the only chance he'd had of getting Josh back alive, and now the boy was doomed. There hadn't even been a fight.

Stratton didn't even want to think about Jack and Sally who were probably looking down on him at that moment with untold disappointment – although they could never be as angry with him as he was with himself. He looked around, at the two men opposite, the chains, the iron box they rode along in with its door bolted from the outside, the key with the driver. If there was a way out of this he could not see it. Ten, fifteen, twenty minutes and he would arrive at the Federal lock-up where his life behind bars would begin. This was not how he had expected to end his career. Dead, perhaps, at the hands of crazed terrorists in some godforsaken corner of the world. That would have been acceptable, though he would of course have fought to stay alive. But at that moment this seemed far worse than dying. At least if he was dead he would not be tormented by feelings of guilt and failure.

He lowered his head into his hands and looked down at his feet, the clean metal floor beneath them. Then his eyes focused on something on the side of his boot. It was a tiny piece of some white substance, poking out of the tread of his sole. He stopped breathing while he willed it to be what he hoped and not a piece of chewing gum.

Stratton looked up at Hendrickson and the police officer who were staring ahead at nothing. He sat back, crossed his legs, looked away and let a hand wander to his heel where he could feel the substance, a glance revealing that it ran into the tread for an inch or so. He picked a tiny piece off and casually wiped his nose while sniffing it. It was indeed RDX and must have got stuck there while he'd been in the mine. Interestingly, RDX was sensitive but not overly so. For instance, he would have had to jump off a three-storey building and land directly on his heel to detonate it. The fall would probably have killed him anyway.

He sat for a moment, the tumblers of his mind turning through the possibilities for its use. A plan quickly fell into place. Without further hesitation he popped the tiny fragment of RDX into his mouth, swallowed it and then sat back to wait. He remembered reading somewhere that RDX was not lethal if ingested in small amounts and had symptoms similar to those produced by cordite, which had on occasion been used by soldiers in the past who had wanted to avoid duty. He only hoped that his memory served him correctly and that he had taken a small enough dosage. Within a few seconds the cramps began and he started to feel hot and feverish. But he kept himself from throwing up for as long as possible to make the most of it. The pain grew steadily worse and the bile began to rise in his throat as his breathing quickened and his hands began to shake.

The police officer was the first to notice Stratton's distress but did nothing initially. In his line of work he had seen it all, from prisoners feigning injury to actual suicide. It was his experience that some would do anything to avoid going to jail but on the other hand he had a responsibility to ensure their safety and well-being. Even if a prisoner had been sentenced to death it was his duty to save him so that he could suffer his legal fate. Making sure that a prisoner stayed alive technically took precedence over his responsibility to keep them incarcerated.

Stratton started to shudder as his eyes rolled up into his head and a white, frothy mucus oozed from his mouth.

'Holy shit,' the officer said, lunging forward as Hendrickson looked to see Stratton lean over and moan.

'He's gone white as a sheet,' the officer said, grabbing hold of Stratton.

Hendrickson jumped to his side as Stratton began to shake violently.

'What's wrong with him?' Hendrickson asked, out of his depth with a medical emergency and at a loss about what to do.

'He's having a heart attack, I think,' the officer said. 'We've got to get him on his back.'

Stratton's convulsions grew worse as he began to vomit.

'Get him outta the cuffs,' the officer said.

'Should we do that?' Hendrickson asked.

'A prisoner's first right is to life. Get him outta the chains,' the officer said as he dug a key from a pocket and struggled to get it into the padlock of the restrainers.

Hendrickson unlocked Stratton's handcuffs as the officer pulled away the chains that secured him to the bench. The van rattled violently as it travelled over some rough road and as Stratton felt his bonds loosen he suddenly lashed out, his first blow to the officer's throat sending him across the van onto the opposite bench. Then he grabbed Hendrickson by the hair and rammed his fist up into his jugular, cutting off the blood supply for a second. Sputum ran out of Stratton's mouth uncontrollably as he fought the severe stomach cramps to channel his strength into his limbs, driven by the all-consuming incentive that this was his last chance.

Hendrickson made an effort to reach for Stratton who slammed him in the jaw, almost knocking him out. Then Stratton grabbed the handcuffs, threw Hendrickson over onto his front, cuffed his hands behind his back, ripped off his tie and secured the police officer's hands in a similar manner. Stratton's gaze flicked up to the small hatch into the driver's compartment. He prayed it would not open as he dragged both men off the bench to the floor on their bellies. He put his mouth close to their ears and dangled Hendrickson's keys in front of their eyes.

'Either of you struggle or shout out, so help me I'll gouge your eyes out before this van comes to a stop. Do you hear me? Ask yourself if being blind for the rest of your life is worth it.'

Both men blinked wildly, still struggling to breathe properly, their throats swollen due to the blows. But they understood Stratton and, more importantly, believed him.

Stratton raised the bench, pushed the two men beneath it and let the bench come down on them, partly to keep them immobile but mostly to help protect them from the next phase of the escape.

He worked quickly as the van turned down the slip road onto a freeway and joined the slow-crawling mass of traffic as it snaked along the four-lane road towards the towering city centre several miles away. He dug the rest of the RDX out of the tread of his boot with the end of the key, pausing to control a wave of nausea before throwing up again and wiping his mouth on his sleeve. He pressed the explosive into a cube the size of a dice.

Stratton got to his feet and dismantled part of the other bench until he was holding half the sitting section that had chains hanging from its centre. Taking the central chain he lifted its free end to the small vent in the ceiling and threaded it past one of the bars. Then he secured it. He aimed the end of the bench at the door and released it, letting it dangle from the ceiling. The end slowly turned away from the door like a compass needle so he took a second chain and secured that to another bar in the roof vent. He released the bench again and this time it swung back and forth like an ancient battering ram, its end staying true and not turning away from the door.

As a final test Stratton pulled the bench back away from the door and then released it so that it swung forward and up. It was a bit noisy when it struck the door and Stratton quickly glanced around to see if the driver's hatch might open. It didn't. He went to the door and inspected the mark where the bench had struck it. It was near the lock. Deciding that it would have to do, he took the small piece of RDX, spat some mucus on it and pushed it over the mark, pressing it home until it stuck.

Hendrickson strained to look over his shoulder at whatever Stratton was doing. All he could make out was the improvised battering ram, which he did not think would be enough to break open the door.

Stratton got down on his knees, checked the floor area beneath the remaining section of bench where he would take refuge and looked to make sure that the two men were secure beneath their bench. Hendrickson stared back at him.

'I'd cover your face if I were you,' Stratton said.

Stratton pulled the battering ram all the way back and then threw it forward while at the same time diving for cover. He hit the floor at the same instant as the bench struck the RDX. The resulting explosion rocked the vehicle and filled it with smoke – and with daylight as the doors blew open.

Stratton immediately rolled onto his knees and cursed as he hit the swinging bench with the side of his head. He got to his feet just as the driver slammed on the brakes, sending him hard into the front of the van beside the hatch, which then opened. Stratton looked at the back of the van as the smoke quickly cleared and launched himself out.

He flew from the van, landing hard on the bonnet of a car which had stopped close behind. A family inside, frozen in horror, stared at him. He felt the blood trickling down the side of his head where he'd hit the bench, rolled off onto the road and started to run, aware that the next immediate danger might be shots from the two officers in the front of the van.

Stratton did not look back as he ran faster, dodging between the lines of cars that had now stopped. No one dared to challenge the desperate-looking individual who had emerged from the exploding doors of a police van. One officer who jumped out of the van's front did bring his gun up on aim but as Stratton weaved between the cars he decided against the risk of hitting a civilian. At the same time he wrote off any thought of giving chase to the guy who was running as if he was on fire and whom the cop was clearly never going to catch.

Chapter 35

Hobart and two police officers approached the entrance to Skender's building, which had returned to some form of normality as staff continued to prepare for the big event. Hobart had taken a moment in the square to make some calls and confirm any initial contact that had been made to set wheels in motion to evacuate Skender's business centre, set up a police cordon and bring in EOD teams. He also checked that the relevant utilities such as power, gas and water which might need to be shut down had been notified, as well as emergency services like hospitals. The two police officers had arrived in response to the alarms that had since been switched off and Hobart asked them to accompany him to the building. As he walked across the concourse he paused to look at the statue of Skender, shook his head, and carried on to the entrance.

Klodi was in charge of an enhanced search team at the main doors. When he saw Hobart and the cops approach he stepped forward to meet them.

'Hey, officers, can I help you?'

Hobart ignored the large thug with the bandaged hand and forced smile to talk to a woman who appeared to be a senior member of the event staff. 'Who's in charge here? I'm talking about the catering and everything?'

'That would be Mr Mathews,' the woman said, looking at Hobart and the two cops either side of him.

'And where would I find Mr Mathews?' Hobart asked, like a schoolteacher talking to a child.

'He's inside,' she said.

'Get him out here – now, please' Hobart said.

As the woman walked inside Hobart turned to face Klodi, trying hard not to show an anger that was gradually bubbling up inside him. He was expecting to receive resistance from Skender and was getting ready to meet it head on. 'I want to see Skender.'

'Mr Skender is a little busy right now,' Klodi said with a cocky smile, wiping his nose with his bandaged hand. 'We got an openin' ceremony today.'

'I didn't *ask* to see him. I said I *wanted* to see him which is the same as saying I'm *going* to see him. Do you understand me?' Hobart said.

'Do you wanna hold on a moment? He could be anywhere in the building.'

'You've got one minute and then I'm looking for him myself.'

Klodi moved to one side and raised his radio to his mouth. 'Mr Vleshek. This is Klodi at the front door.'

'What is it?' Cano's voice crackled over the radio.

'That FBI guy's down here. Says he wants to see Mr Skender.'

'Tell him to come back in an hour when the bar's open.'

Hobart was listening and bit his lip. He was here

473

to kick some Albanian butt but he needed to save himself for the top man. 'You got thirty seconds,' Hobart said.

'You better get down here,' Klodi said into the radio. 'I don't think he's here on a social visit.'

There was a pause, then the voice came back. 'I'm on my way.'

'He's on his way,' Klodi repeated, maintaining his smile.

A man stepped through the doors with the female event-staff member in tow and presented himself to the police officers. 'I'm Mr Mathews, the event manager. Can I help you?' he asked with a smile.

Hobart took out his badge and showed it to the man. 'I'm head of the FBI in California. Does that mean anything to you?'

'Well, yes – quite a lot,' the man said, his smile waning a little at the edges. He was beginning to look a little nervous.

'You're right. It does mean a lot. I'm giving you five minutes to evacuate this building and move all your people and transport out of here. Is that clear?'

'Five minutes?' the man said, looking deeply perplexed.

'If your vans aren't out of here by –' Hobart checked his watch '– twelve minutes past the hour you'll be cited for obstruction of justice, your vehicles will be impounded and could be held for months and I doubt very much whether your business licence will be renewed. Do you understand everything I've just said?'

'I do, sir,' the man said as he turned on his heel and pushed his way back into the building.

Hobart watched him go. Then he faced Klodi who was standing between him and the front doors. 'You're in my way,' he said.

Klodi stepped aside in the face of a superior power. Hobart and the officers marched in.

As they walked into the lobby beneath the massive chandelier Cano was coming down the broad stairs at the other side of the elevators. As he stepped onto the marble floor it became evident to him by the excited activities of the event staff that something was happening about which he was unaware.

'Where's Skender?' Hobart asked as Cano approached.

'What's going on?' Cano asked, ignoring Hobart's question and looking past him as several event-staff personnel hurried from the ballroom and out through the main doors.

Hobart hated being ignored and this place was sorely trying his patience. But he stuck by his plan and held on to his temper, though with increasing difficulty. 'You want to know what's happening?' he asked, forcing a smile. 'I'm closing down your building, your opening ceremony, everything. And now you listen to me. You speak to me one more time like I'm the bellhop and I'll run you downtown so fast your feet won't touch the ground. Now take me to Skender!' he shouted.

Cano remained cool as ice. Hobart's efforts to impress him were as effective as hail on armour. 'One moment,' Cano said, holding up a finger as he took his cellphone from his pocket and stepped to one side to use it.

Hobart gritted his teeth as he looked at one of the cops. Cano spoke quietly on his phone for a few seconds before pocketing it and walking to the elevator. 'Mr Skender will see you,' he said as he pushed a call button.

Hobart turned his back on Cano who was just beyond earshot and talked to the cops. 'Your chief is on his way. This is an emergency situation. We have a suspected bomb in the building. Skender's bodyguards can stay for the time being but I want everyone else out of here. That includes security staff, administrators, janitors, cooks and busboys, everyone. Got it?'

The cops looked at each other and nodded.

'Go to it,' Hobart said before turning to head for the elevator. 'Lead on, Mr Vleshek,' he said, making a meal out of the name.

Cano walked inside and Hobart joined him. The elevator doors closed. Cano thought he could sense that Hobart was unusually confident about something, then dismissed it as one of the FBI man's little moments of power.

The elevator arrived at the penthouse. Hobart followed Cano out, past two suited thugs who were guarding the elevator doors and along the curving corridor to the conference room where Skender was studying his model town and making notes.

Skender looked up as the glass doors opened and the two men walked in.

'Hobart's emptying out the building,' Cano said.

Skender studied them both as if he had not quite heard correctly. 'Say that again?' he asked.

'He's sent the caterers away,' Cano said.

'Home,' Hobart corrected him. 'I've sent them home.'

Something inside Skender almost snapped as he realised the significance of the information. But he held himself in check as he looked at Hobart, reassessing the man.

'Just in case you don't understand my English, I'll spell things out for you,' Hobart said, wearing the hint of a grin. 'Your party's over. The opening ceremony – it isn't going to happen. Not today at least.'

'You want to tell me why?' Skender asked, putting down his notepad.

'I have reason to believe there's a bomb in your building,' Hobart said.

'You do?' Skender said, glancing at Cano.

'That's right. I'm not here to argue with you, Skender. I want everyone out of the building.'

'Why do I get the feeling that you suddenly grew a pair of balls, Hobart?' Skender asked, walking towards him. 'You used to walk in here with your cap in your hand like some busboy and now suddenly you're – how is it you Americans say? – walkin' tall. What happened? Your wife give you your annual blow job last night?'

Hobart wasn't fazed by the insult. 'You're right about the change. This is just the first step. I warned you about crossing the line.'

'Warn?' Skender said, closing on Hobart, barely holding on to his temper. 'Is that like a weather warning, or a tough-guy warning?'

Hobart suddenly felt a pang of unease in his core

477

as Skender moved into his space, looking more dangerous than he'd ever seen him before. Everything he knew about the man, his history of violence since his youth, appeared to be written on his face. He suddenly felt uncomfortable being this close to it.

'So what was this line I crossed?' Skender asked, his voice sounding more croaky as it got quieter.

'Kidnapping, for one,' Hobart said, feeling as if he might get the upper hand at this meeting if he showed Skender some purpose.

'What are you talking about?' Skender said, genuinely surprised. Then his suspicions flashed to Cano but he did not look at him.

'Sally Penton's kid,' Hobart explained. 'The woman your two boys killed, Leka and that moron Ardian,' he said, deliberately staring at Cano, knowing that the man was furious but did not dare show it. 'They're the reason you have a bomb in your building,' Hobart continued, looking back at Skender. 'Come on. Don't you know what's going on in your own house? Maybe I should be talking to this guy. I bet *he* knows what's going on. What do you say, Vleshek? Or should I say Cano, Ardian's brother?'

Cano choked back his surprise. But at that moment he was more concerned about Skender who had thrown him a most dangerous look.

Skender was beginning to boil over inside. Had Hobart been able to see the danger he might have held back a bit. He had Skender on the run but did not know how tight was the corner that he was chasing the Albanian crime lord into.

Skender instantly believed Hobart about the

kidnapping though he genuinely knew nothing about it. Nor did he know of the supposed bomb in his building but he believed that too. Cano had kept everything from him. Skender knew that Cano's deviousness was rooted in fear as well as in the hope that he could resolve the problem on his own but matters had gone beyond that now.

'The walls are closing in, Skender,' Hobart said, unable to hide his satisfaction at seeing these two evil men in mental turmoil. 'I've been waiting for you to drop the ball. It was only a matter of time.'

Suddenly Skender's fist slammed into Hobart's solar plexus under his heart, stopping it just for a second and knocking every ounce of wind out of him.

'Time is what you ain't got a lot of,' Skender said. As Hobart toppled forward, grabbing his chest in pain, Skender took him by the throat with a gnarled peasant hand, pushed him upright against the central pillar and powered a fist into his side, cracking something. 'You need to learn your place in this world, little man.'

Hobart's legs buckled. As he went down Skender kneed him viciously in the face, knocking the back of his head against the pillar as his nose burst open.

'Now tell me. How much do I give a damn?' Skender demanded.

Hobart dropped to the floor, trembling as he tried to roll onto his side. Skender kicked him brutally in the face and as Hobart collapsed onto his front the Albanian loomed over him like a salivating wolf savouring his kill.

'Let me tell you your future,' Skender said. 'My deal with the Feds goes on. I have what they want and I'm gonna deliver, from time to time. One of my new conditions is that they dump your ass. You know they will, because I'm more important to them than you are. Now I'll tell you what else I'm gonna do, and I want you to listen carefully. Are you listening to me?'

Hobart was in a bad way but Skender callously rolled him onto his back with his foot. Blood trickled across Hobart's face and he blinked to hold on to consciousness as Skender went in and out of focus.

'One day,' Skender went on, 'a year, maybe two years from now, you're gonna be somewhere, driving along, maybe leaving a restaurant with your fat wife and you're gonna have an accident. Hit-and-run maybe, a mugger, whatever. The point is, you're gonna die, Hobart. That's an Albanian promise, my friend. I want you to spend every waking minute until that day thinking about it, knowing that it's going to happen.'

As Hobart stared up at Skender he heard a ringing sound that seemed to go on for an age. But he was so consumed by what Skender had done and said to him that he was unable to realise it was his mobile phone. Hobart had never been so physically abused in his life and nothing had prepared him for it.

Skender sneered at the pathetic figure before turning away to rest his callous stare on Cano. 'Where is he?' Skender asked with a malevolence that shocked even the other Albanian.

'He got into the building somehow—'

'I'm talking about the kid!' Skender yelled, his face going red as he closed on Cano.

'The floor below,' Cano said, wondering what his

reaction would be if Skender struck him too. To hit back would mean that he would have to kill Skender, for that would be his own fate if he did not.

'You brought him here?' Skender growled. 'Are you *completely* stupid?'

'No one would think—'

'*You're* the only one who doesn't think around here. Where?'

'In the janitor's cupboard.'

Skender wanted to kill him there and then. But this was not the time to execute a man who was obsessed with killing another who was a more immediate threat. Besides, he would expect Cano to fight back and that could be problematic. He fancied his chances against Cano, even with their age difference. Cano was brutal but he lacked Skender's experience. Nevertheless, this was not the time. 'How does Hobart know there's a bomb in this building?' he asked, turning his attention to the immediate and potentially more dangerous situation.

'I don't know.'

'The Englishman?'

Cano nodded.

Skender was aware of Stratton's abilities with explosives but the truth was that he had no concern for his own life, feeling secure in such a large structure. What angered him was the thought of even a speck of damage to his beloved new building.

'When was he here?'

'An hour ago.'

'Inside the building? You're sure of that?'

'He nearly killed one of our people in the garage.'

Skender looked away in thought. 'This guy will have a plan.'

'He wants the kid,' Cano said.

That was fairly obvious, thought Skender as he stepped towards the glass doors, pausing at them. 'Get that creep outta here,' he said, indicating Hobart. 'And Cano – if that guy does anything to this building, and I mean one broken window, I'm gonna kill you myself.'

The two men stared at each other. Cano did not doubt the threat for a second.

Skender walked along the corridor behind the frosted-glass wall to the emergency exit. Cano lowered his gaze to Hobart who was trying to pull himself up, using the edge of the table. But his damaged ribs, among other things, were causing him extreme pain.

Hobart persevered and pulled himself up enough to slump awkwardly into a chair, every breath accompanied by a burning stab inside his chest. The pain was one thing but much worse was the degradation and humiliation. He had entirely miscalculated Skender's contempt for authority and lust for brutality.

'You know where the elevator is,' Cano said as he walked out of the room, too much on his own mind to care what happened to Hobart.

Hobart wanted nothing more than to get out of there but at that moment he was not sure if he could get to his feet without help, let alone out of the building. His face hurt like hell, his jaw was probably broken and God only knew how bad his ribs were. He cursed himself for being so stupid and putting himself in such a situation. He should have asked the cops to accompany him but he had been too arrogant to predict for himself what he might have warned others of. And there was yet more to come when he faced his staff and superiors. They would hold him partly to blame for his stupidity in confronting Skender alone. Without a witness Hobart was helpless.

His phone rang again but he ignored it, unsure if he could actually speak properly. He made an effort to get to his feet, wobbling slightly, fixing his stare on the doorway and staggering towards it.

Chapter 36

Skender stepped through the sixteenth-floor fire exit and went to the floor below his penthouse suite. One of his guards remained at the door while the other followed him along the curving corridor and stopped by the elevator. Skender continued on to the end of the corridor where there was a small kitchen with a janitor's closet opposite. A key was in the lock. He turned it and opened the door.

Sitting on the floor in the dark, his legs and hands tied with cloth in front of him, was Josh. The boy blinked rapidly against the sudden light in an effort to focus on Skender. He had long since stopped crying even though he'd been in the cupboard since the early hours of that morning when the horrible man with the eyepatch had released him from a sack. He'd been inside *that* since he'd been put into the back of a car after other men had taken him from the protection centre. The eyepatch man had checked on him a couple of times and given him water and some biscuits that were still in front of him, untouched.

Josh did not know this new stranger who now looked down on him. He waited nervously for whatever was going to happen next. He knew that he was in a dangerous situation but beyond that it was all a mystery. He wanted to be back with George and Vicky and, of course, most of all, he wanted Stratton, the only link he had left with his life in England. He had hated leaving his homeland from the moment he'd boarded the plane with his mother. All that now seemed a long, long time ago.

'How you doing?' Skender asked in a low, calm voice as he squatted to untie Josh's bonds. 'You okay?' he asked.

Josh nodded. He was frightened, mostly by the man's strange gravelly voice. But this one did not look as angry and hateful as the eyepatch man even though there was still something scary about him.

'Get up,' Skender said after removing the ties.

Josh obeyed and stood stiffly, looking at him.

'You want some juice?' Skender asked.

Josh shook his head.

'Something to eat?'

Josh shook his head again.

'You scared?'

Josh wanted to say yes. But he had been brought up in the company of men who did not reveal such emotions so he shook his head.

'That's good,' Skender said. Then he noticed that the boy's trousers had a large pee stain around the crotch. 'You wanna go to the toilet?'

Josh looked down at the stain, then back up at Skender. He clenched his jaw, embarrassed but also angry. He had not peed himself out of fear but simply because no one had thought of taking him to a toilet and he had been too embarrassed and shy to ask. Josh shook his head again.

'How old are you?' Skender asked.

'Six,' Josh said after clearing his throat.

Skender remembered his own sixth year. The images of his slaughtered village and the screams of his family being gunned down were still quite vivid. They'd replayed in his mind often throughout his life, usually without any warning or prompting, scars as indelible as the one across his throat.

'Let's get outta the closet, shall we?' Skender said.

Josh stepped out of the cupboard and joined Skender in the corridor.

'That yours?' Skender asked, pointing to the floor of the janitor's room.

Josh saw the little camel that had fallen out of his pocket. He quickly picked it up and held it carefully.

'Where'd you get that?' Skender asked, seeing that it meant a lot to the boy.

'It's from Iraq. My dad gave it to me. He was a special forces soldier,' Josh said.

'Oh? Where's your dad now?' Skender asked, suddenly wondering if it could be Stratton.

'He's dead,' Josh said.

Skender had given the boy hardly a second's thought before this moment but now he recognised some of the parallels between them. 'Tough losing your parents, eh?'

Skender heard his own words although he had never felt sorry for himself or disadvantaged by growing up without a family. It was only in his later life that he had begun to wonder what they had been like. He had never been particularly close to them – except his mother, a little perhaps – and he had no glowing memories of a classic father-and-son relationship. As he grew older he better understood the difficult circumstances of his youth and the pressures his father must have been under, the constant fighting and periods of cold and hunger. It did nothing to stimulate his total lack of emotion, however. He'd had no experience of love of any kind from a motherly figure or girlfriend and any spark of happiness or contentment he felt was for material things or accomplishments in business. The first man he'd killed had been when he was eighteen – for sitting on the bonnet of his new car. The second, a couple of months later, had been for something so trivial that Skender could no longer remember why. His reputation for brutality had come effortlessly but he never saw himself as others did. His rule of life, as he saw it, was a simple one. Work hard for your gains, any way you can, don't take what is not rightfully yours, severely punish those who take from you and honour your clan beyond everything else.

'I lost my mother and father when I was the same age as you,' Skender said.

Josh looked up at him, unable to imagine this man ever having parents.

'The people who killed them also slit my throat,' he said, leaning forward and pulling open his shirt to show Josh his neck.

The boy gaped at the scar, fascinated by it. 'Did it hurt?'

'Not at the time – I guess I was too scared. They threw me in a river right after to drown me.'

'Wow!' Josh exclaimed. 'How'd you get away?'

'I nearly didn't. The river was cold and flowing fast but somehow I managed to crawl onto a rock and pull myself onto the river bank.'

'Did you get your own back on them?' Josh said, staring at him in awe.

'Of course,' Skender said. 'It took me twenty years to find them, though. They were communists. You know what communists are?'

Josh shook his head.

'Communists used to be the old bad guys. My father fought against them when they tried to take over my country. How long was your father a soldier?'

'Don't know.' Josh shrugged. 'A long time.'

'Well, he probably fought against the communists when he was young. They wanted to take over everyone's country.'

'My father and your father were on the same side?' Josh asked.

'Kind of. My father fought for the king of my country.'

'A king?'

'Yeah. King Zog.'

'Zog?' Josh repeated, finding it a strange and amusing name.

'Zog fought against the communists alongside my father. Anyway, the guy who led the communists who killed my father moved to Paris in France when they lost the war.'

'I know where Paris is. I've been there with my dad.'

'Did you like it?'

'It was okay, I suppose. We went to Disneyland.'

'I've never been to Disneyland,' Skender said. 'Well, I found this guy in Paris and I killed him.'

'How'd you kill him?'

'I slit his throat, of course,' Skender said, thinking about that day. Skender had also killed the man's wife and three children in the same manner and left them in their Paris apartment.

Josh tried to imagine Skender drawing a knife across a man's throat. Stratton had never been so graphic with his stories. 'Do you know Stratton?' Josh asked. 'He's killed loads of people all over the world.'

Skender looked at him. 'Yeah. I know Stratton.'

'Do you know where he is?' Josh asked, a note of hope in his voice.

'I believe he's on his way here to get you.'

'He is?' Josh exclaimed excitedly.

'I'm just guessing, really,' Skender said, wondering what Stratton was planning and for the first time feeling a touch of unease. The man was no doubt a planner of some experience, judging by his hits on Leka and Ardian and if one was to read anything into the boy's description of him. Perhaps there was something to be concerned about.

Skender's private cellphone rang in his pocket and he took it out, hit a button and put it to his ear. 'Yeah?'

'This is Stratton.'

Skender glanced down at Josh who was inspecting his camel. He walked into the kitchen to look out of the window. 'What a coincidence. I was just talking about you,' he said, surveying his square that was now empty. He noticed some police activity at the corners.

'This is your last chance.'

'That right?' Skender said, watching several cop cars arrive and park across the ends of the side streets, the officers climbing out to direct people away from the square. 'You know how many times I've been told that in my life?'

'You've never heard it from me before.'

Skender looked away from the window, trying to remember what Stratton looked like, the image of him at the foot of the stairs in the courthouse not entirely clear. 'I see you have the police all stirred up. What do you have in mind?'

'You do not want to find out the hard way, I promise you. Where's the boy?'

'You think I'm going to negotiate with you because of threats?'

'I'll bring your empire down around your ears if you ignore me.'

'This isn't about the boy, not for me. If I start allowing myself to be dictated to by any individual who takes a dislike to me where will I end up? What will my people think of me? What will happen to my own self-esteem? I'm sure you understand. Now why don't you run along and do whatever it is you feel you need to do to express your anger. Seems to me your fight is against everyone.'

'Skender, listen to me!' Stratton shouted, his desperation coming through. 'I don't want to do this but I will if you force me. Once I start this there'll be no turning back. I'll kill you, Skender. Today you will die, believe me – unless you give me back Josh. Then I'll give you your life.'

'Stirring stuff. Now get lost,' Skender said before disconnecting. He looked back out of the window at the increasing build-up of cop cars, a couple of fire trucks and what looked like some military personnel in a camouflaged Hummer. He accepted, based on what Hobart had said, that Stratton's threat was not entirely empty and that he had planted some kind of explosive device in the building. Perhaps Stratton was trying to flush him out of the penthouse and down to where the device was. Whatever, Skender felt comfortable at the top of his building and would remain there until this little incident was sorted out.

He stepped out of the kitchen, put a hand on Josh's shoulder and guided him along the corridor. 'Let's go upstairs and see what we've got to eat. You could eat something now, right?'

Josh nodded.

Skender walked to the fire exit where his two guards were waiting and they all headed up the stairs. Josh and Skender went into the penthouse while the guards remained in the stairwell.

Chapter 37

Stratton hung the payphone back on its cradle and took a moment to muster his thoughts. This was it. He was going ahead with the plan. There was no turning back now and no point in delaying it further since Hobart knew about the manufactured explosives. A search of the building was no doubt imminent.

He buttoned up the Yankee baseball jacket that he had found in the trunk of Grant's car where he had left the rest of his equipment and pulled the baseball cap down low over his face. Then he headed across the road past a television news crew preparing for a stand-up report.

The attractive female correspondent held a microphone in front of her while the cameraman focused the camera. 'We're just around the corner from the new Skender Square in Culver City,' she announced seriously, 'where police have set up roadblocks to keep people back from the brand new Skender business centre which was to have had its grand opening ceremony today. Reports are unclear at the moment but what we do know is that the building has been evacuated, apart from some security guards. There are rumours of a bomb inside which, as you can see, police are taking very seriously.'

Stratton made his way past the news van into an alleyway that paralleled one side of the square. Halfway along it he turned in through the door of a building, past a large kitchen, along a narrow corridor and into a restaurant that was empty but for a man sitting behind the bar and reading a newspaper.

'We're closed,' the man said as Stratton walked through without acknowledging him and opened the front door. 'Ain't no one s'posed to go out there. Cops say there's a bomb.'

Stratton let the door close behind him and paused on the doorstep. He had approached the building from the side opposite to where he had been arrested and, seeing the square was now empty, he set off across the road. He stepped onto the square and as he crossed a flower bed to reach the side of the building a voice called out from behind him. He ignored it and continued around the corner.

He headed for the concourse, scanning in all directions, glancing quickly over his shoulder to check that he was not being pursued. As he approached the front of the building he unzipped his jacket to reveal the complex radio transmitter hanging from its strap around his neck.

Stratton stepped onto the marble concourse, flashed a look in the direction of the doors in the entrance portico to see that they were closed and made his way to Skender's heavy bronze statue. He stepped between the outstretched arms and looked up to see the glass face of the building sloping all the way up to the pinnacle. As he extended the antenna of the transmitter, movement and a sound in front of him caught his attention. His gaze flashed to one of the heavy Indian doors as it slowly opened. Stratton's hand flicked to the power switch and turned it on, a small red LED light glowing to indicate that it was operational. His stare stayed fixed on the door.

It opened just enough to let Hobart step through before it closed to leave the FBI man standing alone.

Stratton stood perfectly still, staring at the man who had arrested him a short time ago who was now looking seriously beaten up.

Hobart paused to take a breath and gather his strength. As he took a couple of hesitant steps forward he saw Stratton standing between the outstretched arms of Skender's statue and stopped.

Stratton noted the pain that Hobart's movements seemed to be causing him and could only assume the man had received an unexpected and unwelcome reception from Skender. But he could not even imagine why.

Hobart continued walking slowly towards Stratton, keeping stiffly upright and doing his best to maintain his dignity, and stopped several feet away. He saw the device with its complex panel of switches slung across Stratton's chest, one of his hands hovering over it. Though Hobart knew little about electronics he knew enough to figure out that the box and its antenna were related to the explosive device.

'Move on,' Stratton said. 'You're all done here.'

Hobart looked into the man's eyes, the resolve in them obvious. But more interesting was the similarity to the eyes he had looked into a short time ago before their owner had beaten the hell out of him: a dark madness, perhaps, or simply an unharnessed ruthlessness. The Albanian and the Englishman might be very different animals but there were parallels – most notably, they were stubborn and tenacious to the point of self-destruction. Skender was the egotist and king of a ruthless empire who could not comprehend an individual's challenge to his will. Stratton, on the other hand, was a human cruise missile and once launched would weave past all obstacles until his objective was reached.

Hobart could see ways out of this madness for both men but they themselves could not see beyond their own needs. They were on a collision course and nothing now was going to stop them, certainly not Hobart. The ultimate loser would of course be the boy, wherever he was. Hobart appreciated how Stratton had little choice, though his solution was extreme to say the least. But above everything else it was Skender's last words to him that echoed in Hobart's head: the threat to him and his wife. Hobart would never admit it to anyone but he hoped Stratton succeeded in destroying the man if for no other reason than his own survival.

'I'll give you a minute to get clear,' Stratton said. 'Make sure no one is anywhere near the square.'

Hobart stared at Stratton, reminded of a failed suicide bomber he'd once seen in a jail. But that man had planned nothing on this scale, of course. He glanced up at the building behind him, his contempt for it and its owner impossible to hide, then back at

Stratton. 'Blow him to hell for all I care,' Hobart said. Then he moved off painfully, past the statue and towards the edge of the square.

A movement caused Stratton's gaze to flick to the balcony above, where Klodi and another of Skender's thugs had arrived to look around. Klodi looked down onto the concourse and at the statue. The two goons were about to move on when the signal finally reached Klodi's brain that someone was standing between Skender's statue's arms. Then he recognised who. Klodi disappeared instantly and Stratton ran his fingers along the transmitter to the first of four buttons. They hovered above it while Stratton drew the jacket across his body to hide the device from view.

Hobart crossed the street at the corner of the square towards the roadblock, moving faster, despite his injuries, than when he'd left Stratton. He was thinking of the remaining seconds of the minute that Stratton had given him that were ticking away.

Hendrickson hurried through the roadblock on seeing Hobart hobbling towards him. 'Sir, are you okay?' he asked, falling in alongside his battered leader.

'Get these people back out of sight of the square. Now!'

'Stratton's escaped, sir. I tried to call you—'

'I know!' Hobart shouted, hurting his ribs in the process. 'Get these people out of here! Tell the cops the bomb's going off any second!'

Hendrickson ran off towards the chief of police who stood surrounded by his officers and members of the fire department on the other side of the checkpoint.

They were immediately goaded into action. Seaton appeared alongside Hobart who had stopped to lean against the wall of a building and was glancing around the corner towards the pyramid at intervals.

'You okay?' Seaton asked dryly.

Hobart looked up at him in between clearing some congealed blood from his nostrils into his handkerchief. 'I will be in a minute,' he said to Seaton who was unaware of the irony.

'What about Stratton?'

'What about him?' Hobart asked.

'Any idea where he is?'

'Take a wild guess,' Hobart said, looking back around the corner.

Klodi hurried into the ballroom to find Cano briefing a dozen of his men, organising a search of the building. 'He's here!' Klodi shouted.

Cano looked up at him, knowing exactly who he meant, a rush of excitement coursing through him. 'Where?'

'Outside. By the statue. He's just standing there.'

'Cover him,' Cano said as he hurried past Klodi and across the lobby to the main doors, followed by half his men. The others trotted up the stairs behind Klodi.

Cano removed a large silver-plated semi-automatic pistol from a shoulder holster and pulled the slide back enough to expose a bullet in the chamber, making sure that it was loaded. He took a deep breath, adjusted his eyepatch, exhaled through flared nostrils, put his free hand on the door handle and paused a moment in thought, like a gunfighter about to head out of a

Wild West saloon into the sunlight to face the sheriff.

He turned the handle and pushed open the door, slowly at first, exercising caution. Then the statue came into view as he opened it further. Stratton stood in front of it as Klodi had described, staring straight at Cano.

Cano kept his pistol held low as he examined the man for a few seconds before searching around for a trap of some kind. There was no obvious place in which to hide a bomb in the immediate area, no planters, alcoves, boxes – nowhere to conceal anything that would harm Cano and his men and not Stratton.

Stratton's stare remained fixed squarely on Cano. He was confident that an attack would come from no other source without the Albanian's say-so and was counting on the man's desire to kill Stratton personally.

Cano's one-eyed glare went back to Stratton, specifically to the hand inside his jacket that he assumed held a weapon, wondering why the Englishman was out in the open and blatantly facing what he knew would be vastly superior firepower. Perhaps it was desperation: the man had few other options and, Cano speculated, was so consumed with hatred that he had decided to go down fighting.

Cano took a couple of steps outside as several of his men filed out through the door behind him, guns in their hands, moving either side of Cano to where they could get a clear shot at Stratton. Half a dozen more appeared on the balcony above to stand alongside Klodi. Some of them had sub-machine guns.

Cano was beginning to feel more like a bullfighter than simply an executioner. He started to relax and enjoy the role, supremely confident that this was the end of his brother's killer. There was no way out for Stratton now, not with over a dozen guns against him. Even if the cops were watching, Cano had been threatened with a bomb and was within his rights to defend himself. A smile spread across his face. 'Come to die, Stratton?' he asked.

'Where's the boy?' Stratton asked calmly. 'Hand him over now and I'll let you live.'

Cano's smile spread further across his disfigured face before he burst into laughter, which spread infectiously among his men as those who could not understand English well enough heard the translation from others.

'You got balls, Stratton. I'll say that much for you,' Cano said as the laughter subsided. 'Forget about the kid. Mine is the last face you're ever gonna see in this lifetime. No one shoot before me!' he yelled as he raised his gun, aiming it at Stratton as his men did the same. 'How d'you like my firing squad?' he asked.

Stratton's finger pushed the first button on the transmitter. Less than a second later, the top of every lamp-post surrounding the square exploded with a thunderous crack and boom as six and a half thousand ball-bearings blasted from them, like a battery of howitzers primed with grapeshot firing simultaneously, the steel wall spreading as it screamed towards the glass pyramid. The massive shock wave travelled just ahead of the metal wall, covering the distance to the building in less than a second. It hit the palm trees first, shredding their foliage and banners and bending them towards the building as if a tornado had swiped them. Then the metal balls struck the back of the bronze statue of Skender, smashing away all minor details such as ears and fingers. Before Cano's finger could finish squeezing the trigger of his gun the tiny steel spheres slammed through him and his men with such force that they were lifted off their feet and their butchered bodies slammed backwards into the building's doors and walls, dead before impact. Every sheet of glass on the face of the pyramid from the ground to the twelfth floor exploded into fragments, filling the air like a crystal cloud before descending.

Hobart and Seaton hugged the wall, squeezing their heads between their arms as the shock wave ripped down the street bouncing off buildings, trashing windows and tossing those police officers who'd remained on the corners to the ground like paper. The blast cut the tops off the lamp-posts, one landing through the windscreen of a police car, another a few feet from Seaton and Hobart on the sidewalk. Debris rained down everywhere and onlookers screamed, trying to find cover as the television correspondent slammed into her camera and both went rolling.

The glass in the air around Skender's building briefly held its upward and outward drive, then hung suspended for an instant before gravity took charge and it began to drop, much of it falling inside the sloped sides now devoid of protection. The rest fell onto the surrounding pathways and gardens like hail. Stratton pushed back into Skender's statue's arms, covering himself as the debris bounced around him, carpeting the concourse with tiny crystals. Within a few seconds, as the echoing boom subsided into the distance, it went contrastingly quiet except for the occasional chunk of loosened metal window frame dropping with a clang.

Skender hugged the floor where he had dived when the force struck the structure several floors below. After the thunder and shaking had ceased he pushed himself up onto his knees, all his senses alert, wondering what on earth had happened. He shuffled to the window and saw wisps of smoke rising from each buckled lamp-post but due to the angle of the glass that his face was pressed against he could not see the damage directly below. He got to his feet and, stepping over items that had fallen from shelves, hurried through the glass doors to the other side of the building to find a similar picture.

Skender came back to his desk, grabbed up the radio and found the send button. 'Cano?' he shouted into it. '*Cano?*'

His guards came rushing down the corridor from the elevator and emergency stairwell looking as confused as their boss.

'What happened?' Skender shouted.

'Don't know, boss,' one of them said.

'I thought the friggin' building was gonna fall down,' said another.

'One of you go down and find out what happened!' Skender shouted. 'And get Cano up here!'

As the man ran off, Skender paused to think. It was obvious that the building had been struck by something and there had no doubt been some damage. But it had held, he himself was in one piece and that was the most important thing. He then considered the possibility that it might be a diversion of some kind. He went over to a cupboard built into a wall and pulled out one of a selection of semi-automatic shot-guns, his preferred close-quarter weapon. But after calming himself and taking stock he felt certain that the planned attack was over. Though it had been violent and possibly destructive, he had survived it.

'What are you standing there for?!' he shouted at his remaining guards. 'Cover the stairs and the elev-ators.'

The men hurried back to their posts. Skender checked that the gun was loaded, then took a box of spare cartridges from a drawer and placed it on the desk.

'Cano?' Skender shouted into the radio once more. 'Where is that prick?' he muttered as he tossed the radio onto the table and went back to the window to look down onto the square. He then remembered a window in the kitchen that opened and hurried down the corridor.

Josh was in the kitchen under a table, a sandwich on the floor in front of him where he had dropped it. Skender hurried in, opened the window and looked below. His jaw went rigid as he took in the sight of the shattered façade of his glorious pyramid. Every window from four floors below on down was gone.

He stepped back in, thought for a moment and then looked down at Josh who was gaping up at him, wide-eyed and confused. 'Come with me, kid,' Skender said as he took hold of Josh's hand, pulled him to his feet and urged him out of the room. The camel dropped from Josh's pocket in the corridor and as the boy tried to retrieve it Skender yanked him on into the conference room, pulling him forward and over to the far wall.

'Sit down and don't move,' Skender growled, any pleasantness gone from his tone. Josh obeyed, looking at the shotgun in Skender's hand and wondering what was happening.

Chapter 38

Stratton stepped away from the protection of the statue, his feet crunching on the glass as he walked towards the ornate front doors that were now dotted with small, splinter-covered holes. He paused to look down on Cano's disfigured, lifeless body. It was covered in shards of glass, blood oozing from countless holes.

'How d'you like mine?' Stratton asked.

Cano's gun lay by his side and Stratton picked it up, stepped over him, pulled open the heavy door and walked into the lobby.

Two of Skender's men lay dead behind the doors, killed by a dozen steel balls that had penetrated the wood. The marble floor was covered in shards of glass from the shattered windows on the balcony above where Klodi's body and those of his colleagues lay bloody and broken.

Stratton walked to the elevators and pushed the call button. One of the doors opened. He stepped inside, hit a button and the doors closed behind him.

A few seconds later they opened on the tenth floor. Stratton stepped out into a strong wind blowing through the building, unchecked now that the windows and virtually every glass partition on the floor had been smashed by the ball-bearings.

Lying dead were three of Skender's thugs. Stratton hoped that a similar fate had befallen the rest of the guard force.

He walked to the fire exit and opened the door. As soon as he stepped onto the landing the sound of running footsteps came from below. He looked down through the spiralling banisters to see a mob of Skender's men heading up in support of their boss.

Stratton pulled back his jacket, grabbed hold of the rail to brace himself and pushed the second and third buttons on the transmitter. The explosions, almost simultaneous, were deafening as the entire building rocked violently. The lights went out and Stratton almost lost his balance as a huge crack appeared in the outer wall in front of him. Dust and shards of concrete fell all around.

The main spars radiating from the central pillar to the outside corners of both the fourth and eighth floors buckled and dropped, the supports disintegrating as large sections collapsed. As Stratton had calculated, the sides of the pyramid were compromised at this point and they bowed inwards, reducing the overall structural strength. But the umbrella effect remained intact, maintaining the configuration of the floors above.

Stratton regained his balance as the rocking subsided and the thunder gave way to shouts and screams from below. When that ceased all he could hear was falling debris. He looked down to find the metal banisters twisted awkwardly and long stretches of the staircase

505

broken off, with daylight coming in through a massive hole. There was a hand sticking out into the well but it was not moving, the rest of the body having been flattened beneath a large chunk of reinforced concrete.

Stratton looked overhead, unable to see beyond the next floor due to the dust, and made his way up the stairs.

Skender was holding on to a piece of furniture to steady himself while the entire penthouse gradually stopped shaking. It had been whiplashed by the blast travelling up the central pillar and expending itself through the top, sending ornaments flying from shelves and pictures off walls. Several windows cracked and tiles and debris fell from the ceiling, a large chunk landing on Skender's model village and flattening a row of luxury apartments. Skender was stunned, and not just physically, as the real impact of what was happening struck him. He was under serious attack and by just one man. Stratton was indeed not a bluffer. Yet the building remained standing and Skender was alive: he could not help wondering if that was because Stratton had failed or because it was not yet over.

Skender looked for Josh, the reason for this assault, and saw him cowering in a corner, holding his knees against his chest and looking terrified. Then a sudden thudding outside the window startled Skender and he spun round to see that it was a helicopter flying past. Then it came around and hovered, a sign on its side declaring it to be from Channel 7 News. A cameraman sat in the doorway, aiming his camera at the building.

Skender wondered where Stratton was at that

moment. No doubt he was watching from a rooftop somewhere or perhaps even catching it all on television. Then Skender looked back at Josh as he considered holding the kid up in front of the window to let Stratton see, the obvious drawback, of course, being that the Feds would also know that he had the boy. But as the dust settled he warned himself not to be too hasty. Perhaps it was indeed over and, if so, it was now Skender's turn. He promised that Stratton and anyone to whom he was remotely related would pay for this day. And the first victim would be the boy.

Josh never took his stare off Skender, afraid of him now, the more so because of the way the man was looking at him. The explosions had scared Josh witless and his thoughts had been constantly of Stratton since Skender had said that he was coming. He wished that his godfather would soon appear and take him away from this nightmare. But the doubt grew steadily stronger that his hero was not going to save him now.

Vicky sat in her office, looking at a file on her desk but unable to concentrate. She'd been like this since Josh had been kidnapped and Stratton had left her standing in the street. She fought to focus herself and started reading the page from the top again. After a couple of sentences Dorothy walked in and Vicky sighed heavily at this latest interruption.

'I got something to take your mind off things,' Dorothy said, a bandage around her head covering a wound she had received from Josh's kidnappers.

'So have I but I need some peace and quiet to do it,' Vicky said, a little testy.

'Excuse me for livin',' Dorothy said, turning around to leave.

'Dorothy,' Vicky called out, regretting her rudeness.

Dorothy stopped and looked at her, wearing a fake frown.

'Sorry,' Vicky said, but not entirely meaning it. 'What is it?'

'You're forgiven,' Dorothy said. 'Some new building in Culver City is getting blown to hell by some crazy guy. He blew out all the windows and now he's setting explosives off inside. Can't beat the news for entertainment these days.'

'Thank you,' Vicky said, going back to her file. 'I'll catch it tonight. I'm sure they'll repeat it.'

'That the same file you've been reading since this morning?'

Vicky put down the file and looked at Dorothy who rolled her eyes and walked away. 'Okay, okay, I'm going,' she said.

Vicky picked the file up again but was now distracted by something that Dorothy had said. The word 'explosion' reminded her of Stratton and their last night together when the car blew up in the alley behind his apartment, and also of the FBI agent who had asked her several questions about Stratton and bomb-making.

She pushed it out of her mind and started to read the file once again. But it was now impossible. She put the file down, got up, walked around her desk and out of the office.

Dorothy and two other staff members were in the recreation room, watching the television and Vicky stood in the doorway where she could see it. A banner across the bottom of the screen declared breaking news as a recent tape was replayed showing the initial explosion that shattered most of the windows of the pyramid building. It then flicked back to the live scene from the roof of a building overlooking the square where a correspondent was standing in front of the camera, the building in the background.

'Moments ago we heard another explosion, possibly two explosions together, this time inside the building itself. We're told this is not the work of terrorists but of just one man who police think could actually be in the building. Police gave no details about the man, who he is or why he is doing this. The building here in Culver City belongs to Albanian billionaire Daut Skender. Why he is under attack remains a mystery.'

Vicky's mind raced when she heard the word 'Albanian'. Stratton had said something about Albanians being involved in Josh's kidnapping and that he was going to face them. But surely this was a co-incidence.

The next view of the building came from a media helicopter circling it. Vicky left the doorway and sat down on the couch beside Dorothy.

'Told you it'd take your mind off things, didn't I?' Dorothy said.

Stratton arrived on the fourteenth floor, walking carefully up the stairs to reduce the noise of the glass underfoot. The building constantly creaked and groaned as supports complained about the added stress.

He stepped through the fire exit, checking the floor

as he made his way into the central room, and went to the massive pillar. He had reconsidered the dangers of blowing the twelfth floor, the final explosion, because the upper floors might completely collapse. But another part of his mind urged him to keep to his plan and have confidence in his initial calculations that although the floors might sag they would hold together since the weight on the spars radiating from the pinnacle would be far less. Whatever happened structurally, the safest place to be was close to the central pillar since it was the strongest part of the building and would not collapse.

Stratton opened his coat, checked the transmitter, then paused to reconsider once more. The purpose of this whole business was not suicide but to get Skender to release Josh: if Skender died so did the mission. Then Stratton reached the end of his deliberations. The component parts of him – planner, soldier, revengeful protector, self-destructive annihilator – fell into place. He pushed the button.

The explosion's force powered up through the floor and slammed against his feet, rocking the building much more than before despite the charge being half the previous amount. Ceiling tiles fell around him and windows shattered as the frames surrounding the room buckled. The rumbling continued for several seconds, like an earthquake, as the outside corner supports of the pyramid bowed and the floors below weakened, the horizontal struts unable to hold them by themselves.

A loud cracking sound suddenly filled the air and the floor beneath Stratton's feet sagged. A second later the ceiling gave up and followed it. Every glass wall and window shattered and doors crunched in their frames. For a moment Stratton believed he had gone an explosion too far.

He pushed himself back against the pillar with nothing else to cling to but hope. As he held himself in readiness, the groaning subsided and the floor did not drop any further.

Stratton could not afford to hang about a moment longer. He made his way down the sloping floor directly to the fire escape, only to find the door jammed in the buckled frame. He had to kick hard to make a gap wide enough to squeeze through. As he stepped onto the landing another shudder sent chunks of concrete cascading down the stairwell. He looked up in anticipation of another falling piece and saw a fleeting movement on the floor above.

Stratton pulled the pistol from his belt and held it, barrel up, in both hands next to his head. Hugging the wall, he made his way up.

As he reached the midway landing he held out the gun in front of him, waiting for a target, warning himself that if it was Skender he had to maim, not kill. Another tremor shook the building as a support strut below gave way. But the stairs held. Stratton took advantage of the diversion and moved up to the next landing.

A figure suddenly appeared above, looking down. It was one of Skender's men and he saw the gun in Stratton's hands. As the man pointed his own weapon at him Stratton fired a round through his head and kept his pistol on aim in case a second shot was required. But the man slumped over the banister rail, his gun falling past Stratton to clatter down into the dust-filled void.

Stratton moved quickly up to the landing to find the emergency door twisted in its frame and jammed solid. He carried on up to the next turn in the stairs, moving on towards the penthouse. The sound of movement above heightened his senses to maximum alertness.

The muzzle of a gun appeared and the man behind it fired several unaimed shots. The first hit the wall inches from Stratton while the others went wide.

Stratton moved up several more steps to change his location in case the shooter chanced another wild bullet. Then he heard the sound of someone scrambling over rubble. A foot came into view as the owner negotiated the obstacle. Stratton aimed quickly and fired a single shot into the heel. This was followed immediately by a howl of pain. Stratton leaped up the steps in time to see the man lying on the rubble. Disorientated though he was, on seeing Stratton he raised his gun. But Stratton fired first, sending a bullet smashing through the man's eye. Stratton moved closer, ready to follow it up with another. But there was no need.

Stratton immediately saw why the man hadn't been able to escape. There was a large slab of jagged concrete jammed against the fire exit. Stratton put down his weapon and as he grabbed hold of the body to pull it aside the building groaned loudly. Something below snapped and a loud wrenching sound followed. The floor dropped several feet to lean down at an angle away from the central pillar. Stratton grabbed the banister rail to stop himself from falling into the void. As he regained his balance and pushed himself back onto the landing he saw that the slab had shifted from the fire-exit door.

Stratton picked up his pistol and took hold of the door. He was about to pull at it when he stopped himself, his senses warning him of the potential dangers: Skender and others could be waiting for him the other side. He needed to go ahead quickly, sure, but safely too. He put down his pistol again, grabbed the body and dragged it to the edge of the opening. Holding the dead man under the arms he pulled open the door and lowered the corpse's head past the door frame. A shotgun blast instantly took the side of the head away. Stratton let the body drop as he once more picked up his weapon, hoping that whoever had fired the shot thought that the stiff was him.

Stratton was undecided about his next move when the building made up his mind for him. Supports ripping from their mountings caused a sudden massive jolt and the entire floor tilted, the outside wall of the stairwell crumbling away to reveal a view of the city. Stratton fell back and let go of his gun to grab the banister rail that had come free of its mounting for several yards. He hung over the centre well, a drop of fifty feet or so underneath him, bouncing up and down as if on the end of a wire. He swung his body, using the sprung tension of the rail to gain momentum, and managed to grab hold of an edge and pull himself back onto the crumbling staircase. The door had popped fully open and he clutched at the door frame, concerned that another jolt might make the entire floor collapse. With the stairs pretty much shattered and descent that way no longer possible there was nothing for it but to get closer to the central pillar, which meant getting back inside. He tensed himself and sprang forward.

Stratton scrambled through the doorway and up the sloping floor without a shot being fired. He raced along the corridor. Its glass walls were gone, their jagged edges jutting down from the ceiling like lethal stalactites.

He twisted into a doorway, expecting a shot any second, and hugged the floor while he scanned the shattered room. The central pillar remained solid and upright but one or two of the outside corner supports must have given way because the floor slanted acutely. As he looked around his gaze fell on something a few feet in front of him. When it came into focus the implications hit him like a bolt of lightning. It was Josh's camel. Stratton reached out a hand, picked the carved object from the debris and inspected it. The realisation that the boy had been somewhere in the building at the time Stratton had begun his attack and that Josh was possibly now dead filled him with horror.

Stratton pulled himself up and stepped out into the room, holding on to whatever he could to stop himself from sliding down. As he moved to where he could see the conference room, the wall along its entire length gone, a desk at the far side moved up the floor a couple of feet, apparently defying gravity, and was then heaved aside to reveal Skender who had been briefly trapped behind it. Skender got to his feet and then saw Stratton above him on the sloping floor.

The two men instantly knew that one of them was not going to survive the day – though considering the present precarious state of the building neither's life was exactly guaranteed. Skender's stare dropped to the ground in search of the shotgun he had lost during the tremor that had left him trapped by his desk but it was nowhere to be seen. Then he saw something else that might prove equally if not more useful. It was Josh, hanging on for dear life outside the room where the wall had fallen away, his little hands gripping a piece of window frame, his feet on another section below.

Stratton followed Skender's gaze and saw the small hands. He was immediately filled with dread but he did not have time to think about it.

Skender was only a couple of metres from Josh and now he took a step closer to him. Stratton was twice the distance away and got off his knees, ready to make a move.

Skender then saw something by his feet in the rubble and leaned down to pick it up. It was one of his decorative swords, and he pulled off the scabbard to expose a long, slender blade with a slight curve in it. Without further hesitation he made a leap towards Josh. At the same time Stratton released his grip and slid down the tilted floor. Skender arrived first just above where Josh was hanging on but was not prepared for Stratton who crashed into him while simultaneously grabbing the remaining piece of glass-wall framework to stop them both falling out of the room.

The men dropped onto their backs on the sloping floor and began punching and clawing at each other like wild beasts. Skender managed to raise the sword and bring it down close to Stratton's skull but a savage blow from Stratton sent Skender reeling and he let go of the sword. But Skender was a powerful man and he showed no signs of his age as he spun round, gripped Stratton around the throat with both hands and began to strangle him with real ferocity.

Stratton immediately started to gag. He tried to push Skender back but his arms were not strong enough. As his vision blurred he dropped his hands to grip Skender's, felt for both the Albanian's little fingers and grabbed them, bending them back. No one can resist such a countermove unless they are prepared to have their fingers broken in their sockets. Skender let out a yelp as one of his snapped at the joint. He released Stratton's throat. Stratton slammed him back and to his surprise Skender rolled off the floor and out of sight.

Stratton scrambled to the edge, praying that Josh was still there, to find the boy in the same position. But to Stratton's horror Skender was only feet away, hanging on to a reinforcing bar. His baleful stare was fixed on Josh and it was quickly obvious that if he fell, which seemed unavoidable, he meant to take the child with him.

At that moment the media helicopter thudded around the side of the building and hovered a stone's throw away.

★   ★   ★

Vicky slowly stood and moved closer to the television, her mouth agape as she watched the helicopter's camera zoom in to show a man and a boy hanging outside the room at the top of the building. Then another man inside came into view as the news anchor excitedly described what they were seeing.

Vicky turned on her heel and ran from the room. She raced along the corridor and out of the building.

Hendrickson was watching the television monitors inside the open back of the media truck when he saw the feed from the helicopter. He quickly looked around for Hobart and saw him standing at the corner of the block, watching the building. Seaton was at his side.

'Sir!' Hendrickson shouted as he ran over to them. 'You'd better come take a look in the media truck, the TV monitor. I think it's Skender and Stratton.'

Hobart looked around him, then over at the media truck. He hurried towards it, Seaton following. 'I think the kid's up there too,' Hendrickson said, following.

They arrived at the truck and crowded into the back, much to the consternation of the engineer who was shoved aside.

'Excuse me—' the engineer said, an overture to a complaint, but he was cut short.

'Shut up,' Hobart spat as he scrutinised the image.

'I can see at least three people, one of them a boy!' the correspondent in the helicopter shouted excitedly as the cameraman did his best to zoom in close without increasing the camera shake. 'They're hanging on for their lives. The building is crumbling away, much of it already disintegrated by the powerful explosions. It looks like the man inside is moving to try and save the others but time may not be on their side. I can see cracks appearing at the top of the pyramid. There is no telling how long it can hold together . . .'

'Can you believe this guy?' Hobart said, mainly to himself.

'Josh!' Stratton shouted above the wind and the noise of the helicopter's rotors.

Josh looked up at him. The little boy was terrified beyond the point of panic and was frozen to his perch. The side of the building had collapsed immediately below and it was clear that the long fall onto the jagged spars and rubble would be the end of him. His small body was painfully stretched, his feet resting on a ledge. But another violent shake – or if the foothold gave way – and he'd be lost.

Skender was in an even more unstable position, outstretched like Josh but with his feet on a shaky horizontal bar that did not look as if it could hold his weight.

'You hang on, Josh! Do you hear me?' Stratton shouted as he dropped to his knees, trying to get into position to lift the boy to safety.

Josh nodded quickly as he shuffled to improve his hold, his hands aching where the edge of the window frame cut into them.

Skender looked at Stratton, then at the boy as the Albanian adjusted his grip, glaring viciously.

Stratton stretched himself fully as he reached down for Josh. But at that moment another heavy jolt hit the building and the floor jerked down once more. And Josh lost the grip of one of his hands on the window frame.

Media stations across the country had by now picked up the story and several million people gasped as they watched the small boy almost fall.

Hobart, Seaton and Hendrickson watched the media-truck monitor in cold silence.

Stratton put his shoulder against the bottom of the frame and took hold of one of Josh's arms. 'When I say, you let go and I'll pull you up!' Stratton shouted.

Josh looked up at Stratton, terrified.

Skender then made a sudden effort and swung himself towards Josh, letting go of his own hold. He grabbed Josh around his waist with both hands as Stratton took Josh's arm. Josh let out a scream as he let go and dropped, but only for a few inches. Both Josh and Skender were now held by Stratton.

Stratton struggled to bend his other arm around the frame to get a better hold on Josh but could not. His own head was in the way and at an awkward angle. Josh was slipping from his grip and it was only a matter of seconds before he fell. Stratton felt helpless.

Stratton glanced down at Skender and the two men stared into each other's eyes.

'Screw you, Stratton!' Skender shouted.

Stratton wanted to tear the Albanian's heart out and as he struggled to find a purchase for his free hand it fell on something. Stratton knew instantly what it was. He grasped it and pulled it around so that he could see it. Both men knew the advantage had suddenly changed as Stratton lowered the tip of the sword towards Skender's face and, taking a second to line it up, shoved it through the man's eye.

Skender remained holding on to Josh, his feelings a tortured mix of disbelief and stubbornness. He knew it was all over – not just the fight, but his life. He saw those days of his youth in the mountains of Albania, saw his brothers and sisters killed and the communist brute slit his throat, saw all this and much more one last time. The sword burned his eye and he took an even firmer hold of Josh, hanging on to life.

Stratton gave a shout as he dug deep into his last resources of strength and thrust the sword even deeper, penetrating Skender's brain. Then, as the life left Skender's body, the crime lord dropped silently away, the sword sticking out of his head.

Stratton gripped Josh firmly and raised him up over the frame and to the floor. He held the boy as he lay exhausted, looking at Josh who was staring back at him.

'You having fun, Josh?'

Josh shook his head. A second later another massive jolt rocked the building and the floor dropped even further. Skender's desk slid past Josh and Stratton and off the edge. Stratton scrambled to his feet and pulled Josh out of the way as the model village on the conference table went past and sailed through the hole to crash into the debris below.

★　　★　　★

A million people were watching the events unfold on television. Still in shock after seeing the man hanging onto the boy stabbed through the head, they gasped as they saw the entire floor collapse. The helicopter spun around, the pilot momentarily panicked. As the correspondent shouted at him to get the side of the chopper back in line the audience saw the pinnacle of the pyramid lean over and fall, bringing the penthouse down with it. No one inside could have survived.

Chapter 39

Seaton exhaled audibly and slowly walked away from the media truck, leaving Hobart to stare at the screen. He walked to the corner from where he could see the building, already planning ahead, his thoughts on damage control for the Agency as well as for the Brits. Stratton's body would more than likely be found and if it was left to the police they would investigate his identity and the part he had played in the incident. That had to be avoided at all costs which meant that Stratton's and Josh's bodies would have to be separated from the others and removed. Seaton would clear it with Hobart since he would need his help but he did not expect any resistance from that quarter as it was also in the FBI's interest.

Seaton took his cellphone from his pocket, hit a number on the menu and put it to his ear. 'Sir? This is Seaton in LA. Yeah, it's over. That's what I'm calling about. I need a clean-up crew here for when they find the body.'

Several hours later roadblocks surrounded the square, keeping the public well back while the emergency services began their work. Engineers conducted safety surveys as well as initial demolition planning and the designation of areas where the fire department could safely search for bodies. The explosives and ordnance department had cleared much of the building although it would take a thorough examination lasting days before it was officially declared safe.

Seaton sat in the open door of Hobart's sedan, staring at the building and sipping a cup of coffee while contemplating his immediate future in LA. The way things were going, it might take days to get to the spot where the penthouse had landed and Stratton's and Josh's bodies could be found. Hobart had given him the okay to remove the corpses when they were unearthed from the rubble but the delicate part was going to be managing it without raising the interest of the police. Worse still, the media were hovering all over the place and were as keen to find the mysterious man and boy as Seaton was.

Beside Seaton on the back seat were some of the items taken from the pick-up that Stratton had stolen. Seaton took a look at the pyramid blueprints, curious to see how Stratton had planned the placement of the explosives. The horizontal struts on the fourth, eighth and twelfth floors were marked: he was impressed at Stratton's assessment of how to do maximum damage with the minimum amount of explosive since it was not obvious to Seaton. But the results were there for all to see. The guy *was* a surgeon, that was undeniable. Still, although Seaton had regained all the respect he had lost for Stratton when the Englishman had been arrested he could not help feeling disappointed in him for not having figured out an escape route.

Seaton would have expected Stratton to have made some kind of plan to get out of the building once he had killed Skender, no matter how impossible it might have seemed. He refused to believe that Stratton was the suicidal type. Seaton appreciated that Stratton had not known that Josh was in the building, otherwise he would never have detonated his bombs. It would have been second nature for him to have considered a way out.

Several pencil marks looked like places where Stratton had changed his mind about charge placement. But as Seaton studied the blueprint while sipping his coffee the design of the central pillar conjured up an image from his memory. He held the plans out at arm's length to get a broader perspective and realised that the central pillar was the shape of a champagne bottle. It was wide at the base until the tenth floor where it gradually narrowed until the fifteenth and then became straight the rest of the way to the top. It reminded him of Stratton's trick in Jack's garden where the challenge had been to get the glass inside the champagne bottle.

Seaton took a closer look at some of the pencil marks and discovered that one at the base of the pillar corresponded to another at the top. The centre of the pillar was hollow, with conduits and piping of every description running to each floor. There was also a ladder that extended from the garage to the roof, with a hatch on each floor hidden behind the wall fabric. The hatches were not intended to be used once the building was complete except when major work was required.

Seaton climbed out of the car to take a look at the

building. A flush of excitement ran through him at the possibility that had just occurred to him. However, he could not remove from his mind the image of Stratton and Josh on the edge of the floor barely seconds before it had collapsed.

As he closed the car door and headed for the square he was stopped by a voice calling out to him.

'Sir!'

It was a police officer who was walking towards him from the barrier where a crowd of rubbernecks were packed, watching and photographing the scene.

'Are you with the FBI, sir?' the young officer asked.

Seaton was more interested in investigating his theory. 'Yeah,' he said, hoping he would not be delayed long.

'I got a woman says she knows the man and the kid who were in the building.'

Seaton looked past him at the woman standing alone and watching him. It was Vicky: although he did not know her, the need to block every source of potential information about Stratton and Josh was essential.

Seaton walked over to her and said hello.

'My name's Vicky Whitaker,' she said, wringing her hands nervously. 'I just wanted to know if John Stratton and Josh Penton are okay – the young boy who was in the building?'

Seaton saw bystanders starting to take an interest. He stepped to the side of the barrier. 'Come with me,' he said.

The police officer moved a section of the barrier aside to let Vicky pass. She joined Seaton several yards away.

'How do you know them?' Seaton asked.

'I work at the child-protection centre, where Josh was kidnapped. I'm his case officer.'

Seaton remembered having heard Hobart talk about her. She looked pensive and concerned and holding on to her emotions by a thread.

'I'm sorry,' he said. 'We don't believe anyone survived inside the building.'

Vicky looked down at her hands. 'Have . . . have they found . . . ?' she said. She could not continue.

'No,' Seaton answered, trying to be as considerate as he could.

Vicky's lips trembled as she nodded. Then she squeezed her eyes shut in a vain effort to hold back her tears.

'Come with me,' Seaton said, taking her elbow. She walked alongside him as if in a trance while he led her to the sedan and opened the back door. 'Why don't you sit inside?' he said. 'I'll go and check if there is any news.' He wanted to get away, not only to check on the possibility that Stratton might be alive but because there was no one more uncomfortable to be around than the bereaved.

Vicky sat on the back seat and stared down at her hands on her lap.

'Can I get you anything?' Seaton asked, feeling lame.

She shook her head without looking at him, lost in her thoughts.

Seaton walked away from the car across the square and around the side of the building to the garage entrance where an engineer was talking to a senior police officer and a fire department chief.

As Seaton headed past them the engineer reached out an arm to stop him. 'Excuse me, sir. Where are you going?'

Seaton reached inside his jacket, pulled out a small leather wallet and opened it to reveal his badge.

'CIA,' the engineer said with surprise, looking at the other two men and then back at Seaton. 'Can I ask you why you wanna go inside?'

Seaton looked at him. The thin smile on his lips clearly said no. He put his badge away.

The engineer was out of his league. His body language became that of someone stepping back without actually doing so. 'Well, it's not officially cleared but as long as you accept responsibility—'

'I'll take full responsibility,' Seaton said. 'And I'd also appreciate it if no one else came down here while I'm inside,' he said to the police officer.

The men looked at each other and shrugged. 'Sure,' the officer said.

Seaton left them watching him as he walked down the concrete ramp and into the darkness.

He headed into the centre of the garage where a handful of cars were parked, all of them covered in dust, and paused to check around. There was no sign of damage, no collapsed ceiling as far as he could tell in the poor light. He took a look at the pillar in the gloom as he drew near it. The drawings had the hatch on the west side opposite the elevators and he followed the curved wall until he found a large metal hinged bulkhead similar to that on a ship. It was held shut by six bolts evenly spaced around it. He was going to need a tool. Without wasting another second

527

he turned around and headed back to the garage entrance.

After a brief exchange with the fire chief a fireman was sent off and a few minutes later returned with a huge wrench. Seaton thanked him and carried the tool back down into the garage, much to the interest of the men watching.

Seaton returned to the pillar, adjusted the wrench to fit the first nut and pulled down on it. The nut moved easily, being new, and within a few minutes he had removed all six of them.

But the hatch did not readily budge and he had to used the end of the wrench to prise an edge open enough to let him get his fingers inside. He placed the wrench on the ground and pulled hard on the hatch. Putting his weight behind the effort he managed to push it open.

Seaton looked back towards the garage entrance to ensure that no one had followed him. Then he looked inside the pillar. It was too dark to make out anything and he did not have a flashlight. Too impatient to go and get one he climbed over the lip of the hatch, which was a couple of feet from ground level, and with his leg felt for the bottom inside. It should have been no more than a foot or so lower than the garage floor.

Seaton found the bottom and dropped inside the hatch. It was barely a minute before he climbed out, closed the hatch without bolting it and walked back across the garage towards the entrance. He took his phone out of his pocket.

He walked out into the sunlight, ignoring the

engineer and fire and police chiefs, and raised the phone to his ear. 'Where are you guys?' he asked, and as the person at the other end of the line answered he heard the toot of a horn. He looked up to see a clean grey van with two men in the front. The passenger was holding a cellphone to his ear.

Seaton put his phone away. He waved at them to follow him as he turned and headed back to the garage entrance.

As he reached the engineer and the other men he beckoned the van to continue into the garage. 'Excuse me, gentlemen,' he said.

The men moved to one side as the van drove down the ramp into the garage. Seaton followed.

The van came to a stop at the foot of the ramp. As Seaton walked past it started to move again and slowly followed him.

Seaton stopped at the pillar. The driver brought the van to a halt and turned off the engine. He and the passenger climbed out. They were two nondescript characters in their fifties and wore grey overalls, gloves, boots and polite businesslike smiles.

Seaton looked towards the garage entrance where the engineer and police officer were silhouetted in the light. They were obviously unable to see any detail from where they were. Seaton headed to the hatch which he pulled open more easily than he had the first time.

'You'll need a stretcher and body bag,' he said to the two men. They understood, went to the back of the van and opened it. A moment later they appeared with the requested items.

Seaton climbed in through the hatch, followed by the men. It was a good five minutes before Seaton climbed out again, dusting off his hands.

One of the men climbed out, then reached back in to take hold of the end of the heavy stretcher with the now full body bag on it, zipped completely closed. He dragged it out until the other end rested on the rim of the hatch so that his partner could climb out. They carried the loaded stretcher around to the back of the van and placed it inside. Seaton closed the doors behind them.

Seaton walked back to the hatch and closed it. He quickly replaced the nuts without bothering to tighten them, then walked to the front passenger side of the van and climbed in. The driver started the van and headed for the entrance.

As they emerged out of the darkness and arrived at the top of the ramp Hobart was standing in their way. The van stopped.

Seaton opened his window as Hobart walked around to him. They looked at each other for a moment, communicating somehow without speaking. But that was not enough for Hobart.

'You got what you were looking for?' he asked.

'Yes,' Seaton said.

Hobart looked past Seaton at the body bag on the bench.

'How'd you find them?' he asked.

'A hunch,' Seaton said.

Hobart nodded. He would have liked to see the bodies, mainly because of something niggling away at his intuition. But, as per his agreement, Stratton and

530

Josh were now out of his hands and for that reason he put them out of his mind as well.

'Good luck,' he said to Seaton as he stepped back.

'You too.'

'Maybe we'll bump into each other again sometime,' Hobart said.

Seaton wondered briefly if Hobart meant it to suggest that he still had the CIA man in his pocket. But then he discounted it. Once Seaton was clear of the square the case would be closed as far as Stratton, Josh and the FBI were concerned. Hobart would provide a sufficiently convincing cover story about the Englishman and the boy to keep the media and police happy and in doing so the issue of the explosives and information that Seaton had given Stratton would be similarly buried.

'You ever need anything, you give me a call,' Seaton offered as a parting gift.

'I will,' Hobart said. 'Same goes for you.'

Seaton tapped the driver's arm and the van pulled away as the two agents continued to look at each other.

Not exactly the beginning of a beautiful new relationship with the CIA, Hobart thought as the van drove off. But it was a start. 'Hendrickson?' he called out.

Hendrickson came trotting over. 'Sir.'

'Take me home,' Hobart said tiredly, squeezing the back of his neck, his face twisting in pain as he moved his head around to loosen the muscles. 'How are you at giving massages?' he added.

'Sir?' Hendrickson said, looking somewhat alarmed.

'Lighten up, Hendrickson. I'm kidding.'

★　　★　　★

The van pulled up to the barricade and waited while the police officers moved back the crowd before opening it.

Seaton glanced out of his window at Vicky sitting in the back of the sedan, looking sad and forlorn. Then, as if she felt his gaze on her, she glanced up and stared at him. He looked away, wishing that she had not seen him. He climbed out of the passenger seat and into the back of the van.

Seaton sat on the bench opposite the body bag, contemplating it. Then he reached out, took hold of the zip and pulled it down.

Stratton and Josh lay motionless, Josh on top of Stratton, completely still, his eyes closed, as he had been told to. Stratton opened his eyes and looked at Seaton and Josh did the same.

Seaton undid the zip all the way down. Josh climbed out, relieved though still very confused. But at least he knew he was going to be all right now.

Stratton sat up painfully and eased his aching body into a more comfortable position.

'You okay, Josh?' Seaton asked.

Josh nodded.

'Better sit down. We'll be moving off in a minute,' Seaton said.

Josh sat on the bench by the back window that was covered by a small curtain. He looked at Seaton and then at Stratton, starting to relax as his feeling of security and protection grew.

Stratton remembered something and reached into his pocket. He pulled out the camel and handed it to Josh. 'Better hold on to that. It's lucky.'

Josh took it, happy to have it back.

The van lurched forward and stopped again as people milled around, getting out of the way. The movement made the curtain shift enough for Josh to catch a glimpse outside. He recognised someone and stood up and moved the curtain aside to see Vicky standing beside a car, looking towards the van.

'Vicky,' Josh called out as he waved.

Vicky could not hear him. But as her gaze roved along the back of the van her heart leaped into her throat as she saw Josh's little face in the window.

Stratton reacted to the name and joined Josh at the window.

Vicky put her hands to her mouth, scarcely able to contain herself as she watched the two faces that she had prayed most to see again. Deep down she somehow understood that they could not stop to speak with her and, even worse, that she might never see them again. Although the sadness of that would not hit home fully until later, nonetheless the joy of seeing them alive was beyond anything that she had ever felt in her life before.

The tears streamed down her face as the van moved away. She waved until it was out of sight.

Stratton sat back tiredly, about to reflect on Vicky, then Seaton cleared his throat, wanting to talk.

'So, what now?' Stratton asked.

Seaton nodded, thinking the question through. 'Well. You'll go back to the UK, you and Josh, never to darken the doors of Los Angeles again. John Stratton was never here and so he didn't blow the hell out of that building, nor did he do everything else that he, er, didn't do — as far as we're concerned. I can't speak for your own people but I should think they would see it the same way. You might find yourself stationed in Outer Mongolia for a decade or so but other than that . . .' Seaton shrugged.

Stratton exhaled heavily, agreeing. It was the most likely upshot of the several that he had speculated about while waiting in the base of the central pillar.

Josh sat down beside him. Stratton put his arm around the boy and kissed him on the top of his head as his thoughts went to Jack and Sally. He hoped that they would be content with the outcome and would forgive him for the dangers that he had put their son through. Wherever they were now, they were still practical people and would know that, as in any war, it wasn't always the conduct of the campaign that mattered as much as the end result.

The Hostage

DUNCAN FALCONER

When an undercover operation monitoring the Real IRA goes horrifically wrong, British Intelligence turn to the one man who can get their agent out: Stratton, SBS operative with a lethal reputation. It's a dangerous race against time: if the Real IRA get to the Republic before Stratton gets to the Real IRA, his colleague is as good as dead.

But the battle in the Northern Ireland borders is just the beginning. For there can only be one way the Real IRA knew about the British agent: someone within MI5 is tipping them off. Then the surveillance mission in Paris to identify the mole ends in disaster: Hank Munro, US Navy SEAL on secondment, is captured.

Munro's wife Kathryn is distraught, and turns to priest Father Kinsella for support. Kinsella, though, is not the holy man he seems, and Kathryn becomes an unwitting part of a deadly Real IRA plan, a terror attack the likes of which London has never seen . . .

First Into Action

DUNCAN FALCONER

They are the most elite and mysterious special forces unit in the world – but they are *not* the SAS.

The Special Boat Service is a small, clandestine and highly professional unit whose team-based ethos and exemplary combat record has created an intense rivalry with the SAS. At the age of nineteen, Duncan Falconer was the youngest man in recent years to join the unit and rose quickly to become one of its most skilled undercover operatives.

Through his own extraordinary experiences, Falconer recalls his leading role in SBS operations in Northern Ireland, the Falklands and the Gulf. He recounts the missions that have contributed to the unit's astounding success in the fight against terrorism and drug-smuggling, and charts the long-standing power struggle between the SBS and the SAS.

A fascinating insight into the secret world of the special forces, *First Into Action* is the *Bravo Two Zero* for the SBS.

Other bestselling Sphere titles available by mail:

☐ The Hostage	Duncan Falconer	£6.99
☐ First Into Action	Duncan Falconer	£6.99
☐ The Hijack	Duncan Falconer	£6.99

The prices shown above are correct at time of going to press. However, the publishers reserve the right to increase prices on covers from those previously advertised, without prior notice.

———————————————— sphere ————————————————

SPHERE
PO Box 121, Kettering, Northants NN14 4ZQ
Tel: 01832 737525, Fax: 01832 733076
Email: aspenhouse@FSBDial.co.uk

POST AND PACKING:
Payments can be made as follows: cheque, postal order (payable to Sphere) or by credit cards or Switch Card. Do not send cash or currency.

| All UK Orders | **FREE OF CHARGE** |
| E.E.C. & Overseas | 25% of order value |

Name (Block Letters) _____

Address _____

_____

Post/zip code: _____

☐ Please keep me in touch with future Sphere publications

☐ I enclose my remittance £_____

☐ I wish to pay Visa/Access/Mastercard/Eurocard

Card Expiry Date
